# WICKED ACADEMIA
## STORMWIND OF SHADOWS

Jasmine Jenkins & Sophie Suliman

LUNA FOX
PRESS

# Wicked Academia

## STORMWIND OF SHADOWS

Jasmine Jenkins & Sophie Suliman

*To the Wicked Academia community, our very own
cluster of star-gazers and shadow-seekers*

*Wicked Academia is an adult fantasy book. It contains mature themes and is intended for audiences 18+. For a complete list of content warnings, please go to www.wickedacademia.com*

# THE
# CELESTIAL ACADEMY
## FOR FALLEN STARS

MEADOW OF
SHATTERED STARS

ENCHANTED FOREST

POND OF GALAXIES

THE GLASS CATHEDRAL

FARMS

THE ACADEMY

SELENE CRESCENT

# ISLE OF
# ARGOS

# 1
# IN WHICH MARION SEES THE MAKING OF A MONSTER

*ATCH A FALLING star and the world becomes yours. Create new destinies. Change your fate. You will become Starlings and Thraina shall bow before you.*

These were the words that had carried Marion Greywick, the middle triplet of the star-crossed Greywick siblings, through her Celestial Rite.

She stood on the hill leading down to the Meadow of Shattered Stars. It was a beautiful night, a night that would go down in history. For the children of the gods had caught their stars.

But Marion Greywick was bothered.

She was bothered by the incessant crush of bodies against hers, as each member of her new Morning Star house suddenly decided they were best friends. She was bothered by the *wisp wisp wisp* of Loremaster Setviren's breathing as he stared aghast down at the field. She was bothered by the newfound heat within her chest, a heat that had burst into flames during her trial earlier this night.

But most of all, she was bothered by the legion of Celestial Knights surging into the meadow, straight for her brother.

*No.*

Timothée. He couldn't be...

Marion shoved herself out of the flock of Morning Stars, all chattering like startled birds.

"What's he doing?"

"Shadows! All around him. Look!"

"Dark Star..."

"Not like any Dark Star I've ever seen."

"You don't think... Noctis?"

Marion ran to the edge of the hill. "Timothée!"

In one flash of moonlight, he looked like her brother, panicked, hands deep in his hair, standing amid a pool of shadows. In another flash, he appeared someone else entirely, the living darkness rising with every shift of his body.

A host of guards surrounded him, their white-gold armor glinting in the night.

"Get away!" Timothée shouted. "I don't want to hurt you."

Marion's heart leapt. She had to do something. But what? She looked around. Her sister, Vivian, was at the forefront of a group of Evening Stars.

What a mess this was! Only a few days ago, they had just been the Greywicks, three orphans living—or surviving, more accurately—in Wolfhelm. One little slip up on a moonless night, a stupid decision to save the Prince of Andúrigard, and a silly legend about the Lost Star Children, and now the Greywicks were here: the Isle of Argos, destined to attend the illustrious Celestial Academy for Fallen Stars.

Of course, the prickly bit of that was you had to catch and swallow a star to become a student. Vivian, the eldest triplet, had succeeded first, emerging from her Rite with an Evening Star burning inside her breast. Marion had been next, surviving her trial of earth, water, wind, and flame, to rise with her Morning Star.

But last was Tim. Last was always Tim. He was always late or missing or asleep somewhere.

But this time, he'd done it. He'd done it in the worst way possible.

He'd swallowed a Dark Star, the feared magic once wielded by the first child of Xydrious and Rhaemyria.

*The one they call our brother. Noctis.*

The guards stepped closer, but Timothée's shadows surged outward, knocking away their weapons.

"Get away from me!" her brother screamed.

Marion whirled to look at Kassandra, the Archpriestess of the Celestial Church and the headmistress of the Academy. And the Greywicks' adopted mother. She was the one who had created these trials for them. Surely, she could help Timothée—

A single tear ran down the Archpriestess's face.

"My lady?" Setviren, the green-haired loremaster said, coming up beside her. "Is this your will?"

She took in a deep breath. "He must be contained."

Timothée stumbled across the meadow. Shadows kept springing from under his feet, slithering up his body. He looked down at them, horrified. They were like black flames, devouring the air.

There was so much noise: the students in a frenzy, Vivian screaming their brother's name, the rush of blood in Marion's head.

"Stop it!" Marion shrieked. "Don't hurt him!" Tears rushed down her face. Her body was hot, too full of fear and hatred for these knights and Archpriestess Kassandra—

Arms enveloped her. "You can't stop it, Marion. It has to be this way." It was Khalid, holding her tight. Khalid Ali Bagheeri. Her one friend in this horrible place. The noble who knew her sister's secret and vowed to help them.

Marion thrashed against his hold. "We have to do something!"

Khalid swung her around, so she stared into his emerald gaze. "Look at him. Your brother isn't in control. The last thing he would want is to hurt you."

Marion caught movement across the field: Yvaine, her brother's ugly cat, tearing through the dark. A flash of something lilac staggered up the hill, away from Timothée and the Celestial Knights.

Valentine Sun.

The Dark Star boy had tormented her brother since they'd arrived, locked him in a sewer, stared at them all with that sardonic smirk. Then he'd been sucked into the Celestial Rite trial with Timothée. Somehow, this had to be his fault.

"Let me go," Marion growled to Khalid. He released her, and she stumbled over to Valentine. "What's going on?"

Val was rigid beside her, his feet digging into the muddy ground, fists balled at his side. His mouth was a thin, firm line.

"Faster!" Archpriestess Kassandra called to her guards. Panic laced her words. "Seize him *now!*"

The Celestial Knights tromped forward, drawing weapons. Weapons! Why did they need those?

"What happened in the Rite?" Marion screamed at Val.

He opened his mouth but didn't speak. His violet eyes looked everywhere but her face.

"Talk to me!" she demanded. "People have swallowed Dark Stars before. Why is the Archpriestess sending knights after him?"

Finally, Valentine said, "The darkness has never chosen someone like him." He looked at the field. "At least... not in a very long time."

Marion stared helplessly down as more shadows coiled around her brother, spiraling out of him in wild funnels, tearing across the grass. Guards encircled him, but even they kept their distance.

"What do we do?" Her voice was a trembling sob.

But Valentine was already staggering away from her. "Don't ask me, Morning Star."

Marion ground her back teeth. Useless. Everyone here was useless. And her own body was making it so hard to think, a fever burning through her skin.

Through her hazy vision, she saw Vivian shouting for Darius. The Prince was a blue beacon at the crest of the hill. Pain etched his features.

"Students, back to your dorms!" Setviren bellowed. "Follow Prince Darius. He shall lead you back to school."

Darius lurched to a stop, clearly torn between wanting to go to Vivian and his duty to the loremaster.

He chose his duty.

Marion ran to her sister. She looked radiant in the dying night, eyes full of tears and starlight. "How do we help him, Mare?"

This was so beyond them. They were the Greywicks! They made bread and sold candles and collected leeches. They shouldn't be here, floating on an Isle that could swallow them up and douse them in deep magic, all in the name of the gods that hadn't done diddly-squat to help them when they were starving and fighting for their lives on the streets of Wolfhelm.

Whatever force had taken Timothée was evil. It wasn't part of him. It couldn't be.

"It's best not to watch," a voice tinged with a heavy Kirrintsovan accent said, and the sisters turned to see Carmilla Vladimirovna.

A grand princess whose home, title, and family had been stripped during the Trinity War twelve years ago. A ward of the Andúrigardian throne. The one who had stabbed the Dark Prophet that fateful night when the Star Children were discovered. And a recent Dark Star herself.

"Tell us," Marion pleaded. "What happened to you when you swallowed your Dark Star?"

Carmilla's face did not have the same pain as Darius's or Khalid's. There was something else in her steely gaze. "A flicker of shadow, but that was it."

And Carmilla Vladimirovna, who had struck down the Dark Prophet, trembled as she stared at Timothée.

His body was dressed in shadows that flickered like murky flames. His back was arched, mouth open to the dying night.

Marion swore she heard her name, and Vivian's, in the torrent of his screams. Vivian collapsed to the ground, head in her hands.

Another horror—Vivian could not open her mouth, not when she was this scared or angry, lest everyone see her sickness.

All of them… so helpless.

Timothée was almost completely covered in shadows. They had fully wrapped around his legs and clawed up his torso, pulling his arms down.

A Celestial Knight held up his hand, slowing as he approached Timothée. But one of Timothée's shadows shot out, striking the guard through the chest like a lance. The guard gave a gurgling retch as the shadow lifted him off the ground.

Timothée stared in horror. Black tears streamed down his face.

Two more knights spurred forward. Shadows lashed at them like a whip. Khalid was right. Timothée couldn't be in control. He would never hurt anyone.

"Contain him!" Setviren shrieked.

"I don't—I don't—" Timothée screamed.

But they kept rushing him. Shadows flayed the ones in front, sending them sailing through the air. Dark tendrils wrapped another; the breath squeezed from his lungs. More shadow lashes sprung out, spiking bodies to the earth with darkness.

These Celestial Knights… They were the best-trained soldiers in all of Thraina. They were the Archpriestess's royal guard.

And they were no match for Timothée, crying tears of shadow.

"All magic goes away with the stars," Vivian whispered. "Dawn approaches." She pointed to the pink line of the horizon.

But dawn was still minutes away. There was too much chaos: Setviren screaming, the students rushing from the field back to the Academy, the dark swirls surrounding her brother and lashing out against the Celestial Knights.

Light cracked across the sky, a flash like a falling sun. And a voice boomed, ancient and terrible: "No shadow dare crest Rhaemyria's holy ground. Put down your dark villainy, acolyte of Noctis. Your reign has ended. Choose peace. Or death."

And Archpriestess Kassandra appeared a giant entity, her mortal body ensconced with a halo of light in the form of great wings. She swooped down the hill; her red and orange armored dress seemed to be made of glittering embers.

Marion wanted to scream. Wanted to run and throw herself in front of her brother, shadows and all. But she was struck still. The warmth within her chest blazed, nearly bursting out of her, as if called to Kassandra's magic.

They were both Morning Stars, disciples of Rhaemyria. Kassandra created so much light, sparks bursting out of her body, that the remaining students ducked down and shielded their gaze.

But Marion did not look away. The light didn't hurt her. And she needed to see.

Kassandra strode across the field, her black staff held high in the air. The bodies, murdered by Timothée—no, not Timothée, by his star—illuminated within her wake.

And Timothée fell to the ground, his shadows curling behind him. He stared up at the Archpriestess. Marion had never seen such fear.

"This ends now," her terrible voice boomed.

Lashes of light emerged from her halo, surging for Timothée. But his darkness whipped back. Light and dark merged, twisting and squeezing. Timothée cried out but stayed still, his brow furrowing. Kassandra was unreadable, expression hidden beneath the bursting white light radiating from within.

Marion could barely take in a shallow breath. They'd lost Father three years ago. She couldn't lose Timothée too.

On shaky legs, Marion stumbled over to the loremaster. He looked down at her with watery eyes, his face ashen. "Professor, is she trying to kill him?"

"Never!" Setviren threw a hand upon his chest. "She only got her son back a day ago. But this darkness…"

"You've seen this before?" Marion urged.

Setviren licked his thin lips. "I've… I've seen this before."

"With other students?"

The loremaster opened his mouth. Closed it.

Upon the field, Kassandra's light formed a great shield around Timothée. But dark spikes shot through, shattering the barrier. Kassandra stumbled back.

Pink light dusted across the field now. But a few stars still twinkled in the sky, giving their power to the Starlings below.

There were too many shadows crawling out from Timothée's chest, his fingertips. Light flickered beneath Kassandra's skin, like stars winking out. Marion could see the great intake of breath even from her vantage upon the hill.

The Archpriestess rose her staff with the strange black stone at the top. And then she slammed it, stone down, upon the earth.

Timothée cried out, grabbing his head. His shadows curled inward. And Kassandra took the advantage. Her light, a dying fire, shot out and enveloped Timothée.

A man whipped past Marion and Setviren, sprinting down the hill. An indigo cloak flowed behind him.

"Barracus!" Setviren cried. "You'll get yourself killed!"

But he didn't stop. Kassandra ground her teeth, knuckles white upon her staff as she struggled to keep Timothée within her light prison. She turned as the man ran up to her, nodded.

The radiant barrier broke away, and the man leapt upon Timothée. His shadows curled, then there was a flash of something black in the dawn.

And the shadows melted into the ground.

The purple-clad man sat atop Timothée's back. Timothée lay in the mud, face scratched, and a black choker around his neck.

Archpriestess Kassandra slumped against her staff. "There." Her voice rang across the meadow. "The Dark Star has been contained."

# 2

# IN WHICH TIMOTHÉE IS BOUND FOR BATS AND COBWEBS

THE WORLD WAS a blur of blackness. Of moist withered leaves and grass and grasping fingers. Timothée couldn't breathe. He kept gasping for air, but his lungs were empty. The sky swirled. At least he thought it was the sky. But there were no stars— and the sky had stars, right?

*Steal the stars from the sky.*

*Shatter the magic.*

*Shake the earth with my reckoning.*

A voice beat against his mind, veiled and foggy.

He'd been sucked into the very Isle. Almost burned by Rhaemyria in a dream… and nearly burned by her upon the field. No, no, that wasn't right. The gods were still in the sky. It couldn't have been Rhaemyria—

Val. Val and Yvaine. They had been swallowed with him.

Where were they?

Light, unbidden, unwanted, broke across his vision, and he still couldn't breathe. But now he could see, and Celestial Knights towered above him.

Something was strangling him. A tight strap around his neck. Some distant part of his mind registered it: a choker.

He couldn't breathe, couldn't exhale. Something was trapped—no, *caged*—within his chest.

"Don't touch that!" the knight yelled. "Don't move! Stop!"

He didn't know what he was doing. He saw a flash behind the guards: Vivian and Marion. They were yelling too.

"It's all right. I'll handle it," a deep voice said.

A man stood over him. He was tall and wore a dark purple cloak. His attention was focused on the knights.

"You're making it worse. Back up," he continued. "We've got the choker on him. I'll take it from here. Come, Carmilla."

Then Carmilla leaned over Timothée, and the pink sun crested the horizon, making her red hair glow like flames themselves.

"Carmilla, get him out of here. I'll clean up this mess," the deep-voiced man said, casting a glance back at Archpriestess Kassandra. "Take him to the Cauldron. I'll find him at twilight."

"Yes, Professor." Carmilla placed a steady hand on Timothée's chest. "Timothée, look at me. You need to breathe."

Didn't she know he couldn't? But when his eyes found hers, he knew she understood. The black choker around her neck, the same one Val wore. The same one Val had taken off the night he'd used shadowcraft.

Carmilla and Val were Dark Stars.

And so was he.

But where was Val? Was he okay? Had Timothée—

"Breathe, Timothée." Carmilla pressed harder on his chest.

He opened his mouth. Cold air seeped into his lungs.

"Good." Then her arms were around him. He staggered to his feet.

"Val." He finally pushed out a word. Of course that was the first one that made it out of his mouth.

"He's fine," Carmilla said simply. "The cat as well. They ran good and clear of you before... before your magic took over."

Blackened streaks slithered through the dark grass. There were still knights in a fighting stance. Still knights on the ground.

"Did I—" Timothée stuttered. "Are they?"

"Stand up and start walking," Carmilla ordered.

He followed her instructions, kept his gaze down, saw Vivian and Marion's skirts.

"Yvaine," was all he could manage. "Please find her."

"We will," Vivian said.

He couldn't bear to look up at the expression on Marion's face. He'd seen her fear when Vivian was at her most monstrous. Didn't think he could survive that expression cast upon himself.

But even without looking up, he felt something different about them. They too had caught stars.

"Do you want to stay with them?" Carmilla whispered.

"No." Then they were walking again, up the hill, cutting through the fog. After a few minutes, he mumbled, "I couldn't talk to them."

"I couldn't either." Carmilla was so much shorter than Timothée, but she supported his weight easily. "Our whole lives it was Darius, Khalid, Celeste, and me. We knew we would go to this Academy. And it sounds silly, but our biggest worry was that we would be split into different houses. Because Dark Stars are so rare, aren't they? It couldn't be any of us. And then Darius caught his Evening Star. And I was next. The Dark Star wrapped its grip around me, and this thing has been choking me ever since.

"I suppose I shouldn't have... but I secretly hoped Khalid would catch a Dark Star, as well. It took him straight 'til morning to catch his. But, alas, he came back with a Morning Star, dawn chasing his heels. Typical of that boy."

Timothée realized they were almost back at the Academy. A couple of other students surrounded them, all dressed in the same purple and silver accented uniform. The uniform of the Dark Star house. But he didn't see Valentine.

The entire trial of Argos seemed a dream. But the part where he and Valentine worked together, where Val had looked at him… For a moment, Timothée had felt understanding and something else, something more, pass between them. And that seemed the most dream-like part of all.

Timothée followed behind Carmilla's heels, and eventually the other students skittered ahead or fell behind.

"Do you know about shadowcraft, Timothée?" Carmilla asked.

He did. He didn't. He didn't know what he knew anymore.

Those who caught an Evening or a Morning Star used starcraft: the magic to change or create. But those who caught Dark Stars could summon and wield the very darkness of night, known as shadowcraft.

"I know it's banned. I know it's evil." *I know it was the magic of Noctis. The magic of my brother.*

"There will be time for a history lesson later." Carmilla paused at the entrance to the school. "For now, there's only one thing you need to know about shadowcraft. The Celestial Academy of Fallen Stars is run by the Celestial Church with support from the Kingdom of Andúrigard. The two most powerful forces in this world." She turned to face him. "But they fear Dark Stars. They fear us."

"AND HERE IS the entrance to our house," Carmilla said.

"Is there a key or secret password?" Timothée asked.

Carmilla gave a little laugh and shook her head. "No. That would mean people actually *wanted* to come here."

Inside the castle, they'd fallen into silence, weaving through the halls like it was a maze. He'd kept his head down. There had been stairs, though. Lots and lots of stairs.

It all led to an old door with a purple bat sloppily painted across it.

They entered a large circular room—which made sense. They must have climbed so high they were in one of three large towers at the top of the Academy.

"Welcome," she said, "to the Cauldron."

The room was filled with… clutter.

Purple flames crackled in an ashen fireplace. Bookshelves were crammed full and loose parchment spilled onto the stone floor. A long table, which was probably meant for eating, was littered with vials half-full of neon liquids, and various colored splotches splattered the ground beneath. The distinct smell of coffee beans and acid filled the space. A few windows let in the first rays of morning light, but most had patchwork curtains covering them.

Several students lounged on mismatched sofas and chairs. They had blankets bundled around them, and Timothée could already feel the draft this high up. All the students wore chokers.

"You must be tired," Carmilla said. "Let me show you to your room. Your things will be delivered here shortly." She then placed a hand on her hip and addressed everyone in the Cauldron. "You're all doing your best to be polite, and I appreciate it. But as you know—because you were all there—this is Timothée Greywick. He's a Lost Star… and he's one of us. Let him be tonight. There will be plenty of time to annoy him tomorrow."

He felt more than heard the command in her words and the soft obedience in the surrounding students. If it hadn't been for the war, she would have inherited an empire.

A young man rose from the crowd. He looked slightly older than Timothée and Carmilla. He had short brown hair, pale skin, and a face of hard angles and hollow cheeks.

"But who would I be to not *formally* introduce myself to *the* Timothée Greywick?" the man asked.

Carmilla let out an annoyed huff. "If you must."

"My name's Erik Borstigsson." The man—Erik—took Timothée's hand. His palm was sweaty. "You might have heard of me."

Timothée thought the name Borstigsson might sound familiar, but his mind was foggy. He looked beyond Erik to the common room. So many students were staring at him, their gazes curious and… fearful. Didn't they all swallow a Dark Star too?

And even here, Timothée felt the innermost core of himself—his differentness—no matter where he went.

"Excuse me!" Erik snapped his fingers in front of Timothée's face. "I thought we were having a conversation."

Timothée startled at the sound. Carmilla sighed, then said: "Erik's father is Jeremysson Borstigsson, Darius's uncle. He will be the steward of Andúrigard until Darius graduates and takes his place as king."

Timothée might see the relation to Darius if he looked closely, if he squinted. But Erik's features were harsher, he was shorter, and he held himself in a way that was too calculated to be casual. *He's trying to appear at ease,* Timothée thought, *but he's frightened of something.*

"Is that all I am to you, little ward?" Erik smirked. "I'm also a fourth-year here and the house leader."

"It's nice to meet you," Timothée mumbled.

"Indeed." Erik narrowed his eyes, then said, "You gave us quite the entrance. Think you took out a couple of Kassandra's favorite knights."

"What—"

The knights on the ground… Had his magic hurt them? Images of violent strips of darkness played in his mind's eye.

"Professor Barracus is taking care of it, I'm sure," Carmilla said. "Timothée didn't know what he was doing."

"No." A slow smile crept up Erik's face. "But can you imagine when he does?"

There was something about the house leader's eyes and his smile— they were misaligned, two mismatched puzzle pieces. Something flared inside Timothée as he looked at Erik. It was his star—a warning.

"He might have what it takes to rival the Dark Prophet himself," Erik murmured.

"Do you think so?" Something passed between Carmilla and Erik. Something acknowledged without being spoken.

"But then again, maybe not. He is rather scrawny." Erik grabbed Timothée's arm. Perhaps his gesture was meant to be lighthearted, but the grip was too tight.

A knock sounded at the door and everyone in the Cauldron went wholly still. Timothée got the impression few outsiders made the trek up the tower.

Slowly, the door opened and in popped Darius Störmberg's golden head. Timothée could have wept at who was curled in his arms, looking as content as she ever had.

"Yvaine," he cried.

But as relieved as he was, Timothée couldn't help but notice the whole Cauldron had suddenly changed with the appearance of Thraina's monarch. Students sat straighter, and some delved deeper into the shadows of the room. But the person who changed the most was Erik Borstigsson. His grip tightened around Timothée's arm.

Erik finally released Timothée and turned to the Prince. "Welcome, cousin. What a sight to see you. You've been at the Academy for almost an entire moon, and yet this is the first I've seen you at the Cauldron."

Darius stepped further into the room. His gaze swept from one side to the other. Jenny Cotswood had the same expression on her face the one and only time he had brought her back to their apartment on Enola Avenue. It was meeting up in her parents' attic after that.

*How different is the Evening Star common room?*

"I'm here to deliver one more member of the Dark Star house." Darius placed Yvaine down on the ground, where she sleepily stretched.

Whatever hesitation had flashed in the Prince's eyes was gone, replaced with the easy grin of royalty.

Erik didn't seem too impressed by his cousin's shift. He strode forward. He was shorter than Darius, lean of build, and a strange, dark confidence settled over him here, in this place he called home. Like he'd led the Prince into a trap.

"Wait, Darius. Won't you stay and have a drink?" Erik gestured to the messy table.

"No," Darius said. "In fact, I must return. Vivian desperately wanted to know her brother was reunited with his pet."

Yvaine flicked her fluffy tail against Darius's leg before running across the room to Timothée, as if such a word was beneath her.

Timothée immediately scooped her up and held her tight against his chest. "Hi girl," he mumbled into her fur.

"Vivian." Erik licked his lips, cocked his head. He didn't say anything more, not with words. But Timothée noticed Darius's slow swallow, how his fingers curled into fists.

"Excuse me," the Prince said, turning.

"I'm curious," Erik said. "How does it feel to be the ruler whose festival was ruined by a raving cultist half his height?"

*He's talking about the Dark Prophet,* Timothée realized. *Making fun of Darius.*

"I wouldn't know," Darius said, and his voice dropped to a pitch Timothée hadn't heard before. His head turned, glimmering blue eyes catching in the low light. "You'll have to take it up with the steward who's currently reigning Wolfhelm. But wait until he tucks you into bed at your childhood home, as Steward Borstigsson doesn't allow Dark Stars in his court."

The Prince slammed the door.

Erik turned, storming to the back of the Cauldron. Students shifted out of the way. Then he snarled, swiping a hand over the table, vials smashing to the ground in a clatter.

"We should go," Carmilla whispered, then pulled Timothée to a staircase across the room. She paused at the bottom. "That's Erik and Darius for you. Of their encounters, that one was mild."

Timothée stayed silent, still thinking of Darius's tone when he'd said 'Dark Stars'. Like it was a vile word.

"As you can see, this is our common room," Carmilla said. "This is where most of the studying happens, and the arguing, and well, everything. There's a small kitchen over there, though it's a bit of a disaster. Some students also use it to practice our assignments. You'll eat most of your meals in the dining hall, anyway. And up here is where all the dorms are."

"Is there a room for me?"

"Morning Stars and Evening Stars have private rooms with personal washrooms," Carmilla said. "We have twenty rooms and four washrooms, and they're all shared. Well, except one." Carmilla placed a finger to her lips. "Where to put you? Sylvester would be kind, but we've already got six people in that room. And you would not want to share with Ashwyn and Bess. I *could* stick you in Nate's room, but he has an allergy to cats."

Timothée shifted from foot to foot. "I don't care where I go."

"Okay then," Carmilla said slowly, "it better be…"

She tugged on his arm, and they started up the staircase. Torches lined the stone walls. "Dorm. Dorm. Washroom." Carmilla named the many doors as they passed by.

"Here's my room," she said. "I would have put you with me, but it's already quite crowded. Keep climbing the stairs. You'll reach the attic—your dorm. It's the only door from here on out. It's a double so you'll share with one other student, but you'll have your own bed and dresser, and it's got a private washroom."

"No one wanted to share a room with a private washroom?" Timothée asked. He was out of breath, but he relished the use of his muscles after everything.

"No one wanted to be his roommate," Carmilla said. "He values solitude, but the Academy forces us into this small space. They claim Dark Stars are so rare, we don't need as much room as the other houses. Then explain to me why we're crowded in here? But never mind. It would seem neither of you have a choice."

"I, uh—"

"Professor Barracus will sort out your uniform and texts in the twilight," Carmilla said. "You relax. Get to know your roommate. He keeps everything tidy, at least. Try not to kill him, okay? The Dark Star house—or as we're otherwise known, the Apothecary's Guild—already has a bad enough reputation."

She entered her room and closed the door before he had a chance to say goodnight. Timothée looked up. If he never saw any stairs again in his entire life, he would be okay with that.

The stairs narrowed, and there were no more windows or doors. He missed Carmilla's presence. Why hadn't she come with him? Soon enough, he realized why no one wanted to be in this room. Who would want to climb all these stairs every day? Finally, he arrived at the black door with a silver handle.

Inside would be the roommate no one wanted.

But no one wanted to be around him either, so maybe that fit.

He rapped his knuckles against the door. When no one answered, he looked down at Yvaine and shrugged. "I guess I should have asked Carmilla if they were up here."

He opened the door and blinked as the dark room slowly came into focus.

It wasn't a room: it was the tomb of one.

Stains of black crawled up the walls. The stone flooring was torn up, chipped and crumbling, with the same black markings. It was like a fire had exploded in the room and all that was left was the silhouette of flames. There may have been dressers or beds, but everything was broken, draped in torn sheets, a patchwork of cloth and splintered wood. A fireplace burned with purple crystals, but underneath were the remnants of an actual fire. Timothée saw bits of burned books and papers in a pile of ash. The dark curtains over the window were the only intact objects.

The common room had been a mess, but this room was destroyed. He stumbled inside.

A powerful scent filled his nose. It was the acidic taste of magic. Dark magic, the same as he had smelled in the field earlier. He wasn't sure how he knew, but he could tell someone had cast shadowcraft in the room, but not recently. The smell was faint, faded.

Something cool clenched around his heart.

Had Carmilla sent him to the wrong place? He couldn't have taken a wrong turn. There was nowhere else to go. But someone couldn't possibly live here.

Yvaine jumped from his arms and her fur shone silver as she hopped through a pink line of rising sun, drifting through the window. Running water sounded from behind the closed curtain on the other side of the room.

Timothée slowly shut the door behind him. He could go ask Carmilla, but the thought of waking her up—and doing all those stairs again—sent a shiver down his spine. He wanted this day to end. Rotten luck had stacked itself over and over on him. It couldn't get any worse.

Here, in the silence, his thoughts started creeping in. He didn't want to think about the Dark Star that had leapt down his throat, the burning sun on that black beach, Erik's unsettling smile, the knights' drawn weapons, or their still bodies in the meadow.

"Hello?" he called uncertainly.

The water stopped running. Rapid movement sounded.

The curtain slid aside, and out stepped Valentine Sun.

# 3
# IN WHICH VIVIAN ENTERS THE DEN

**V**IVIAN WALKED BEHIND Tafieri Hartton, the house leader of the Evening Stars. Although Darius had returned to the field, he'd taken it upon himself to retrieve Timothée's cat. "I'll take Vivian home," Taf had offered.

*Home.* The word rang through Vivian's head as she and Taf walked to the castle. They had to make their way over the Meadow of Shattered Stars, then cut through the village proper—Selene Crescent—full of shoppes, and taverns, and homes for the non-enrolling citizens of the Isle of Argos.

While the Starling students were all heading to bed, the other residents were waking. Smoke rose from the brightly colored wooden houses, and farmers emerged among bountiful fields. A windmill glistened pink in the predawn light, and a sparkling river cut through crops and straight off the edge of the Isle, roaring falls dissolving into misty clouds.

Tafieri looped an arm through Vivian's, her presence reassuring. As they stepped onto the pathway that led to the Academy,

Vivian caught the first view of towers peeking out above the high circular wall.

Her heart stumbled over itself, and warmth flickered in her breast. *Home.* It seemed different to return to the Celestial Academy for Fallen Stars now. Now that she had caught and swallowed her star.

Now that she was a Starling.

Everything felt crowded. Like there wasn't enough room inside her chest for a heart and a star.

"See those three towers?" Taf pointed at the castle.

Vivian followed her gaze, seeing three towers right in the center, the glass roofs glistening.

"Those are the common room spires for each house," Taf continued. "The Den for the Evening Stars on the left, the Nest for the Morning Stars on the right, and there in the middle back is the Cauldron. For the Dark Stars."

That back tower, where her brother would be, didn't reflect the morning light. No glass windows or ceilings. And why would they need it? The Dark Stars didn't use their magic.

Was all shadowcraft as uncontrollable as her brother's had been?

Vivian kept her eyes on her feet, but when they came to the bridge that entered the Academy, she could not help but glance over the edge, to the white, fluffy clouds dancing in the wind.

A school in the sky. A star in her heart. Her feet would never firmly be on the ground again.

Vivian wanted to take in the beautiful architecture of the school, the sprawling grounds of willow trees and flowers, gardens, and little ponds. But her mind buzzed. *Home.* Tafieri had said she was going home.

But as she walked through the doors of the Celestial Academy, she only felt alone.

Home was with Marion and Timothée, at the old lavender field or the run-down apartment on Enola Avenue.

She shut her eyes. *They're still here. We're still together.*

Despite being triplets, all three of them had swallowed a different star.

This Academy had already separated them.

"A verdallion for your thoughts?"

Vivian blinked, realized Taf was stepping backward up a set of long polished stairs.

"I…" Vivian began. "I suppose none of this feels real yet."

Tafieri turned to walk alongside her. "I know what you mean. Sleeping during the day is strange at first. But," she pressed a hand on her sternum, "your star knows when it's time to rest. I can already feel mine simmering down."

"Sleep with the sun, rise with the stars." Vivian echoed the common phrase for Starlings. Starcraft could only be summoned under the light of the stars. Thus, the entire Academy learned at night and slept during the day.

"We're here," Tafieri said and stopped in front of a set of immense doors.

Vivian had seen them before, colored blue with designs of silver stars and constellations and handles of white wings.

"Forged on the Wings of Starlight." Vivian read the words carved atop the door, and they filled a deep ache inside her as she stepped into the Den.

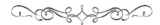

ENTERING THE DEN was like stepping into another world. The room was circular and vast. Glass windows etched with constellations led up to a fractal glass ceiling, the last of the starlight filtering in above them.

Vivian stepped further inside, immediately hit with the sweet scent of maple and sugar and pine. It drew her gaze to the right side of the room, to a grey stone kitchen, lined with ivy, and hanging brass pots and pans on the stone walls surrounding it. A tiered cake with creamy blue frosting was topped with white chocolate stars, and pitchers of glittering blue liquid were laid out on wooden tables.

"We made stuff to celebrate," Tafieri said, "in case a triplet swallowed an Evening Star."

"Oh." Vivian swallowed in a dry throat, gaze sweeping over the cake. Knowing even if she didn't feel sick to her stomach about Timothée, she wouldn't be able to taste a bite.

"And it'll still be good after you sleep," Tafieri said.

She missed nothing, did she? Vivian would have to be extra careful at hiding her illness around her.

"Come look around," Taf continued.

Vivian's boots clicked musically over the marble floor, a deep blue like a cosmic sea. The Den was divided into parts. There was the stonework kitchen, a study nook with towering bookcases that stretched nearly as tall as the ceiling, and tables spread with papers, inks, and art supplies. In the center was a sunken circular pit with cushioned seating, pillows, and plush blankets surrounding an open fire pit. But instead of logs, glittering crystals burned in a pastel fire.

One part of the wall was painted with an intricate mural, a pegasus mid-flight, an armored warrior atop its back. Xydrious, the Moon Father. He brandished a sword in his hand. There was something familiar about that sword...

Starlings wandered through the Den, stopping to stare at her. There was the low rumble of words as she passed, and she caught the whisper of *godling, Evening Star*, and *brother, brother, brother*.

Taf ignored them all. She led Vivian through a door beside the bookcases.

"This is our unofficial work space," Tafieri said. "It used to be storage for extra uniforms, but with so much space, we made the best of it."

A long wall was filled with folded clothes and hanging cloaks, but before it lay a calamity. Long tables spread with half-finished paintings, sculptures, bolts of fabric, and sprawling dresses hung on mannequins.

Vivian walked to a shelf filled with jars of paint, blocks of clay, vials of glitter, boxes of pastels, bound notebooks, untouched paint brushes, and rows and rows of parchment. She ran her fingers over the thick canvas.

"Do you paint?" Tafieri slid beside her, a bundle of clothes in her arms.

Vivian's father used to return home from his trips with paper and brushes and seashells. He'd taught her how to make her own paint by gathering materials from around Seagrass, using everything from flower petals and pollen to the earth itself for colors. She'd painted the adventures from Timothée's stories, and cards to sell the lavender, and the word *Greywick* above their door.

When Father died during the vampire attack in Wolfhelm three years ago, there hadn't been money for paint and canvas. Marion had bought her a sketchbook and charcoal for their eighteenth birthday last year, and she'd known Timothée and Marion had gone hungry because of it.

But the gift had only brought her pain. She'd never felt like drawing in it. Couldn't even make herself pick up the charcoal sticks.

Vivian dropped her hand from the parchment and turned to Taf. "I used to."

"Evening Stars are known for their creativity. You can use the supplies anytime you want." Taf handed her a pile of clothes. "Here are some basics to get you started, and some lounge clothes. We wear uniforms to class, but you can alter them a bit. The professors don't mind. Someone in our house would be happy to help you. Shoes are on the bottom row if you want to grab your size."

Vivian leaned down and plucked a pair of short black ankle boots and black flats, putting them on top of her pile.

"On the weekend, you can wear whatever you want. There are shoppes in Selene Crescent, but most people enjoy taking the sky shuttle down to the capitals like Wolfhelm, Novagrad, or Baz-Kazar. They have the most options."

"Okay," Vivian said. "Thank you."

Taf smirked, then hooked her arm around Vivian's. "Time to see your room."

As they left the workspace, Vivian noticed most of the students still mingling around the room had settled into a post-dawn routine. Many wore blue lounge clothes and carried around steaming cups of tea. One student touched something on the wall, and a shimmering velvet curtain circled around the windows, shrouding them from the morning light.

Some students came up to offer a quick welcome or congratulations on catching her star. She didn't hear any whisper of *brother* this time.

"Every dorm room is private with their own washroom." Taf led her to a winding staircase at the back of the circular space.

Doors lined either side of them. They were all painted in shades of blue, from robin egg to the deepest night. Curved at the top, in glowing silver light, were the names of students. She read through them: *Jacen, Olivier, Tafieri, Fiona, Sif, Sapphire, Safiya, Wren.* Vivian paused at a bright blue door, couldn't help but place her hand on it. *Darius.*

Taf eyed her. "Knowing Darius, he won't come in until he finds that cat."

Vivian nodded, then followed Taf up a few more stairs until she paused in front of a room with no name. It was the light ice-blue of a frozen lake.

"Go ahead." Taf nodded. "Touch it."

When Vivian did, her inward star fluttered as glowing lines appeared at the top of the door. *Vivian* in bright silver letters.

*Welcome, daughter of Xydrious.*

The voice came from the walls themselves. Timothée had told her and Marion on his first night here the castle spoke to him. And when she'd been swallowed by the Isle and taken to her trials, the voice had been there too.

It was as if the whole Isle of Argos was alive.

"I'll let you settle in. They serve breakfast in the dining hall starting at seventh toll. I'm sure Setviren will sort out your schedule at twilight. Please let me know if you need anything."

Vivian nodded. "Thanks, Taf."

Taf disappeared down the hall, then Vivian pushed open her door to the room.

It was more spacious than she could have imagined. Square in shape with a door that must lead to the washroom, marble floors, and a circular moon rug. There was both a vanity and a desk. Vivian placed her new clothes atop a white dresser. In front of a window was a sitting bench with the plushest-looking pillows she'd ever seen. She wondered if they had given Timothée a similar room. It looked like a spot she'd catch him reading.

She looked past the fluttery curtains and saw a rocky cliff and a sparking waterfall. Slowly, she closed them, blocking out the morning light.

There was a strange cabinet along the wall and when she opened it, cold air blew in her face. A starcraft enchantment? She knew some powerful Starlings' magic could last beyond the light of the stars. Inside, the cabinet was filled with chilled bottles of water, fresh fruit, and chocolates.

She unhooked her muddy bag from around her chest and dug in the bottom until she found the jar of leeches. Perhaps it was the stress of the trial, but she didn't feel hungry. She had to eat though, so she sucked down one of the slimy creatures. Then she grabbed a pair of silk pajamas from the dresser and made for the washroom.

It was bigger than their entire apartment on Enola Avenue. With a copper clawed tub, sink, large mirror, and shower enclosed with stone working, Vivian felt like she was sullying everything just by looking at it.

Carefully, she stripped out of her clothes and tossed them into a wicker basket. Then she stepped into the shower, admiring the sill lined with vials and sweet-smelling oils, and a hard stone for scrubbing. She went to work freeing her near-translucent skin from caked mud.

Gently, she touched a sudsy finger between her shoulder blades and a flashing memory of her trial coursed through her: the monster from her Rite. A vampire who had lost all sense of its former human self, a starving, stretched body of ashen flesh, sharp claws, and membranous wings.

But her back felt smooth, and the leech blood satisfied her for now. Perhaps that star beside her heart had given her a little extra strength.

She locked the memory away as she stepped from the shower. Even the towel over her body felt wondrously soft. But she wouldn't get used to this.

Everything could be lost in a moment.

She dropped the towel into the bin and looked in the mirror.

Her dark, wet hair lay limp around her face, her eyes were swollen, her skin pale, bringing out the few freckles in stark contrast. But as she stared into her grey eyes, she imagined the tiniest fleck of blue there. A light from within. Her star was strengthening her.

As she slipped on some silken pajama pants and a loose shirt, a knock sounded. Vivian rushed to the door, and there, mud splattered on his cloak, was Darius.

"Hi," she whispered softly.

He leaned on the doorframe, silent, as if he had to take her in for a moment before saying anything. Then he took a deep breath and ran a hand through his wayward blond hair. "I found the cat."

"Yvaine. Oh good."

"She came right when I called. I reunited her with Timothée."

"So, he's okay?"

"Carmilla is looking after him," Darius said. "I'm sure he just needs to rest, as you do." He caressed a wet strand of her hair. "Do you like your room?"

"It's lovely."

He dropped his hand, stared at her for a moment, then said, "We can speak in the evening. Sleep well."

He had just arrived and now he was leaving? He was probably exhausted. Darius turned, and she almost reached out to grip his arm, to ask him to… to stay.

The notion was preposterous. He was the Prince of Andúrigard. Even if he had displayed affection for her, he certainly wouldn't consider spending the night in her dorm room.

"Goodnight, Darius."

She watched him disappear down the stairs, then closed the door with a soft click and headed to her bed.

Vivian nearly sunk into the layers of plush blankets and pillows. She pulled the comforter up to her face. This bed was larger than the one she shared with Marion back in Wolfhelm, or the simple one Father had built from driftwood at Seagrass. She wondered if Marion would enjoy sleeping in her own bed today without accidentally being kicked in her sleep by Vivian's ice-cold feet.

She'd never had her own room in her entire life.

It was terribly lonely.

And when she closed her eyes, all she could see was Timothée devoured by shadows, and the monster from her vision, biting and scratching. And when she desperately tried to run from that nightmare, she was back in the square, her eyes glowing under a moonless sky. Vampires burning beneath her gaze, as if the light in her eyes was the sun itself.

Guilt simmered. But vampires weren't human. They only cared about drinking the blood of mortals. Somehow, she differed from other vampires. She could walk beneath sunlight without burning, and she'd like to think she'd held onto her human heart. She'd never bitten a human, and survived on the leeches Marion had gathered from her bloodletting shoppe.

They had some stores, but how long would they last? Khalid Ali Bagheeri said they would find answers here, but that could be false hope.

There was no belonging to be found here. She wasn't really a student, but an imposter, a monster in a uniform.

She groaned into her pillow, desperately trying to quiet her roaring mind, but every sound—from the crackle of the crystal fire to the tinkle of wind on the glass window—felt too loud.

Vivian threw back the covers, and before she knew what she was doing, padded across the floor. She didn't want to be alone tonight.

And couldn't ignore the pull of her heart.

Before she could change her mind, she opened her door and walked barefoot down the cold stairs.

*He's here.* His back was to her. Darius had changed from his uniform into a loose white shirt and tan breeches, his hair glistening wet. He took a few steps down the stairs, then turned to head back up, gaze still downcast. Then turned back down again.

As if he couldn't decide which way to go.

"Darius," she said.

He looked up, blue eyes wide as he took her in. And then she knew. He knew. Somehow, they had felt the call to each other.

She flew down the rest of the steps and leapt into his arms.

He caught her and pulled her against him. Then his lips found hers, a devouring kiss.

She sighed into it, thankful for the leech blood. Kissed him back hard, her lips exploring the planes of his face, tasting the soap and water on his jaw.

"Stay with me," she murmured against his neck. "Stay with me tonight."

# 4
# WHICH TIMOTHÉE GETS THE VERY WORST ROOMMATE

VALENTINE'S EYES WENT wide, water flying off his hair. "What are you doing here?" A dark rasp of words.

He wore a grey robe, tied loosely at his waist, open enough so Timothée could see the smooth white planes of his chest. Water caressed his exposed skin. His face was bare, shadows and liners washed off. Without it, he looked different: softer, younger almost. Timothée's breath caught in an odd way. *Of course, it's Valentine...*

"You better answer me, Greywick." Val stalked toward him, navigating around the rubble of the room. The whole place was trashed.

"This is… This is my room now." *If you can call it a room.*

"Did Borstigsson put you up to this? Oh, this is a funny joke." Val bent down to a pile of clothes and threw on a tight black shirt and some loose pants before dropping his robe and hauling the door open. "Well, let's see how he likes—"

"It was Carmilla," Timothée said weakly.

"Carmilla?" Val hesitated, then slammed the door so hard the wood splintered. "What was she thinking sending *you* here?"

The question didn't seem directed at him.

Timothée barely dodged Val as he stormed back to the window and drew the curtains, blocking the rising sun.

Why was Val upset? Lots of people had roommates they didn't like. It wasn't as if *Val* had been attacked by Celestial Knights while *his* sisters got to celebrate. It wasn't the worst day of *his* life.

Well, maybe getting sucked into the abyss of the Isle of Argos and fighting a phantom god had made it the worst day of Val's life, but he hadn't had to endure the other stuff like Timothée.

Timothée wanted to scream and cry and curl up in a ball—but he couldn't do that. Not in front of Valentine.

He clenched his fists, forging his sadness into anger.

"This room is a disaster!" Why was Val staying in a room so destroyed? How could a school treat its students this way? "How do you live like this?"

"You don't." Val stepped over a pile of books, bracing his hands on the wall. He was silent for a long time. So long the crystals in the fire broke down to glittering embers. "You don't live at the Celestial Academy for Fallen Stars. You survive."

And Timothée thought with sickening clarity: Marion had been right. His father had been right.

"You think I want to be in here with you?" Timothée whispered.

Because that was all he could say. How could he talk about what happened when he and Val had been pulled into the Isle? Both his sisters had endured their trials alone. But Val had come with him by accident... or by some other reason.

But Timothée didn't know how to look at him now. Val had admitted so much to him when they thought they were going to die, but one thing he said stood out in startling clarity: Val regretted swallowing his Dark Star.

"I don't think you know what you want," Val replied.

Timothée swallowed in a dry throat. He *had* known: he had wanted a purpose. He had wanted to be a hero, to find out where he belonged. But he had been scared to wish it. Been scared to voice that desire. Until all at once it had come to him: place and purpose. Then it was ripped away in a single night.

As if it had never been there at all.

He gritted his teeth then clawed at his choker.

"Careful. If you take that off wrong, you'll bleed all over my room." Val licked his lips. "Not that I wouldn't find that amusing, but I don't want to be blamed for you getting hurt."

Timothée dropped his hands. Not because of Val. But he knew it would be worse if he took off the choker. It wasn't the choker that was wrong. It was everything about him. The magic writhed inside of him, coiling and slithering and searching.

Shadowcraft—that type of magic had leveled kingdoms, defied the gods, been banished.

*My magic.* The voice that was not his own spoke inside his mind. *Blacken the sky until the gods have no home to return to.*

*Steal the stars.*

Now there wasn't something shuddering inside him, but all around. The crystal fireplace sparkled and burst, and for a moment he swore he saw something—glowing eyes staring back at him from the flames.

He stumbled, tripped, and barely righted himself.

"What?" Val sneered. "More ghosts?"

"Like you care. Are you going to pretend it didn't happen?" Timothée went to what he thought might be a bed. He threw off broken pieces of wood and books—very old books—until he saw the semblance of tattered sheets and pillows. He whacked it with his palms a couple times, sending plumes of dust into the air. Then he picked up Yvaine and plopped her down on the dirty blanket.

"Unfortunately," Valentine sneered, "I have an impeccable memory."

Timothée looked over at him through the wayward waves of his hair. And he remembered another moment, the moment after he'd swallowed his star, before the darkness took hold. They were falling. Falling through space and time and stars, and he'd clutched Val's face between his hands...

Anger swirled inside him as he looked at his roommate. "This is your fault. Why did you come to me in the meadow? You made me catch that Dark Star."

"It was that or nothing," Val said simply.

Timothée had the oddest urge to shove him—but he was afraid if he put his hands on Val's shoulders they would get stuck there. "I'd rather have nothing," he said instead.

"You don't know what nothing is—"

"And you do?"

"Imagine a horizon so vast there is no end." Val reached up his hand, fingers coiling dangerously around Timothée's choker. "Before you is a great sea, smooth as glass because there is no wind, and everything is grey, because everything that had brought color to the world is gone, and nothing will ever bring that back. But somehow you endure—even though there is nothing to endure for, and you're as still and grey as that vast horizon, unmoving water. Until your blood solidifies to crystal, your skin hard as stone, and you are as alive as carved marble, a painted picture—nothing but an imitation of life. That, Greywick, is nothing."

Timothée swallowed, realized he was clutching Val's shirt. "If that was a poem, it did not move me. If that was a song, I'd say your voice lacked a certain cadence. And if it was a spell, it did not work." Timothée trembled beneath Val's gaze. "I'd rather be that than what I am."

"We'll see." Val stepped away.

"See what?"

"One day you'll understand what nothing is. And then you'll know."

Val turned from him and walked to a corner of the room, wrapping a large black cloak around his shoulders, and slid to the ground.

Timothée kicked off his shoes. Still in his clothes, he crawled into the bed and soon felt the warm press of Yvaine on top of his legs, her low purr the only sound.

He stared at the ceiling. "Where do you even sleep?"

The darkness answered, "I avoid it. If I can."

Timothée rose on his elbows, saw the flicker of purple light along the boy's jaw. He remembered when he'd first seen Val wandering the halls. *He told me he couldn't sleep then.* "Why?"

Val gave a long sigh, tilted his head back. Wet strands of silvery hair slid over his shoulders. "There are things I'd rather not see when I close my eyes."

Timothée wanted to ask more but held back at the hesitation in Val's voice.

"Go to sleep, Greywick," Val said, his voice lined with shadow and promise. "I won't murder you… tonight."

Timothée clutched Yvaine to his chest, lay back. Sleep caught at the edges of his mind, and somehow he knew he would slumber like every other night.

Even wicked monsters needed rest.

## 5
# IN WHICH MARION RECEIVES
# A PHANTOM SIGN

ESPITE DAWN LIGHT sneaking over the huge balcony and through the large windows, a party raged within the Nest. A party of which Marion was the guest of honor.

Which explained why she was outside, leaning on the railing, in a sulk.

The Nest was as beautiful today as it was when Khalid snuck her in, everything gilded and ornate. And there was so much food: hot soups in kettles, every possible vegetable stuffed with seasonings, and bread made in the traditional way from all of the three nations. They had given her a lovely yellow dress to change into, so she didn't have to wear her muddy clothes from the Rite.

And everyone seemed so happy, laughing and singing songs and playing boisterous card games.

Didn't they feel it?

The weight within their chests?

The heat threatening to explode?

Maybe it was different for them. None of these Starlings had been sucked into the Isle of Argos, like Marion and her siblings. None of them had held their father's head between their hands and squeezed until the flesh melted beneath their fingers. None of them had two monsters for siblings.

She sighed, breathing in the dewy air. It was beautiful on the Nest's huge balcony, bathed in the rising sun. It looked over the edge of the Isle of Argos, clouds filling the horizon, pink as the fairy floss they sold at traveling carnivals.

She should go back inside. The last thing she wanted was for Khalid to come looking for her and start reading her mind—something he seemed all too adept at.

But when she looked through the large windows into the common room, Khalid was standing on a table attempting to throw a bread roll into a basket held aloft by another student on the far edge of the room.

She was safe in her solitude a little longer.

"What are you doing out here alone?"

Marion jumped, clutching her chest as she turned to see Rayna, another first-year Morning Star and Khalid's cousin. "Three above! How are you so quiet?"

Rayna laughed her tinkling laugh. "I always wear slippers. Makes for better sneaking." She gave an exaggerated wink.

Marion stared at her, totally unsure if she was teasing her or not.

"So, why are you out here all alone? It's a party for you, after all! The Morning Stars got a godling! Not that I'm surprised."

"Aren't you all supposed to be asleep by now?"

"The key to creation is balance. That means when we focus, we focus. And when we celebrate," Rayna's robin egg blue hair swished as she laughed, "we celebrate."

Marion didn't feel like she was worth celebrating. She slumped over the railing, pink light playing across her pale hands.

Rayna worried her bottom lip and mimicked Marion's position. "Hey, it's okay. I know this is probably a lot. Your siblings will be fine."

*You don't know that,* Marion thought. But there was no point saying it out loud.

"Don't ask me how I'm sure, but the Dark Stars will take care of Timothée. They're good people, Marion. And Professor Barracus seems gruff, but he looks after the Dark Stars like they're his own kids."

*Nobody knows how to care for Timothée except for me and Father.* A lump formed in her throat. What a good job she'd done of that so far.

"And Vivian will love being in the Evening Star house! I've got loads of friends there, and they're wonderful. And of course, dear Prince Darius will watch over your sister. Oh, wouldn't that be fun? You, me, Khalid, Darius, Vivian, and Taf could all go down to Selene Crescent on our next day off! It will be a triple date."

Marion scrunched up her nose. "I'm not dating Khalid! And Vivian is certainly not dating *that* prince." She shook her head. "I didn't know you were with the Evening Star house leader."

Rayna gave a mischievous giggle. "Not yet, but I've crafted a grand plan."

"You *are* like Khalid. Always with your plans."

Rayna went quiet. She looked through the windows and Marion followed her gaze.

Khalid stood in the middle of a crowd of Morning Stars, his energy as radiant as the sun itself. He'd changed into more casual clothing, a tight black tunic, accentuated with a loose golden necklace. He ran a hand through his perfectly tousled black hair and Marion wanted to scream.

Khalid Ali Bagheeri was the only reason she'd been able to leave the field after Archpriestess Kassandra had forcefully attacked her brother. He'd taken her by the shoulders, reassured her Timothée would be alright. Something in his gaze had made her believe him.

But how much of that confidence was based in reality, and how much was caused by that damn curl between his green eyes?

"Look, Marion," Rayna began. This time she stared down at her small, slippered feet. "You're going to love it here with the Morning

Stars. We're a big, happy family. We might stab each other in the back a little, but we're a family all the same."

"That sounds reassuring."

"It's just the facts. And that's why I want to warn you." Rayna took a deep breath and met Marion's gaze. "Khalid is my cousin, and I love him dearly. But if something seems off to you... Trust yourself first, okay?"

"I only ever trust myself," Marion said.

Rayna smiled. "Good girl." With the grace of a dancer, she turned on a toe and glided toward the doors back into the common room. "I'll let you get back to your ruminating now."

Marion balled her hands into fists and choked out the words: "T-thank you. Thank you, Rayna. For being a friend."

Rayna's brown eyes sparkled. "Hey, just remember, I may be your friend, but don't trust me either. Okay?"

"Okay."

"See you later, godling. Oh, and if you need a break from all this hubbub, there's a door from the balcony that leads through the Nest's kitchen. You can escape if you don't want anyone to notice you."

And as soon as she stepped through the balcony doors, she was a different person entirely, small frame lit up with electric energy, instantly greeting and engaging with people.

Marion stood in the dawn silence, rubbing her chest.

Her skin felt on fire.

She wanted to extinguish. She wanted to plant her feet on the ground and never think of flying. She wanted these clouds to turn to rolling fields, the heat in her breast to cool, and the racing of her mind to quiet.

But there was no relief here.

Marion studied the door Rayna had pointed out, the one that cut through the kitchen, then watched the party. Khalid turned in a circle, looking around.

Looking for her?

Before he spotted her through the window, she fled. She pushed through the kitchen doors, bumping into a couple Starlings pouring pitchers of orange juice and putting together colorful fruit kebabs. From the kitchen, she exited to the edge of the common room, easily darting into the stairwell that led out of the Nest.

There was a bedroom somewhere here for her, a place to call her own. But how could she lay her head down to rest when she was sleeping within the very walls her father had fled from? How could she make small talk with strangers when her brother had killed Celestial Knights?

She darted down the stairs and flung open the doors past the double phoenix statues. The hallways were a labyrinth of velvet carpet and mahogany wood, but she remembered the path to the main alcove. The corridors were mercifully bare, the other Starlings asleep or perhaps also celebrating in their own towers.

All Marion knew was she needed to escape these walls. She burst out the main doors and sprinted down the steps into the open air. A cold wind whipped her blond tresses around her face. The white stone bridge carried her over waterfalls that cascaded off the edge of the Isle and evaporated into mist. Too close, the Academy still felt too close.

Running was a terrible sport and should only be done if one is in immediate danger. And yet, here she was. Running. Sprinting, even. Maybe if she ran fast enough, the heat inside her would extinguish.

Her feet carried her from the bridge out into the courtyard of Selene Crescent. There were people here, workers closing up their shoppes and still cleaning up from the big event last night. Marion felt as if a spotlight had been draped over her. No, no, she didn't want to be seen. Didn't want any of these eyes to know her, sister of monsters, failure, a star too hot for her heart.

Some of them called out to her as she ran past, but she didn't stop, didn't think her legs could. Where was she going? There was grass beneath her feet now, and she left Selene Crescent behind. No one followed her. How could they? She must be made of smoke now.

Ahead, there was a grove. Leafy trees stood sentinel around a small lake. One tree stood out from the others, adorned with blue flowers. But Marion could only concentrate on the lake. Without thought, she plunged into the dark water. Her body clenched from the icy cold, but she dove, heavy skirt holding her back. There had to be a place cold enough in this lake to extinguish her.

A new burning sensation appeared, this one in her throat. Air. She turned upward, bursting out of the lake, and dragged herself onto the shore.

She was still too hot.

Marion dug her hands into the silt and looked upward. The sun burned fiercely, bursting through the clouds in arrogant beams.

Rhaemyria, the first goddess. That's who had blessed her, with this burning star. That's who'd created her twenty years ago. Her mother.

"What do you want from me?" Marion screamed at the sky. "Why would you do this to us?"

If the legend were true, and the Greywicks were the children of Rhaemyria and Xydrious, how could their own mother leave them to suffer? Why would she allow Vivian to be bitten by a vampire? For Timothée to swallow a Dark Star?

Marion heaved herself up and turned in a circle, eyes watering as she stared straight at the sun. "Who are you? Answer me! Are you even listening?"

She collapsed on her back, blinking up at the beams of light filtering through the branches of the grove. Her hands drifted over the wet grass, desperate to feel a semblance of earth on this floating Isle.

She knew there would be no answer; no one was listening. She was alone, with the trees and the lake and the dawn light and the chitter of a squirrel.

"I just want someone to tell me," she whispered, a single tear running down her cheek, "I'm not alone."

Her hand tickled and there was a small rustle. Marion sat up, looked beside her. Strange blue flowers with pointed petals sprung up from beneath her hand, growing and blooming as if resistant to time.

Marion scrambled back, but more flowers grew beneath her feet.

"What's going on?" She looked around. "Is someone using starcraft?" But it couldn't be. The stars were long hidden behind the sun. Besides, there was no one here except for a large black squirrel shrouded in the shadows of a tree hollow, staring at her intently with a yellow gaze.

Marion turned back to the flowers. They'd stopped springing up now, the small cluster blowing in the breeze.

"They're not lavender," she mused, "but they're nice all the same." She looked up at the black squirrel. "What do you think? Are these magic flowers? Is it a sign?"

The squirrel turned in a rapid circle in the hollow, the trunk shaking with the movement. Petals rained upon her as the branches trembled. She smiled a soft smile, letting them catch in her hair, on her wet cheeks, adorn her clothes.

"I hear you," she whispered. She reached down and plucked a few of the flowers. She'd need to put them in water. That would mean going back to the Nest, finding her room.

"They did bloom for me after all. I wouldn't want them to wilt," she said to herself.

And maybe there were no answers to be found about who she was or who her parents were. But she could put these little flowers in a cup and care for them. She could go back to the Academy for that.

And maybe for this morning, that would be enough.

# 6
## IN WHICH VIVIAN SLEEPS WITH THE WOLVES

"STAY WITH YOU today?" Darius echoed her words back. Vivian pulled away slightly, flushing. "I didn't mean…" she faltered. "I just don't want—"

"To be alone?" He finished the words for her.

"Yes."

They climbed the few steps to her room, and Darius kicked the door shut behind them.

"Is this allowed?" she asked.

He crossed his arms and leaned on the wall, observing the room. And her. "Do you always follow the rules?"

"You're the Prince of Andúrigard. Of anyone, you're supposed to be enforcing them."

"Depends on the rule." He ran a hand through his golden hair. "From what I've observed, spending the night in a different dorm room isn't forbidden. We're adults, and the professors trust we'll be responsible."

Vivian's heart raced faster in her chest. Responsible. She could only imagine what Marion would think about her inviting Darius to her room.

"You'll have this room until you graduate," Darius said. "Many students decorate their spaces. I'm sure you'll make this your own."

"Have you added anything to your room?"

"No, not really." He paused, then his voice softened as he said, "Just one thing. An old stuffed animal that used to belong to Celeste."

"Your sister." His sister had been killed three years ago during the attack on Wolfhelm led by the Dark Prophet and his vampire cult. The same attack had taken the life of Vivian's father and claimed her humanity.

"We always thought we'd go to the Academy together. She'd be one year behind me." Darius stared past Vivian. "I suppose I feel like I'm taking her with me."

Vivian crossed to him and thread her fingers through his. Darius was usually so composed, but in moments like this, she caught a flicker of something else beneath his eyes. A storm brewing.

"You may all have caught a different star," Darius said, "but you're lucky to go on this journey together."

"I know." She could do none of this without Marion and Timothée.

"I am lucky too, with Khalid and Carmilla," Darius continued. "They are like family."

Khalid and Carmilla with their sly green eyes, Khalid's like chips of emerald, Carmilla's like shards of jade. There were depths within them both.

"Come on." She tugged his hand. "I have to get used to sleeping during the day."

A smile broke, and the storm faded away for a moment. "Trust me, after some of Professor Barracus's combat classes, you will be thoroughly tired."

"Combat classes?" Vivian pulled back the covers and slipped beneath the silken sheets.

"Indeed. Many graduates will become Celestial Knights. Year 1s and 2s explore all aspects of becoming Starlings before specializing in Year 3 and 4."

He followed her into the bed, arm tucking beneath the pillows, and body curving around her. She was grateful for this connection between them, that she didn't have to explain what she needed from him tonight. His presence, his warmth, the comforting beat of his heart.

She turned so her head lay against his chest, his left arm wrapping around her, his right caressing the hand she lay on his stomach. She clasped the blue ribbon tied around his wrist.

"I've never done this," she whispered. "Slept next to someone other than my siblings."

He threaded his fingers through hers. "I'm glad to be beside you, Vivian."

But this wasn't his first time sleeping next to someone. He'd been her first kiss, the first man who had ever touched her. How many people had he been with? Vivian almost wished she didn't know one. A striking green-eyed woman popped into her mind: Carmilla Vladimirovna. Khalid had told her Darius had been with Carmilla until she'd left him for Valentine.

"Hey," Darius said, sensing her unease. "Is everything okay?"

She curled in closer to him. "Yes, it is."

Darius tapped a clear crystal on the side of her table and the glittering fireplace dimmed, shrouding them in darkness.

"Is this crazy?" Vivian held tight to the ribbon. "Does it feel strange to you to sleep beside someone you hardly know?"

"We have only just met, but I don't think I hardly know you."

She'd sensed it from the moment he'd walked into the candle shoppe. He saw so many parts of her no one else did. But she couldn't show him the darkest part of herself. Not yet.

His lips pressed gently to her forehead. "Sleep sweet, Vivian."

She closed her eyes and fell asleep to the ever-present beat of his heart.

MUMBLED CRIES AWOKE her. She blinked sleep from her eyes, pushing herself up from the bed. Darius tossed in his sleep, his brow knotted, as incoherent words escaped his lips.

"Darius?" She crawled over to him, touching her palm to his face. Cold sweat dripped down his forehead. "Darius? Wake up."

His eyes shot open, flashing wild and animalistic in the crystal firelight. Then his hands were on her, grip tight. She whirled, flat on her back, him above her.

His eyes were cloudy, distant, mouth held in a grimace. She struggled, unable to break free of his grip. "Darius!" she shrieked, then drew up her knees and pushed against his chest. He tumbled off the bed.

She hadn't meant to hit him hard. He lay flat against the marble floor, eyes clearing as he took her in. She realized the topmost buttons of her shirt had come loose, revealing her collarbone, the top of her chest. Her dark hair curled wildly over her shoulders.

"Vivian, I'm sorry." He stood, words low and fast. "I should have known I couldn't—"

"Darius?" She pushed off the bed, but he was already heading to her door. "Darius, wait!"

The door closed as she reached it, and before she could think about her actions, she flew down the steps after him.

She caught his door before it fully shut. Stars, what was she doing? If he was running from her, he clearly wanted to be alone. But the pull toward him was as strong as it had ever been.

"Darius!" she said again, a surprising harshness to her voice. She pushed herself inside. His room was similar to hers, nothing to mark it as his own besides a folded uniform atop the dresser.

He didn't turn. The blinds were open, and he was nothing but a black silhouette against the glaring sun. "I'm not... I shouldn't have stayed with you."

Her heart tightened, the star flickering. "You didn't want—"

"Of course I wanted to. But I should have known I couldn't will away my nightmares. What if I had hurt you?"

She moved close enough to hear his ragged breath and the frantic beat of his heart.

"I can take care of myself. I'm the daughter of a god," she snarled. Was it the first time she'd said that? She wasn't sure. But it was the first time she had felt it. And she pushed against his chest. Not hard, but he stumbled across the room, falling onto his bed.

She gasped and looked down at her hands. "I'm sorry. I didn't mean—"

Was that the god part of her lending strength or something else?

Golden strands of hair fell on his face as he looked up at her. "I'm alright."

"You don't have to be." She shook her head and tears poured from her eyes. "You don't have to pretend. Not with me." She walked over to stand above him.

Rough hands gripped her face, tangling through her hair. "There are so many things I haven't told you," Darius said.

*And I you.*

He pulled her down to his lap. "I'm sorry. I should have warned you."

"That you suffer from nightmares?"

"Yes. It's in the Störmberg blood. That's what my father used to tell me." He paused. "But they got worse three years ago. Before it was just images: forests, trees, a frozen mountain, strange monsters. Running until I thought I'd swallowed my heart, trying to stop and not being able to, wanting it to end, but always just out of reach of snarling claws and teeth. But now, I see the attack."

"What the... what the vampires did to your family?" *The vampires,* she'd said. Like they were so different from her. She had to believe they were.

"Yes." The muscles in Darius's jaw tightened. "And what I did to them."

Her stomach dropped. "Darius…"

"It is not your burden; I should not trouble you with such darkness. Not when you have faced such hardship on your own." He cupped his hand on her cheek. "You never told me what happened when the Isle took you away."

She looked down at the floor. "I saw a room with only stars beyond and a wall of portraits. Some of the past and some of the future."

One such portrait was of herself as the Queen of Andúrigard. And by the way he was looking at her, it was almost as if he could tell what she was thinking.

"And a portrait of my most monstrous self. That's the one that came to life."

"And what did you do to that monster?"

She swallowed in a dry throat. "I killed her. For now."

He stared at her. She knew he understood. Perhaps he understood in a way no one else could.

His hand drifted down her neck, lightly touching above her heart. "My mother used to say we all have a hungry wolf constantly circling our hearts."

"A wolf?" She moved her hand above his heart, fingers dipping beneath the soft fabric of his shirt.

"It's the family crest," he said. "There are many legends of wolves in our history. She'd say the wolf feeds off anger and fear, but if you fill your heart with laughter and love, the wolf will protect you."

She closed her eyes, letting her whole hand drift against his warm skin. "Don't feed the wolf."

"Mother used to say that," he murmured. "Don't you dare feed the wolf, Darius Störmberg. She'd say it with so much fear."

"Then let us not feed the wolf tonight." Vivian gently pressed her lips against his.

He opened his mouth to the kiss, and she let her whole tongue dip into his mouth. It was amazing, the strength she'd received from catching her star. Or had it been vanquishing her monstrous self? Her hidden fangs tingled, but they were easy to control as his tongue slid across her teeth, explored deep in her mouth.

The feeling sent a shiver down her spine, the sensation circling deep. She pressed her body tight against his, realized she was straddling his hips.

The silk of her pajamas was thin, and the long hard shape of him was firm between her legs. She swayed there for a moment, considering.

Pure male arrogance flashed on his face. Heat built in her core, and a soft surrendering sound escaped her lips. He placed his large hands on either side of her waist.

He raised a brow, then guided her hips in a rocking movement. The sensations of the fabric against her skin, his hardness rubbing, rubbing, rubbing—

A strangled breath released, and she grabbed his shoulder to steady herself.

"Remember what I told you before? You have to tell me what you like." Darius's breath was warm on her ear before he gently took the lobe between his teeth. "Tell me what you like."

She managed in a breathy cadence, "What if I don't know?"

"Shall I give you some options?" Then they were spinning, and she fell into a heap on the soft bed.

"Okay."

"First, what don't you want to do?"

She swallowed. She wanted him, all of him. But she needed to go slowly, especially as she wasn't sure how her... illness would react to too much stimulation. "I want to do everything. But I think it would be best to take our time."

"I can take my time." Darius grinned.

"Are you upset?"

He took her face between his palms. "Of course not. I would be content to sleep at the foot of your bed if you desired it so." He kissed her softly on the mouth. "If this ever gets too much, say the word."

"'Kay."

They kissed, long and lingering, until the taste of him was the only thing she knew.

Voice rough, he murmured into the column of her neck, "There are many places I desire to use my mouth on you."

And there were many places she desired to use her mouth on him. It came in a flash, fangs plunging into his skin. How sweet and warm his blood would be as their naked bodies moved together.

She shuddered at the image and squeezed her eyes shut, concentrating on not letting her fangs drop.

"Does it scare you?" he said. "How much I want you?"

*It scares me how much of you I want.*

She shook her head, curls falling in her eyes. "No. Tell me."

He rested on his elbows, hovering his body overtop of hers. The gap between them was maddening.

"I will never tire of kissing your lips." He brushed his thumb over her mouth. "But I also haven't been able to stop thinking about…" His rough hand stroked her throat before cupping her breast, the silken fabric of the pajamas sliding across her skin.

She swallowed. "You've touched me there before."

He gave a challenging grin, then hovered his mouth over her body as he lowered himself. Lips not yet touching her, only the warm caress of his breath.

"D-Darius."

"I've also been insanely curious of how you taste."

He grasped her thigh and slipped his hand between her legs. Each featherlight stroke sent her reeling. He pulled back a slick finger.

With a smirk, he rose to hover above her. "So wet for me?" This time he pressed his hips down on hers, and an almost animalistic sound broke from her lips. She writhed, moving her body to deepen the contact, hooking a leg around him.

"Do whatever you will," she gasped, tugging at the buttons of her shirt. "Do whatever you will to release me from this agony."

"Agony?" He pressed a hand to her back, lifting her out of her shirt, before lowering her back down to the bed. "Is that what you'd call it?"

"Is there any other word? Every touch of yours trembles along my skin."

And there was the other deep agony of desire to take the part of him he could not give. Oh, but how good it would feel. How good it would *taste*.

"You know nothing about trembling under my touch." He dove toward her, but she pushed her hands hard against his chest.

"Wait."

He stilled, and slowly she reached for the ends of his loose shirt, and at his nod, she pulled it up over his head.

His body was immaculate, a muscled chest and soft patches of light hair. Well, immaculate except for a jagged scar, edges like a bolt of lightning, that puckered along his shoulder blade.

There was only one weapon that could make a scar like that. *The Dark Prophet's sword of gravastarium.*

She hooked her arms around his neck and kissed the scar. Her breasts rubbed against the hard contours of his chest.

"Fuck," he growled.

Then he pushed her back to the bed, kissing his way along her collarbone. His tongue swept over the top of her breasts, and he took one of her pointed nipples into his mouth.

Pure liquid heat shuddered through her body, and she threaded her fingers through his soft hair. He took her other breast in his hand, lightly pulling at her nipple with his thumb and forefinger.

She squirmed beneath him as he switched breasts, sucking hard on the other one. She touched her now freed breast, fingers sliding over the slick surface of her enlarged nipple, gliding over the parts where his mouth had been. He sucked deeply on her other one, then tugged on the point with his teeth before flicking with his tongue.

She moaned, rocking her hips against his manhood.

The sensation stopped, and she fluttered her eyes open in confusion. But he was staring at her, transfixed, lips glistening and pupils dark. Something feral flashed in his face as his breath rose in cadence with the beat of his heart.

"Darius." She tilted her head to the side, hair falling over her shoulder. "What is it?"

"A mere glance of you renders me speechless." Muscles bobbed in his throat as he swallowed. "But seeing you spread out before me on my bed... Every part of me is undone."

No words came to her. His eyes followed her every movement as she shifted her body. She continued to move her hand over her breast. There was a power in this.

The star beside her heart burst awake, sparking in wild excitement.

"Are you going to keep gaping at me?" she purred. "Or actually use your mouth like you promised?"

He gave an arrogant laugh, then dragged his tongue down her bare stomach, dipping into her navel, before his lips pressed against the hem of her pants.

"As much as I would love to remove these," he flicked his ice-blue eyes up at her, "we are going to take our time."

Her molten body regretted her earlier words, and as she opened her mouth to protest, he smirked up at her and said, "Don't worry. This will be very enjoyable for you as well."

His lips pressed overtop the silken pajama pants, dampening the thin fabric, before he pressed a kiss between the heat of her core. His tongue dragged a leisurely stroke along her center.

"Darius," she gasped, her body trembling.

"You called?" He was above her.

"Darius, you're—"

"A great kisser?" He pressed his lips to hers before pulling away, laughing.

She laughed too, a semi-release, her mind half in the stars, half in the bed, and all full of bliss to be near him.

"Fret not, my darling," he said. "There is not a thing in this world I would deny you, especially not your pleasure."

He trailed his hand between her legs, moving in soft circles and long rubs with the heel of his palm. He grabbed her hips to press against the shape of him through his pants, long and hard and eager.

That she liked the best, though she couldn't help but imagine what it would be like to feel him fully inside her.

"I want to touch you," she gasped, or tried to, her words muffled against his skin.

"Anything, Vivian."

She dragged her hand down the hard edges of his body, feeling for the long shape of him through the loose fabric, rubbing at it.

It seemed to drive him wilder in his pursuit. His hand moved faster between her legs, pushing the soaking fabric across her swollen heat.

A growl tore through him, and she captured his mouth with hers, kissing him hard, until they were nothing but twined bodies. He crested her to the edge, a wave about to crash, only to slow, to stop, to pull his hand away for a moment, a smirk against her lips. Then they started again, heat building and building and building. He moved his hand away, her body aching.

When he did it for the third time and followed it up with a laugh and tug at her ear with his teeth, she growled in frustration, and wove her legs around him. They rolled until he was on his back, and she pressed her hips hard against him.

"Vivian," he breathed, cheeks reddened, eyes sparkling.

And she moved and moved against the shape of him between her legs, and his golden hair tangled, and she saw the moment when his face shattered, because it was the moment a rippling of pleasure, of starlight, coursed through her. She cried out, her star bursting and burning hot within her chest. A wave they rode together, until she fell into his embrace.

STARLIGHT DIPPED BENEATH the curtain, and slowly she blinked her eyes open. Darius's arms were wrapped tight around her. She laid her hands on his chest, listening to the ever-temping beat of his heart.

They'd changed, and she wore one of his long tunics, her bare legs twined around his.

At least no nightmares had plagued him further this night. If the stars were out, it was almost time to wake. But she wasn't quite ready to rise from the warmth of the bed.

Something caught her eye: two lumpy shapes on the bedside table. Slowly, she reached overtop of him to snag two knitted stuffed animals.

Darius blinked his eyes open, a soft smile appearing on his face as he looked over at her.

"I thought you said you only had one."

"You caught me. Two. Celeste and I bought each other one from a vendor in town."

Vivian studied the animals, one a white horse with a blue mane, the other a patchwork cat. "Which one is yours?"

"The horse," Darius said. "Riding was one of our favorite activities to do together." Darius's large hand roamed over the horse's mane. "Khalid and Carmilla liked to sleep in, but Celeste hated it. She always had to be doing something. So many times she'd jump on my bed, waking me before dawn. We'd shoot targets. She could rival the hunting goddess Suseter with a bow. She'd spar at the drop of a hat or stuff her face with sweetcakes she pilfered from the kitchen."

"What an adventurer." Vivian picked up the stuffed cat. "I've never ridden a horse before. Father had a horse, but she was for pulling the cart only. Oh, and we had an old donkey named Murdie. Father used to lead us around the field on him."

"I could teach you if you like," Darius said. "The campus has a stable. My horse was brought up from Wolfhelm."

"I'd like that," Vivian said. "Tell me more about your sister."

"Celeste..." Darius lightly touched the ratty knit animal. "She loved cats. Skoog, our chef, kept many around to rid the kitchen of mice. She'd always be carrying them around the castle. If one had a litter, she would make sure it had blankets, and she'd bottle-feed strays." He gave a light laugh, a sparkle appearing in his eyes. "She and Khalid used to mix up treats in the kitchen, then they'd leave a little trail back to her room so the cats would come up there. It drove Carmilla mad. Her room was right across the hall, and she hated the little beasts."

Vivian curled deep into his embrace. She adored him like this, the softness of the boy. A glimpse of who he was beneath the royal mask he wore so well.

"And that's why I can't rest," he said, chest rumbling as his voice deepened. "I'll never truly be at peace until I eradicate every one of the monsters that murdered her. And if I have to kill every single vampire myself, then so be it."

# 7

# IN WHICH TIMOTHÉE MAKES HIS HOME IN THE CAULDRON

A KNOCKING ON THE door startled him awake. Timothée threw himself upright, causing Yvaine to jump off in a hissing fit. He blinked, eyes crusted and blurry. He'd been deep in a dreamless sleep.

Silver bands of moonlight peeked out from beneath the curtains, falling like a sheet over the sprawled-out boy on the floor beside his bed. Valentine Sun was laid out long, his hair swirling like lilac ribbons around his face, one arm draped over his eyes, long fingers curled, his chest slowly rising and falling.

*Can't sleep, huh?* Just another one of Valentine's dramatic lies. Val had been asleep below his bed. The thought was as unsettling as it was… some other emotion Timothée couldn't name.

Val blinked awake, and his face was so soft, unrecognizable from the constant snarl. Val smiled. Timothée's heart stuttered. There was an ethereal sort of beauty about him.

"Your hair is as wild as your eyes this night." Val's voice was raspy from sleep.

A knock sounded again. Timothée jumped, fell, and tumbled over the edge of the bed.

Right on top of Valentine.

The blurry gaze and soft smile were gone so fast, Timothée thought he must have dreamed everything. "What are you doing, Greywick?" Val snarled, pushing against him. "Get off of me!"

Another knock, then: "Timothée, Val, are you awake?" Carmilla's voice, dripping with the Kirrintsovan accent. "Come on! Barracus is downstairs looking for Timothée."

Timothée was about to answer when Val's hand clasped over his mouth.

"Do not let her in," Val said.

And Timothée would have done anything he asked in that moment, with Val's hand across his lips. When he opened his mouth to reply, he tasted Val's skin, the same as he smelled: pomegranate and pine.

Val just pressed harder against Timothée's face, and his other hand coiled into the blanket on the ground. He looked… afraid.

"I don't care what you're doing in there—" The door opened and Carmilla burst in, but her gaze didn't fall on Timothée, partially sprawled on Val's lap. Her eyes swept across the room. "What happened in here?"

Val's hand dropped from Timothée's mouth.

Timothée almost laughed, then said: "So, the rooms don't all look like this?"

"No," Carmilla said simply, hard gaze locked on Val. "They don't."

Val pushed Timothée away and stood, running a hand through his hair, and pacing the room like a caged animal.

"Professor Barracus is waiting for you in the common room, Timothée," Carmilla said, but her eyes didn't leave Valentine's.

Timothée stood slowly, feeling like a trespasser. *In my own room too.*

He tugged on his boots and tried to tame his hair before backing out the door. Halfway down the stairs, he had the distinct feeling of forgetting something. Yvaine. He couldn't leave her up there with Valentine, and who knew where they would send him in the Academy today?

Timothée sighed, then turned back up the stairs, breath already heavy in his throat. He was almost to the top when he noticed Yvaine, sitting a few steps from the door.

"There you are—" He cut himself off, heard voices from behind the door, urgent and frantic.

He knew he should grab Yvaine and head downstairs, but curiosity tugged on him like an anchor.

"So, you thought no one would ever see what you did?" Carmilla's voice. She sounded *angry*.

"I didn't expect to have company," Val snarled back.

"You're unhinged. Do you have any idea what could have happened if you'd lost control of your magic—"

"I am *always* in control."

"This room," Carmilla stated, "is proof you're not. Watch your temper, Valentine."

Timothée's breath caught. Val had destroyed the room... with shadowcraft? The stale smell of magic told Timothée it must have been like that for a while. What had made him do that? Timothée's curiosity gave way to sadness, and he felt a strange kinship with Val as he imagined the boy's dark magic spreading across the room, tearing it apart.

He knew what it was like to be out of control.

"How can you expect me to," Valentine said, voice low and dark, "when you sent *him* up here?"

Carmilla gave a nasty laugh. "He's just your roommate."

"He took everything from me!" Valentine screamed, and it was the first time Timothée had heard him raise his voice. The sound was sharp as a blade.

What did Val mean? How had he taken everything from him? By pulling him into the trial? It didn't make any sense.

"You can't lose what you never had," Carmilla said. "Stop blending your dreams with reality. You're losing sight of what's important."

"Why would you do this to me, Carmilla?"

"You're too clever to ask that question," Carmilla stated. "If you stopped for a single moment and thought of the forest beyond the trees. About who he is and what he can do."

"I know better than anyone what he can do," Val said. "He killed Celestial Knights the moment he swallowed the star. When his magic is supposed to be the weakest, when it was still bonding with his heart."

"Exactly. Would you rather I let him cozy up next to Erik?" Carmilla asked. "Imagine what he could do once—"

Timothée couldn't listen anymore. He was gasping, his heart sputtering in his chest. Those knights on the ground... He had killed them.

Blood rushed in his ears, and the choker around his neck felt too tight. It couldn't be true. He bumped into other students in the packed stairway. They yelped in protest. But his heart was racing, he couldn't breathe, and he didn't know where he was going, only he had to get out of the stairwell. He staggered into the common room of the Cauldron and was hit with a wave of starlight through wide-open windows. Every Dark Star student had their attention fixed on him.

His presence had frozen everyone around him, a flurry of activity come to a standstill. They didn't wear their purple and silver uniforms, but rather a mishmash of clothes and accessories unlike anything Timothée had seen before. There was inspiration from all three nations in the designs.

He could imagine how he appeared still in his grass-stained clothes from last night, with tears streaming down his face.

So much for a good third impression. First, smelling like the sewer, then losing control of his star, and now a teary mess.

"What did Valentine do to make you cry, Greywick?" It was Erik, the house leader. He leaned against the long table, a steaming mug in his hand. "Heard you were bunking up all the way at the top."

Behind Erik, Starlings were brewing coffee and potions, the scent of nuts and earth filling the room. And now the silence was broken with chuckles and anxious breath.

Timothée wiped a dirty sleeve across his face.

"That'll be quite enough, Mr. Borstigsson." A man stepped forward. Timothée distantly remembered seeing him on the field last night. He was the one who had called the knights off, who'd gotten Carmilla to help him. "I'm Professor Barracus, head of the Apothecary's Guild."

Timothée sniffed, the sound so loud in the silent Cauldron.

"Come with me, Timothée," Professor Barracus said. "The rest of you, get on with your own business. It may be the weekend, but you've got homework and practicing to do."

A mumbling of "Yes, Professor" and the students went back to their routines.

Timothée studied the professor as they walked. He was tall with dark brown skin and shorn hair. His clothes were not as crisp and formal as Setviren wore, no flowing robes. Instead, Professor Barracus favored brown trousers and a cream cable-knit sweater.

Timothée followed on Professor Barracus's heels. Now they headed down the Cauldron's tower, winding and winding, and through a hallway into another tower until they arrived at a simple wooden door with a silver nameplate in need of a polish: *Quincy Barracus*. The professor ushered Timothée to follow after him.

"This is my office." Professor Barracus took a seat behind a large desk. The desk's legs were polished branches, and the top was a large slap of granite, though it was hard to tell because it was so covered in papers and bottles and vials and coffee mugs. The room was no bigger than his dorm, but circular. Another offshoot tower.

Quincy Barracus's office felt like a breath of Timothée's old life. A large open window spilled starlight over a station of bubbling vials and little burners. A fireplace burned wood, not crystal. But it wasn't until Timothée stepped fully into the room that he realized it was the lack of something rather than the presence of it that brought this sense of home.

"You haven't swallowed a star," Timothée stated. There was no lingering presence of magic in the air, and Timothée couldn't decide if he mourned the feeling or relished it.

Barracus motioned for him to take a seat opposite his desk, and Timothée slid into the worn leather chair.

"No," Professor Barracus said. "You won't find any professors here who have swallowed a Dark Star."

Timothée wiped his eyes again, sure his sleeve was slashing dirt across his face.

"I never swallowed a star," Professor Barracus continued. "I am but a humble potion-maker amongst those with the power of gods."

There was a meaning hidden under his words, Timothée thought, something said without really being said. But his mind was too muddled to piece it together.

"I'll take you to wardrobe to find your uniform after this," Professor Barracus said. "The other houses like to alter theirs with magic, but you'll find our students can be just as creative in their own way."

"Okay," Timothée said.

Professor Barracus gave a long sigh then shifted through some papers on his desk and pulled out a folder. "Your class schedule is in there, and the books and supplies you'll need. The shoppes in Selene Crescent will have enough to get you started."

Timothée opened the folder and skimmed his timetable: History of Thraina, Introduction to Potion-Making, Physical Combat, Modern Potions and their Uses, Natural Foraging, the Study of Sacred Literature. The paper behind it was a list of supplies: parchment and ink, glass vials, and over half a dozen text books.

His stomach sank.

The worry must have shown on his face because the professor added, "I've already asked Carmilla to show you around. It won't be a problem."

"That's not it." Timothée fumbled with the paper in his hands. "I don't think I'll be able to pay for all of this." It seemed silly to worry about that right now, when his magic had almost killed him, when it had killed others, when he'd somehow unknowingly ruined his roommate's life, and this thing around his neck made every breath a struggle.

"We have students from all walks of life here," Professor Barracus said. "From the paupers to the princes, none of them go without. But in particular, Archpriestess Kassandra will provide for you and your sisters; she's already set up an account in your name."

"W-why would she do that?" Timothée asked slowly.

"She's… your adopted mother?" He said it like a question, and Timothée still wasn't sure of the answer.

But he was sure of one thing: he couldn't keep going on like this. Pretending everything was okay.

"I shouldn't be going to classes. I should be in the dungeon." Timothée wanted to scream, but all the power of his voice was trapped in his throat. "I *killed* people."

"Listen to me, kid." Professor Barracus rubbed the bridge of his nose. "We put you on that field, we told you to catch a star. We all saw how the Isle took you under. The fault lies with the Academy in not being prepared for…"

"Prepared for me," Timothée finished.

And there was no denial. Professor Barracus didn't seem the type to hide behind kind lies. But his words didn't ebb the guilt simmering within. Timothée whispered, "I want to know their names. My fault or not, those deaths are… I need to know who they were."

"I'll see it done." Professor Barracus narrowed his eyes. "Starting at the Academy is never easy, and I imagine in your case it's going to be a difficult road. Did I hear you are roommates with Valentine Sun?"

He knew what the professor was doing, trying to draw out the storm clouds of his mind and focus him on lighter topics. But what the professor didn't know was at the mention of Valentine, the storm clouds moved from his mind to sweep around his heart.

"I don't think he likes me very much," Timothée said.

"Valentine is one of the most brilliant students we've had in the Apothecary's Guild for a long time. He's only been here a few weeks, but he's already accomplished extraordinary things." Professor Barracus looked out the window. "However, I think he had a hard time his first few weeks, as all of them do, after they swallow that star. I don't think anyone comes up to the Isle of Argos thinking they'll inherit Noctis's magic. It's a special sort of adjustment."

And again, Timothée felt a pull toward Valentine. Had he come to the school hoping to be a hero like Timothée, only to have his dreams dashed by dark magic?

"I think," Professor Barracus continued, "he was starting to find his stride here. He might be a little jealous of someone so inherently special showing up and claiming all the attention."

"I'm not special," Timothée said. "I'm dangerous."

"It wasn't your fault, Timothée," Professor Barracus said. "I'll say it to the day I die. But if you really want to make sure everyone around you is safe, keep that choker on, and concentrate on your potion-making. There's as much magic in that as in the stars, you'll come to see."

"Yes, sir."

"And Valentine will come around. I didn't think anyone would ever want to climb all those stairs. It's a nice room though."

Maybe it was until Valentine destroyed it, and he wondered again what exactly had happened in there. Val had used his banned magic, torn apart the room. But why?

"Professor," Timothée whispered, "have you ever heard the castle… talk to you?"

He regretted the words as soon as he'd said them. But Professor Barracus didn't laugh. "No. But sometimes the school feels alive. A deep magic created it. It's said it was Rhaemyria herself. She cleaved the top off of Mount Argos and rose it in the sky."

"Are the gods that powerful?"

"I don't know." Professor Barracus knocked the wooden leg of his desk. "But we haven't crashed to Thraina yet!"

Timothée managed a smile.

"Lucky for you, it's the weekend. You'll have a few days to settle in before your first class." Professor Barracus stood. "I'll take you to wardrobe now."

"Thank you, sir." Timothée stood as well and started to the door when the professor cleared his throat.

"I knew your father."

And Timothée realized this was the first person who had referred to his father as his father, not the man who raised them, not the former headmaster, not the heretic, but his *father*.

"I was a young man when he hired me," Quincy Barracus continued. "He took a chance on a poor lad with no magic to speak of, but a desire to create it. Even if I could only do so with the proper mixtures."

*A young man?* Aging must be an anomaly in a place like this. He knew those with powerful star magic, like all the Evening and Morning Star professors, aged slowly. *How strange*, he thought, *to grow old so close to the stars.*

"He raised you with compassion," Professor Barracus continued. "Don't let that fade, no matter what they say of you here. What they say of Dark Stars."

They left his office and Professor Barracus led him back up to the Cauldron in silence, but Timothée's mind hummed.

What Timothée couldn't say to the professor, what he couldn't express, was that it had been him. In control or not, the shadows were an extension of his arm, his hand, his entire being. And he had felt it all—every pierce of the flesh, drop of blood spilled, and the lives that had leaked into the green meadow.

And he thought of the words Carmilla had spoken to him: the Church and the kingdom were afraid of Dark Stars.

That voice that was not his own spoke in his mind:

*They're not nearly afraid enough.*

*They don't know what you can do.*

*But I do.*

# 8

# IN WHICH MARION IS OUT OF HER ELEMENT

CHOOL WAS FOR layabouts who didn't have the gumption to teach themselves. At least, that's what Marion told herself as she stood before the door leading into her first class at the Celestial Academy for Fallen Stars. Her heart drummed loud enough to be heard outside her chest, and she was fairly certain the pastry she'd nabbed from the Morning Star kitchen was going to come up over her new uniform.

Two days had passed since the Celestial Rite. The weekend had allowed the triplets time to recover and settle in before beginning instruction. Marion had found her room—a gorgeous golden place with a proper desk and her own washroom—and been taken on a tour of the Academy. She made herself memorize each path from the Nest: how to get to the dining hall, to the library, to the other house's towers, and especially how to leave the castle itself.

Everyone had been perfectly lovely to her.

But she knew better.

It was the Isle itself that had swallowed her up.

No one told her where to go or what do to, except for orientation or getting uniforms or supplies for classes. She'd even been able to take meals and walks with Vivian and Timothée. Both seemed settled. As settled as they could, for a vampire and a shadow creature.

Though no one seemed near enough concerned Timothée was sharing a room with the same boy who had locked him in a sewer. And of course Tim, the soft-hearted sob he was, refused to complain and get switched. It didn't seem fair both she and Vivian got their own rooms while Timothée was forced to sleep so close to that vile human.

But it was easier to worry about that than the trials. None of them talked about it with each other, about the deep magic that had pulled them under. It seemed too private a thing, even for the triplets.

The Academy couldn't fool her. They gave her soft clothes and fed her hot food and offered her lessons in extraordinary things.

But Father had taken her from this place for a reason. Archpriestess Kassandra had nearly killed her with the deep magic. And if Vivian's secret was revealed, the Academy's most beloved royal student would slay her without thought.

She rubbed her chest, feeling the heat of her skin beneath the rich thread of her embroidered gold jerkin. *The deep magic.* Everything had felt so real there. Surely, if the Isle was capable of such magic, there was a cure for Vivian here.

But she'd have to attend class to find it.

Other Morning Star students approached the Introduction of Organic Synthesis class. They laughed and chattered with one another, arms full of parchment and quills and books. But they all seemed too quiet as they passed her, flicking their eyes down.

She unnerved them.

It wasn't like she meant to be unfriendly or sullen the last few days. It was just she lacked any sort of desire to get to know these people. What was the point? Friendship seemed a distraction amidst the stakes.

But there was one person who was completely undeterred.

"Well, well, well, look at the little wishing star all ready for school." Khalid Ali Bagheeri turned the corner. His eyes crinkled at the sight of her. "I thought you might wait for me this evening. But what was I thinking? Marion Greywick waits for no one."

He was done up in full uniform today, snug black trousers with a bright yellow tunic adorned with bronze clasps. It didn't look like he'd brushed his hair from sleep, though Marion was beginning to think he purposely styled it that way. And with every step he took toward her, her chest grew tighter and tighter.

What was it about him that sucked the air from her lungs? Was it a good feeling or not? How did Khalid draw her to him like a pathetic bug to a lantern? And why did no one stop and stare as he approached? Did they not see him as she did, how he walked under a spotlight?

But she'd had good practice at pretending she felt nothing at all. Marion stuck her nose up in the air but kept her gaze on him. "I've got a map."

"Pish! A map won't tell you all the fun facts about the school, like how the stone was apparently crafted by the god Xydrious himself." Khalid leaned in, his warm breath blowing a golden curl away from her face. "Or that rumor has it, Professor Kunuk's been teaching this class for hundreds of years. *Hundreds.*"

"That's impossible." The word came out barely a whisper. His lips were awfully close to her skin.

"I heard it from a reliable source. Trust me."

Marion pulled back, Rayna's warning ringing in her ears. Every step she made had to be carefully calculated. And Khalid had told her the night of the Celestial Rite that to survive at the Academy, she was going to have to cheat, steal, and lie. Might as well start now.

"I trust you," Marion whispered.

He pulled back, that roguish grin on his face. "I know you do."

He stepped through the doorway, then turned back when she wasn't following him. "You coming?"

Marion opened her mouth. Closed it.

"What is it?"

Students jostled her shoulders as she stood in the way. She should go back to her dorm room, claim a weak constitution from all the hubbub—

"Marion?" Khalid was in front of her, his hand under her chin, lifting her face to his. He wore black leather gloves that were cool against her skin.

"I-I've never been to school. Father taught us what we needed at Seagrass, reading and writing and arithmetic. But I've never been... We had to work as soon as we were in Wolfhelm, and now we've already missed almost a moon of lessons here. I'll be behind, and it will be so embarrassing—"

"Marion." He drew the word out, as if it tasted good in his mouth. "You think too much. Nobody here knows what they're doing. And besides, the fastest learner is the one who has learned how to learn."

Marion blinked. "What?"

Khalid laced his gloved fingers through hers. "And how do you learn how to learn? Simple, Ms. Greywick. You possess the complete and utter audacity of trusting yourself that you are capable of learning anything, but never everything. Do you understand?"

He was absolutely in love with his own voice, but she didn't care. She was following him into the classroom. At the final moment, she yanked her hand away. Last thing she needed was everyone gossiping about her and the Prince's ward.

"Come on," Khalid said. "Let's sit near the top."

The classroom was a small lecture hall with individual desks on an upward slope. Marion followed behind Khalid and squeezed into one of the small chairs.

Everything in the Academy seemed ancient and yet perfectly maintained. This lecture hall was no different, with wooden engraved goddesses along the wall. The roof was cut out with large skylights, revealing the crystalline night.

"So this is Introduction of Organic Synthesis," Khalid explained. "Only Morning Stars take it. It's where we first start understanding the rationale behind the creation of various elements and put it into practice."

Marion nodded, throat dry. Khalid's fingers thrummed on the desk. Students buzzed around them, settling in. The chamber seemed too big, the stars too bright. She took in a deep breath and concentrated on Khalid's rhythmic tapping.

Her own hands clenched and unclenched. She reached forward and touched the smooth leather of his gloves. "Why are you wearing those inside?"

He smiled, flexed his fingers. "Poor circulation."

The door slammed shut, and a woman strode in front of the green chalkboard. She was short, dressed in heavy gold robes embroidered in silver thread. Her black hair lay loose to her shoulders save a small bun in the back, braided with gold leaf. Her dark eyes searched the room, the mere gesture rendering the class speechless.

"As above," she said.

"So below," the students returned.

The professor nodded, as is reveling in the greeting. "Welcome back, students. I hope you all had a restful few days off." Her eyes landed on Marion, and for a moment, she was terrified the professor would ask her to stand up in front of the rest of the students, introduce herself to the class. Mercifully, she looked away and began the lesson.

"Professor Inga Kunuk," Khalid whispered. "She's warm enough outside of class but super strict—"

"Mr. Ali Bagheeri, unless you're teaching the class, I shouldn't see your mouth moving, hmm?" Professor Kunuk crossed her arms. The class giggled.

Khalid leaned back in his chair, hands behind his head. "Hey, if you need a break, Professor, I'm sure I could do it."

"After you set a desk on fire last week? I don't think so."

The class laughed again, and Marion rose an eyebrow.

"Hey, this starcraft stuff is hard." Khalid shrugged. "I'm still working out the kinks."

Professor Kunuk paced back and forth, hands behind her back. "Today, we're continuing where we left off last week. We finished our lecture on the synthesis of air and manifesting it into wind power. Today, you will practice the theory."

*Marion.*

All the breath rushed out of Marion's chest. She could see it in her mind's eye: the castle being ripped apart by a gale, the tempest tearing at her clothes and skin. She had failed the trial of air during the Celestial Rite, been unable to find her star. Because of that creature.

*Marion.*

The great animal had killed her father. It had been in the prescient vision shown by the deep magic. Why had it known her name? Why had it said her name *like that*?

*Marion.*

That single gleaming yellow eye staring at her—

"Marion!" Khalid shook her shoulder. "You alright?"

She shivered despite the warmth of the room. She clutched the desk, felt her feet planted firmly on the ground. Only the lecture hall. No giant bat in sight.

"I'm fine," she murmured.

"To practice your abilities," Professor Kunuk's voice carried throughout the hall, "you shall attempt to lift a leaf in the air. Remember what we learned last week. Can you create air of different temperatures? How does that affect your ability to create currents?"

Professor Kunuk walked behind the chalkboard and grabbed a box. She set it on her podium and opened it, revealing a stack of red maple leaves. Then with the smallest twitch of her nose, the leaves lifted into the air and sailed toward the students.

Marion gasped, her skin pricking with magic. A warm breeze flew through the classroom, each leaf landing perfectly in front of a student.

"See how powerful she is?" Khalid whispered, grabbing his leaf mid-air. "She doesn't even use her hands as a conduit for her starcraft.

And see how much control she has? I'm telling you, she's got to be at least a million years old."

Marion laughed and ran her finger over the red stem. "Maybe a billion."

"As always when practicing starcraft," the professor called, "your goal is to feel close to Rhaemyria. She is the one who gifted this magic to you. Feel the peace within your star as you summon your craft. This is no place for ego or emotion. Only when your heart is still will the strength of your star emerge."

Soft voices murmured through the room as the Starlings began to practice. Marion looked around. Already, a few leaves were lifting off the desks. Little breezes of hot and cold air flittered over the back of her neck.

She stared down at her leaf. "How am I supposed to do this? I never attended the lecture."

Khalid blew through his teeth. "You don't need that. You're Rhaemyria's daughter. Who could be closer to her?"

Marion crossed her arms, said nothing.

"Take notes from the master." Khalid pushed his hair back from his dark brows and gave a toothy grin. He held his hands level with the leaf on his desk and stared down at it.

"Don't you want to take off your gloves?"

"No way. If Professor Kunuk can do it by twitching her nose, I can keep my fingies toasty warm."

He worried his bottom lip and Marion sucked in a breath. There was something boyish in his overly determined gaze.

He murmured, "Here. We. Go."

A torrent of air rushed from Khalid's hands, pushing him back from the desk and falling to the ground. The leaf flew forward, and the wind was so strong, the student in front of Khalid toppled forward and fell from their chair.

"Khalid!" Marion cried, reaching down to him.

He rubbed his elbow. "Something needs tweaking."

"I'd say so." She yanked him back into his chair and began dusting him off. "Maybe you were feeling a little *too* close to Rhaemyria."

He grabbed her hand, his touch firm. "I don't know. I could be closer."

"Mr. Ali Bagheeri, first you try to set my classroom on fire and now you're blowing gales." Professor Kunuk walked up the stairs and stopped beside Khalid, hands on her hips.

"Sorry, Teach," Khalid murmured.

Professor Kunuk sighed. Then she shifted, staring at Marion. Marion squirmed beneath her gaze. She knew Khalid had been joking before, saying Inga Kunuk was millions of years old. But there was the similar feeling to her as the rest of the Academy: something that had seen the ages of Thraina and yet remained untouched.

"Ms. Greywick, I've heard so much about you. I'm pleased to finally make your acquaintance. Rhaemyria blesses the Morning Star house with one of her children."

Marion smoothed an invisible wrinkle in her skirt. "Pleased to make your acquaintance as well, Professor."

"Right then, let's get to it. Lift your leaf, Ms. Greywick."

Marion's spine straightened like a rod. It was bad enough to be expected to do this at all, but with the professor watching... "I've never attended a lesson."

"Do you think Rhaemyria took lessons before creating Thraina? Come now. Let's see what god's blood can do."

Students were turning around and watching her. Marion took a deep breath, face heating. During the trial, she had summoned flame enough to burn down an entire cabin and field. This was just a spot of wind.

She held one hand above the leaf and rubbed her chest with the other. It simmered beneath her skin, that star too hot. Somehow, she had to channel that strength. Professor Kunuk had said to be close to Rhaemyria, to feel stillness in her heart.

But when she thought of Rhaemyria, all she thought of was a stupid legend that people kept pushing her into. And how could her heart be still when it was fighting with this terrible invasion in her chest? And if she was to summon wind... Would it be as strong as the gale that nearly tore her apart on the edge of the castle? The one that sent the giant bat smashing against the rock?

Hot tears sprung to her eyes, steaming down her face. She stared at the leaf, gritting her teeth, willing it to move, to twitch, to do bloody *anything*.

Khalid grabbed the hand that was rubbing her chest, squeezed it. "You can do this, Mare. Keep going."

The hand above the leaf shook. *Concentrate*. Rhaemyria. Stillness. No emotion.

*Marion!* Wind, Father's killer, a storm to break the Academy—

"Ah!" Khalid leapt out of his seat, yanking his hand from hers and clutching his wrist. Steam drifted from his leather glove.

"Enough!" Professor Kunuk ordered, and Marion gasped, flinging back in her chair.

Her skin... It was so hot. Too hot.

The leaf remained unmoved on her desk. Students began to murmur, staring at her with strange eyes.

Marion's breath was heavy. She wanted to leave. She looked to the door.

Archpriestess Kassandra stood there, staff held with white knuckles. For a moment, Marion thought she was a statue, like one of the goddesses carved into the wood. But her ice-chip gaze burrowed deep into Marion. And with an enigmatic look, she turned away.

"Argh!" Marion grabbed her leaf, tore it into tiny pieces.

Professor Kunuk twisted back and forth between her and the door where Archpriestess Kassandra had stood just a moment ago.

"So much for god's blood," Marion grumbled.

"Don't be discouraged, girl," the professor said. "Your father was the greatest professor the Academy has ever had, and even his craft required much practice."

"My father?" Marion leapt up. "You're talking about Bram Cavald." He had been Henry Greywick to her, a lavender farmer from Seagrass.

But to the Celestial Academy, he was the former headmaster, an Evening Star. Bram Cavald.

Professor Kunuk cleared her throat and looked aside. "I mean, the traitor. The one who you called father. Now, let's get you a new leaf—"

Marion jumped up, grabbed her arm. "Wait! I need you to tell me about him. I need answers."

Professor Kunuk spun on her toes, faced the class. Clapped her hands. "You are to take your leaves with you and practice as homework. Class is dismissed."

A loud murmur rustled through the students as they packed their bags and shuffled down the stairs of the lecture hall and out the door. Marion held her breath, standing and staring at the professor. She would not be moved.

Last of all, Khalid shambled down the stairs.

"You too, Mr. Ali Bagheeri. Out you go," Professor Kunuk said.

"I thought I'd wait for Marion—"

"*Out.*"

Khalid feigned a hurt expression and then winked at Marion as he passed by. "Remember," he whispered, "you can learn anything."

There was silence as Marion stood across from the Morning Star professor.

"I need to know," Marion said, "why did Bram Cavald take me and my siblings from the Archpriestess?"

"Listen to me, girl," the professor's voice was a harsh whisper, "you must know the Archpriestess loves you as her own kin. Her favor will ensure you and your siblings a life of status and wealth—"

"All my siblings? Even Timothée who was attacked and dragged into that dark tower?" Marion snapped. "Forgive me if I am not swayed by status or wealth. My father was *afraid* of this place. My father who you called the most powerful professor in the Academy's history. What was he so afraid of?"

Inga Kunuk's face shifted to a scowl. "What do you think, girl? You saw it yourself. The deep magic. Do you think Kassandra keeps this isle afloat? No. The *isle* keeps the isle afloat."

"What is it?" Marion breathed. "What is in this castle?"

Professor Kunuk gave a low laugh. "Whatever it is, it's enough to keep Kassandra afraid. I pray every night I never find out."

Marion left the classroom shortly after, walking through the halls aimlessly. What did it mean? What had her father discovered within the deep magic?

She turned a corner and stopped. All the glittering gems that lit the hallways winked out one by one. Her heart thudded in her chest.

And a voice whispered in her mind, *I suppose, little Greywick, you're going to have to come and find me.*

# Hunter's Blood Moon

Many legends and fables originated from this time of transition for Thraina. Farmers harvest the last crops, including pumpkins that will be used for decorations during the universally celebrated All Hallow's Eve.

The final night of the Hunter's Blood Moon is saved for feasting, merrymaking, and praying to ward off any fabled evils. Parties are thrown so the ghosts may haunt to fulfillment and rest for the moons to come. Kings and peasants alike wish each other the old adage: *May the skeletons dance and then sleep.*

# 9

# IN WHICH TIMOTHÉE MAKES AN EXPLOSIVE FIRST IMPRESSION

"**A**ND ANOTHER IMPORTANT thing," Carmilla explained as they walked to class, "is to pay close attention. Professor Rosewyn is a bit of a mumbler, and if you mistake root powder for a rose petal, you're going to be in serious trouble."

"I'll try to remember," Timothée said.

They cut their way across the school grounds. The rainy days of the Singing Harvest Moon had swiftly ushered in the misty mornings of the Hunter's Blood Moon. Dreary and cold, where greyness settled over everything. The stars hid behind a curtain of thick clouds.

Timothée had dutifully attended all of his classes so far this week. Most of them were focused on one thing: potions. The history, the ingredients, the practical uses. One lecture that wasn't entirely about potion-making was the History of Thraina—or what Carmilla called 'The Celestial Church's Account of History'.

But today was his first day of Introduction to Potion-Making. This was the purpose of his house. If he couldn't do magic, making potions and elixirs was the next best thing.

He and Carmilla walked into the classroom. Long wooden tables were cluttered with glass vials, mortars and pestles, gas burners, and small trays of ingredients: herbs, flowers, clay pots, and things Timothée couldn't name.

"My station is over there." Carmilla squeezed his shoulder.

Timothée found an empty table at the back of the classroom. The equipment looked well-used, but that was typical of everything in the Dark Star house. His classmates were masters of reusing, recycling, and making things better.

Yvaine hopped on the bench, and he stroked her black ears. She started to purr. No one else sat beside him.

That was okay. He didn't need a partner. Sure, he was starting a moon later than the other students, but he was a quick learner. He had snuck a peek at Val's books when his roommate was in the bathroom. Val spent an exorbitant amount of time in the bathroom applying all manner of powders and liners to his already beautiful face. It provided Timothée with lots of space to flip through his texts. They were all full of jargon he didn't understand... yet.

It was a blessing he could find the books. On the weekend when Professor Barracus had taken Timothée to get his uniform, he'd returned to his room to find it clean and organized.

Two beds, two dressers, two study desks, and a fire burning purple crystals. There were still stains of darkness rippling up the walls, but Timothée was pretty sure nothing could get rid of those. Val had returned a little while later, looked him up and down, and sneered: "Does this room now satisfy the child of the gods?"

Without Valentine Sun, the room would have been perfect.

Presently, Timothée snuck a glance at the professor at the head of the class. She looked young, with pale pink hair and a button nose. Green and pink flowers crawled up her white dress.

"Careful," a smooth voice curled over Timothée, and he looked up to see Val leaning on his desk. Val wore a twisted scarf around his neck and a slim black shirt that clung to his narrow waist, tied with a corded purple belt…

"Or don't." Val gave him a strange look and straightened. And Timothée realized he had missed a whole string of Valentine's words.

Timothée ran his hands through his hair. It didn't matter. Val was probably insulting him like usual. The two of them had formed a strange alliance over the last week—and by alliance, Timothée didn't talk to or acknowledge Val, and Val didn't lock him in any sewers.

"Whatever," Timothée snarled. Val was already out of earshot, having settled into a spot beside Carmilla.

Val spent all his time with Carmilla. They ate together, they went to class together, they sat together, and the nights Val wasn't in the dorm room, he was probably with Carmilla. Timothée's sisters had told him how they used to be a couple—and for not being a couple anymore, they certainly spent a lot of time together.

But Timothée couldn't hate Carmilla the way he hated Val. Every moment she wasn't with Valentine, she was with Timothée. Taking him to and from his classes, pointing out what to avoid in the dining hall, and checking on him every morning before bed. She certainly offered more support than the official leader of the Dark Star house, Erik Borstigsson.

Life was okay. He wasn't great. But he was okay. If he couldn't do magic, then he could do the next best thing. He could create magic encased in glass.

*And I'm not here for magic,* he reminded himself. *I'm here for Vivian. To find a cure.* Maybe that cure wasn't in starcraft, but in potion-making.

The professor clapped her hands three times, drawing the class's attention.

"Welcome to Introduction to Potion-Making." Her voice had a hint of musicality to it. "My name is Professor Rosewyn. It is my understanding we have a new student."

Here it went again. He was with the same students every class; they had all heard his lame introduction so many times. But the class shuffled and turned to Timothée regardless, and when he looked up, he was staring straight at Val's smirking face, with a look that said he knew just how uncomfortable Timothée was.

Timothée slowly stood. "Hi," he mumbled. "I'm Timothée Greywick. Uh, I'm excited to learn how to make potions."

Professor Rosewyn's smile lengthened. "I'm glad to hear that, Mr. Greywick. Making potions isn't just about mixing up little elixirs. It's about finding the essence of matter and adjusting it to our desires."

Timothée wondered if he was going to be allowed to sit down soon.

"An apothecary's passion is to always strive for more. By understanding what others have made, we can broaden our ideas and produce something new. The goal of the Apothecary's Guild is to create seemingly impossible elixirs. Do not think it is too high a feat, even for first-years. Our own Mr. Sun created a brand-new potion in his first moon. It is already in review by the Guild's council, and if I may be so bold, the talk of the potions world!"

Now the attention shifted to Val, who blinked his long lashes, as if he, of course, hadn't predicted the conversation shifting this way. Timothée glanced at Yvaine and rolled his eyes.

"Mr. Sun combined the brewing method of the Everlasting Memory Potion with ingredients like scorpion grass, amnesia root, and forget-me-nots for a truly incredible result."

There was another impressive murmur through the whole class. Timothée tugged uncomfortably at the band around his neck and fell back into his seat. He should feel pleased the conversation had been directed away from him, but he couldn't muster the energy.

"So, you see, Mr. Greywick," Professor Rosewyn continued, "even though you have a Dark Star inside you, even though you are the legacy of the God of Shadows, it does not mean you cannot still achieve great things for the Academy."

There was that name again. God of Shadows. The Dark Prophet had called Timothée that. And the portrait that hung in the Academy—the portrait that looked like him. His brother, Noctis.

"We know," Rosewyn said, "not all the gods' gifts are good. We must make our own decisions for the betterment of Thraina. That is why you cage the cruel magic inside you."

All the students in the room touched their chokers, fingers brushing against the black bands. Had Professor Rosewyn swallowed a star? He couldn't feel any magic from her.

No Dark Star professors, Professor Barracus had told him.

"When the last child of the gods reigned, darkness swept across the land. Shadowcraft, vicious monsters: it was all brought forth by Dark Stars." The class was eerily quiet, hanging onto the professor's words. "Noctis has been dead a long time, and yet Thraina still bleeds from his past. When the next children of the gods were born, it was said they would heal the world. We all thought the three lost, but you have been returned. Archpriestess Kassandra believes you and your sisters will do great things, Mr. Greywick. And so do I."

IT TURNED OUT being the son of the gods did not, in fact, make Timothée Greywick good at potions.

He rubbed away the red clay that covered his face, then hesitated. At least it was covering the flush of his cheeks as the class filed out around him.

He didn't miss the snickers as other Starlings passed by, looking over at the red explosion on his desk. The assignment had apparently been an easy one. A simple sleep aid created by mixing lavender and a pinch of fire-snow in a base of poppy milk. Timothée had smelled the lavender and expected to feel sadness. Loss. But when he'd brought the small flower petals to his nose, a sense of dread passed over him. His father's cold blue eyes flashed in his mind.

He'd felt off for the rest of the lesson and missed a step—or twenty—and accidentally added bone powder instead of fire-snow. As soon as he put his mixture on the burner, it had bubbled and spilled and hardened all over his desk and the floor.

Two Starlings he'd met briefly before stopped at his desk.

"Hey!" Sylvester Dashwood said, a broad smile on his face. "Maybe Valentine can give you some of his Forget-Me potion and you try again tomorrow?"

"Have a better start." Nathaniel slithered up beside him.

"Really, there's no shame in trying Val's stuff." Sylvester leaned in close to Timothée. "Fenix was so embarrassed after Carmilla rejected him, he drank the potion and now has no idea. Poor bastard still talks about trying with her someday."

"You also took some of that potion, Syl. It would be unfortunate if you remembered what you wanted so badly to forget," a cool voice said as Carmilla slid up beside them. "I could remind you—"

Sylvester's eyes went wide, and he stuttered, "Carmilla!" before he and Nathaniel exchanged worried glances and slunk away.

"Valentine's potion has already become quite a bartering chip among our house." She scrubbed the clay off Timothée's nose. "If you take the potion, you can forget your last few hours. But if someone reminds you of it, it will all come rushing back."

Timothée shrugged out of her reach. He searched the crowd for Sylvester. "What did he choose to forget?"

"Oh, he never took the potion—but he's going to drive himself mad now thinking about it."

Timothée laughed, following her out of the classroom and into the murky night.

Introduction to Potion-Making was their last class of the evening. He'd head back to the Cauldron to drop off his bag before finding his way to the dining hall for dinner. He wanted to read more of his potions book, determined not to make a fool of himself in another class. Most of all, he was tired of Val showing him up in every subject.

"I wish I could be good at something," Timothée mumbled.

"Oh, you are good at something," a low voice said as Valentine walked in step beside them.

Timothée's heart seemed to stop and pound at the same time. He sighed and turned to his roommate. "What's that?"

"Snoring." Valentine smirked. "I barely get any sleep."

Timothée furrowed his brow. "I don't snore!"

Carmilla laughed as she watched them. "At least you're getting any sleep at all, Val."

"You're a disaster, Greywick." Valentine started to undo the buttons of Timothée's vest.

"What are you—" Timothée started, then realized his buttons had been done up wrong.

"Disaster in life, disaster in potions," Valentine murmured, long fingers sliding the last button into place.

"You may be top of the class now, Val," Timothée said, "but just wait. I'll get better. I'll create and change things, and I won't even need magic to do it."

"Oh, Greywick." Val smiled. "Who said we don't use our magic?"

"What do you mean?"

Carmilla looped her arm through Val's and strode forward. "Stay alive, little Greywick, and who knows? Maybe we'll show you."

# 10
# IN WHICH MARION LEARNS OF A LOVER'S QUARREL

**S**WEAT DRIPPED DOWN Marion's nose and pooled on her upper lip. She blew a limp curl out of her vision and clutched the wooden sword tighter in her hands.

Why wasn't Physical Combat a voluntary elective?

Rayna danced forward, her incessant speed making her near impossible to hit. "Come on, Mare! Don't give up yet!" She waved her own wooden sword teasingly before Marion.

Curse this bloody class! She'd much rather be sitting through one of Setviren's history lectures than running around the training hall hitting—or *attempting* to hit—other students with a toy sword. But she seemed to be the only one who thought that way. Every other Starling was in grand spirits, laughing and taunting their partners as Professor Barracus wove between them, correcting stances and muttering praise.

The one good thing about combat class, though, was all the Years 1s from every house took it together. She liked being able to have Vivian and Timothée within eyesight, wanted to feel close to them.

But seeing them with their own houses made her feel further away.

They'd been attending classes at the Academy for two weeks now, and today was their first class for sparring. None of the Dark Stars had wanted to partner with Timothée. Marion saw it in their gazes: the fear. And it made sense. Who would want to stand against the boy that had killed Celestial Knights, even with his choker binding his magic and only a wooden sword in his hand?

Regardless, she was about to charge over there and snap at them all for being unfriendly cowards when that little purple-haired weirdo, Valentine Sun, sighed and snatched Timothée's hand, dragging him over to spar with him and Carmilla.

Marion had watched with a twitchy eye to see if the former imperial princess and her little crony were doing it to bully Timothée, but it had all seemed on the up-and-up. And certainly less concerning than her other sibling.

Vivian had no problem finding a sparring partner. Prince Darius Störmberg, in all his golden glory, had taken it upon himself to coach Vivian in the art of swordplay. Marion worried her bottom lip. Why was the Prince so intent on Vivian? Did he truly believe her the daughter of the gods and wanted in on some holy blessing? Did he see how pale and weak she was and think himself some knight in shining armor? Or did he truly see her kindness, her creative spirit, the beauty in which she saw the world?

Whatever his plan, she wanted it gone. Wanted him gone.

Vivian might be fooled, but Marion would never be. The Prince's kingdom was the closest ally to the Celestial Church. If he found out the true nature of Vivian's secret, the Greywicks were doomed.

*Crack!* Pain lanced through Marion's arm.

"Ouch!" Marion narrowed her gaze at Rayna, who shuffled back after smacking her with the wooden sword.

"Hey, I could tell you were overthinking something! Overthinking isn't good for you, you know. If this was a real sword, I'd have sliced you open."

"Well, good thing I don't intend to be in a proper battle," Marion grumbled.

"You never know, Ms. Greywick." The deep baritone of Professor Barracus echoed through the training hall as he walked over. "Thraina has known peace for many years, but peace is tenuous. We must be prepared to understand where our convictions lie and what actions we will take to protect them."

Marion did not like to be corrected, but she didn't mind it so much from Professor Barracus. He had short black hair and dark skin, and he was always sharply dressed in violet and black, even in the training hall. Despite being head of the Dark Star house, he never favored them over his other students the way Professor Kunuk coddled her Morning Stars or Setviren his Evenings.

"Very true, Professor." Khalid wandered over, black tendrils of hair stuck to his sweaty brow. "And who's to say one person's peace isn't another's turmoil?"

Marion blinked. The exercise uniform—tight black leggings and a wool top covered by fighting leathers—clung to Khalid's long body. Images flashed in her mind of the last time Khalid had appeared so sweaty and tussled: when he'd taken her in his bedroom and put his hands all over her.

*Why hasn't he asked me back?*

Not that she would say yes. But it was curious. He'd been so friendly, sat with her at lunches, taken her around, partnered with her for classes. Yet, he hadn't touched her.

Had he not liked it, seeing her naked and sprawled upon his bed? She looked down at herself. A few strands of blond hair fell over her shoulders, having come loose from the high ponytail. Her own uniform accentuated every curve and mound of her body. Combat class was the only time she didn't wear skirts or dresses, but perhaps she should try pants more. Carmilla and Rayna both favored them.

"Yes, yes, Khalid." Professor Barracus sighed. "Very good, Year 1s. Please put your swords away. Class is dismissed."

There was a great deal of shuffling and chatter as the students tidied up the training hall and mingled about. Marion weaseled over to Vivian, clutching her thin wrist and yanking her away from the Prince. Then she aggressively waved her arm to get Timothée's attention from where he still stood with Carmilla and Val. Darius cocked a smirk then drifted over to talk with Khalid.

"I wasn't very good." Vivian laughed. "I kept dropping the sword."

"Well, no wonder. Look at you. Pale as a ghost. Have you eaten today?"

"Yes. Three leeches."

*Three leeches already today and she still looks ghastly?* "Are they staying frozen in your icebox?"

"Yes."

"If you had three today, and that was four yesterday... We've got about another moon left. We'll figure it out, Viv. We'll go down to Wolfhelm on a break. Maybe there's a new bloodletter and I can make a deal. I'll figure it out," Marion said.

Something flickered in Vivian's grey gaze. "Y-yes, Mare. I know."

Before the conversation could continue, Timothée rushed over, throwing arms around each of their shoulders. "I wasn't half-bad! I even got a hit on Val."

Marion looked over to the scowling Dark Star in the corner of the training hall. "I don't doubt you."

Professor Barracus neatly rearranged the training swords in their bucket then walked by the Greywicks, nodding at them, and headed for the exit.

"Come on! Let's go talk to Professor Barracus. You said he knew Father. Let's try to get some information out of him."

"I don't know, Marion." Timothée threw a hand behind his head. "I don't want to bother him."

"You're in his house! He'll talk to you. This is our opportunity while he's by himself."

Timothée sighed. "Fine."

"Coming, Viv?"

But Vivian's gaze was across the hall, where Darius and Khalid had taken up wooden swords against each other and were playfully sparring. "I'll be… right behind you."

Marion rolled her eyes but there was no time for arguing. She didn't want to lose Barracus. And if she was going to find out the truth of her father and the castle, persistence was a necessity.

Marion dragged her brother out of the training hall and into the corridor. Professor Barracus was up ahead, striding with a casual confidence.

"Professor!" Marion cried and sprinted forward. Bother, she'd done enough physical exercise to last her a decade.

Barracus turned, stopped. Rose a brow. "Greywicks?"

"Professor!" Marion wheezed, keeling over. She shoved Timothée forward, unable to speak through her panting.

"U-u-uh," Timothée said. "We, uh, wanted to ask you something."

The professor crossed his arms. "Out with it, then."

Timothée looked pleadingly at Marion, but she was still gasping like a fish on land. Timothée sighed and continued, "How long have you been a professor here?"

Barracus started walking. "Not long compared to most of the faculty. Twenty-odd years now?" He gave a little huff—half chuckle, half sigh—under his breath. "Don't suppose I'll leave anytime soon."

"Twenty-odd years," Timothée echoed and followed beside him. Marion quickly caught up on his other side. "You said my father, or the man who called himself my father, hired you."

Barracus looked between them, obviously uncomfortable being sandwiched by two eager Greywicks. "That's correct."

Starlight bounced through the giant windows as they turned a corner down another hallway. "Please tell us about who he was when he was headmaster," Marion urged. "Was he—"

Barracus stopped abruptly. Pinched the bridge of his nose. "Look, kids. I know this must all be wondrous. Farmer's children turned gods. But I didn't know your father very well, and I know even less about the gods' wishes."

Marion stepped closer to him. "We just want to find out more about him. What he was like as headmaster. If you could tell us—"

"I don't have time to recall memories from the past," Barracus grumbled. "You are the children of the gods. You've been granted an incredible opportunity to come to the Academy and *make* something of your lives. Concentrate on your future, not your past."

"I don't care about the future," Marion snarled. "I want to know about my father!"

Barracus sneered down at her. "You know what I want to know about? I want to know why there's a sudden influx of rogue vampires attacking villages across Andúrigard. I want to know who's defacing Rhaemyria's shrines and cathedrals. I want to know why pilgrims bearing a sigil of a blue handprint are gathering at the Ruins of Argos. That's what I want to know about, Ms. Greywick. I'm sorry if your grief doesn't rank higher for me."

Marion took in a sharp breath. Hot tears pricked her eyes. "This is not just about my grief. They call my father a traitor and a heretic."

"What does it matter what they call him? He's dead."

The words were so blunt, Marion stepped back. She could hear it—his screams, the beating wings of the great animal. The bat's voice: *Marion!*

"Come on, Mare," Timothée murmured, touching her arm. "We're not going to get any answers here."

She turned away and her brother wrapped an arm around her shoulders.

A deep sigh fell behind them and Barracus mumbled, "Wait."

The Greywicks turned.

The professor rubbed a thumb between his brows, looked down. "Listen. I didn't know Bram for long, but he was paranoid. Could be he was what they say—a religious outcast. Maybe he did want to steal Rhaemyria and Xydrious's children for himself. But if you ask me… He took you out of vengeance from a lover's quarrel."

The words were a breath: "A lover's quarrel?"

"All I'm saying is at the time, Bram was the headmaster and Kassandra was the Archpriestess. And they spent an awful lot of time alone in close quarters."

"Thank you, Professor," Timothée said, and turned away, leading Marion down the hall.

She was silent, her only tether her brother's arm around her.

Had Bram loved Kassandra? Had he truly taken them—become their father—out of spite?

No. She couldn't believe that. Wouldn't.

"None of these professors know anything," Marion grumbled.

"No." Timothée stopped in the hallway, stared forward. There was only the moonlight pooling through the windows and the purple flicker of the crystals on the walls. "I think there's only one person who does." He swallowed. "Only one *thing* who does."

As if in answer, the hallways echoed with dark laughter.

# 11

# IN WHICH VIVIAN HAS A PHANTOM VISION

**V**IVIAN WATCHED HER siblings dart out of the training grounds after Professor Barracus. A knot tightened in her chest. She should go with them, but what was one more Greywick pawing at Barracus's coattails?

Marion sought answers about their father as fervently as she searched for a cure. But Vivian knew in her heart no one could tell them the truth behind their father's lies except for Father himself. And he was gone.

She took in a deep breath, re-centering herself to the moment. She never imagined herself enjoying combat class, yet she looked forward to it. It felt good to move her body, to push it to exhaustion in a way that was so different from her usual weakness. And there was something exhilarating about seeing Darius in his element.

Currently, he and Khalid had thrown down their sparring weapons and Darius had his best friend in a headlock. Khalid laughed and clawed at Darius's arms. They reminded her of schoolchildren, constantly teasing and pestering each other affectionately. Darius obviously loved Khalid like a brother, and even Vivian's own sister had found herself taken by the Medihsan ward.

And yet… Vivian worried her bottom lip. Khalid had never given her reason to be untrusting of him. So, what was this feeling churning inside?

She pushed it away. Khalid was the only one apart from her family who knew her secret. It was rational to feel cautious of him.

Maybe she felt strange because she was hungry. She'd eaten three leeches this morning, but it wasn't enough.

Darius let Khalid go and put his hands on his hips, laughing. Vivian's heart skipped. She wished she could see him like this always: playful and carefree, without the weight of the kingdom on his shoulders. Or how he had been as they sparred together during class. Fluid and confident, erring on a male arrogance that made her core heat.

The last Dark Stars to remain were Carmilla and Val standing shoulder to shoulder with matching sardonic expressions directed at Darius and Khalid. "Did you really think you could take him, Khalid?" Carmilla asked, admiring her sharp red nails.

Khalid ran a hand through his hair. "Hey, one of these days, he won't be expecting it." He gave an exaggerated wink. "Maybe I'll even get you too, Mills."

She grimaced. "That's the difference between me and Darius. I'm *always* expecting it."

A beat passed and then Khalid threw his head back with laughter. "Guess we'll have to take Darius down together!"

"I'd rather align with a snake than you."

Khalid smiled slowly, gave a pointed look at Val. "You already have."

Another long pause. Then Darius stepped forward, offering a generous laugh. "Come on, now! Admit neither of you could ever take me in a fight. Though," he glanced up, his storm blue eyes shooting across the room at Vivian, "Vivian kept me on my toes."

Vivian looked down, knowing her cheeks would have been completely flushed if she had more mortal blood in her. He was joking; she hadn't so much as gotten the footwork right, let alone landed a blow against Darius. But he was grinning at her in a puppy-dog way that was so evident, Carmilla rolled her eyes.

The training grounds were empty now, except for she, Darius, Khalid, Carmilla, and Valentine. She felt like she was trespassing in some insider's club.

As she was about to excuse herself to run after her siblings, boorish laughter filled the hall. A group of young men in a variety of uniform colors strode into the training grounds.

"Oh joy," Val mumbled. "The cavalry has arrived."

Vivian saw it immediately, how all four of her classmates stiffened as the group approached. Heard the quickening of their heartbeats. At the head was a young man dressed in purple training garb, a black choker around his neck. A Dark Star. Vivian didn't think she'd seen him before, and yet he looked familiar—

The man noticed their group. A crooked sneer crawled up his face, and he strolled toward them. "Ay, look at this, lads. The first-years are trying to get their feet wet with the wooden sticks."

The group snickered. Darius crossed his arms.

The man sauntered right in front of him. "And if it isn't King Greenhorn himself. Hello, cousin."

Darius looked down at the man. "Hello, Erik."

*Cousin?*

Vivian sensed a presence beside her and looked to Khalid. How quietly he'd approached! And how strange only minutes ago she'd felt distrusting of him, and now she was grateful for his presence.

He put his lips right by her ear and whispered: "That's Erik Borstigsson, Darius's cousin, and a fourth-year Dark Star. He's the son of the current steward of Andúrigard, Jeremysson Borstigsson. Darius's uncle, Jeremysson, handles the general ruling of the kingdom until Darius graduates from the Academy."

Vivian nodded. That's why Erik looked familiar.

"Why am I not surprised to see you here with your two little pets?" Erik gave a pointed look at Carmilla and Khalid. "I know how it is.

My grandmother won't go anywhere unless she's accompanied by her dogs. She appreciates faithful companions." His cronies snickered.

Khalid mimed an arrow going into his heart. "What gutting commentary, Erik!"

Vivian noticed the pulse in Darius's jaw, could see the losing battle to rein in his temper. Erik was baiting him.

Khalid leaned against Vivian again, his warm breath caressing her neck. "Look how full of himself the little rat is. Only because of his Father's position. He would have been next in line after Jeremysson if he hadn't swallowed a Dark Star."

"What does that matter?" she whispered back.

"A Dark Star will never sit on the Andúrigardian throne, no matter what blood or title they have."

Vivian stared at the coldness in Erik's gaze. "He's resentful of Darius."

Carmilla stepped forward, heavy boots stomping on the ground. "Don't be rude, Erik, or I won't help you with your herbology assignment." She smiled a viper's smile. "I heard you failed last year. Rest assured, I would never be such a disappointment."

Erik scrunched up his face. Despite being cousins, he and Darius could not look more different. Erik's hair was the brown of winter, earth leeched of color. Sharp hawklike features made up his face. "Careful, ward."

Khalid gave a mock shiver. "Oo, you say that word with such disdain."

Darius stepped chest to chest with his cousin. "It's you who should be careful."

Erik furrowed his dark brow, glowered at Khalid. "Classic Medihsan. Always getting big brother to stand up for you."

A silent beat passed through the training ground. Khalid ambled forward, hands in his pockets and stood touching shoulders with Carmilla. "Must be quite the blow that your own blood takes us traitorous foreigners to every meeting, values our advice, and trusts our counsel over yours. Maybe it's because we're not awful human beings." Khalid offered a grin as serpentine as Carmilla's. "Or maybe it's because we're not terrible at herbology."

Darius narrowed a gaze behind him at his two friends. The meaning was clear: *Easy.*

"Alright, then." Authority coated Darius's voice. "Enough poking at each other. We're all Thraina now. It's up to us to be a cohesive unit, so another war never happens like the one that stained our childhood."

Erik licked his upper teeth. "Wouldn't that be a shame."

"We'll let you get to your training," Darius said and turned his back on Erik. Vivian couldn't say how, but she sensed something significant in the action.

Vivian huddled in close with Darius, Khalid, Carmilla, and Val.

The short, lilac-haired boy curled his upper lip. "I feel the need to bathe anytime I'm in his presence."

"He is an acquired taste," Darius murmured.

Vivian hadn't seen Val be friendly with anyone besides Carmilla, but there seemed to be camaraderie in all hating the same person.

They gathered their things and wandered past Erik and his friends, who were weighing training weapons in their hands and stretching.

"I meant what I said." Darius looked down at Vivian. "You were keeping me on my toes out there. You're going to be a proper duelist in no time."

Vivian smiled at him. "Well, I had an excellent teacher."

"Ay, wait!"

Her group stopped in unison. Hesitantly, she turned around to see Erik leering at her, two wooden swords in his hands.

"Is that one of the godlings?" Erik said to Darius. As if Vivian wasn't even there. As if she were an object toted around. "Barely noticed you before. You certainly don't look like much."

Vivian could nearly feel the force of Darius's blood rushing within him. She stepped away, head dizzy from it. *I need to eat.*

"Yes, this is Vivian Greywick, daughter of Rhaemyria and Xydrious," Darius growled. "Excuse us—"

"And you're teaching her to fight, cousin? Can't keep your paws off anything, can you?"

"Let's go," Khalid mumbled. "If I wanted to listen to a self-indulgent boaster, I'd look in a mirror."

"Finally, we agree on something." Carmilla put a hand to her head.

But it was like they were invisible. Darius stepped forward, arms crossed. "Yes, I am. Why? Do you have a problem with my teaching?"

Erik scowled. "If you're anything like the little blond whiner you were back at Wolfhelm, then I do. If she actually wants to be half-good, the godling should train with me."

"Don't I have a say in the matter?" Vivian leveled Erik with a glare. "I'm quite satisfied with my instruction, thank you very much."

He rose a brow. "Is that so? Then let's see how good of a teacher my little cousin is." He held out a wooden sword. "Let's have a practice match."

Immediately, Darius, Khalid, Carmilla, and even Valentine started protesting, but Vivian blocked them out. Ran a tongue over her flat teeth.

She'd been a weakling in Wolfhelm, an object of derision for Tilda Dovetail and her friends. There was no way she could actually beat a fourth-year with palace training. But she could at least show Erik she wouldn't be cowed.

She had an Evening Star beating inside her, after all. And she'd wielded more than a wooden sword.

"Fine then." Vivian took the training sword from Erik. "One practice match."

His white teeth flashed. "Excellent."

"Vivian!" Darius grabbed her shoulder. "You don't have to do this."

"I know. But I want to." She smirked at him. "I meant what I said too. You are an excellent teacher."

His smile was enough to send her star fluttering around her heart.

She met Erik in the middle of the training hall. He paced across the stone floor with the agitation of a caged lion. Toned muscles lay beneath his tight training garb like knotted whipcord. The heavy pound of his heart thudded in her ears.

Vivian knew then, if Erik couldn't beat Darius, he would beat the next best thing.

All those close to him.

She took in a deep breath, positioned herself in the wide-legged stance she'd been practicing. There was no backing out now.

"Ready, godling? Or do you have to pray first?"

Darius, Carmilla, Khalid, and Val all stood on one side, while Erik's friends huddled on the other. So many eyes on her. She lifted the sword up in attack position. "Don't worry, Erik. I prayed for you."

He lunged at her.

She completely forgot all the defensive maneuvers Darius had shown her, instead rolling across the ground and scrambling away from Erik on all fours.

"Show me what you're made of, godling!" Erik roared, spittle flying from his mouth.

Vivian stood, adjusting her grip on the training sword. *It's just wood.*

Yet, Erik's bark-brown eyes held something feral, anger long repressed. Vivian crouched, circled the noble. Darius's instruction played in her mind's eye.

She pounced, sword arcing down to strike Erik's shoulder. He twisted, meeting her blade with his. He had a two-handed grip on his wooden hilt, the force sending her blade skittering across the ground.

"Say when you're done, Vivian," Darius called.

"You're not done yet," Carmilla said. "Not until you've smacked that ugly smirk off his face!"

Vivian retrieved her weapon, circled slowly back around Erik. He pressed her, darting forward, feinting his attack under her sword, and slamming the wooden hilt between her shoulder blades.

She fell like a wet rag, pain shooting down her spine.

"Vivian!" Darius cried. "That's enough!"

Erik tossed his sword from hand to hand. "Come on, now. It's all a bit of fun, isn't it, lads? Vivian knows it. Don't you, godling?"

Her vision was blurry from the pain. She blinked. Placed her hand down on the ground to steady herself.

But it wasn't the cold stone.

It was sand.

She took a deep breath; the air was dry and thick with human sweat. And there was a roaring in her ears, a cheering crowd.

Vivian stood on shaky legs. She was no longer in the castle. Her world was hazy, half-formed, with only some details in sharp clarity. A star-swept sky lay overhead, and she was surrounded by a circular arena filled with applauding patrons. Sitting in a dais was a family dressed in brilliant blue and gold. A young man with a sapphire crown and black hair stared down at her intently.

She swallowed in a dry throat. An actual sword was in her hand, a jagged blade covered in scratches.

*What is this?*

"Come on, Vivian!" a shadow with the voice of Erik wavered before her. "Can't you even fight back? Or has our dear Prince Darius found himself another pathetic sob story to hold on to?"

Vivian breathed in the sandy air. Her body positioned itself in a new way, her legs grounded in the gravel, her sword now feeling like an extension of her arm.

The shadow darted forward, and Vivian moved, twirling around it. The shadow snarled and turned around, charging again. And again, Vivian moved, quick as a cat, dancing around the blade.

"That's a bit more like it!" the shadow cried and lunged mid-sentence.

She blocked the attack, then countered, slamming the flat of her blade against the shadow's side. It let out a startled yelp.

Vivian crouched low, blade turned upward. She knew and yet didn't know the steps. Her sword was wooden and also a jagged metal blade. Darius's voice cut through the cheering crowd. The black-haired boy on the dais was staring down at her. His face changed becoming Darius's, then Val's. No, it was the black-haired boy again.

She noted inwardly, as she cat-footed forward toward the Erik-shaped shadow, that this was both present and past, a reality forming before her mind's eye. Blood rushed through her body, but it did not feel her own.

"Do you yield?" she asked.

The shadow laughed. She pounced. One foot, two foot, a leap, and a downward strike. The laughing turned to gasping as her blade thrust against the shadow's rib cage.

She leapt, rolling across the sand to land on the shadow's other side. *Whack!* Her sword swept under his arm, landing a blow to the torso. The shadow crumpled and Vivian leapt again, easily feinting right before swiping left and cracking the sword that was maybe wooden and maybe steel against the shadow's windpipe.

He fell backward, wheezing. "Y-Y—"

Vivian stopped before him. Her body felt strong, muscular. "What?"

"Yield," the shadow's rasping voice said. "I yield."

Vivian stumbled back, stared around the arena at the sky shrinking inward, the roaring crowd whose cheers seemed to come out of her head, at the intense gaze of the black-haired prince in the dais—

She blinked. And when her vision cleared, she was back in the training hall, with Valentine Sun staring at her.

The cheering—that was real though. Carmilla and Khalid were clutching each other's hands and jumping up and down. Darius had his hands on his hips and laughed. And Valentine was still staring at her like she'd grown a tail.

*Why is he looking at me like that?*

A gasp sounded and Vivian looked down at Erik who clutched his throat and rolled on the ground. His friends hurried over, heaving him up to a sitting position.

"It was just a practice match. You didn't have to take it so seriously," one grumbled at her.

Vivian dropped the wooden sword. *What was that?* Her body hadn't felt her own. On shaky legs, she made her way over to Darius.

He clutched her shoulders. "You've been holding out on me, Vivian! At this rate you'll be the one training me next combat class."

She ran a hand through her hair. "Just the thrill of the fight."

"Amazing!" Carmilla cooed. "Let Erik chew on that loss for a few days. Now he knows who he's messing with."

The five of them turned and started making their way to the door.

She'd… beaten Erik in a sword fight. How was that possible? Especially when she was weak and so hungry—

She heard the hard hammer of a heart first, before she turned, and saw Erik charging at her, wooden sword drawn. "I demand a rematch! NOW!"

She held up her hands to block the blow, but it was too late—

Darius leapt in front of her, the wooden sword striking him right across the temple. *Crack!*

Erik dropped the sword. Stepped back. "Sorry."

Darius sneered, touched his forehead. "Dammit, Erik. Why'd you do that? The match was over—"

And they kept talking. And other voices started arguing. But Vivian couldn't make sense of it.

Because blooming along Darius's golden hairline, where the sword had hit, was a brilliant spot of blood.

Vivian inhaled. Her heart battered against her breast. Oh gods. It was like nectar, sweet and coppery and rich. Dark red drops dripped down the side of his face, painted his blond hair. She licked her lips. Her mouth was suddenly full of saliva. Inhaled again. Oh gods, oh gods. *The smell.* If it smelled like that, she could only imagine the taste.

Her stomach rumbled, gnawing at itself. A taste, a taste would be enough. She stepped forward. Her vision was blurry and absently she wondered if her pupils were dilated. She ran a tongue over her lips, but they caught on her sharp fangs.

People could see. They would know. But he was right there, and if she could have one taste—

"What do you know!" Khalid cried and suddenly his arms were around her shoulders. "I hear Marion calling for you, Viv. We best go find her before she gets mad! Carmilla, get Darius a bandage for his head, won't you? And Erik, stop being such a giant knob."

There was more chatter, but Vivian was swept toward the door by Khalid. The smell, Darius's blood, if she could—

"Get a hold of yourself," Khalid murmured. "I'm getting you out of here, just keep it together for a few minutes more."

Khalid was... helping her. He'd known.

Her brother and sister weren't here, but he was protecting her in their stead. She clutched a hand to her mouth and let herself be led out of the training hall. As soon as they were back in the corridors, she took in a deep breath, clear of Darius's blood.

"Come on, let's go a bit further so we don't chance them running into us." Khalid kept his arm tight around her, took her turn after turn deeper into the castle.

Tears pricked her eyes. What would have happened if Khalid hadn't been there? And he'd noticed her hunger... The shame of it overwhelmed her.

"So, what the hell happened back there?" Khalid said under his breath.

"I-I'm just so hungry—"

"No, not the whole wanting to eat Darius part. That's understandable. I bet his blood smells like freshly baked cookies." He turned to her, green eyes flashing. "I mean the whole beating Erik to a pulp thing. I watched you during combat class. You could barely hold a sword."

"I don't know. My body knew how to move before my mind had a chance to think."

Khalid stared at her. "You looked like a moving shadow out there. You fought like..." He inhaled. "You fought like the Dark Prophet."

She blinked at him. It was all too much. The vision, Darius's blood. Her head was too foggy to consider anymore. Her legs buckled, and she fell against Khalid. He threw his arms around her waist, and looked both ways down the corridor, before opening a door and dragging her inside.

It was a dark, empty classroom. He leaned her up against a desk. With his hand steadying her shoulder, and his handsome face a breath away from hers, he said, "Bite me."

She blinked, eyes adjusting to the dark. "What?"

Khalid pulled down the collar of his training uniform, revealing a sinewy neck. "Bite me, Vivian."

She tried to push away from him. "Khalid? What are you saying?"

"You're worried about Darius, aren't you? Worried you'll hurt him?"

Vivian looked down. "No, I wouldn't. I would never hurt him. I won't be a monster."

"Why not? Be a monster. Bite me to protect him." Khalid tugged lower on his shirt collar. She could see the veins clearly, hear the rapid beat of his heart. "Take my blood and get better, dammit."

"I'm not drinking your blood."

"You'll die if you don't figure something out soon." Khalid tugged her closer. "I doubt you'll survive much longer on your sister's leeches."

Vivian swallowed. Her fangs sat heavy in her mouth, and she knew how easily they would slide into his skin. "If I drink your blood—"

"I'll be fine. It won't kill me. I heard it happens all the time in the Kirrintsovan underground."

"But what if it… turns you?"

"Do you know how that happens?"

"No. Do you?"

Khalid shook his head, dark curls falling across his face. "Not exactly. But I'm willing to take the risk. For you."

"Even if you survived, you'd hold it over me. Make me do whatever you want."

Khalid gave a frustrated groan. "If I wanted your secret out, it would be out. I'll even keep this a mystery from Marion."

His heart was frantic, and she could see the veins pulsing in his neck.

"Why would you do this?"

He blinked, then looked down at her. "For Darius. He's like a brother to me. And he cares about you, Vivian. If this keeps you both safe, then I'll do it."

Was it as simple as that with Khalid? He would give his blood for Darius's safety? Or was there more?

Tears spilled over her cheeks. "I won't become a monster for any-one or anything. Not even for Darius. Not even for love. I need to stay *myself*."

"But Viv—"

She stood up and staggered to the door. "If you want to help me, then find me a cure. A real one. One that kills the monster inside."

# 12

# IN WHICH TIMOTHÉE AND VAL AWAKEN LONG SLUMBERING SHADOWS

TIMOTHÉE BLINKED RAINDROPS out of his eyes and stared down at the soggy piece of paper trembling between his pruned fingers. He held his lantern up to the page and squinted at the bleeding ink. "One saffron crocus, two orange mulberries, and three cinder mushrooms."

Ingredients for a protection potion. He looked down at his basket. There was one wilted purple flower, a couple mulberries—that honestly leaned more red than orange—and not a single black mushroom.

So much for impressing Professor Barracus in their Natural Foraging class. Timothée tugged on his too tight black choker. Maybe he was tired, still adjusting to the Starlings' schedule of sleeping during the day and being awake all night. But more likely it was just like everything else: he was bad at this.

It had been two weeks since they'd swallowed their stars, and he'd fallen into the routine of school: waking as the first stars rose in the sky. The Cauldron may have been ramshackle compared to the other houses, but he was getting used to calling it home.

At least all Starlings ate together. The dining hall had to be one of his favorite parts of the whole school. Hot breakfast, lunch, and dinner, and snacks available whenever you wanted. He'd never eaten so much in his life. There was even special food for Yvaine, which she gobbled right up. Some of the other Starlings had pets. Birds were quite popular. He'd seen a few dogs, a couple other cats, small creatures like mice, and Nathaniel had a snake that dangled from his neck during class.

Every day, Timothée woke up, went to class, ate and ate, attempted to study, and—of course—tried to appease Marion. She was constantly shuffling her siblings and Khalid into the library to research. It was another beautiful room, with floor-to-ceiling windows, and plenty of comfy seats. But he hadn't even had a chance to check out the fiction books yet.

Not with Marion's demands. They were here for one reason. A cure for Vivian.

So far, their research had come up empty, but there was knowledge to be gleaned, he was sure of it. And he was sure the castle's voice had the answer. But it had been strangely quiet since his first night. Maybe it didn't want to be found.

Vivian had told him and Marion of a vision she had during Physical Combat, of an arena with a sandy floor and cheering crowd. How her body had moved of its own accord. She'd sketched out the image for them, a dark-haired prince with a sapphire crown. Had the castle created the vision like it had the trials? Or was it something else?

In the meantime, he had to play the role of Starling student. And that meant not failing any of his classes.

Even cold, wet classes held outside in the middle of the night.

Professor Barracus had taken them to the edge of the Enchanted Forest for a gathering exercise. After he had laid out the terms and boundaries, they were set free. Foraging would have been hard enough during the day, but at night it was near impossible. Gloomy clouds covered the moon, and his lantern only cast a small glow around him. Why did Starlings love the dark so much?

Some students had already found everything they needed, returned to the professor, and were no doubt heading back to the Cauldron to rest before their next class.

Meanwhile, Timothée had stepped ankle-deep into a pool of mud, ripped his new cloak on a thorn bush, and somehow had brambles tangled in his hair.

Low voices tugged him from his thoughts, and he looked past the yellow leaves of an old oak to see Sylvester and Nathaniel tramping through the forest, baskets and lanterns swinging from their hands. Something clenched inside Timothée's chest.

This class had all but confirmed his suspicions: people were avoiding him. His classmates were avoiding him.

They still whispered about what happened the night he'd swallowed his star: *Murderer, darkness, shadows, rising again…*

Timothée shook his head, tried to push the thoughts from his mind. After Professor Barracus had given him the names of the Celestial Knights that had fallen, he had written a letter to each of their families. He'd stayed up late in the professor's office as they revised the letters together. Professor Barracus had promised to send the letters off, but Timothée sensed hesitation. When he pried, Barracus said he'd promised to send them, not that they would be delivered. The Church would read the letters, and it was up to the officials if they'd pass them on to the families or not.

Timothée had thought he'd feel better after, but he didn't.

And now, all he felt was alone.

Sylvester and Nathaniel's laughing banter cut straight through him. *I could ask to join them,* he thought.

He walked a few paces forward, but stopped, nerves roiling in his stomach. He was sure they wouldn't want his help. If someone had wanted to pair up with him, they would have asked.

Something caught his eye at the bottom of a tree, almost blending in with the dark rich forest floor: a tiny black mushroom.

Timothée reached for the mushroom—just as a pale hand plucked it from the ground. Timothée opened his mouth to protest when he was suddenly stuck in Valentine's gaze.

Val's wet hair clung to the edges of his face, falling over his full lips that curved into a mocking smile.

He laughed as he stood, then tossed the cinder mushroom to Carmilla who stepped out from behind him. "That's your last one."

"Thank the Three," Carmilla said. "I'm soaked through. I need a hot bath before lunch."

"Go on then." Val waved an idle hand. "I'll find more for myself."

Val didn't carry a lantern like the rest of the students. Instead, his cloak was covered with a strange powder he'd made, causing it to glow a shining purple. Professor Barracus had gushed over it for *forever*. Many other students had asked Val to make powder for them. At this rate, Val wouldn't need a job after graduating. Students were always knocking on their door, buying everything from Forget-Me potions, to sleeping drafts, to who knows what.

And Val would toss all the verdallions in an overflowing drawer beside his bed as if he didn't care about it at all.

It was annoying.

He was annoying.

His stupid, pretty, glowing, blinding purple cloak was annoying.

And he was the one part of his new school routine Timothée had not gotten used to.

Didn't know if he ever would.

Didn't know if he could survive a year of living right next to Val. Or would it be four years? Timothée shuddered.

Carmilla kissed Val on the cheek before turning her attention to Timothée. She let her piercing gaze roam over him, from his mud-soaked pants to wayward hair, then she glanced into his basket. "You know those are salmonberries, right?"

Timothée let out a frustrated sigh before tossing them from his basket. Then Val disappeared into the forest. Timothée darted after him, slowing to a walk a few paces behind his roommate.

"So," Timothée said. Maybe Val could be useful for something. "You know where more cinder mushrooms are?"

"Yes," Val said lowly, "and you're about to crush a mulberry patch with your big feet."

Timothée stumbled to a stop and held his lantern over a thorny patch of small orange berries. "I would have completely missed that."

"No doubt," Val said dryly.

Timothée dropped to his knees in a pile of squishy wet leaves and plucked the berries off the bush.

"Did someone say mulberries?" Sylvester dropped beside Timothée and stripped the bush bare. Backed by the red and orange trees, Timothée realized how much autumn suited Sylvester, with his auburn hair and dark eyes. Even his personality flitted like leaves bouncing on the wind. "We've been looking for these forever."

"Of course, it was Valentine who found them," Nathaniel said.

Timothée looked up at the other Dark Star boy. If Sylvester were early autumn, Nathaniel was late autumn. He had all the reediness of bare branches and his lanky dark hair reminded Timothée of mud-soaked leaves.

Val had already walked away, his purple cloak a glowing speck in the distance. Timothée quickly plucked the last berry from the branch and scrambled to his feet. "Val knows where the cinder mushrooms are."

Sylvester's eyes widened. "We haven't been able to find those either."

The three of them shuffled through the brambled forest as fast as they could after Val, who gave a great sigh as they approached.

"Heard you know where the good stuff is." Sylvester gave a scandalous wink then moved to throw an arm over Val.

"Don't touch me." Val darted swiftly out of the way.

Sylvester flinched back and stuck his hands in his pockets.

Timothée had made the conclusion within a week at the Academy that Val didn't have many more friends than him. But it seemed by choice.

Timothée cautiously approached. "So, you'll show us where the mushrooms are?"

"If you can keep up."

Nathaniel and Sylvester gave him a hopeful grin, and something strange bubbled in Timothée's stomach. Was this happening? Was he actually working with people? Even if those people included Valentine.

There was no path in the Enchanted Forest, at least none Timothée could see. Val made his own trail, effortlessly slipping between the trees and gracefully skipping over the roots. The three of them followed clumsily in his wake.

The rain at least had slowed, but the forest still dripped over them from every too-heavy leaf or fir shaking in the wind.

A slow-running creek appeared in front of them, brown water full of rotten leaves and sticks stuck on stones and muddy banks. Val swiftly leapt over the smooth rocks to the other side.

Timothée hesitated at the edge. "Didn't Professor Barracus say not to cross the creek?"

Val looked over his shoulder. "He also said to collect all the ingredients."

Sylvester and Nathaniel crossed to the other side, much less gracefully than Val, with wet and muddy ankles.

But Timothée had followed Val before and gotten locked in a sewer.

He'd followed Val's advice and caught a Dark Star.

Val tilted his head to the side, a sly smile crawling up his beautiful face. "Coming, Greywick?"

Of course he was.

IT SHOULD HAVE been darker across the river, where the trees knit together overhead, denying even a sliver of moonlight. But it wasn't.

This side of the forest... glowed.

Everywhere he looked were fluorescent green-capped mushrooms. Flowers blew sparkling dust when brushed by his boot, and vines shimmered as if they had the sun's light inside them.

"I guess this is why it's called the Enchanted Forest." Timothée reached toward a strange flower growing on the side of a tree: pale yellow with a gleaming pink center.

"Among other reasons." Val snatched his wrist. "Don't touch that. Don't touch anything."

Val's hand was cold against his skin, and his pulse fluttered beneath Val's fingertips. Val scowled up at him, then dropped his hand.

Timothée swallowed in a dry throat. Sylvester quickly tossed a plucked purple leaf to the ground.

"How are you so good at this?" Timothée asked. "Finding things, knowing your way around the forest?"

Val hesitated then said slowly, "I've had a lot of practice."

Timothée heard the reservation in his words. There was more he wasn't saying.

"What, did your parents make you practice potion-making in case you swallowed a Dark Star?" Sylvester grinned.

"Maybe you picked up potion-making after you realized you weren't going to marry an empress," Timothée chided. Both Sylvester and Nathaniel burst out laughing. Everyone gossiped over why Valentine and Carmilla had broken up. A warm feeling crept through Timothée as Sylvester clapped him on the back.

Val didn't answer, but his body stiffened as he walked. Finally, he said, "Don't be ridiculous."

Timothée stopped talking after Val's retort. The world dissolved to the sounds of the forest, the rush of the wind through the trees, the slosh of their feet moving through old dead leaves, the snap and crackle of breaking branches.

There were animal signs too: skittering, birds screeching, and the gleam of bright eyes through dark trees.

*What lives in here?* Certainly nothing too frightful. He could hardly see Archpriestess Kassandra letting anything dangerous live on her Isle.

She kept all the dangers inside it.

A branch broke to his left, and he leapt, bumping into Sylvester. "Sorry."

Then again, the forest was huge, and the Isle had been in the air for many years. Who knew what had grown and thrived undisturbed all that time?

Light shone through a gap in the trees up ahead. Not the unusual luminescent glow of the deep forest, but the natural shine of a bright autumn moon. The clouds had parted.

Val held up a hand as they approached the clearing, a vast grassy field. In the center lay a spool of thorny vines that disappeared beneath the ground. Bright red flowers bloomed like pinpricks of blood. Moonlight shone through the scattering clouds. They'd been in the forest a long time. Soon, Professor Barracus would wonder where they went.

"Well," Val said, "here we are."

A grove of cinder mushrooms spread out between them and the field. Sylvester gave a yelp of excitement as he and Nathaniel dropped to collect the mushrooms.

Timothée looked over at Val. "Hey, thanks for taking us here. You didn't have to."

"No, I didn't." Val shoved some mushrooms into his basket.

Baskets full, they turned to head back. But Timothée hesitated, looking at the red flowers on the vines.

"Those flowers look familiar."

"They should."

Timothée wrinkled his nose, tried to recall where he'd seen them before. "Torias flowers. Starling surgeons use them to numb their patients and put them to sleep before they perform intense healing."

"So, you have been looking through my books." Val gave him a sideways glance.

"They're an important medicinal ingredient. Shouldn't we grab some and take them back to the school?"

Val raised a slender brow. "Oh, I'm sure Professor Barracus would be oh so grateful to anyone who could bring him back such a precious petal." He started to walk away.

Timothée stared into the clearing. If he could bring a couple flowers back, he could provide a real service to the Academy. He wouldn't just be the new godling who had lost control of his magic. He could make a positive difference.

A difference Valentine didn't seem to care about. Timothée put down his lantern and tentatively stepped into the clearing.

When nothing jumped out to kill him, he let out a deep sigh and walked quicker toward the spool of thorns.

"What are you doing?" Sylvester called.

"Grabbing the Torias flowers."

"Uh, I don't think you should touch that thing," Nathaniel said. "Torias flowers are…"

Timothée glanced over his shoulder to see the three boys watching him from the clearing's edge.

Val crossed his arms and smirked. "As long as he doesn't touch the thorns, he should be fine."

"Of course, I know not to touch the thorns," Timothée called back. "I'm not an idiot."

*He doesn't think I can do this,* Timothée thought. But Val knew more about this plant than he was letting on. *Don't touch the thorns.*

A strange tingling sensation crawled up his spine. *No fear,* he told himself. *Grab the flowers and go.*

As he drew closer, he realized the strange vines were bigger than they had appeared from far away, some thicker than his arms. *Not that that's saying much.* The vines rippled from their cluster and out into the field like crescent moons. There were three or four flowers on the entire plant, and lots of thorns.

Carefully, Timothée wove through some of the smaller vines to get closer to the center of the plant, where the flowers grew. The vines were bigger closer to the center, the tightly wound spool at least two heads taller than him. But there! A small red flower right in front of him, partially obstructed by criss-crossing vines.

*The opening is wide enough for my arm.*

Timothée wasn't sure what would happen if he touched the thorns. Some sort of poison probably, but he wouldn't give Valentine the satisfaction of asking.

He reached his hand through the narrow opening, holding his breath. His fingers brushed the red petals. Slowly, he angled his hand down and plucked the flower from its base.

He let out a long breath.

"Almost there!" Sylvester cried before clamping a hand over his mouth.

Timothée didn't think silence was necessary; it wasn't as if the plant could hear them. But he did need to concentrate. Gradually, he drew back his arm. He cleared the opening and straightened, the red Torias flower in his palm.

"See this, Val?" Timothée smirked and waved the flower in the air.

"You did it!" Sylvester called.

"And you didn't even wake the Lyrastera." Nathaniel grinned. "I heard some of the big ones can swallow you whole."

"The Lyra-what?" Timothée startled, stepping back. "Swallow?"

He heard a crunch and looked down to see his foot on a vine, a broken thorn beneath his heel.

"And there we are," Val said coldly. "I knew he would wake it."

The ground beneath him rumbled. Vines sprung from the earth. Every thick thorn split open, revealing rows and rows of sharp green…

Teeth.

Timothée screamed and stumbled back, dropping the red flower and his basket. The vines trembled and wove in and out of the ground like an eel cresting through water.

Timothée dashed toward the forest. Sharp thorn teeth nipped at his legs. Sylvester wailed and ran into the trees. Nathaniel looked sick. And Val… Val was smiling.

*'I knew he would wake it.'*

Timothée had walked into another one of Val's traps.

Sharp pain carried up his body as a thorn snagged his ankle, and he fell to the hard dirt. He pushed himself up, spitting out grass. The ground split before him, hard dirt and rocks spreading as the Lyrastera broke through the earth, showing its colossal form.

Timothée screamed as he gazed up at it. The vines on the surface had only been a small part of it, all attached to a globular green body. Its head was like the bulb of a flower, blooming to reveal a gaping maw of sharp thorny teeth.

"If you actually read anything," Val called from the side of the clearing, "you would have known what horror protects Torias flowers."

"We need... We need..." Nathaniel stuttered. "We need to get Professor Barracus."

Timothée could look at nothing except the plant towering above him. His heart beat wildly in his chest. Thorny vines crawled on either side of him. One slammed across his basket—all his supplies!

He yelped and darted back, trying to weave through the thrashing vines. Something sharp twisted around his ankles, and his world spun.

Cutting pain coursed through his legs and he realized the plant was holding him upside down by his ankles. He cried out with frantic terror.

"Oh, the Three!" Nathaniel cried. "We have to help!" He turned on his heel and bolted into the forest.

"If he's truly a god, he shouldn't need our help," Valentine snarled at the fleeing boy. His words were so venomous, Timothée thought he'd rather stay tangled above the man-eating plant than go near Val.

Until it began to swing him. The plant lifted him above its gaping maw. The petals of its face curled back, a circle of teeth wide-open, revealing a pit of sticky plant goop and decaying bugs.

"Val! Val, help!" Timothée let go of his dignity, wild terror crawling through him.

"Admit it," Val said.

"Admit what?"

"Admit you're not a god. You're an imposter!" Val yelled. "Tell me what you really are."

In that moment, Timothée would have given Val anything. Anything. But he couldn't give what he didn't have.

"I—I don't know."

"Not good enough. Tell me the truth! Why do you look like that?"

"Why I *what*?" Timothée clawed at the vine wrapped around his ankle, the little thorn teeth nipping at his fingers. "Help me! *Please!*"

"Help yourself, God of Shadows."

The Lyrastera lowered Timothée. His head spun, choker too tight. The creature's warm breath reeked of rot. More vines wrapped around his body. Blood and mud dripped down his leg.

*No, no, no. NO!*

Val couldn't actually let this plant devour him. But when he looked over, there was a hunger more intense than the monster's in Val's eyes.

Timothée Greywick had not come all the way to the Celestial Academy to be eaten by a plant.

His heart beat madly in his chest, body trembling with terror. He could almost feel the petals on his face.

Suddenly, he was thrown through the air. He fell among the vines, thorn teeth clamping and biting at him before shuddering still.

Timothée blinked through clouded vision and saw the plant screeching. Behind it was a massive shadow.

No, not a shadow... A panther. With wings.

It unhinged its massive jaw and clamped onto the Lyrastera. The plant gave a horrible hiss, vines smacking up and down before shriveling to mulch.

Timothée untangled himself from the decaying vines, shoving something in his pocket. He wasn't quick enough. The panther was already stalking toward him.

It was like no creature Timothée had ever seen. Shadows dusted its edges. *Shadowcraft?* But whose? Val still had his choker on, and so did he.

The creature wasn't all black; parts of it blinked in the moonlight like trapped stars, ripples of purple. It prowled across the peat, leaving a black sparkling trail.

Timothée held up his arms as it approached, almost wishing he could go back to the giant man-eating plant.

The panther paused in front of him. Timothée must have been dazed for he could have sworn it inclined its head.

Then it turned, spread its wings, and charged.

Right toward Val.

Val's eyes went wide with terror. He frantically clawed at his choker. He was going to use his magic, but he wouldn't be able to remove his choker in time.

"Val!" Timothée sprinted toward him, cutting off the panther. He leapt, grabbing Val around the waist, and they tumbled back into the forest.

The huge cat crashed through the trees, hissing and snarling above them.

"No!" Timothée cried. "Stop."

And the shadow panther stopped.

Val and Timothée stared up at the cat's bright purple eyes, its jaws full of fluorescent teeth that dripped dark saliva overtop of them. It slid over his arms, his chest.

The feeling was oddly reminiscent of Val's magic in the stairwell.

The frantic beat of Val's heart matched his own. Val slowly shifted his head to him. "What now, Greywick?"

"This is your fault," Timothée hissed back. "You wanted me to get eaten by that plant."

The panther paced back and forth, as if deliberating the best way to devour them.

"It wasn't going to eat you. I had a vial of chloroblast that would have withered the plant in a second."

"I'm supposed to believe you were actually going to save me?" Timothée groaned, but still didn't release his hold on Val. He could push Val in front of the giant cat and run…

But if that had been his plan, why had he rushed over to save Val?

"A Lyrastera is easy to kill," Val snarled. "Not so much a—"

Suddenly, the shadow panther arched back, wings flaring, and bright red flames appeared behind it.

Sharp pain coursed through Timothée, his nerves alight as if they were on fire too. "No!" Timothée cried, though he wasn't sure why.

A glass vial flew through the air and crashed into the giant cat, consuming the shadow beast in flame.

It crackled and hissed and withered, and Timothée had to look away, instead watching the flames dance in Val's eyes.

Then there was a *thunk*, and the creature dropped to the ground.

A figure stood silhouetted behind it.

Professor Barracus's face was stern as he glared down at them. "Do I even want to know what you boys were doing this deep in the forest?"

Timothée looked at Val, pale with shock. He could tell Professor Barracus Val had led him out here to die a painful death by plant. But he went with another truth. Slowly, he untangled himself from Val and dug into his pocket.

"I wanted to get this." He held out the wilted Torias flower in his palm. "For the school."

Val coughed and stood behind him. "You actually got it."

Professor Barracus gave a long sigh, then snatched the flower from him. "Timothée Greywick, indeed. You and Mr. Sun can harvest the rest of the flowers off the dead Lyrastera. The Three know it will take us moons to grow another one this large and fruitful. And that's the first of your punishments. Detention, every day until I decide otherwise. And you can bet I'll think of some interesting tasks. I know you got him out here somehow, Valentine. And Timothée, I thought you were smarter than to fall for this."

"I—" He had wanted to help, and now he'd disappointed the only professor who cared a little bit about him. "You knew this plant was here?"

"Of course," Professor Barracus said. "We professors harvest it once a moon in a controlled state. Now we'll have to outsource our Torias flowers."

Shame rolled through Timothée. Of course, the professors had known it was here... and he'd ruined everything. His eyes caught the body of the panther. It had changed color in death. Its fur had turned blue and rippled with the pattern of stars and constellations, wings silver and still.

"What is that thing?"

"That," Professor Barracus said, running a hand over his shorn hair, "is another matter entirely."

Val came up behind him. For the moment, it seemed he'd lost his arrogance. He held his elbows, observing the creature with a discerning look.

"What you're looking at now," Professor Barracus said, "is one of Xydrious's mythical beasts."

"But," Timothée stammered, "they're all gone."

"Apparently not." Professor Barracus cast his gaze to the sky. "And it appears this beast was corrupted. A shadowling."

"Shadowling..." Val echoed the word.

"As the legend goes," Professor Barracus said, "Noctis desired to create his own creatures. But since he could not craft them himself, he found a way to make his father's beasts his own. They wore the shadows of his making and came at his command. It's said Rhaemyria destroyed them all with her wings of fire, which is why I tried my morning glory potion on it. Seemed to work well enough."

Timothée's mind reeled. "Mythical beasts. Shadowlings. They don't exist anymore. They're creatures of legend."

"Were," Val said. "They *were* creatures of legend. Not anymore."

"The proof is before us." Professor Barracus stroked his chin.

Timothée stared at the crystalline eyes of the dead beast. "How is this possible?"

"My guess?" Professor Barracus looked straight at him. "When the children of the gods woke up their magic, so did they."

"Woke up…" Val whispered.

"Now, don't think this discovery is going to make me go easy on your punishment. You two could have been seriously hurt," Professor Barracus said. "Come along. I need to get back to the other students. I'm pretty sure Sylvester shit his pants when he came running to me. This must be reported to administration as well."

"You're going to tell Archpriestess Kassandra?"

"I'm going to tell her we came across a mythical beast." His gaze cut into them. "And if anyone asks, that's all you two saw as well."

*He's not telling them it was a shadowling,* Timothée thought. *Why?*

Timothée watched the professor head into the forest. He took one last look at the Lyrastera and panther.

Then he heard Val's voice: "I was wrong about you."

Timothée turned to him. "What do you mean?"

"Maybe you are a god."

Setviren had told him that. Archpriestess Kassandra had told him that. The world had screamed it at him. But to hear Val say it, with glistening eyes and tears cutting lines down his mud-splashed cheeks… It felt different.

It felt wrong.

And right.

"I—" Timothée started.

"That creature. That shadowling. It didn't just appear," Val said. "It was called."

Timothée trembled and wrapped his arms around himself.

"What?" Val hissed. "I thought you'd love that I was wrong."

Timothée looked up into the dark sky. "Not about this."

# 13
# IN WHICH MARION PICKS A FIGHT WITH ARGOS

MARION TOSSED IN her bed. The sheets were ropes tangled around her ankles, her skin hot and sweaty. She needed to sleep. But her mind spun, sending her thoughts skittering like motes of dust.

Khalid had told her what happened the other day at Physical Combat when she had run after Professor Barracus. Darius had an abrasion on his head and started bleeding. And if Khalid hadn't gotten Vivian out of there, Andúrigard's future king would be an empty bag of skin and her sister would be…

What would Archpriestess Kassandra do to a kingslaying godchild?

They'd been at the Academy for nearly an entire moon and were no closer to any answers than their first night here.

With an angry roar, she threw herself out of bed. They'd wasted enough time pouring over old books and interrogating spineless professors. Marion knew who could cure her sister's illness. And she'd pry the answer out brick by brick if she had to.

She flung herself to the floor, knees pounding against the stonework. Her fingers dug between the cracks of the brick. Blond curls fell raggedly around her face. "Listen here," she growled, voice raspy, "I know you can see me. Hear me. I'm done with your little games and I'm not afraid of you. Show yourself, castle. I demand it."

A minute passed. And then another. Marion looked around her room. What was she expecting? A ghost to materialize out of the walls? A flash of light?

She slammed her palms flat against the rock. "You helped me during the Celestial Rite. Help me now. I demand it!" Tears spilled from her eyes. It was foolish, talking to the stone. But what else was there? It was only a matter of time before the leeches ran out. Before Vivian couldn't control it anymore. Marion wouldn't let her die the way she'd let Father. "*Please!*"

No answer. Marion struggled up, walked over to her bedside table. There was a glass vase with a small bouquet of blue flowers with pointed petals. She snatched the flowers, spraying water across her bed.

"Look at this!" she screamed, shaking the flowers at the ceiling. "You grew these flowers for me, didn't you? And every time I leave my room, thinking they look wilted, I come back and they're blooming all over again. Isn't that you? Aren't you showing me I'm not alone?"

She collapsed onto the bed, the flowers discarded to the floor. "Tell me I'm not alone."

*I have nothing to do with those flowers.* The fireplace in her bedroom lit to life with purple flame. *In fact, I have a great aversion to living things.*

"Castle?" Marion's feet crushed the petals. She fell before the fire, body bathing in heat and purple light. "You're here. You heard me."

*Your shrill voice could penetrate the thickest stone.*

Marion bit the inside of her cheek. "I cannot believe I'm being insulted by a piece of architecture."

A dark laugh sounded, and the flames flickered. *I'm much more than that, little firebird. I am the force that draws the Isle into the air. I am the space between the stars.* The fire dimmed then grew, making Marion sit back. *I am your only hope.*

"Yes, yes," Marion breathed. "I need your help. My sister is sick. You must cure her."

The curtains whipped away from the closed window with an invisible wind. Daylight broke across the floor. *I must cure her? What do I owe the Greywicks? Three little piglets willingly walking to slaughter.*

"What are you talking about?" Marion snarled. "We only came here to help Vivian. If you're powerful enough to keep the Isle afloat, surely you can make her well again. What does it matter to you?"

*It matters a great deal.*

Marion pounded her fist against the side of the fireplace. "I have had enough of your games and little light tricks."

*I quite like my little light tricks.* Suddenly, the fire exploded in size, flames curling and taking form. A face made of fire.

Father's face. Father's face melting into ashes, revealing only charred bone beneath.

"Stop it!" Marion screamed.

*Don't you remember what I told you? Face your fear and rise stronger than before. All I see are three little cowards. Why should I help you when you all hide from your true selves? The blood remembers. Embrace what you are or suffer in stasis.*

The face was still there, bones and charred flesh silently screaming. Father's eyes melted from their sockets.

"I said STOP IT," Marion shrieked and threw her hands into the fireplace, cutting through Father's face. She clutched the purple embers, choking the life from them. Burning pain laced over her skin.

A strangled laugh echoed through the room. Marion didn't stop. Sweat poured down her face, tears fell from her eyes, and yet her arms were in the fire, hands squeezing, squeezing, squeezing the coals.

*Embrace what you are. What you have become. Perhaps then I will let you find me.*

All at once, the firelight disappeared, the curtain fell back over the window, and the room was shrouded in darkness. It was silent.

"Castle?" Marion whispered. She shuffled beneath the curtains covering her window. Daylight caressed her skin. With a deep breath, she looked at her forearms.

They were perfectly unmarred.

THE HUNTER'S BLOOD Moon brought brilliant blood-red leaves to the trees and a stinging cold to the air. Marion wrapped her cloak tighter around herself and rubbed her mittened hands together. Selene Crescent smelled of pumpkin, cinnamon, and pecans as the shopkeepers prepared food and drink for the coming night.

There was no point in trying to go back to sleep after her encounter with that damned castle. She shot a look back at the Academy. What did the stupid hunk of stone mean? *Embrace what you are.*

She didn't know what the hell she was. Who her father or mother were. She was no Starling, not even able to conjure a little wind to move a leaf. She didn't even enjoy the night, like Starlings were supposed to. The bright sun and pure blue sky stole her gaze. The daylight was where she belonged.

But at least being awake during the day meant there was no one around to bother her.

She walked to the edge of Selene Crescent and was about to turn around when the flash of white robes caught her eye out in the field near the farms.

Setviren stood with his hands on his hips looking into the sky. His shoulder-length green hair tossed in the wind. And standing behind him was…

"Khalid?" Marion whispered. What in the Three were Loremaster Setviren and Khalid doing together in the middle of the day?

She crept forward, staying along the edge of Madame Tabitha's Dress Shoppe. Crouching behind a bush, she was close enough to see the gleam off Khalid's single gold earring.

"Ah, there he is now," Setviren said.

A whirring sound carried with the breeze, and a silver sky skiff appeared over the edge of the Isle. It puttered into a landing near the loremaster and Khalid.

The propellor stopped turning and a tall man stepped out of the metal contraption. He removed his goggles, revealing wind-strewn blond hair, a tight mouth, and storm blue eyes. Prince Darius Störmberg.

At first, Marion thought he was wearing a red jerkin and matching pants. No. His clothes...

They were caked in blood.

"Your Highness!" Setviren rushed forward. "The hunt was successful, I presume?"

Darius didn't answer. He paced forward, face in a dark scowl. His hands clenched and unclenched into fists.

"Your Highness?" Setviren pressed.

Darius whipped around and kicked the sky skiff with a roar. "This damned thing! It's not fast enough! How am I supposed to find him if I can barely cross the Iron Vale in a night?"

"But, Your Highness, the blood—"

Khalid bumped Setviren's shoulder to silence him. "No sign of him, Dare?"

Darius's knuckles were white as glaciers on the edge of the sky skiff. "Not a fucking sniff of him. Caught a coven of the monsters preying on a fishing village near the mouth of the Vale. They claimed no knowledge or allegiance to him."

"Can you trust them?" Setviren asked. "They are monsters, after all."

A joyless smile crossed Darius's lips. "After what I did to them, they wouldn't dare lie."

Marion's heart hammered against her chest, and she stayed as still as she could, though the branches of the bush tickled her face. There was something feral, inhuman, in Darius's expression.

She'd known it all along, and she was right. He was dangerous, this prince, and not just because of his position. Darkness lurked within him.

But who was he hunting?

Darius turned away from the skiff, ran blood-caked hands through his hair. "Every hunt I go on, more and more rogue vampires appear out of the woodwork. Why are they suddenly so brazen if not under his orders?"

"You'll find him, Dare." Khalid placed a hand on the Prince's shoulder. "It's only a matter of time."

Darius's body jerked to stillness like a crossbow ricochet. "Time?" He turned and Marion shrunk back at the look in his eyes. "You speak to me of time? That demon has stolen the last three years of my life. And until he's choking for breath beneath my boot, I will not rest. Cannot rest. Thraina will not know peace until the Dark Prophet is dead." His body trembled with the words. "And all his vampire scum with him."

Khalid nodded and looked down, hiding the enigmatic look in his eyes.

"Let us return to the Academy," Darius ordered. "Letters must be sent to the noble houses of Andúrigard. All personal guards should report to Wolfhelm for redeployment on scouting missions. I want no rock unturned until the Dark Prophet's blood returns to the soil."

"At once, Your Highness." Setviren hurried behind him.

"And schedule an audience with the Archpriestess."

"The Archpriestess, m'lord?"

Darius didn't stop his stride. "More Celestial Knights are needed on this mission."

"B-but, m'lord, the Celestial Knights are already spread thin. You've heard the news." Setviren's voice lowered. "The blue handprints defacing Rhaemyria's statues and temples. The strange pilgrims gathering at the Ruins of Argos. Rumors spread of this so-called *Exalted One*—"

Darius turned and towered over the trembling loremaster. "If Rhaemyria is so distraught by the vandalism of her relics, then she can come down and deal with it herself. I have no time for pilgrim rats. We remove one false deity, and they'll just find another to worship. I will have more Celestial Knights and I will have the Dark Prophet's head. And if Kassandra doesn't like that, she can take it up with the King." He stepped away. His shoulders shook with harsh laughter. "Oh wait. That's me."

Setviren's throat bobbed, but he scuttled after Darius.

"Coming, Khalid?" Darius called.

Khalid kicked the propellor of the sky skiff with his foot. "Yeah, in a minute. I'm going to look at your skiff."

Darius waved a hand in acknowledgment then he and Setviren entered the Crescent. Marion held her breath, pushing further into the bush. Darius's boots pounded on the stonework.

She counted each one—*thud thud thud*—until he and Setviren were out of sight. Then she shoved herself out of the bush, pulling twigs from her hair, and walked into the field.

Khalid hunched over the sky skiff's propellor, his back to her. She cleared her throat.

"Adding espionage to your repertoire, Ms. Greywick?" he said without turning. "You are learning."

Marion stiffened. How did he know it was her? "What are you doing with Darius's skiff?"

He spent a few moments more prodding the propellor before looking up at her. His black hair curled around his ears. "Looking if I can add some thrusters. He wants it to go faster, I'll make it go faster."

She stepped closer, yellow cloak dusting the grass. "You know how to do that?"

"Of course. Professor Rimmer teaches mechanics to the third-year Dark Stars. They make different devices to deploy their potions. But she lets me use the lab after-hours to build stuff."

"Why don't you spend that time practicing your starcraft instead? Then you can make whatever you want with magic."

Khalid smiled at her. "Those who rely on magic are burdened by it. But to create with just your hands and your wits… Isn't that a type of magic in itself?"

"I suppose." Marion had none of those things. She had no magic, wasn't particularly good at building things with her hands, and certainly felt her wits had long escaped her. Especially when Khalid peered down at her with that intense gaze of his.

"So, were you spying on me?"

"Of course not!" She straightened. "I couldn't sleep and went for a walk. And lo and behold, what do I find? My sister's paramour filled with bloodlust over slaughtering her kind."

"Listen to yourself." Khalid turned back to the skiff. "Your distaste for Darius colors your view. Those vampires aren't your sister's kind. She's not like them."

Marion rubbed her dirty boot against the shiny skiff. "I know that. But Darius wouldn't see her differently if he found out. Did you see his face? He was practically frothing at the mouth."

Khalid sighed and leaned against the skiff. He seemed downtrodden. Marion worried her lip and leaned beside him. "I'm sorry. I know how much you care for him."

"Look." Khalid placed a hand against his forehead. "Darius is my best friend, but we don't share the same views on many things. His father believed in assimilation disguised as unity. And Darius views his father as a saint; to think otherwise would be heresy to him. He has to see his family, *himself*, as a hero." Khalid shook his head. "What other choice is there?"

Marion took in a deep breath. "Embrace what we are."

"And what are we?"

"Monsters," Marion said. "All of us."

"Well, that's a nihilistic view of the world, isn't it?" Khalid sat up, stretched. "Honestly, you two are more similar than you'd like to admit."

"Take that back!" She swatted at him.

He caught her wrists in his rough hands, pulled her chest to chest with him. "Stubborn, single-minded, likely to raze an entire kingdom if someone hurts your family—"

Marion's breath was heavy in her throat. Khalid's body was warm against hers, his long lashes casting shadows below his green eyes. "But I'm not pretending to be a hero."

"You're certainly not a monster."

Marion looked to the castle. Bright, midday light reflected sunbeams off the glass windows. "No," she whispered.

*Not yet.*

# 14

# IN WHICH TIMOTHÉE JOINS THE SECRET SOCIETY OF STARBOUND EXILES

TIMOTHÉE'S LAST CLASS of the day had been canceled, affording the Dark Stars a free block. Val had disappeared, with no word for where he was going or when he'd be back. Naturally, Timothée cooped himself up in his room to read. He had a stack of history books Marion had assigned him to comb through, but he was re-reading his favorite series instead. They'd already poured over so many ancient textbooks, and none of them had answers. None of them discussed vampires unless they were talking about killing them.

Besides, at breakfast Marion had shared a message from the sentient castle: *Embrace what you are.* Embrace what he was? How could he do that when he didn't even know who he was? For all their best guesses, the castle wasn't even alive, and they were all going insane.

When a knock sounded on his door, he leapt up, breathing a sigh of relief at any distraction from his thoughts. Carmilla greeted him, a strange look in her eyes. Her short red hair hung in sharp angles around her face. "Come on." She yanked his wrist. "It's time we showed you something."

"We?"

Val appeared out of the shadows, arms crossed, a scowl on his perfect face. "Don't look at me like that, Greywick. This isn't my idea."

Carmilla rolled her eyes. She turned and walked down the stairs, Val and Timothée following dutifully behind her.

In the kitchen, she pulled aside the large pantry, revealing a cobwebbed passage.

"Do the professors know about this?" Timothée asked.

Carmilla and Val looked at each other and laughed.

He'd spent a lot of extra time with his roommate lately, serving Professor Barracus's detentions. The Dark Star professor had devised some creative punishments for them: everything from mucking the stables to sorting through stacks of potion ingredients. He'd even tried to get them to weed the Academy gardens while the rest of the students slept, but Val had complained so adamantly about it, Professor Barracus had relented.

Val didn't talk to him much, but sometimes he'd deign to offer a response or two. Timothée had settled on passing the time by telling Val the plots to all his favorite books. And while Val didn't exactly acknowledge him, he didn't tell him to stop either.

Presently, the three of them walked through the secret passage for a few minutes before it opened to the outside. Stiff wind tore at his messy hair. Before them lay a swinging rope bridge. Night still blanketed the school, and Timothée looked down upon the sprawling turrets and glass ceilings of the Academy below. The bridge itself led to a purple tower with a ramshackle roof. The whole thing had an odd lean to it.

"I'm not crossing," Timothée yelled over the wind.

"Gather your courage, Greywick. I'm going to get things prepared." Carmilla walked easily across the bridge, so carefully balanced she barely made it sway. Once past, she entered a door to the tower.

But Timothée stayed rooted to the spot.

"Are you scared?" Valentine taunted before dancing onto the bridge.

Timothée stumbled forward, not wanting to be left alone. He grabbed Val's sleeve. "Wait!"

"Need me to hold your hand, Greywick?" Val said mockingly. But then he laced his fingers through Timothée's and walked backward over the bridge, pulling Timothée with him.

Timothée let out an audible gasp as his feet stepped over the wooden planks, swollen with rot, and placed half a foot apart. Valentine's grip was tight. The swaying made his stomach tumble.

But then Val stopped, right in the middle of the bridge.

"What?" Valentine smirked up at him, lilac hair swooping across his face. "Afraid you're going to fall?"

And Timothée was.

"But what a view," Val said more to himself.

Timothée followed his gaze, barely able to register anything besides the touch of Valentine's hands over his. On one side of the bridge was the intricate architecture of the Academy, and the fields and forests across the Isle of Argos. The other side showed the end of the Isle, a sharp drop off of rock and water leading to a sea of stars.

"You must think I'm terrified and bad at everything," Timothée said.

Valentine raised a delicate brow. "I'm sure you're only terrified and bad at most things."

Timothée laughed. "Once, I even got told I was a bad kisser."

"Oh?"

Timothée flushed the moment he realized what he'd said. "I mean, I—"

"What?" Val placed his palm flat on Timothée's stomach. "Are you wanting me to evaluate that too?"

"I shouldn't have—" He was wavering now, and not just from the wind and the bridge. Val's full lips parted, his smile dangerously curved. He looked serious.

*This has to be a joke.* What sane person went from saying you took everything from them and trying to get you eaten by a giant plant, to almost kissing you? But the wild glint in Val's eyes reminded Timothée that the boy in front of him was very much *not* sane.

"You're crazy," Timothée breathed.

"You're the one that's crazy, Greywick. This is a dangerous place to try." Val's voice lowered. "The pleasure of it might make you pass out, and I don't know if you're enough of a god yet to survive a fall this high."

"I wouldn't pass out."

"Are you so sure?" Val's hand slipped beneath his shirt, and his cold fingertips brushed Timothée's bare skin.

"Of course," Timothée said. "I'd be the worst kiss you've ever had."

"That's quite the statement." Valentine stood up on his toes, his chin angled up. "You've piqued my interest."

And before Timothée knew what he was doing, he grabbed Val's shirt collar, pulled him closer. Val's face blanched, genuine surprise flashing over his features. But he didn't pull away.

"Are you coming?" Carmilla yelled, the door to the tower flying open. "Come on! We're already late."

Timothée stumbled back, felt open air, but Val grabbed his shirt, straightened him. "Remember, Greywick." He smirked. "Don't fall."

Then he laughed the rest of the way over the bridge, without taking Timothée's hand.

Another one of his cruel jokes. *I knew it.* But he had fallen for it anyway. With shaking legs, Timothée crossed the rest of the way and followed Valentine into the slanted tower.

"About time," Carmilla said. "Welcome to the Secret Society of Starbound Exiles."

The torches on the wall flickered, as if also bidding him welcome.

The small room was crowded. Timothée recognized first to fourth-year Dark Star students. Something crackled around them. His body hummed with it, and he grabbed his choker which suddenly felt too tight. None of the other students were wearing theirs. Shadows swam around their hands.

"You're practicing shadowcraft," he whispered.

"We're summoning that which our stars gifted us," Carmilla said. "Destruction?"

"It's more than that." Val was in front of him, choker dangling between his long fingers. "Noctis was called the God of Shadows, but his magic came from the space between the stars. We don't just summon darkness; we summon the very fabric that binds the universe together."

A shivering dark shadow spiraled from Val's palm. Timothée was captivated by it as he seemed to be by all things Valentine did. It wasn't just a black shadow, but edged with flecks of purple and flashes of white where it captured the flicker of light in the room and swallowed it up.

Then as quickly as it came, the shadow poofed out. Val gave a self-deprecating laugh. "Still working on holding it."

Someone came up and placed a tight hand on Valentine's shoulder. "Don't worry, that's why we're here. To practice."

Erik Borstigsson. This was the first time Timothée had seen Val and Erik side by side. They were about the same height, but Erik held himself differently, a wide-legged stance and arms on hips, as if he needed to take up more space.

Around them, the other Starlings paused to watch the interaction.

Val shrugged out of Erik's grip. "Well, we can always look to our faithful leader for guidance."

Erik opened his palm, summoned a swirling black ball. "Maybe you'll achieve my talent in a few years, Valentine."

Val gave a mocking laugh. "And maybe you'll get to Greywick's in ten, but I doubt it."

Erik squeezed his fist shut, darkness dissipating, and red spotted his face. "What do you think, Greywick? Ready to show us if all that power was a fluke?"

"I can take your choker off for you!" a bubbly voice said. A blue-haired girl popped up in front of Timothée.

"Huh?" Timothée stumbled back.

"Surprised to see me?" Rayna, Khalid's cousin from the Morning Star house, said. She wore grey trousers and a yellow blouse with the emblem of a phoenix. She was shorter than even Valentine. *What's a Morning Star doing here?* "Taf and I can assist you in taking off your choker."

Rayna nodded to a girl with long black hair in the corner wearing a blue uniform, nose deep in a textbook. "Oh, hi, Timothée. I thought I'd eventually see you here."

Tafieri Hartton stood and Timothée did his best to hide his shock. He knew her as a friend of Vivian and Darius's, but from what he'd heard, she was daughter to the captain of the Störmberg guard, and a high achiever at school. "You're here. With the Dark Stars?"

"As much as the school might like to pit everyone against each other, most of the students don't see it that way," Taf said, looking up. "I mean, at least a lot of us don't. My older brother is a Dark Star. He's graduated now, working in the army as a chemist."

"Morning and Evening Stars created the chokers." Rayna bobbed up and down. "So if you say pretty please, we can alter them so you can take them off whenever. And we're so good at our jobs, the professors never know!"

"Take mine off?" Timothée repeated, even though he was now the only one in the room with his on. "We could get expelled. Or worse!"

"Is there anything worse than living without your freedom?" Carmilla's voice was harsh.

Timothée wrung his hands together. "But what if... What if someone loses control?"

Carmilla bit her lip, hesitating. "What happened when you swallowed your star, Timothée... Nothing like that has ever happened before."

Of course it hadn't. Because he was a freak. He would always be a freak. Always be different.

Rayna bounced up to him, blinked her big eyes. "So, what do you say, Star Child? Ready for us to take it off?"

Humming sounded between his ears, heartbeat becoming erratic with an unnatural cadence. A voice inside his mind cried: *Yes, yes, yes.* His magic screamed to be released.

"No." He gripped his hand around his neck. Professor Barracus told him if wanted to atone for what he'd done, he had to keep his choker on. "I will not use my magic."

There was a worried look on the other Dark Stars' faces. He quickly added, "I won't say anything about this though." He wasn't sure if what they were doing was right or wrong, but they certainly weren't as dangerous without their chokers as he was.

"It's alright, Timothée." Carmilla placed a calming hand on his shoulder. "Why don't you watch for a bit? There are some books over there. We've tried to collect all the resources we could on Noctis's shadowcraft. Though most of those have been destroyed or are kept hidden by the Celestial Church. The copies we've gathered are missing pages or falling apart, but you might find something of interest there."

Timothée's heart leapt. He may not want to use his craft, but he could *read* about it. And Noctis had an army of vampires. Perhaps there were books about them here, a clue to help Vivian.

Timothée picked his way across the room. There were several tables, but also worn couches and chairs. The room was lit by torches and a fire at the far end. It had the smell of musk and smoke. Bookcases lined the walls, and when he got up close, he realized Carmilla had been right: most of the books were more dust than paper.

"Your sister told me you're a big reader."

Timothée turned to see Taf behind him. Her bright sapphire uniform was neatly pressed, and a matching blue clip held her long hair back. Her deep brown eyes narrowed inquisitively at him.

"I read most of these books during my first year, though Carmilla was able to sneak some new ones out of her collection from Novagrad," she continued. "Though don't tell anyone."

"I won't." Timothée offered a smile. "Vivian said you were from Wolfhelm, but the lettering on these books... Is it Kirrint? How did you read them?"

"My mother's from Kirrintsova and taught me how to speak her language." She tilted her head, purple torchlight playing across her dark brown skin. "Do you speak any other languages?"

"Only Liturgical." He shrugged. Though all three nations had traditional languages, the Church had created a universal language to be instilled as the common tongue. It was the language the Greywicks spoke. They'd never learned the traditional dialect of Andúrigard, but that was not uncommon for the working class. Timothée had occasionally overheard Carmilla and Val whispering to each other in Kirrint, the old language of Kirrintsova.

"Are you looking for something in particular? I can help."

He didn't want to sound suspicious, but he probably wasn't the only one with morbid curiosity. "Um, I'm kind of interested in vampires."

Taf lowered her brow. "Of course, vampires. They attacked you in the square. I was in the crowd. We thought we were dead until you three lit up like the sun come to Thraina."

"Yeah," Timothée said.

"Well, if you're curious about vampires, then you have to start at the beginning." Taf stood on her tiptoes, fingers straining. "Hey, grab that dark brown book at the top and follow me."

Timothée easily pulled the book down. The cover was scarce except for a few connected stars. A familiar constellation, but he could not name it. The Kirrint letters were foreign to him.

Taf sat in a tucked-away window seat laid with comfortable cushions. Rain pattered on the shackled roof, slid down the window. A thin line of moss grew on the inside of the sill. She patted the seat next to her. "I can translate it for you."

Timothée sat down beside her and looked back over the classroom. Thankfully, most of the Starlings were now concentrating on using their magic.

Their shadowcraft.

Many of the fourth-year students mentored the younger ones. Well, except Erik who had his own little group encircling him as he sliced various pieces of fruit with his shadows. But Timothée's gaze fell as it always did: on Valentine. He was standing at a table, letting shadows flicker through his fingers like a deck of cards. A girl with the ends of her hair dyed bright red leaned on the counter beside Valentine, staring up at him with a wide grin.

"That's Melissa Cormick," Taf said. "Rumor has it, she's had a thing for Val since the beginning of the year. All her perseverance has paid off. To be honest, I never thought he'd actually go for her. Or anybody for that matter."

Timothée liked that Taf was so blunt, how she talked to him with none of the flowery flattery some of the other students used. Her honesty was refreshing.

He bit his lip, watched how Val placed his hands under Melissa's, how she pushed her wide hips back into his, and he whispered something in her ear. Shadows flicked on and off of Val's hands as if he couldn't hold them.

But Timothée remembered when they had been in the staircase, how Val had used his magic to hide them from Archpriestess Kassandra. That had been no small feat. And the lashes of magic in their room… *Why are you pretending to be bad at it?* To get Melissa's help up close? There must be something more. Valentine had pretended with Erik as well.

Timothée let out an annoyed breath then looked back down at the book. "So, what's this book called?"

"The Tale of the First Vampire: The Prince That Betrayed His Kingdom for a God."

If Darius found out that Vivian was a vampire, would he choose her or his kingdom?

An echoing voice whispered in his mind, *The present is only ever an echo of the past.* Timothee shivered.

Taf flipped the text open, old book smell spilling out. The pages were so crisp with age they crackled.

"It began when the Prince prayed to the heavens and a curious god left his home on Mount Argos to investigate," Taf said. "Noctis, the son of Rhaemyria and Xydrious."

"Noctis," Timothée repeated the name, and the sound trembled in his mouth as it always did.

"It was there he met a prince, said to be the most beautiful person in all the world. In the dead of night, Noctis stole the Prince away."

No wonder he had never heard this story. The royal family would have hidden this blasphemous history as deep as they could.

Taf turned the page and Timothée saw the abstract picture of a man made of shadows, and a beautiful prince with long black hair and piercing blue eyes.

"He was a Störmberg," Timothée guessed. "I thought they were all blond."

"He was the youngest son of King Vegar Störmberg, the Conqueror. His mother was the King's second wife, a noblewoman from the prosperous Seong family."

Taf turned another page. "Then Noctis—and I'm paraphrasing a bit here, because this book is a slog—Noctis was mad at his mother. He's pretty much mad at his mom in every piece of lore about him. Rhaemyria would not let him create, for she had already crafted the most perfect world.

"So, Noctis stole her most beautiful human and made him his own. He forced the Prince to swallow a star of darkness, and it gave him the same magic you have now. And it turned his eyes and hair purple."

Timothée looked over at Val, but then his gaze swept the rest of the room. A few of the students had glints of purple in their hair and eyes, undertones catching the light.

"A legacy the magic of Noctis still grants some to this day." Taf frowned. "But Noctis did not stop at giving the Prince shadowcraft. He wanted to show his mother he could create a more powerful, more deadly, immortal version of fragile humans. Noctis gave the Prince teeth that pierced flesh and let him drink his own god-blood." Taf's voice rose in cadence. "The blood of a god made the Prince strong and kept his youth, but it came with a cost. Noctis was the god of darkness, and his creations could not stand the morning's light. They could not survive on the bounty of the earth alone but needed to feast on the blood of humans. Though many say Noctis intended this, to have his creations best his mother's."

She flipped the page, and a picture spread across the entire book: Noctis, his brother, with his grey eyes. Blood dripped down his body, while the beautiful prince with red-stained lips fed upon him.

"Three Above," Taf said, looking up at Timothée. "That could be a drawing of you. I mean, a more muscular version of you. Even so, the resemblance is uncanny. Let Erik call you a false god now."

Timothée's breath snagged. All the Dark Stars were looking at him. They must have been as captivated with Taf's story as he had been. He tried to look away, but Val's gaze caught his. He still had Melissa wrapped around him, but his lips were parted, the most unusual expression on his face. An expression Timothée couldn't name. Didn't want to name.

Then he blinked and Val's face was blank again. "Something on your neck, Greywick?" Val said, laughter edged with raspy shadows.

Timothée realized he was touching his neck, the same place Noctis had been bitten in the picture. He dropped his hand, looked away from Val, and snickering sounded across the classroom.

"Anyway," Taf said, flipping the page, "the Prince was the first vampire, who became the Prophet of Stars, who stood beside the Shadow God and foretold the future of the path they would walk together: creating an army of vampires, and of those who wielded the magic of the Dark Stars."

The last page of the book had a portrait of Noctis and the Prince dressed in armor.

"The Dark Prophet," Timothée whispered.

"No," Taf corrected. "The Prophet of Stars. Their armor is different if you look closely. See, the Prophet of Star's armor is made up of many types of metal, some stellarite and a bit of gravastarium. But I saw the Dark Prophet in the square. His whole suit was made of gravastarium."

The room erupted in a flurry of words: those who had been at the square, and those who claimed to have seen the Dark Prophet in

Wolfhelm three years ago. Timothée didn't want to think about his experience with the Dark Prophet, the way he'd moved like a shadow given form. The way he'd almost killed his sister.

"So, what do you all think?" Erik's voice rose above the clamor. "Is it the same prophet of years past, or a new hero rising?"

"I'd hardly call him a hero," Rayna chimed in.

"Because you've never needed to fight not to be called a monster," Erik said. "You don't have a choker around your neck."

"No." Rayna's gaze hardened. "Just prison bars around my home."

The crowd went quiet.

"Be careful who you call hero, Erik." Carmilla walked up to the Dark Star house leader. "The Dark Prophet tried to kill your cousin."

"Darius is resilient." That unsettling smile spread across Erik's face. "Like a cockroach, a thing not too easily stamped out."

An uncomfortable silence spread across the room until Sylvester chirped: "So is the Dark Prophet an impersonator of the Prophet of Stars? Or is he truly the ancient one returned? And who is he under that mask? What does he look like?"

"Maybe he wears it because he's hideously marred," Nathaniel said dryly from the corner.

"I don't know," Carmilla said with a sultry rasp. "I imagine something else."

The others turned, as they often did, waiting for her to speak again—to latch onto her newest idea.

"What if he's wickedly handsome," Carmilla's lips curved up, "and good in bed?"

There was scandalous laughter. But Timothée didn't miss the annoyed look Val gave her or the little smirk she returned. Maybe they weren't as over each other as Khalid claimed.

But Timothée was still stuck on what Erik said. He turned to the house leader. "The Dark Prophet isn't fighting to liberate those with shadowcraft. He's fighting to bring Noctis back."

Erik gave an indignant look and opened his mouth, but was interrupted by Val's laughter. Timothée's roommate strode over to him.

"Death isn't always the end," Val said, an odd cadence to his voice. "Especially with the magic of the stars. But Noctis wasn't just killed. He was murdered by another god, had his star ripped from his chest. There's no coming back from that."

"You weren't in the square, Val. He foretold Noctis's return." Timothée crossed his arms. He was so tired of Val knowing *everything*. And no one could understand the way the Dark Prophet had spoken to him. "I heard what he was saying, how he—" *How he said that name when he looked at me.*

"Well, the Dark Prophet was wrong. People have been fearing Noctis's return for hundreds of years. But..." Val looked carefully at him. "Maybe Noctis didn't come back in the way everyone expected."

"What are you talking about now?"

"You're the son of the gods," Val whispered. "And you have the power of a Dark Star. That, Greywick, makes you the most dangerous person in this school." His gaze shifted away, and an almost thoughtful expression crossed his face. "Maybe the most dangerous person in the entire world."

"You—"

Val turned, looked to Melissa. "This place is a bore."

And Timothée stood stunned as Val made his way across the classroom. Around them, everyone was going back to their own business. Melissa hung off Val like one of Marion's leeches. Val hadn't been close to anyone these last few weeks, besides Carmilla. *Why now? Why her?*

"Greywick," Val called.

Timothée hated that he turned the instant Val said his name, that suddenly that stupid boy had his total attention. That he nearly choked when Melissa's lips pressed at the base of Val's throat.

"Maybe don't come to the room for a while." Val gave him a knowing look. "This will probably take the rest of the night."

Timothée stood stunned as Val and Melissa left. He felt sick. Who was Val to tell him he couldn't go back to his dorm? He wove across the classroom.

"Timothée, stop." Carmilla grabbed his arm. "He's being a prick. I'll stay with you on the couch. We can talk about how annoying he is."

"That's not the point. He can't kick me out so he can—" Images flashed in his mind: Val and that girl in *their* room, bodies intertwined. Timothée shrugged out of Carmilla's grip.

He opened the door and the frosty night air hit him, wind and rain like daggers. Val and Melissa stood across the bridge. Her fingers clenched his shirt and her tongue plunged into his mouth. Val's gaze slid open for a single moment.

Timothée stormed back into the room, slamming the door behind him. He caught a flash of the Starlings summoning their shadows before all the lights went out. The room rumbled and shook, and for a moment, he swore the whole tower was about to collapse. Shrieks and yells rang through the air, until a moment later, the torches bloomed back to life.

But the shadows weren't in the hands of the students anymore. They were a black storm.

Around him.

# 15

## IN WHICH VIVIAN REMEMBERS THE COLD TOUCH OF XYDRIOUS

**V**IVIAN SIGHED, BLOWING the hair back from her sweaty brow. She had been staring at the little dish of water for far too long.

She sat beside Marion in their Properties of Matter laboratory, a class both first-year and second-year Evening and Morning Stars attended. Instructed to partner up with someone from an opposite house, Vivian had walked as fast as she could to Marion. Now the two of them occupied a double desk in a spacious classroom with a glossy black floor. Magic crackled in the air but not in front of them.

The room was vast, with rows and rows of desks and cluttered shelves of materials lining the walls. There were normal supplies such as bowls and burners and vials, and then the more unnatural: jars filled with bobbing lights, glowing mushrooms, and glass globes of swirling gas. At the head of the class was a chalkboard, and behind it enormous windows stretched up the walls and turned into the ceiling, letting the starlight shine through.

Although they didn't need to see the stars to summon their magic, their professor said it made it easier, especially for first-years.

Professor Yuriana taught this class, and Vivian liked her immensely. She weaved between the desks on a floating chair. Darius had informed Vivian the device was a clever ingenuity between houses after the professor lost the use of her legs. Professor Yuriana was an older Evening Star, with hair blue as ocean waves.

"It can happen that way sometimes," Marion had whispered at the beginning of class. "Rayna told me. Occasionally your hair turns the color of your star when you swallow it."

Vivian had looked at her own chestnut-brown hair, then at Rayna who was sitting in front of her.

"Maybe that's why Setviren has sea-green hair," she'd laughed, then said: "But Rayna's a Morning Star and her hair is blue."

A rare smile crossed her sister's face. "Her hair's not natural; a third-year Evening Star changed it. Rayna lost a bet with Taf and has to keep her hair blue until All Hallow's Eve." Vivian had laughed lightly, and Marion continued, "I wonder if that's why Valentine's hair is purple, all the *dark magic* coursing through his veins."

The way Marion said it: *dark magic*. So much disdain in her voice. *Our brother has that magic too.*

Presently, Vivian turned her attention back to the professor, with the darker blue hair falling in waves down her back. She was floating among the Starlings, observing and offering pointers. The beginning of the class had been a lecture on the properties of water, and now they had moved onto the practical assignment.

A small wooden bowl sat in front of her with a shallow layer of water. It had been the Morning Star's job to summon water in the bowl, and the Evening Star's task to turn it to ice.

It was supposed to be simple; it was supposed to be a natural progression.

It wasn't any of those things.

Marion had been unable to produce even the sheen of moisture on her fingertips and nearly broken out in tears with frustrated rage.

Professor Yuriana had quickly asked another student to create their water, telling Marion not to worry. But of course, not worrying was not in Marion's nature. She sat, arms crossed, staring grumpily down at the bowl.

Now it was Vivian's turn. But no matter how hard she tried, or stared, or waved her hand, the water remained liquid. Her star inside of her was a constant hum in time with her heart. And it didn't help every time she held her hand above the water, she knew Marion could see her shaking fingers, the sweat on her brow. *Maybe she'll think it's from the task itself.*

There was a great splash, and she looked up to see Khalid casting a giant stream of water into his and Darius's bowl. It spilled over into a huge puddle on the floor.

"*Control*, Khalid!" Professor Yuriana chided. "Until then, go get a mop."

"But Teach!" Khalid moaned. "You could evaporate it with a wave of your wondrous hands."

"I could," Professor Yuriana responded, "but where would your lesson be then?"

Vivian leaned forward, watching Rayna and Taf in front of her. Rayna had cast water to the top of the bowl, and Taf closed her eyes and wiggled her fingers above the water.

Magic crackled in the air, a faint blue glow, and the water froze to ice.

"She makes it look so easy." Vivian sighed.

Finished with their assignment, the two girls began murmuring to each other. Vivian knew she had to focus on her work but couldn't hide her excitement. "Did you hear that, Mare?" she whispered. "There's to be an All Hallow's Eve ball at the end of the moon!"

Marion shrugged. "What of it?"

"Listen!"

The two sisters leaned forward, eavesdropping as Rayna and Taf whispered giddily to one another. "I went last year so I know what to expect," Taf said. "There's a live band and entertainers. And more sweets than you could eat in your entire life. Pumpkin pie, and cinnamon tarts, and apples covered in sweet caramel."

"Don't tell me this before dinner!" Rayna cooed. "What costume are you wearing?"

"Fiona's making me a pegasus costume. It's going to be amazing! You should see if she's got time to make you something."

"What do you think?" Vivian whispered to her sister. "Will we go?"

"Let's think about it." Marion worried her lip. "The last thing we need is a distraction."

Vivian's gut tightened.

Right. Because everything that wasn't curing her was a distraction.

Nothing mattered until she wasn't a monster anymore.

"I should try this assignment again," she mumbled.

She placed her hand over the bowl. And although the steady thrum of magic beat inside her, it seemed none of it would leave her body.

"It can help," a deep voice said, "to think of a memory."

Darius. Her heart twirled in her chest.

Think of a memory? With him standing beside her, there was only one memory she could think of: that first night in the Den, in his room, their bodies moving together. She shook her head and banished the thought before her fangs could drop.

They had spent a few nights in each other's rooms since then, sometimes sleeping, sometimes tangling together. But they had gone no further than that first night. Not because she didn't want to.

Because she didn't know how much longer she could control herself.

Presently, Darius looked down with no judgment at the little dish of warm water.

"Expected more from a child of the gods, did you?" Her voice was light, but she couldn't stop the feelings. Weren't they supposed to be better at this?

"Everyone needs to practice, to learn." Professor Yuriana floated over. There was kindness in her deep eyes. "Even the Star Children. Mr. Störmberg is right. Think of a memory, a cold one, and bring the feeling of ice into your heart and your star."

"That shouldn't be too hard." Darius smiled. "You grew up in Andúrigard. It's always cold."

Vivian closed her eyes and let herself drift away. Her memories glossed over the three years she had spent in Wolfhelm. There certainly had been cold nights there, the three of them huddled together under threadbare blankets. No, she swept her mind back further, to the lavender farm in Seagrass.

"Marion," she spoke out loud though her eyes were still closed, fingers hovering over the water dish, "do you remember the Winter Solstice when we were ten? Timothée had been wishing and wishing for snow, and when we looked out the window, a few flakes were falling."

"Yes," Marion replied.

"Father bundled us up, and we went outside, but the flakes hadn't stuck yet," Vivian continued. "He said he knew a spot by the beach, and when we got down there, there were piles of it. But snow couldn't possibly fall there now I think of it. The water would have washed it away..."

Vivian could almost feel the chill on her cheeks now. She shot her eyes open, saw the entire class staring at her. She focused on Professor Yuriana, asked, "My father—I mean, the former headmaster—was an Evening Star?"

"Professor Bram Cavald." Recognition and sadness tugged at the edges of her face. "He was the most powerful Evening Star who ever lived."

"He turned the seawater to snow," Vivian said, her eyes closing again. She remembered jumping into fresh white powder. Making shapes as Timothée threw snowballs at them, their father tossing them up and down. They walked back to the cabin with frosted fingers and cold toes and frozen smiles.

"Vivian, you're—!" Darius said.

A blue glow crackled around her. Her water hadn't frozen; it'd changed to soft snow that spilled over her bowl. Gasps sounded from around the classroom, and she turned to see snow spilling out of all the little bowls.

She sensed her magic in every flake. Her heart nearly burst out of her chest.

"And the Greywicks do it again." Khalid smirked from the back of the class, mop tight in hand.

Students cheered in delight, touching the snow. The snow she had made.

Rayna barked a laugh. "Incredible!" Then with a wave of her hand, wind whirled through the air. "Something I've been working on."

And the wind picked up the snow from all the little bowls and swirled it into the air. It was snowing in autumn.

"Wonderful!" Professor Yuriana clapped her hands together in delight. "We don't start upon snow until winter!"

Vivian gasped, her hands shaking. She could still feel it—her hold on the magic.

But Marion hadn't said anything, not a single thing.

"Mare, what's wrong?"

"It did snow by the sea," Marion said. "Why does everything have to be attributed to magic? Can't you remember it the way it actually was?"

*She won't believe Father used starcraft.* The realization sat like a hard rock in Vivian's stomach.

Screams sounded through the classroom, and hail pelted the students. Vivian's snow had become ice.

"Alright, alright," Professor Yuriana said, calming the class. "With time, you'll learn to keep a good hold on your starcraft and the changes that can occur."

Professor Yuriana had explained it in one of their first classes. Evening Stars could make permanent or impermanent changes. But until their power grew, everything they made would turn back at sunrise.

Or in her case, right now.

"Starlings," Professor Yuriana said, "let's get this cleaned up."

"I have an idea," Darius said.

Vivian looked over at Marion, knowing she should talk to her sister.

But then Darius grabbed her arm and there was the sharp spark of magic between them. He gasped, but then waved his hand, the blue ribbon around his wrist dangling. All the chunks of hail trembled on the floor then rose into the air, changing into foggy clouds.

The students began to applaud. But then the clouds twisted, shaping into words…

Vivian read them out loud: *"All Hallow's Eve Ball?"*

Darius flicked his wrist, letting the clouds dissipate, then turned to her. "Will you be my date to the ball, Vivian?"

Starling students hooted and hollered. And Vivian blushed under the attention.

Well, she would have if she could.

"See?" Khalid came over, resting an arm on Marion's shoulder. "If I tried that, I'd be in detention and foraging Chef Venneri's mushrooms in the Enchanted Forest for a moon."

"I can only imagine the crude things you'd write," Marion groaned.

Khalid placed a hand on his heart. "Would you expect anything less?"

But their words floated away as Vivian lost herself in Darius's storm blue eyes. "I thought I already gave you the dance I owed."

He placed his hand under her chin, tilting her face up. "That's the problem, darling. That dance has ruined me for all other dances. It's you in my arms or nothing."

"I'll go," she breathed. "I'll go with you."

She wrapped her arms around his neck as he swung her around, and she caught the joyful and awed gazes of her classmates: Khalid's too big smile, her sister's stoic face, the single tear running down Professor Yuriana's eyes as she said, "What a romantic gesture. He is truly the prince of fairytales!"

And she should have been happy.

But she was only afraid.

As class dismissed, Marion grabbed Vivian's arm and pulled her back, telling Khalid and Darius they would meet them in the dining hall for dinner soon.

"We need to talk," Marion said, leading her down several halls until they made it to an abandoned alcove.

"Yes?" Vivian asked.

"I heard you stayed in his room," Marion said. "Several times."

"How did you hear that?"

Marion avoided her gaze. "You have to know things here. To survive. Why didn't you tell me?"

"I thought..." Vivian bit her lip. "I thought you'd be disappointed."

Marion pinched the bridge of her nose. "I'm worried, Viv. Did you sleep with him?"

"No." Vivian looked down, knowing she owed her sister the truth. "We did... other stuff."

Marion looked up and down the empty halls, then pulled her deeper into the alcove. "What about your...?" She tapped her teeth.

*My fangs?* This wasn't her sister trying to be stealthy. She never mentioned the specifics.

"I was in control," Vivian responded.

But that was a lie.

She'd managed to keep control, but the closer they got, the more she wanted him. And not just him, but the blood beneath his skin.

She knew she could never fully give into her desire with him, though every part of her ached for it. How sometimes the looks he gave her felt like a touch, and she could only respond with a closed-mouth smile.

"You need to keep your distance, Vivian," Marion said. And she knew her sister could read the lie along her face.

"We told Khalid about me. Do you think Darius would understand as well?"

"No." The word was swift, sharp, and absolute. But there was something simmering in her sister's grey eyes.

"Marion," Vivian said carefully, "what aren't you telling me?"

Marion studied her for a moment. Chewed her bottom lip. "Nothing. Just keep your distance. Until we find a cure."

"A cure..."

"There're answers here, I *know* it. We have time to find them."
Marion grabbed her ice-cold hands. "Have faith in me, big sister. I
won't let anything happen to you."

"'kay."

Marion gave her one last look before heading down the hall.
"Aren't you coming?"

"I'll meet you there," Vivian said. "I forgot something in my room."

Her shoulders sagged the moment her sister was out of sight. And
quickly, she made her way back to her dorm and locked the door.

She wasn't sure if it was using her magic, being so close with
Darius, the lack of leeches, or just the ever-present enemy of time.

But she was getting sicker. So, so much sicker.

Marion was wrong. They didn't have time. And maybe that was
why she was so careless with Darius—because she knew she was
running out of her last bit of humanity. She wanted to clutch every
bit of life a dead girl could.

One more kiss.

One more day.

Before there was nothing human left of her.

Tears streamed down her cheeks, and she clawed off her uniform.
Maybe she'd had a desperate sort of hope, a hope that swallowing a
star would somehow fix her.

But if anything, it had made her worse. Drawn a deeper line
between the human girl that could have been a god, and the monster
the world made.

She screamed as her uniform fell to the ground. Truly inhuman.
There was a deep need to shed her skin until she stood naked, gasping,
and blood slid down her back and onto the floor.

But her own blood did not tempt her, nor the blood of her siblings.
They had tried it one desperate night. The image was scarred into her
memory: Marion bleeding Timothée's wrist over a cup, like he was
an animal. But that blood had made her sick. She'd spat it up and
vomited over their tiny apartment.

There were so many students here… They trusted her. She could take their blood so easily. Khalid had offered his own up to her, and how good he had smelled—

No, no, no.

Slowly, she turned and looked at her back in the mirror.

Two translucent, membranous wings fell limp along her back. Mucus dripped down their length, pooling on the floor in a gooey mess.

It was such a relief to free them from her skin, as limp and broken as they were. Just for a moment. Just for a moment, to embrace this *thing* she'd become.

They had to go back in, no matter how painful. No matter how much blood seeped down her rigid spine. No matter how—

*Knock, knock!*

"Vivian? It's me. Are you in here?"

Darius's voice.

What was he doing here? He was supposed to be at dinner! Vivian's heart surged erratically, and she turned in a circle, her heavy, weak wings swinging behind her. He couldn't be here! She was a *monster*.

"Vivian?"

She had to remain silent. Maybe he'd think she was somewhere else. She stumbled backward, and one of her godforsaken wings caught the edges of her lamp, sent it tumbling. *Smash!*

"Vivian! Are you alright?"

Vivian laced her hands through her hair and pulled, eyes welling with tears.

The door handle turned as Darius attempted to get in. "Vivian, answer me!"

"Uh," she called. "One moment. I'm getting changed."

"Oh. Of course. Don't rush on my accord." The thick wood door muffled his voice. "It's just, you didn't come to the dining hall. I wanted to make sure you were okay with the whole All Hallow's Eve Ball thing. I know it was a bit much, so public, but I wanted… I wanted you to know. How much I care for you."

Getting changed? What a pitiful excuse! What was she going to do? She fell to all fours, closing her eyes and willing the wings back into her skin. But it didn't work that way. She took a deep breath, tried to steady her voice. "Oh no, that's not it. I got a sudden headache."

"A headache? I didn't see you eat breakfast. You must be hungry, especially after using starcraft. I brought you up a plate from the dining hall." The doorknob wiggled again. "If I could come in—"

"No!" she shrieked. "No, I mean, it's just, uh, I look a mess."

"You know I don't care how you look."

Vivian glimpsed herself in the mirror, back carved with those hideous, translucent wings. *You would care about this.*

She sighed and pressed her fists against her eyes. "It's my moon's blood, Darius. I need a little time alone."

In actuality, she hadn't gotten her moon's blood since becoming a vampire. Was it because of the creature she'd become or how sick she was? There was no one she could ask.

Silence on the other end of the door, then: "Oh! Oh. Can I bring you anything? Hot water bottle? Chocolates? Cloth? Perhaps a potion to dull the pain?"

She smiled sadly and crept to the door. Put her hands against the wood as if she could touch him. "No, thank you. I'm going to turn in early."

"Very well. Please come to me if you need anything." He sighed, and she swore she could feel his hand on the other side of the wood. "Ask anything of me, and you shall have it."

*Don't you know?* A tear crept down her face. *All I ask of you is your heart. And it is the one thing you should not give.* "Thank you, Darius."

His heavy boots sounded down the hallway.

When she was certain he was gone, she stumbled back to the middle of her room and collapsed to the floor. And wrapped tight in the embrace of her monstrous wings, she cried human tears.

# 16

# IN WHICH TIMOTHÉE HAPPENS UPON A FAMILY HEIRLOOM

"**I**T ISN'T ME!" Timothée was screaming, but he could barely hear his voice over the rain and wind. He tried to make his way across the wavering bridge. And this time, he couldn't think about how high it was. "It isn't me! The school is haunted!"

"Timothée." Carmilla grasped his arm.

The shadows swirling around him had dissipated the moment he'd taken a step back. But the looks, the fearful looks on his classmates' faces... Those were burned into his mind. Like the first night he'd swallowed his star.

He forced himself back into the secret corridor that led to the Cauldron. Although he wasn't sure where he was going to go. He certainly couldn't go back to his room. Who knew what disgusting activity Val and Melissa were up to?

"I know it wasn't you. It couldn't have been," Carmilla said. "You're still wearing your choker. Besides, we can't control other people's shadowcraft. Whatever that was, it was strange. I've never seen any-thing like it."

Timothée forced air in and out of his lungs. The corridor was dark, smelling of old water and plant life. "I wish I was normal. I wish people didn't look at me and hate what they saw. I want to fit in."

"You'll never fit in," Carmilla said. "Timothée, you're the son of the gods, you glow, and your shadowcraft overpowered knights with years of experience. There's no way for you to be normal."

"Then can't I at least be liked?" He heard the shattered defeat in his voice.

Carmilla put her arms around him, lightly touched the back of his neck. "Why would you ever wish for something so mundane?"

"The school…" Timothée whispered. "I hear it in my head. During my Celestial Rite, when Val and I got dragged into the Isle, I swear it was… I don't know. Guiding me. I tried to tell Val, but he couldn't hear it."

"What about your sisters? Can they hear this voice?"

"They've sensed a presence too. Especially during their Celestial Rites. I know it sounds crazy—"

"This place is old." Carmilla pulled away. "If the legends are true, it was built by Rhaemyria herself. Perhaps you are connected to the magic."

"Because she's my mother?" Timothée said, almost jokingly.

"There are crazier things in this world." She rubbed a circle around the top of his spine. "You say the school is talking to you. Have you tried talking back?"

Timothée shrugged. "Not really."

"Close your eyes," she said. "Try saying something."

There was nothing left to lose. He let his eyes grow heavy, and this time instead of speaking out loud, he spoke inside his head, the way the voice did to him.

*Hello,* he thought. *Are you there?*

The darkness in his mind answered: *Always.*

The voice was a cold brush in his thoughts. Timothée's heart thumped. *Can you show her you're real?*

There was no reply, but Timothée kept his breath steady, mind open and ready. Then there was a flash of light against his lids, and Carmilla gave a startled gasp.

A glowing purple line weaved through the stone corridor, running between the ridges of the bricks.

"It's the castle," Timothée said. "I asked it to show you it was real."

"It *is* real. I thought you *were* crazy."

"What?" He almost laughed, grabbed her hand. "Come on, it wants us to follow it."

They raced along the corridor, and for a moment, Timothée thought the castle was leading them back to the Cauldron. But the line of light stalled, stopped, and spread, until it made the glowing outline of a door, woven with stars and swirls.

Carmilla placed her hand in the center. "There's nothing here but stone."

*The way is open to those willing to look beneath the light.*

Timothée narrowed his gaze, pushed against the stone. Underneath, his palm glowed purple until the whole wall rippled with shadows. *This is not my magic,* he knew. Though the feeling was eerily similar. *This is the castle.*

"Are we going through?" he asked.

Carmilla gripped his arm. "I fear nothing."

Together, they walked through the shadows.

For a moment, time and space bent around him. One step then they were in a wide-open room, no windows, air heavy with dust and mold. Behind them, the door remained glowing.

"Where did your friend take us?" Carmilla blinked against the dark.

Suddenly, torches sprang to life and Timothée was blinded by glinting light. The room was empty save for three armored mannequins.

Carmilla gasped, and Timothée's heart stuttered as he stared at them. Each mannequin was encased in an upright glass tomb. But he knew without a doubt whom each suit of armor belonged to.

The first was broad-shouldered and glittering navy, with a diamond feathered winged helmet. "The armor of Xydrious," Timothée whispered.

"Is this real?" Carmilla touched the glass casing.

*Yes,* Timothée thought, but he said, "I don't know."

"The legends do tell of the gods coming to earth, fighting ancient wars." She drifted to the next case. "Rhaemyria."

Golden and red, the sleek armor was adorned with chain slats that looked like feathers. A cage skirt of red iron encircled the suit. Timothée touched his palm to the glass, could almost feel the heat of the armor seeping through. *Mother?*

A thick spider crawled up the case, and Carmilla waved it away with the flick of her hand. The movement struck him as odd, but he couldn't say why. Her eyes reflected gold as she stared, enraptured. "What are the gods really, except powerful Starlings? No wonder they are gone now. They gave their magic away to us." Carmilla looked down at her palm, and her breath quickened.

*Her star hates to be caged,* Timothée thought.

They both turned to the final case.

Timothée stared up at his brother's armor: black gravastarium, the forbidden metal. It was all sharp edges, glittering and beautiful and powerful. He placed his palm along the case, and his hand slipped through as if there were no glass at all. His fingers brushed the boot.

*Embrace what you are.*

He gasped and pulled his hand out.

"You can touch that one but not the others," Carmilla said.

He looked back up at the armor, at the long cape pooling on the floor. "I don't know why."

"Timothée," Carmilla walked toward him, "you said you wanted to be liked. But what about revered?"

He turned to her. "What do you mean?"

"I mean I have an idea." Her bright green gaze was locked on the armor of Noctis. "You don't have a costume for the All Hallow's Eve Ball yet, do you?"

## 17
# IN WHICH MARION SPREADS PROPAGANDA ON THE GODS

A S IT TURNED out, being a Lost Star was not all about being taken to a magical school and eating delicious food and wearing lovely clothes. There was work involved. And Setviren was intent on the Greywicks paying their keep.

In this case, it meant showing the world that Rhaemyria's children did walk Thraina.

The triplets sat on fine wooden chairs in a large tent. They'd arrived in the Andúrigardian city of Bøgelund an hour ago and were set to make their appearance as soon as the stars awakened.

It was all part of Setviren's grand idea to have the Greywicks visit a different city around Thraina every moonless night. "Faith is as valuable as gold," he'd said on the hot air balloon ride down from the Isle of Argos. "Nothing will inspire the paupers as much as seeing proof that the gods walk among them."

Marion looked at her brother picking his teeth with a fingernail, then at her sister, two glassy eyes rimmed with dark circles. If she were a pauper, she'd feel ripped off with these sorry excuses for gods.

162

There may have been a time when Marion would have liked the idea of parading before watching eyes in decadent finery. She had passed many childish afternoons daydreaming of being up on stage, performing opera in a troupe.

Now, her stomach twisted. Soon, Setviren would call them out into the courtyard and draw attention to the very thing their father had told them to hide.

At least the royal trio provided some distraction. Darius, Khalid, and Carmilla were here as well, their positions of power also making them commodities to Setviren.

Prince Darius poked his head out of the tent, revealing a host of Celestial Knights stationed around and a growing crowd in the courtyard. "It's a shame we're not staying for more than a few hours. Bøgelund has some fascinating landmarks and a remarkable museum on the creation of the Isle of Argos."

He was done up in his royal finery, all charm and good manners and noble niceties. But it didn't trick her. She saw it every time his blue eyes flashed: the feral monster that lay in wait. *Thraina will not know peace.*

"If by fascinating and remarkable, you mean dusty and decrepit." Carmilla twirled a blood-red strand of hair around her finger.

Timothée sat forward. "I like history."

"Then we must return sometime." Darius clapped Timothée on the shoulder. "It is said Bøgelund used to be a city favored by the gods. We could go visit the ancient ruins of the temples or see the preserved relics. Perhaps we can come back during the winter holiday."

Timothée's eyes lit up, but Khalid cut him off by gripping his other shoulder. "Pfft! Don't listen to this guy, Tim. Bøgelund may have been pretty once upon a time when Rhaemyria shined it up, but now it's a dumping ground for radical pilgrimages."

"The Church will see that handled," Darius said shortly.

"What's going on?" Vivian asked.

Carmilla strode across the tent, waving an idle hand. "The Church is in a tizzy because a bunch of pilgrims bearing a feathered blue handprint sigil are congregating at the Ruins of Argos. You know, the mountain just north of here?"

"The mountain Rhaemyria ripped the top off of and turned into the Isle of Argos?" Timothée asked.

"Precisely," Carmilla said. "These pilgrims haven't proven dangerous, but they've desecrated a bunch of Rhaemyria's shrines and statues. I'm surprised Kassandra hasn't ordered an entire army to the Ruins to wipe them out."

"Kassandra realizes there are bigger issues at stake than statues." Darius's voice was low.

"Well, Setviren's doing what he can to mitigate it. Using our own Greywicks to bolster public support." Khalid smiled at the triplets. "You know what they say. There are two ways to find magic: understand nothing and understand everything."

"Nobody says that," Marion grumbled.

"Seriously though, Bøgelund is a poor holiday." Khalid slung an arm around Timothée. "You want to go somewhere special? I'll take you to Baz-Kazar. Beaches with crystal clear water, the juiciest fruit, and the most beautiful men and women you've ever seen."

Marion rolled her eyes but said nothing. Her stomach was too wobbly to form words.

"We could visit Seagrass," Vivian said, looking from Marion to Timothée. "It's been three years since we've been. Maybe it's time to return home."

Return home... without Father. What ever happened to their little cabin, to their beautiful lavender fields? Marion couldn't imagine opening the wooden door, knowing Father wouldn't be inside, whittling wood or tuning his dulcimer. Couldn't imagine seeing their cabin again after what she'd done to it during the Celestial Rite.

*Embrace what you are.*

Timothée said, "Maybe, Viv."

"I can't believe there's a city of mine I don't recognize the name of." Darius shook his head, then tucked a curl behind Vivian's ear. "We must certainly visit this beloved Seagrass of yours."

"Focus, please!" a nasally voice called. Loremaster Setviren strode into the tent. "There's quite the crowd out there and you all need to be on your best behavior. Your Highness, we'll have you go out first to really jazz up the crowd, and the wards can come after. And then we'll bring out the stars of our show." His eyes got big and watery. "If only I could be one of the crowd, gazing upon your glow for the first time."

Timothée started picking his front tooth again.

With a bird-like flap of his robes, Setviren rushed out of the tent. His voice boomed through the courtyard: "As above."

"So below," the crowd chanted.

Darius stretched and ran a hand through his light hair. "That's my cue."

"Good luck." Vivian stood. "I'll cheer you on from here."

"Please welcome Prince Darius!" cried Setviren.

Darius's blue gaze swept from the courtyard back to Vivian. "I'd much rather have you with me." He swung his arm around her and led her out of the tent with him.

Carmilla groaned. "Always with the dramatics."

Marion drifted to the tent door, watching as Darius waved to the cheering crowd. Vivian stayed tight to his side, a nervous smile on her face before she too hazarded a wave. The crowd erupted even louder.

Setviren cleared his throat. "Prince Darius and, uh, Vivian Greywick, one of our beloved Lost Stars!"

The stars had not quite awakened in the sky, and Vivian's eyes were still a glassy grey. Marion took in a deep breath. She still couldn't get over her sister having the favor of the most powerful person in Thraina.

*He* was *the most powerful person in Thraina,* a voice at the back of her mind whispered. *Until he found us.*

She shook her head. Maybe she needed to remind herself Timothée had been unable to remove a poppyseed from his front tooth for the last twenty minutes.

The crowd was insatiable watching Darius and Vivian. As the Prince droned on about Andúrigard this and unity that, he kept his hand firmly clutched around Vivian's waist. No one could miss the connotation.

"Setviren can hardly contain his excitement." Khalid appeared beside her, his voice a low whisper. "The Church and kingdom have always had strong ties. But a union between Thraina's ruler and a godchild... That would be an unbreakable thing indeed."

"It can never happen," Marion said.

"I agree," Khalid said.

But she saw the look in Darius's eyes from here. It was the look of a man possessed by love. And the whole crowd knew it.

"Even if it works in Setviren's favor, it's true," she whispered. "They really are in love."

"Would it matter if they weren't?" Khalid steeled his gaze upon the crowd. "Is there anything more beloved than a story? The king and the goddess. That tale will spin gold for whoever gets to tell it."

Marion was silent, her heart beating fast against her chest. She had the feeling Khalid was telling her something important. Words within words.

"Do you know Darius's mother was a commoner? King Halvor spotted her selling flowers on the street. She wore a blue ribbon in her hair. It was love at first sight." Khalid pressed his body tight against hers. "Even kings love a story. A candle girl with a blue ribbon in her hair who turns out to glow as bright as the stars themselves. How could Darius help himself?"

Marion gasped in a stuttering breath. Then the warmth of Khalid's chest disappeared from her back. Setviren's voice boomed, "Please welcome His Right Honorable Khalid Ali Bagheeri of Medihsa, and Princess Carmilla of Kirrintsova!"

Khalid stepped out of the tent but looked back with a wink. "Here's another piece of advice, Mare. When your story gets told, make sure you're the one telling it."

Then he was out in the courtyard, waving and parading about like a courtier. Carmilla followed behind.

Marion wanted time to dissect what Khalid had said, to understand it in the context of the fevered crowd, in the adoring gazes shared between Darius and Vivian. But there was no time. Timothée grabbed her wrist. "Come on, Mare. Setviren said our names!"

Had he? She staggered out behind her brother. Everything felt… too much. The crowd was too loud, her name too frenzied upon their lips. The wooden platform they stepped upon seemed too shaky, and Setviren's smile too wide.

And the stars… They were too bright without the moon. She grabbed a lock of her hair. It was still its normal creamy blond, but the sky was darkening fast.

Bøgelund may have been a great city once, but Carmilla was right. Now it was dusty and decrepit. The buildings surrounding the courtyard were rotten wood, the stones of the square cracked and chipped. Even the people appeared ragged and worn. Every wall and door seemed splattered with a blue handprint framed with feathered wings.

"My dear citizens of Bøgelund!" Setviren cried. "It is a great honor to present the Lost Star Children for the first time since their initiation into the Celestial Academy for Fallen Stars! The children of Rhaemyria and Xydrious have each swallowed a star. Please show your reverence to the eldest, Vivian, of House Evening Star!"

Darius spun Vivian around. She laughed girlishly, collapsing against his chest.

The crowd went mad. Falling to their knees, tapping three fingers to each eye, chanting her name.

Marion chewed her bottom lip. Why? Why did they pray to her? Vivian couldn't do anything, besides summon a bit of snow.

And if they knew what she truly was, they'd be more likely to raise pitchforks than hymns.

"Send your prayers up to the stars so the Sun Mother can hear them!" expounded Setviren. "For her child walks among us! Here is Marion, of House Morning Star!"

Oh bother.

If she hadn't liked their worship for Vivian, she liked it even less for herself.

They were a mob, these poorly clad peasants bowing and pleading to her.

"Send the rains to us, Sun Daughter!"

"Please, please, can you bless my womb?"

"The ships are stuck in harbor! A wind, Sun Daughter, a wind, please!"

Marion blinked, took a step back. She had barely kept herself alive the last three years. Who were these people to demand things of her? Who were these strangers to think she could save them? What mercy had any stranger shown her when she barely paid the rent on their apartment? What mercy would they show her family if her sister's illness was revealed?

Bile rose in her throat and her hand trembled.

Someone grabbed it. Squeezed. "You're okay," Khalid whispered. She squeezed back, grounding herself through his touch.

Setviren cleared his throat. "And finally, the youngest of Rhaemyria's children: Timothée, of House Dark Star."

The crowd went quiet. Those kneeling stood. Timothée stepped forward, gave an awkward wave.

A man at the front of the crowd put his hands around his mouth. "BOO!"

Setviren gave the slightest nod, and a Celestial Knight stepped forward, jabbing the man in the stomach with the butt of his spear. The man crumpled to the ground and the Celestial Knight bound his hands and dragged him away from the crowd.

The courtyard was so quiet, Marion could hear Carmilla whisper in her brother's ear: "When you come to Kirrintsova, you will receive a grand welcome."

Before Marion could think on what that meant, a gasp sounded from the crowd. Eyes widened. The townsfolk trembled to their knees.

Night had fallen enough for the stars to blink awake to full brightness.

And the triplets began to glow.

"Move forward!" Setviren hissed.

Marion took a shaky step toward the front of the platform. Timothée came up on her left, and Vivian on her right. The royal trio wandered to the back, allowing the triplets their moment in the starlight.

Vivian blinked her huge eyes, now sparkling with celestial radiance. Setviren darted behind them and pushed Marion's hair over her shoulders, better revealing the crystal light glimmering across her tresses.

"Hold hands," he snapped and crept off the platform.

Timothée gave a sheepish smile and held out his hand, every inch of exposed skin beaming. Marion sighed and took it, then grabbed Vivian's ice-cold one in her other hand.

The crowd gasped louder, then was struck silent as the triplets beamed like starlight itself.

Setviren called, "This holy light conquered the Dark Prophet in Wolfhelm! You are blessed by the Three as it touches you!" Paupers dug into their dirty pockets, pulling out verdallions to chuck at their feet.

These townsfolk with their rough workers' hands and their dirty clothes… were giving money to the Church. The Church that ran the Academy that fed hundreds of students luxurious meals three times a day, that clothed them in fancy uniforms, that decorated their rooms with silk sheets and velvet curtains.

A pit opened in Marion's stomach. What was happening here? These people… They *believed* in this. They believed in her, in Vivian, and Timothée. Setviren was spinning the greatest story of all and leaving out the fact the Greywicks were nothing but three more mouths to feed without anything to offer these people.

It made her sick.

The crowd stood deep in their reverence as the triplets' light shone upon them. Whispered chants spread: "The gods' children live. They have been found! The Sun Daughter is here." Such awe… Marion had never seen anything like it before.

169

And yet she had. A strange sense of remembrance simmered in that space near her heart, the space that always felt warm since she'd swallowed her star.

A sense she'd *been* here before.

She blinked. The townsfolk moved slower, the edges of her vision blurring. That simmering in her chest grew hotter, that feeling of remembering.

"Sun Daughter," the people said. "Sun Daughter. Sun Daughter. Sun Mother."

She blinked. It was daytime. The sun streamed hot and bright upon the platform. Marion fought for her vision to clear.

The crowd... They weren't praying. Now, they were cheering, throwing blue and yellow and purple petals into the air. How strange the people looked, both the men and women wearing long white and brown tunics. They looked like they were in some play, a bunch of actors performing a drama of ancient times.

Gone were the rotten wooden houses and the broken stone square. Instead, the courtyard was made of polished marble, houses of white limestone. Dawn-washed statues adorned the entrance to each street.

"Sun Mother!" the people cried. "Sun Mother!"

Sun Mother? That was a name of adoration for Rhaemyria. And why was it daytime? What were these buildings? Was her hair still glow—

Marion jumped as she looked down. Her Morning Star uniform was gone. Instead, she was clad in shimmering armor that rippled like flame. Plates of gold and orange adorned her body. And her hands... She wore two slender gauntlets with three razor-sharp golden claws protruding outward.

No, not claws.

Talons.

She was the phoenix. The Sun Mother.

Rhaemyria.

Marion took a shaky breath in and looked to her left.

"Oh, Tim—" she began upon seeing her brother. But it wasn't her Timothée. At a glance, it would have been easy to mistake him, but the man beside her was much taller, older. Handsome in a way both ethereal and frightening. His black hair swooped across his brow just as Tim's did, but it was long, down to his shoulders. Even his slight slouch was reminiscent. But it wasn't him.

This man wore black armor that shimmered iridescent purple in the light. He waved to the people with a smile all too familiar. Then he looked at her. "You alright, Mum?"

Each breath was a struggle, her heart in a rapid gallop. Noctis, God of Shadows, was smiling at her.

Her brother. And also her son.

*It's a dream,* she told herself. But it wasn't. It was a memory.

Noctis stood where Timothée had been before. So Vivian...

She looked to her right.

A tall man stood in her sister's place, broad of shoulder, long dark hair peeking out from a winged helmet. Marion knew who it was instantly. Xydrious's armor could have been carved of sapphire with how it sparkled in the sunlight. His face was hidden by the closed helmet, the same startling blue as the rest of his armor.

Xydrious waved to the crowd and chuckled. The sound filled Marion with warmth and comfort.

Father. Husband. Sister.

They were all the same in her multi-memory. She placed a taloned hand against her chest, willing to reach inside and feel the heat of the star living beside her heart. When she'd swallowed that star, she hadn't just awakened her magic. She'd awakened a life lived before hers, the blood memories of Rhaemyria.

Of her mother.

*How is this possible?* She was her mother, and she wasn't. She looked at Noctis. The people were screaming his name, cheering for him too. This must be before he made the vampires.

She wanted to look at him with hatred. But this damned memory was sitting too close to her heart. He crinkled his eyes and laughed in an almost boyish expression. Her heart swelled with familiarity.

The man clad in sapphire turned to her. "Are you well, my dear?" He lifted his visor, revealing his eyes.

Eyes blue like a rain-promised afternoon. Eyes blue as good nights and good mornings and lavender tea and dances in a cabin's firelight. Eyes blue and familiar as love and grief.

Marion stumbled back, tripped, fell. Noctis and Xydrious reached for her.

And then it was dark.

She blinked up, seeing only the swirling stars.

"Marion! Are you alright?"

Her brother above her. Her *younger* brother, the one she'd grown up with. And Vivian too, eyes still shining like a moon-kissed lake.

She staggered to her feet, nearly tripping on the long hem of her dress. A dress, not armor. Everything was how it had been, from the praying crowd to the ramshackle houses.

Setviren hurried over. "What happened? Why did you fall?"

"Get me off this platform," she managed.

Timothée and Vivian swept arms around her. Only when she was back in the tent did she breathe a full breath.

One by one, the royal trio joined. They were all asking if she was all right. Had she felt faint?

Marion gripped the back of a chair, holding so tight her knuckles turned white. She could still feel the weight of the armor, the scorching grip of the talons in her hand.

It had been real. Maybe not now, but once.

It was true. Everything they'd told her.

She was the daughter of the gods.

*The blood remembers.*

# 18
# IN WHICH TIMOTHÉE FINDS FRIENDS IN STRANGE PLACES

TIMOTHÉE COULDN'T SLEEP. There was no specific reason. It was late in the morning, but the sun was safely hidden behind the black curtains in their dorm room. Despite the wind rattling the shingles atop the Cauldron, his bed was warm, blankets soft and not scratchy. Yvaine was curled tight against his legs. And Valentine's breathing was raspy and rhythmic; he couldn't be plotting Timothée's doom in his sleep. Actually, maybe he could. That seemed a very Val thing to do.

Timothée delicately turned over so as not to disturb Yvaine. He needed to rest. He had Natural Foraging first thing in the evening, and he wanted to do well. Professor Barracus was gruff and a little intimidating, but there was something kind behind the hard lines of his face. Timothée wanted to impress him.

If he couldn't have magic, he'd make the best potions.

Something Khalid had said wandered into his mind: *'There are two ways to find magic: understand nothing and understand everything.'*

Professor Barracus wasn't a Starling, but he understood the inner workings of adder's tongue and feverfew and the shards of an eggshell hatched under a crescent moon.

On the other hand, the witch who lived in the shoppe beside the bakery had made her living on tea brewed with lemon just by calling it a love potion.

Slowly, he threw his blankets off, earning an angry yelp from Yvaine. He didn't want to pull back the curtains and have the sunlight wake Val, but the castle seemed to understand his intentions. The purple crystal fire slowly grew brighter.

Quietly, he made some space at the small potion station Val had set up. Surely, he wouldn't mind Timothée using it.

As long as he didn't wake up.

Timothée flipped through his notebook until he found the page for a sleeping draft. Following the instructions, he added all the ingredients into a mortar and ground them together. Next, he carefully dumped the powder into a glass dish with water and poppy milk.

"Boil for two minutes," he murmured, then placed the vial on the small tabletop burner. It bubbled slightly, and a sweet scent filled his nose.

The last time he'd done this, it had turned to goo as soon as the powder met water, so he must be improving some.

Timothée swiveled in his chair and surveyed the room. His lack of sleepiness was made more annoying by the peacefully passed out Valentine.

Or at least he had been.

Val's body was silhouetted by violet light, his slight frame tossing and turning beneath the blanket. Two fists, clenched so tight they were ghost-white, gripped the bedsheet.

Most nights, he seemed not to sleep at all, but when he did... Timothée often wondered about Val's dreams. He would often twitch or mutter in his sleep, sometimes in a language Timothée didn't recognize.

Tonight seemed worse than ever before.

Valentine's lavender hair thrashed across his face and pillow. "Kri... br... it's *me*. I'm... still here."

"Val?" Timothée whispered. *Who are you talking to?*

Val's back arched from the bed, the blanket cascading to the floor. "I won't draw my—!" His voice was a broken cry.

"Val!"

Then Val screamed. Long fingers pressed into his stomach as if he were trying to keep himself together. Timothée's heart lurched, and he flew across the cold floor to his bedside.

"Wake up!" Timothée cried, shaking Val's shoulder. His body was so tense.

Val gave a dry, airless gasp. And his eyes sprung open.

Timothée knew he should let Val go. Knew it in his heart, the way a deer knew to run from the sound of a breaking branch.

Val's violet eyes were filled with stars. Little lights danced within the depths, universes of sight and memory. And all Timothée's knowing came undone. There was something stronger than the fear beating in his heart. Something that told him: *stay.*

Val's head twitched, and he stared at Timothée, but not at him: through him, around him, past him, inside and out of him. "You came for me." A shaky smile begged up his face. "I didn't think you would." He reached up and stroked the pale planes of his own face. "Will you still have me like this, hideous and scarred?"

Timothée brought his hand to cup Val's cheek and Val grasped his fingers with his own. "You're not hideous," Timothée whispered. "Val, you're beautiful."

"Do you mean it?" Val's voice was so far away. Where was he in his head? What dream had stolen him?

Timothée swallowed in a dry throat. "Val, you need to wake up now."

Val's eyes were eerily bright, those stars flashing like erupting suns. Were the stars in his eyes a remnant of his shadowcraft? He was wearing his choker.

"I didn't mean to tell her." Tears fell down Val's face. "I'll always keep it safe—"

"It doesn't matter, Val. Just wake up!"

"I'll get it back for you! Don't leave!" Val clawed at Timothée's shirt, nails dragging through the thin fabric and into his skin. His purple eyes were wide and shining with tears and stars. "Don't leave me again, Morbis!"

*Again?* Shocked, Timothée ripped free.

Val buried his face in his hands, a trembling boy, muttering desperate sounds.

Timothée took a shuddering breath. He wished he could pluck Val from this terrible nightmare. But he couldn't. All he could do was sit with Val through this, be the shore upon which the waves of Val's dreams broke.

He crawled onto the bed and grabbed Val's face between his hands. Stared into those starry eyes. "Wherever you are," he whispered, "I am with you."

Val stared at him. One by one, the stars winked out. It was like a curtain rising between them. One moment Val was *there*, and then he was *here*.

He blinked, looking strangely innocent and boyish, full lips parting. His clear eyes glistened, finding Timothée's face in the dark.

"Why," Val breathed, "are you touching me."

He didn't say it like a question.

He said it like a threat.

Timothée dropped his hands. Heat flushed his cheeks. "Y-you were dreaming!"

"So, you decided to climb on my bed and touch me while I was asleep?" Val's voice was raspy. "That's invasive, Greywick."

"You were screaming," Timothée growled. "You seemed like you—"

Val crossed his arms. "Like I needed your help? I'll tell you a secret. I won't *ever* need *you*."

Timothée slipped off the bed, turned away. "Fine. Sorry for bothering you."

In a flash, Val grabbed his wrist. Timothée turned, shocked. Val wasn't looking at him, instead staring intensely at the sheets. But his hand remained firmly around Timothée's.

*He… wants me to stay.*

Strange warmth spread through Timothée as he stared down at Val, face flushing and eyes focused on an invisible thread. Maybe it was easier for Val to be mean.

Well, that was fine with Timothée. Because it was always easier for him to be nice.

Should he be mad at Val for kissing Melissa? That had been a few weeks ago now, and Val hadn't even talked to her. At least, not that he'd seen. And maybe right now, what Val needed was just a friend.

Timothée took in a breath. "My bed's cold now."

The slightest flicker of a smile flashed on Val's face. "What are you going to do about it?"

"Steal your warmth." Timothée pushed himself into Val's bed, who gave no resistance. "Share the covers too."

Val grumbled but gave way. They sat thigh to thigh, shoulder to shoulder. Timothée heard the croaky rattle of Val's breath. *He's afraid.*

It would be so easy to take his hand or to put an arm around Val's shoulder, bring him close, mumble into his hair that he didn't need to be afraid of dreams, Timothée would protect him from the stars and the space between. But he couldn't do that. Not yet.

But he could do this.

"Do you like stories?"

Val scoffed. "What kind of question is that? Of course. What kind of person doesn't like stories?"

It was true. What kind of person didn't like stories?

"Alright, alright," Timothée said. "Well, I'm going to tell you a story. A story about…"

What would Val be interested in? Another re-telling of his favorite myth about the Emerald Queen and her mystical Riders? A funny story of his sisters, perhaps the time he and Vivian mixed lavender dye with Marion's soap and turned her hair purple? Or perhaps—

A yowl sounded from the end of the bed and Yvaine, looking as scraggly as ever, stared at them with a condescending blue glare.

"Sorry, did I abandon you over there?" Timothée asked. "Best you stay in my bed." *Before Val gives you the boot.*

But Val didn't kick her off. Instead, he sniffed like a child with a runny nose. And patted the blanket.

Yvaine padded up, turned in a circle twice, then sat down on Valentine's lap.

"You should bathe her," Val mumbled. "I'll mix up a gentle shampoo."

"Okay, but you're in charge of holding her."

Val smiled again and Timothée's heart fluttered. He'd do anything to earn one again.

"Okay, my story. It's about the night sky."

"The night sky?"

"Yes." Timothée placed his hand over Val's atop Yvaine's inky black fur. "The night sky. *Yvaine.*"

AN HOUR PASSED as Timothée recounted the story of how Yvaine had come to him. A fake witch who sold pretend potions had found the little cat the night of the Wolfhelm massacre. She'd kept her around as a black cat was good for the witching business. Timothée had worked in the bakery next door, and for three years, the nameless cat kept him company, leaving little pawprints in the flour. The witch never said anything when Yvaine started following Timothée home. Maybe she knew the little cat needed a boy who would give her a name. And that Timothée needed her.

Presently, Val's long, delicate fingers lightly touched Yvaine's fur. "My hair used to be this color when I was a child."

Timothée almost touched the soft lavender waves of Val's hair but thought better of it. "It's hard to picture you with any other color."

Val's gaze drifted away. "It was the same as my mother's. Or so they told me. I never knew her."

Timothée twisted the corner of the blanket, but before he could ask more, Val continued, "I was bored quite a bit in my youth, so I'd have our Starling staff change my hair. Blue as the sky, pink as flowers, or sometimes blond, so I looked more like my brother."

"You had staff?" Timothée smirked. "We were lucky if old Murdie the donkey helped us carry the lavender bundles into town. Where exactly did you grow up?"

Val scratched behind Yvaine's fluffy ears. "Wolfhelm."

"But you were in Kirrintsova for a bit, right? With Carmilla? I must have just missed you when we moved to Wolfhelm. Imagine if you'd come into the bakery. I probably would have said something really embarrassing."

"Is that any different from when you first saw me?" A slight smile curved up his face.

"What about your eyes?" Timothée asked. "They weren't always purple, I suppose?"

"No. They were blue. A trait from my father's side of the family."

"Then your purple hair and eyes came when you swallowed your Dark Star?" Timothée couldn't stop himself from lightly touching the soft ends. Val didn't pull away.

"When I swallowed that star, when I first saw my reflection after..." He paused, a faraway look in his eyes once again. "It seemed like the first color that ever belonged to me."

"It's... beautiful." Timothée grinned. "So, did the magic change all the hair on you or just your head?"

Slowly, Val shifted, looked up at him. Then he rose a brow. A purple brow so dark it was almost black.

Timothée swallowed, and Val's gaze intently tracked the movement down his throat, then back up to his face. He said in a raspy voice, "Are you curious, godling?"

Timothée lightly touched the laces of Val's tunic.

*Shit, shit, shit.* His heart was in his throat. It was beating so fast, he could barely hear himself think. But he grabbed the lace.

Val didn't stop him.

He just held Timothée with that deep gaze, as if he was daring him to keep going.

Timothée pulled, the fabric around his collar loosened, exposing Val's white chest, a light patch of hair the color of—

A bang sounded in the room.

Timothée startled, grabbing Yvaine and throwing himself over Val.

"What in the Three?" Val groaned and pushed up against Timothée's chest.

Slowly, Timothée uncurled, blinking his eyes. The room was cloudy with purple smoke. Tiny pebbles, like bits of snow, had settled over every surface in the room, just missing Val's bed.

Timothée blinked again, "Wha—"

"What did you do, Greywick?" Val darted up and crossed the room to the potion station, where cracked glass littered the counter.

"I—" Timothée stumbled up. Suddenly, his head felt foggy. "I forgot I was making a sleeping draft."

Val let out a long sigh. "Lesson number one in potion-making. Never leave a vial unattended."

*Yeah, well, I wasn't there for lesson number one,* Timothée wanted to say. But his eyes were so heavy.

"I can mix an antidote," Val said.

"I'll get some fresh air in here." Timothée threw back the curtains, blinking in the daylight, and cracked open the window. A breeze of cold autumn air drifted through. He stuck his head out, letting the wind tug at his hair, and inhaled deeply.

He already felt better.

But when he turned around, Val wasn't at the potion station. He was standing behind the curtain that separated the bathroom.

"Didn't you just tell me not to leave my potions unattended?" Timothée gestured to the scattered herbs Val had left strewn across the desk.

"No, I—" Val ran a hand through his hair. "I thought of an easier way. Come here."

Timothée scooped up Yvaine and followed him into the bathroom, eyes adjusting to the dark. Only a small hanging crystal lamp lit the space.

"I could brew a whole antidote to your idiotic mess. But why bother when we can cut the potion with salt?" Val reached across the copper tub to grab a glass jar filled with craggy crystals.

"I'm not eating your weird bath salt."

"It's sea salt with some infusions." Val perched on the edge of the tub and poured a handful of salt into his palm. "If you don't want it, fine by me, godling. I don't care if you fall into an endless sleep. Just don't expect me to kiss you awake."

Timothée was glad the dimly lit bathroom hid his burning cheeks. He wanted to go back to sleep, but he wasn't sure how much of his potion he'd inhaled in the dust cloud. It was better to be safe.

"Fine." He sat down on the edge of the tub.

"This is a rose petal blend, but I have some lavender as well."

"Rose is fine," Timothée said.

"Your sister is always going on about that farm. Thought you'd have a preference."

"Yeah, well, that's Marion." Timothée grabbed a pinch of salt from Val's outstretched palm. "Change can be good as well."

Timothée moved the salt to his lips, but Val snatched his wrist. "Don't swallow it. Let it dissolve under your tongue."

The salt was faintly red, and he placed a pinch under his tongue as Val instructed. Heady floral flavor exploded in his mouth.

Timothée shook his head. "It tastes like I'm eating a flower!"

"Stop whining." Val poked his cheek. "I might have just saved your life."

Timothée stuck out his tongue when the salt had dissolved. "Yeah, but at what cost?"

Val didn't say anything. Instead, he had his hand up to his mouth and was... laughing. It was all so ridiculous, Timothée couldn't help but laugh along with him.

Val dipped back, sliding into the tub, clutching his stomach, feet still hanging over the edge. Timothée fell beside him.

"I can't believe you ate it." Val smirked.

"Hey," Timothée bumped their shoulders together. "You ate it too. Do you think it'll work?"

"I don't know," Val said. "Maybe. But we should probably stay in here until that room clears up."

"Yeah."

"Hey." Val bounced his foot against Timothée's. "What are you even smiling about? I just made you eat the grossest thing in the world."

Timothée licked the salt off his lips. "I don't know if I've ever heard you laugh before."

Val chucked a handful of salt at him. "I laugh. You're just not very funny."

"Oh, I am. I make Mare and Viv laugh all the time."

"Probably because you're being idiotic." Val shook his head. "It doesn't count if they're laughing at you."

"That's only half the time!"

Val's laugh slowly faded until it was only the drip of the shower, and the unfiltered sounds from the open window: birds calling, the distant shouts of the farmers across the fields.

"You're right though," Val said. "I don't laugh much. Not anymore. I used to have friends... like your sisters, I suppose. We could make a joke about anything together."

Val had friends he used to laugh with? *Where are they now?* Did they know Val had swallowed a Dark Star?

Val slowly blinked.

"Don't fall asleep," Timothée said. "We should stay awake until class."

"Ugh." Val rolled his eyes. "How do you propose we do that?"

A meow sounded, and Yvaine jumped up on the side of the tub, then hopped down beside them. She perched herself on Timothée's chest.

"I told you a story," Timothée said. "You tell me one."

Val studied him for a moment, then narrowed his eyes. "Fine, but if you think I'm telling some pathetic sob story about my past, you're wrong. I know some old Andúrigardian myths though. Unfortunately, they're all about wolves and righteous heroes."

"I like wolves," Timothée said.

Val placed his hand on Yvaine's back and began to spin a tale of frozen trees and winter storms. And Timothée couldn't help but think, at least for right now, Val's dreams of the past were gone. They had each other.

# 19

# IN WHICH VIVIAN REVELS IN THE AUTUMN NIGHT

IT WAS THE last week of the Hunter's Blood Moon and preparations for the All Hallow's Eve Ball were in full swing.

Vivian walked with her siblings through Selene Crescent. It was a crisp autumn night and, for Starlings who thrived in darkness, the most comfortable. Warm lights lit up the windows and doors of the little shoppes. Bales of hay were placed throughout the Crescent for students to sit on. Stalls of harvest crops—pumpkins and yams and squashes of every color—lined the cobblestone path.

Even the Starlings seemed filled with the festive mood this weekend, all dressed in warm clothes and carrying steaming drinks and little bags of sugary donuts. They giggled as they ran arm in arm between the clothing shoppes, each one selling finer costumes than the last.

Beside her, Marion took a deep sip of her drink, coming up with a white mustache from the whipped cream. Her eyes trained upward. "I hate looking at that thing."

Timothée chuckled and threw an arm around his sister. "Hey, maybe it'll pass for an All Hallow's Eve decoration."

A hideous statue had been erected in the courtyard of Selene Crescent this moon. A birthday gift to them—a gift to *Vivian*—from the Prince of Andúrigard himself.

A statue of the Lost Stars, the God Children. A statue of them. And the ugliest thing on the entire Isle of Argos.

Vivian avoided looking at it. The Greywicks had celebrated their twentieth birthday and been surprised by the royal trio with a party in Selene Crescent. It had been wonderful. Wonderful until that goddamned statue.

But she pushed it from her mind and turned back to the crackling atmosphere of the square.

"We should talk about the upcoming All Hallow's Eve Ball," Marion said, wiping her upper lip.

At that, Vivian turned excitedly to her sister. "Agreed! Wouldn't it be fun if we had coordinated costumes?"

"I'm not going to match with my *sisters*," Timothée interrupted. "Do you know how lame that would be? Besides, I have a costume."

"What?" Vivian cried. "What are you going—"

She stopped, realized Marion wasn't with them. She was standing a few paces behind, scowling.

"You two can't be serious," she snapped, aggressively throwing her drink into a waste bin decorated with red painted leaves. "We're not attending the ball. It's the perfect opportunity for us to get some answers while everyone's distracted."

Vivian and Timothée looked at each other.

Marion strode forward. "Now, I'm thinking we attempt to sneak into the headmistress's office. If Father was the headmaster, then it used to be his. Perhaps there are some important documents."

Vivian and Timothée were silent.

Marion crossed her arms. "You don't like that plan? Fine. I've got another. This damned castle wants to play games with us. *'Embrace what you are.*' What a bother! I found a map of the Academy. Let's search each corner until we find where this voice is hiding—"

"Let me get this straight," Timothée said slowly. "Instead of attending a party for one night, you want to *break into* the headmistress's office or *aimlessly wander* the hallways?"

She blew a curl out of her face. "Well, it sounds trite when you say it that way."

Vivian inhaled a deep breath of the cold autumn air. She knew where this was going, could tell it from the incredulous tone in Timothée's voice, Marion's stubborn stance.

"It sounds trite because it *is* trite, Mare." Timothée turned away, dug his hands deep in his pockets. "You know it is possible for us to enjoy ourselves while we're here, right?"

Marion wrinkled her nose. "Excuse me if I find it hard to enjoy myself on an isle that literally *swallowed* me last moon."

"What do you want?" Timothée snapped. His voice quieted as a group of giggling Starlings passed by. "Do you want to go back down to our apartment in Wolfhelm? Struggling to survive each day?"

"You know I don't want that," Marion said. She pulled her golden cloak tighter around her. "Is this about the party?"

It was. And it wasn't. Vivian looked around at the Starlings, arm in arm, laughing. Shopping. Sitting on hay bales, testing their magic. Kissing one another outside the tavern.

"I know you're worried about me, Marion," Vivian said softly, "but we all deserve a chance just to… just to *be*."

"You can't seriously be considering attending with the Prince." Marion's voice was tight.

Vivian took a deep breath. "Yes, I am."

"You can't trust him, Viv. You can't trust—"

*You can't trust yourself. That's what she wants to say.*

Marion's eyes were wide and watery. "If you let your defenses down for even a moment, he will kill you."

"I know," Vivian said.

But she was dying anyway. Maybe she hadn't been able to admit it to herself until now. Until it'd gotten so bad, her skin constantly felt stretched over her bones. Until the aching hunger was so intense, she heard the swish of blood through a Starling's veins from across the courtyard. Until she knew lovely smells of pumpkin and apples and warm pies surrounded her, but she couldn't smell a single thing beside the shopkeeper to her left, heady with rich, coppery blood.

She only had so much longer of pretending in her. And she didn't want to waste it creeping around the castle playing games with a voice that may or may not have tried to kill them in the deep magic.

"I want to go to the ball anyway," Vivian said.

Timothée smiled. Marion threw her head back and palmed her eyelids. "Ugh! Fine. Have your dance." She straightened and stared with that grey gaze like an electric cloud. "But after, you know what you have to do."

Vivian nodded.

Timothée clapped her on the back. "Now that's settled, we can—"

"Actually, attending the ball might be the perfect disguise." Marion's stare was faraway. "Timothée and I can inquire about Father. All the faculty is attending—"

"Stop." Timothée stormed up to Marion, snatched her wrist. "Enough, Mare. You need to take a break. Relax. For one night."

Oh, now he'd done it. Vivian pulled her elbows tight, and stared at the fountain, with water spurting in the shape of orange ghouls, wishing she could be anywhere but here.

"Relax? Relax?" Marion stalked forward. "How dare you tell me to relax, Timothée Greywick? I'm trying to piece together Father's history. You think you'd show a little more interest!"

The wind whipped Timothée's curls across his freckled nose. "What's the point in any of it? Are you in denial?" He threw a hand toward the heinous statue. "He wasn't even our real father!"

Marion stepped back as if slapped. "The castle told me the blood remembers. And my blood remembers him!"

Vivian walked beside her sister. "A father is more than who sired you," she said. "Henry Greywick raised us, fed us, clothed us. Loved us."

"Loved you two, maybe." Timothée kicked a pumpkin with a carved face at the base of the fountain. "You both said he was in your Celestial Rite trials. Well, he didn't show up for me. Just like he never showed up for me."

"What are you talking about?" Vivian breathed.

Timothée's grey eyes shined in the lantern light. "Of course, you two didn't see it. Because I don't think he even admitted it to himself. But I felt it. All sixteen years I felt it." He shook his head. "He never wanted to hold me for long. Couldn't look at me without this... veil coming over his eyes. And never once did he ever tell me he loved me."

"That's not true," Marion cried.

"It is true," Timothée snapped. "He loved on you both day and night. I knew I was different and now I understand." His trembling hands touched the choker around his neck. "Father knew I was dangerous. He was afraid of me."

Vivian saw him then not as he was, a skinny young man in too fine of clothing, but as a boy. Small and mop-headed, always wanting to play out grand stories. A boy standing to the side as Father wrapped his girls in his arms and told him he would always be there, always protect them.

And she turned to her sister, saw the war going on behind the grey eyes. Had Father known it from the start? Had he taken the triplets away to ensure Timothée would never swallow a star? And how could someone who loved them so much hurt someone they loved so much?

Marion opened her mouth. Closed it. Opened it again. "Well, I'm not afraid of you, Tim."

He sniffed, nose shiny. "I know."

Vivian grabbed Marion's hand in hers, and Timothée's hand in the other and pulled them together. The triplets wrapped their arms around one another and held on.

"I want to go to the party, Mare," Tim whispered. "The castle told us to embrace what we are. I'm a Dark Star."

"As you wish," Marion said.

The three pulled away, eyes and noses dripping. They laughed lightly, wiped their faces. "So, what do we do now?" Marion asked.

"Only one thing to do." Vivian looked down the street, at the shoppe at the far end with a brilliant display of fabric in every color. "Get you a costume."

# 20
# IN WHICH MARION MEETS THE GOD OF SHADOWS

FOR SOMEONE DRESSED as a woodland elf, Marion Greywick certainly felt serious.

It was the night of the All Hallow's Eve Ball, the moment everyone had been looking forward to during the bitter days of the Hunter's Blood Moon. Everyone except her, of course. She was only attending because of her soft and gentle heart. Oh, what a bother it was to be so generous of spirit!

Vivian and Timothée wanted to go. They had both wanted to go to the Unification Day Festival and look how that worked out. Vampires and prophets and nasally loremasters.

At least on the Isle of Argos, they were the most protected they could be. There should be none of that nonsense.

Perhaps her siblings were right. It might not be the worst idea to… relax. For a night.

Floating candles lit the corridors, and the scent of pumpkin and apple cinnamon infused the air. The Evening Star professors had crafted the eyes of the various portraits to follow where you walked, and the Morning Stars had cast a strange fog that sat just above the floor, so tendrils of mist curled with each step.

Marion and Vivian walked down the halls together toward Professor Barracus's office where they were to meet Timothée. Once Marion had relented to attend the All Hallow's Eve Ball, she of course agreed with Vivian that their costumes must match. But Timothée had insisted he'd found his own, and he wanted to keep it a secret.

If that wasn't bad enough, Vivian had the fabulous idea Darius could complete their trio costume. *Darius.* Marion liked Darius as much as she liked the hideous statue he'd built for them in Selene Crescent. And she liked the idea of matching with him as much as she liked the idea of sewing her forehead to the carpet.

Marion chewed her bottom lip, tasted the heavy ocher lip paint, spat. They were dressed as legendary heroes from one of Thraina's most beloved fairytales. Vivian, clad as the Sapphire Ranger, wore sparkling blue hunter's garb, hair pulled up high upon her head, a heavy application of rouge applied to her cheeks. Her costume, at least, had a semblance of practicality to it.

Marion, on the other hand, must have lost her wits when she agreed to dress as the Emerald Queen. Her costume, created by one of Vivian's friends in the Evening Star house, was made entirely of sheer silk covered in glittering green leaves and vines. It hugged her body, showcasing every curve and roll in a most scandalous way. She'd tried to grab a cloak as they left, claiming she looked absurd, but Vivian had insisted against it: "It's a costume party, Marion. Absurd is the point."

And in a miracle moment of trust, she'd allowed one of the fourth-year Evening Stars to alter little bits of her to suit the character. They'd turned her grey eyes an emerald green and pointed the tips of her ears to better resemble the fairytale elves. And most shocking of all, they'd turned her golden tresses a burnished copper. And she was most proud and protective of her hair.

But it was okay. It would all fade with the daylight.

Despite constantly yanking up the sweetheart neckline to better cover her spilling bosom and plucking bunching fabric out of her bottom, she had to admit…

She looked pretty good.

The sisters stopped before Professor Barracus's office and knocked.

"So odd Tim's getting ready here," Vivian murmured. "And Professor Barracus would allow him use of his personal space."

"I have no idea why he's been so secretive over this whole thing." Marion shrugged. "He's probably going to be dressed in a shoddy cat costume—"

The door opened.

Marion screamed.

IT SHOULD HAVE been fun. It should have been joyful. But the God of Shadows stood before her, telling a story about his cat yakking on his roommate's pillow.

No wonder Timothée had been cagey about his costume. He was dressed as the *literal embodiment of evil*.

Marion and Vivian sat on the couch as Timothée paced back and forth, his cape flowing like a shadowy river. His heavy gravastarium armor was black as pitch, and the violet torchlight flashed off the purple jewels embedded on each shoulder.

And it wasn't just the armor. He, too, had been altered by Evening Star magic. His curls were now straight and touched his shoulders. The warm brown had been changed to black. His eyes were lined with kohl, cheekbones hollowed out and accented with powder.

*He's still my little brother,* Marion told herself. But if it wasn't for his nervous rambling, even she would mistake him for the man she saw in her vision at Bøgelund.

*You alright, Mum?*

"Are you sure this is a good idea, Tim?" Vivian twirled her long ponytail.

He gave a weak smile. "It's only a costume."

*A costume of Noctis!* Marion wanted to scream. A thousand objections roared through her mind. But somehow, she kept her mouth shut. She'd barely said a word, knowing if she said one, the rest would come rushing out.

*I can't control him,* she reminded herself. And she kept thinking of the look on his face back in Selene Crescent. *'Father knew I was dangerous. He was afraid of me.'*

Maybe Timothée needed to prove he could walk the path of darkness and still be light.

She sighed. "You've got a cowlick, Tim. Come here."

And the God of Shadows bent down to her, and she licked her palm, and flattened the top of his black hair.

There was a knock on the door, and a man slipped in. "Ah, I knew I'd find you somewhere, Greywicks."

Marion's breath hitched.

Khalid stood before them, wearing tight breeches with tall leather boots and a billowing white shirt, open at the front to reveal the smooth brown plane of his chest. A red bandana was tied around his neck, and he wore a tricorn hat with a huge white feather. His usual golden hoop glimmered from his left ear, and he wore his leather gloves.

If she had stepped out of a fairytale, he looked like he'd stepped off the cover of a scandalous bodice-ripper. He was as fine a pirate as she could ever conjure.

Khalid crossed his arms and stared at her brother. "Wow, Timothée, talk about a statement piece. Love the cape. Always thought I should get myself a cape, but I don't know if I could pull it off—" Then his gaze drifted to her.

She uncurled from the sofa and stood, drawn to his voice. He ran his eyes over her body. He must think she looked ridiculous. What a stupid idea, to wear such an outrageous dress. And these damned pointed ears! And her beautiful hair, ruined with this color—

And yet...

Unable to stand his silent staring any long, she rose a brow and put her hand on her hip. "Well?"

Breath rushed out of him, and he gave what could only be a nervous blink.

"U-Uh," he stammered. "Hey, M-Marion." Finally, his eyes met hers. "You look beautiful."

Delicious heat swept up her body, and she swore he could see the beat of her heart against her breast. She added a slight sway to her walk and grabbed his hand to button the cuff of his billowing sleeve. "You're not so bad yourself, Mr. Ali Bagheeri."

Maybe there was something to this relaxing thing after all.

MARION AND KHALID stepped out of the office. Vivian had left to meet up with Darius, and Timothée was waiting for Carmilla. Khalid had asked Marion to accompany him straight to the ballroom.

Marion picked at the green glitter along her skin. What was this feeling? Nervousness? She'd walked alone with Khalid nearly every day since arriving at the Academy. She was used to the quickening of her heart when his voice lowered in a husky retort, or when he'd casually brush her arm. But this stomach-turning, heart-galloping, rapid-breathing *sickness* was entirely new. Was it the way she kept catching his eyes straying to her bursting bodice? Was it the energy of All Hallow's Eve? Was it that damned tricorn hat?

"Pretty unnerving sitting beside the personification of the greatest evil to ever walk Thraina," Khalid said, mercifully tearing her from her thoughts. "I'm surprised you're letting Timothée do this."

She sighed. "At some point I have to come to terms with the fact I can't control everything."

Khalid laughed. "Isn't that the beauty of it? Realizing there is no control. Only chaos. Every system is on the edge of collapse. The question is not can you control the collapse, but can you walk the edge of it without falling?"

She poked his chest, if only for an excuse to feel his skin. "You, sir, are mad."

He grinned roguishly. "Or do I just walk the edge of madness?"

They turned a candle-lit corner, and Marion nearly slammed into the small, fiery shape of Carmilla. She was dressed in silvery blue, her dress inlaid with lightning bolts. Marion recognized her from a mural in the Glass Cathedral: Niya, a goddess under Xydrious, who hunted lightning.

Carmilla looked at them with her usual calculating expression. Said nothing.

"Ah, Carmilla! You look positively bewitching." Khalid whipped out his smarmiest grin. "Dressed as a storm-chaser. I couldn't imagine anything more fitting. You're always chasing trouble, aren't you?"

Carmilla's green eyes flashed. Then she pulled out her own smirk. "And you're a pirate. A thief and mutineer." She bumped hard into his shoulder. "Didn't you know you were supposed to wear a costume?"

She walked past them, her tinkling laugh lingering in the hallway long after she'd turned the corner.

"What's her problem?" Marion scowled. "Dress too tight?"

Khalid gave an exhale, attempted a smile. "Ah, it's alright. I should have known wearing this would make me an easy target."

"An easy target? What was she talking about?"

He jabbed her cheek. "You know, I've seen that outraged pout many times before, but there is something particularly endearing when you're outraged on my behalf."

She swatted his hand away. "You're avoiding the question."

He sighed. "You know, the old phrase. *Never trust a Medihsan.*"

"What? How about never trust a snotty redhead who can't say a nice thing to save her life?"

"You don't know the expression?" Khalid rose a brow. "Never mind it. It's an old prejudice from the war."

"What does it mean?" Marion pushed. "Never trust a Medihsan?" It wasn't the first time she'd heard the phrase, muttered both jokingly and not-so-jokingly across dining tables and down long corridors.

Khalid sighed and tilted his hat up. "You know sixteen years ago, Medihsa and Kirrintsova formed an alliance? Kirrintsova promised to aid Medihsa's rebellion for independence against Andúrigard."

"Of course. I actually stay awake in history class."

"I don't need to hear Loremaster Setviren's version." Khalid's eyes trained forward. "I lived it. I was a child, but I remember."

The Trinity War... orchestrated by Khalid's parents in Medihsa and Carmilla's parents in Kirrintsova. "But Medihsa and Kirrintsova didn't stay aligned."

"No. Medihsa and Kirrintsova were fighting for the same thing, but we weren't fighting the same way." He shook his head. "The Empire secretly had an army of Dark Stars and vampires. Wherever their armies walked, destruction followed. Fields blackened. Towns razed. Dark clouds in the sky."

"Shadowcraft is forbidden," Marion breathed.

"For good reason," Khalid said. "Up to that point, the Celestial Church had mostly stayed out of it. I'm sure they were secretly funding Andúrigard and providing Celestial Knights to dress up as kingdom soldiers, but at least they were attempting to appear impartial. But when Kirrintsova started using shadowcraft and vamps... Well, things got messy to say the least."

Marion saw the slightest tremor of his lip as he re-told the history, the only sign that this wasn't just a piece of the past to him. This was *his* past.

And she had been so ignorant. The battles had never made it close to Seagrass. "What happened?"

"Medihsa didn't want war on the Celestial Church. And it was becoming clear the Kirrintsovan Empire didn't care about Medihsa's independence. They wanted dominion over everything. There are cities along the border between Kirrintsova and Andúrigard where no life will grow again."

"So, Medihsa betrayed the Empire."

"Imagine the choice, Marion." Khalid's voice lowered. "Continue your quest for independence, knowing the world you reclaim will be one of death and violence? And that's if your allies don't decide to take you as collateral too. Or turn tail and apologize to the one who has kept you under their boot for years, knowing at least you get to live to fight another day?"

They passed a floor-to-ceiling window with billowing scarlet curtains. The color reminded her of blood. "There would have been no freedom either way."

"No, but my mother and father kept their heads, unlike Carmilla's." Khalid gave a roguish smirk that seemed all too cavalier for the conversation. "And now the children continue what the parents began."

*That's why Carmilla can't stand the sight of him,* Marion thought. *She thinks if Medihsa had stayed aligned with the Empire, she'd still have her throne. And her family.* The idea made her sad. For Carmilla. For Khalid. For the families they both lost.

Khalid ran a hand down her side, fingers trailing over the silken leaves. "It's kind of like the characters in that book you Greywicks love so much. You suit it, by the way."

"What?" Marion's head spun from the speed of the conversation.

"You suit it," he said again and stared at her fiercely. "The Queen."

"Oh! Hah. Well." Marion looked down, feeling her face flush under his gaze.

"Enough talk of sad old stories and politics." He grabbed her hand and coaxed her into a twirl. "It's All Hallow's Eve. I'm going to dance the night away, and I've got the most beautiful girl in Thraina on my arm. Nothing can destroy my night."

She fell against his chest, hands landing on the warm skin revealed by the deep V of his shirt. She inhaled a deep breath of his scent and sprawled her fingers wide. His heart beat fast beneath her palm.

"I trust you."

"Hmm?" He blinked.

"I trust you," she said and smiled. Because it was true. Because in the last moon, he'd saved her sister and been her friend and because she saw *him*. Not the him for Darius or the him for Carmilla or the him for the rest of the world.

Just him.

She tucked her head beneath his chin, inhaling the scent of his skin.

Khalid whistled through his teeth. "Is this your way of telling me I should dress up as a pirate more often?"

She turned her head, so her mouth lay against his throat. "You don't have to be anyone else for me, Khalid. You can just be yourself."

A silent moment passed, and then his arms wrapped around her. "I'll keep that in mind."

It was lovely, to be hugged by him, to have her whole self enveloped in his arms. She felt greedy and free all at once. But it was All Hallow's Eve, dammit. And she had been instructed to relax.

Her voice came out a husky whisper: "How come you haven't touched me again?"

He pulled back slightly. "Hmm?"

"I've been here a whole moon. You haven't even tried."

He looked at her sidelong. "Is that what you want, Marion? For me to touch you?"

Oh, gods. Was he making fun of her? She should laugh and pretend it was all a joke.

As if he saw the thoughts warring inside her head, he said gruffly, "Tell me the truth, Marion. Do you want me to touch you?"

Oh, fuck it. She took a deep inhale. "Yes, Khalid. That is what I want."

In a single movement, he shoved her back against the wall, body pressed tight to hers. His hands dug roughly through her hair. "Well, why didn't you say so?"

It was all she could do to keep from collapsing. She grabbed his biceps and managed a shaky breath. "I-I couldn't just… ask."

"Why the hell not?" he growled. "I thought you trusted me."

"I do." Her vision crackled and sparked; the candles flickered wildly, and the fog stirred beneath their feet. "And I'm asking now."

"Have you been thinking about it?" He wedged his knee between her legs, her silk dress tearing higher up the thigh. She didn't care. "Thinking what would happen if I took you in my room again?"

"Yes," she said more urgently.

He dipped his mouth to her bare collarbone. "Tell me what you imagine me doing to you."

She licked her lips, ran her hands upward to curl in his hair. His hat fluttered to the ground. "I imagine the feel of your skin against mine. Of your hands running over my legs, my thighs, my breasts." Her face was on fire, the words coarse in her mouth. But it was All Hallow's Eve, and the wicked things came out. "The feel of your cock in my hands."

"Oh, you have thought about this." He ground his knee harder against the apex of her thighs and nipped at her skin. "Do you think about it when you're sitting so attentively in class? Everyone thinks you're such a good girl, but I know better." His hands roamed the curves of her waist. "I know how wicked Marion Greywick truly is."

"Tonight?" she breathed and curved her mouth upward, lips on his jaw.

His gloved hand trailed up her body, over the tops of her breasts, landing lightly on her neck. "Tonight? Tonight, you want me to take you to my room and rip you out of your lovely dress and fuck you like the queen you are?"

Heat swarmed in her belly and her fingers raked the back of his neck. Her voice had lost its cowering waver. "Gods, yes."

His hand left her neck and lifted her chin up. Nose to nose, his warm breath blew over her face, his lips an inch away from hers. "Then I am at your command."

And he kissed the barest edge of her mouth. Not a real kiss, but the promise of one.

Or the threat.

Then Khalid stepped back and held out his arm. On shaky legs, she took his elbow.

And then they were at the grand doors leading into the ballroom. There was light and music and delicious smells and friends saying hello.

Khalid looked down at her, a roguish grin upon his face. "Tonight, Ms. Greywick, we eat until we burst, we drink until the room spins, and we dance until we collapse. Tonight, Ms. Greywick, you do not know the meaning of satiated."

# 21

# IN WHICH TIMOTHÉE EMBODIES THE DARKNESS OF ALL HALLOW'S EVE

**E**ERIE MUSIC DRIFTED from under the ballroom doors. A calamity of low-pitched instruments, a cadence as beautiful as it was unnerving.

*Is it almost time?* Timothée looked up and down the darkened hallway and shifted from foot to foot. His movements felt unnatural, arms and legs not used to the weight of his costume. Not that the armor didn't fit. Each piece seemed molded to his form despite the fact they'd looked too big before he put them on.

It was just *heavy.* He wore a tight black shirt and pants underneath, but the rest of him was all metal and sharp edges. Panels of gravastarium glinted and swallowed any light that touched it. And then there was the cape. It wasn't black, but the deepest purple, clasped on either shoulder with a pin the shape of a crescent moon and star. When he moved, the cape flowed behind him like a living shadow.

It reminded him of the cape the Dark Prophet had worn.

Buttery light spilled out of the ballroom doors as Carmilla ducked into the hallway, looking as stunning as ever.

"It's almost time," she said.

"Aren't we a little late?"

"It's all part of the show." She wet her thumb and slicked down a piece of his hair.

His much longer hair, thanks to a few talented Evening Stars. Tonight, he wasn't just wearing his brother's armor—he was becoming him. And what they couldn't change with starcraft, they'd done with a different type of magic: makeup. His freckles had all but disappeared under a layer of powder, and dark kohl lined his eyes. He scrunched up his nose. It was sort of itchy.

"Remember, the moment you walk in you're not Timothée anymore. You are the God of Shadows. Nathaniel is going to dim the lights, Rayna will bring in a little spooky fog, and the rest is up to you."

"All that attention." Timothée felt sick thinking about it.

"You said you wanted to be liked, that you wanted to fit in," Carmilla said. "This is none of that. This will make them fear how much they want your love."

"I'm a god that was executed by his own mother for what he did. You're talking about love?"

"Everyone craves darkness, Timothée." Carmilla ran a hand along the armor. "All Hallow's Eve is the only night they'll admit it."

Three taps sounded on the door.

"That's the sign. Count to ten then enter." Carmilla gave him a quick smile, then ducked into the ballroom.

He thought his heart might race out of his chest. How many seconds had it been? He was about to walk in front of the *entire* school dressed like… dressed like…

He couldn't do it. Everyone would look at him. What would the professors think? And Val…

The music from the orchestra stopped. Timothée had swallowed a star, faced the trials of the Celestial Rite. At the very least, he could walk into a room dressed up for All Hallow's Eve.

With heavy gloved hands, he pushed apart the doors into the ballroom. The room was huge, and yet the only sound was his boots down the grand staircase. Starlings stopped in place, turning their gazes to him. This attention was different than he'd ever received before.

His brother wouldn't have been afraid of entering a room. He would have made every single person in it *his*. He'd take their love and their fear and their worship and become drunk on the power of it.

*And tonight, I'll do the same.*

Which seemed sort of silly, because in actuality, he only wanted that from one person.

Fog cut between his feet, making each step more purposeful. All the wide-eyed gazes, mouths open in awe, trembles of fear, filled him with a strange confidence.

He stopped at the bottom of the stairs near the edge of the dance floor. His long cape, which had flown behind him as he moved, now pooled at his feet. Timothée observed the ballroom.

He'd seen glimpses of the Celestial Academy's ballroom before, but this was the first time he'd been inside. The room was decorated for All Hallow's Eve; red, orange, and yellow leaves floated through the air. Woven pinecone and maple leaf boughs hung from the pillars, parts of them shining as if tiny stars were hidden inside. Gilded pumpkins were piled in the corners, carved with frightful expressions. Pale ghosts drifted from the ceilings, while fake skulls and spiders were scattered amongst the tables of towering food. Everything was a mix of the terror and beauty of autumn.

The ballroom was situated right at the edge of the Isle of Argos, this room built over a cliff itself. The dance floor, made of glass, looked down over Thraina. When the Starlings danced, they did so over oceans and mountains.

A whisper that almost sounded like a chant drifted from their lips.

"Noctis."

"God of Shadows."

"The Greywick boy."

Timothée found his sisters' faces in the crowd, a strange mix of pride and uncertainty. The professors ranged from amusement to outright fear. And Archpriestess Kassandra gave a strange, lingering look as she exited the ballroom, knuckles white around her staff.

There was one person Timothée didn't see, the one he was searching for. Then he saw a glimpse of lilac, almost hidden by the shadow of a large pillar. Valentine's gaze was not the awe or desire or fear that played on the faces of the other students—it was that unreadable expression. Then a flash of sadness—no, disinterest—as Val turned away from him.

Timothée stepped forward, drawn to follow. But Carmilla grabbed his arm.

"So," she said, her voice loud enough to carry. "Does the God of Shadows dance?"

"Yes," he said. And it was true because they had been practicing. Every night after class, he and Carmilla had pushed his and Val's beds to the side and danced across the tiny dorm room.

Carmilla had explained his illusion of fear and awe would shatter if he flailed on the dance floor like a fish gasping its final breath. So, they'd danced, while Val had made fun of his footwork and slouching, and called him a disaster the whole time.

Timothée hadn't told Val what his costume was going to be, and well, Val hadn't asked. But now he wondered if he should have told him. He supposed a small part of him had hoped Val would be, he didn't know, impressed? But he'd looked about as disinterested in this as everything else Timothée did.

*Everyone else is impressed though,* Timothée thought. *What's his problem?*

"Timothée," Carmilla hissed under her breath, "lead me to the dance floor."

He blinked and took Carmilla's arm. As if on their cue, the orchestra started a waltz, and the other couples joined in.

Stars and sea whirled underneath them, and his stomach flipped. He forced himself to look into Carmilla's bright green gaze.

"So," she said lowly as they started their steps, "how do you feel having everyone's eyes on you?"

"Honestly?" Timothée said. "Queasy."

"You'll get used to it."

They swung around the ballroom, and he fell into the practiced movements. He wasn't a talented dancer by any means, but this was enough. The song closed and as he dipped Carmilla low, she tilted her head back, short red hair skimming the glass floor.

He pulled her up and she whispered: "This room is enraptured with you, my little Dark Star."

A crowd of awed faces watched him. He was sure he was blushing, not that anyone could tell under all the powder.

"You could ask them to kneel and they would," Carmilla said. "So, what is it you want from them?"

He searched the crowd until he found him again, standing at the drink station. It was done up as a mad alchemist's experiment: twisting tubes and bubbling colored potions, ready to inebriate and enchant. Was Val even wearing a costume? His lilac hair fell loose, and he wore a light low-cut shirt and tight dark pants and high shiny boots. He wasn't looking at the dance floor. Maybe Val hadn't even seen him come in…

Carmilla gave Timothée a knowing look. "Trust me when I tell you there are some things too dangerous, even for All Hallow's Eve."

"I—"

Carmilla addressed the crowd with a flourish. "Now, who wants to dance with a god?"

# 22
# IN WHICH MARION WALKS THE EDGE OF LOVE AND HATE

"IT'S JUST A suit of armor," Marion said. "Everyone's looking at Tim like he's... like he's..."

"Like he's a god personified?" Khalid responded.

They sat together at one of the small tables covered in an autumn-orange fabric, adorned with a golden pumpkin centerpiece. A fabulous band played hauntingly beautiful music that filled the air. The Isle of Argos was floating over the coastal ranges of Andúrigard this moon, and the sea smashed against mountains beneath the glass floor of the ballroom. The party buzzed around them, a tense and fervent energy, with Timothée in the eye of the storm.

Despite her brother's hubbub, Marion had to admit she was having a good time. Khalid and Darius had raced to eat the most mellow puffs. Rayna had persuaded Taf to dance with her—though she hadn't needed much convincing. The two had been inseparable upon the dance floor. Marion and Vivian had promenaded the whole ballroom arm in arm, blushing as students complimented their costumes.

And of course, Khalid kept running his fingers along her bare back, or tracing his hand over her thigh under the table. A promise of later to come.

Everyone seemed to be having a good time.

Well, not everyone.

Archpriestess Kassandra had been sitting in a golden chair, surrounded by Celestial Knights, when Timothée made his entrance. She'd had a line of Starlings waiting to wish her greetings for All Hallow's Eve.

And then in walked Noctis.

Or at least, the near-perfect embodiment of him.

Marion had watched the Archpriestess's face, waiting for it to melt into rage, for her to send Timothée away. But she'd only stared unblinking at the tip of her staff. With a swish of her robes, she'd exited the ballroom and not yet returned.

"It's just a suit of armor," Marion said again, more to herself than Khalid.

"Not to them," he responded, stretching his long legs out before him. "To them, it's a sinful fantasy safe for them to play with. All their most evil desires presented in front of them, ripe for the picking."

"Surely, that's not what Timothée intended."

"Of course not." Khalid's eyes drifted to the dance floor. "But who's to say it wasn't someone else's?"

Marion followed his gaze to where Carmilla swayed in Timothée's arms. She was positively gloating.

Energy crackled in the air; an excited, electric fear. Students hovered, all wanting a chance to be held by the God of Shadows. Other couples joined, but all eyes were on Carmilla and her prize.

But no gaze seemed so particularly pointed as the one coming from the drink station.

Glass beaker in hand filled with a misting green liquid, Valentine Sun leaned against the table and drank. And brooded. And drank. His presence stopped anyone else from getting close, a magnetic repel. He was dressed in neither costume nor fancy attire, and yet still outshone everyone around him.

*What's his problem?* Marion wondered. But Khalid put a plate of sweets down in front of her, and she pushed that Dark Star boy out of her mind.

The party wore on and Marion and Khalid stepped outside to get some air. The Tealight Garden was a cobblestone path that led through a maze of topiary hedges. They were manicured into the shape of rabbits and elephants, flying horses and phoenixes, praying saints and sword-wielding knights.

Usually, the hedges were imbued with twinkling lights. But now, the verges were dark, the path lit only by the glow of the moon and stars.

"Something doesn't feel right," Marion whispered.

Khalid took her hand and her heart pulsed. He pulled her into the maze.

The music became an eerie echo from the ballroom. The air smelled of the rich greenery, of the cold of an autumn night. Of pomegranates.

They turned a corner to the center of the garden. Towering marble statues of the minor gods and goddesses bordered the courtyard, standing like sentries. Marion recognized them from her Study of Sacred Literature class: Lubuwefe, with their fingers pointed to claws; Yueb, fallen to his knees, a knife before him; Eldy, the one-armed; Niya, a lightning bolt held up to the sky in one hand.

And sitting on a marble bench in the middle was Val.

Or what was left of Val.

He slumped back against a hedge, legs extended out long, arms drooped down to his sides. Except, they weren't exactly arms and legs anymore. His limbs dripped into black, oily goop. Lilac hair fell limp around his face, and his eyes were closed, face a mask of sorrow. Wracking with sobs, his shadowy goop-body grew longer. The black choker lay discarded to the side.

Marion nearly screamed, ready to pull Khalid away from whatever fiendish terror sat before them. But he only took a deep inhale.

"Alright, buddy." Khalid dropped Marion's hand. "Let's get you cleaned up."

"Wait!" Marion clawed at his shirt. "Don't get close! He looks possessed. And he's not wearing his choker!" Images flashed in her mind of what Timothée had done before they'd forced the black band around his neck.

Khalid patted her hand. "Don't worry. He's not dangerous. He's just sad."

Marion wanted to yell being sad didn't turn one into a dripping monster, but she held her tongue. She'd told Khalid she'd trusted him, after all. She supposed now she had to show it.

Khalid took a tentative step over one of Val's massively long black-shadow-leg-tentacle things. "This better not stain." Making a face, he picked up Val's drooping, oily arm goop and threw it over Val's lap so he could sit beside him on the bench.

He clapped Val on the shoulder. The Dark Star boy didn't even acknowledge him. Black tears streaked his face.

What was Khalid doing? He barely interacted with Valentine beyond basic acknowledgements in class.

"You need to put your choker back on, buddy," Khalid said. "Marion, will you grab it?"

Grab his choker? She flung her head back and forth. Who knew what kind of shadowcraft lingered on it? She didn't want to turn into a goop monster.

"Oh, come on. Grab the choker," Khalid said.

"I'm not touching it!"

"I don't want it!" Valentine cried. His voice was raw, like a child just finished a tantrum. "I won't wear it."

"You've got to wear it, friend." Khalid cast a wary glance over the hedges back to the huge windows leading into the ballroom. "If one of the professors sees this, you'd be lucky to be expelled if not executed."

Val fixed Khalid with a lilac stare. "I can control it." As if to prove it, the black goop limbs retracted, sucking back into his body as if they had never been at all. Until he was just a regular boy with black tear stains down his face.

Khalid offered a charming smile. "Valentine, dear, you're drunk."

Valentine ran a tongue over his thick lips. Blinked lazy eyes. Then snarled, "It's a party, Khalid. Of course, I'm drunk. We're all here to worship fucking *Greywick*." With the last word, his gaze shot toward Marion.

Oh, if that little freak wanted to dance, she'd dance. She returned his snarl with perfect accuracy. "Say another word about my brother, eggplant, I dare you."

Val's eyes widened. "What did you call me?" He looked to Khalid. "What did she call me?"

"I think she said 'excellent pal'. Now about that choker—"

"I called you eggplant," Marion snapped. "Because of your stupid purple hair."

Val let out a cry like a hunted animal. He clutched the ends of his hair. "Khalid, you cruel monster. You bring her here to mock me?"

A sick satisfaction washed through Marion, though Khalid looked like his jaw might snap if it got any tighter.

"Your hair is beautiful. We all know it." He shot a pointed look at Marion. "Tell him his hair is beautiful."

Hah! That would be the day. She crossed her arms, stuck her nose in the air.

Val flung himself across the marble bench. Now shadows emerged around his body, circling him like eels. "What does it even matter? Everything is ruined. I hate him, Khalid. I *hate* him."

Something squeezed inside Marion's chest at the pain in his voice. How could it be possible? Timothée had done nothing to deserve such hatred. Unless it wasn't about Timothée at all.

Delicately, she stepped forward and crouched down to be near Val's head. "Why?"

He bared his teeth. "They dress him up like he's got power, like he's even done a single thing except glow." His voice was hoarse. "He's too fucking scared to take off his choker."

"Which you should put on presently." Khalid picked up the strip of fabric with the metal clasp at the back.

"It doesn't matter." Valentine dropped his head back on the marble. "Everything is pointless."

Marion sighed and rubbed at the gooseflesh on her arms. "Look, I know you're some great prodigy. I've heard all about your wonderful potions. I understand it must have been hard to be special for a moon then suddenly… we appear. Timothée didn't ask for this if that makes it any easier."

"It doesn't," Val mumbled through his hair. He pushed up, stared into the windows of the ballroom. "I can't stand the thought of him in there, in *that* armor, parading around like it's nothing but a costume."

Marion furrowed her brow. *Why does he care so much about the armor?* Val hadn't struck her as an overly pious type.

Khalid crossed his arms, said, "That's kind of the point of All Hallow's Eve." Then he looked up at the stars. "I see the problem now."

"And what's that?" Valentine said dryly.

"You're jealous." Khalid smiled. "We already know he took your importance in this school, and now everybody's eyes are on him. Half the ballroom wants to fuck him, and the other half just hasn't admitted it to themselves."

"Ew!" A gust of wind blew through the bushes, rustled the leaves on Marion's dress. She stood and smacked Khalid's arm. "That's my brother."

"Come on!" Khalid threw his arms out to the side. "He dressed himself up as the most forbidden and fuckable god that ever lived."

Marion wrinkled her nose. "Double ew. Apparently, that's *also* my brother." She exhaled. She wanted to go back in and enjoy the party. After all, this was her night to relax. "Look, I'm freezing. And I don't want to leave Timothée in there too long unattended."

Khalid took off his hat with the lovely white feather and placed it on her head. His smile sent a shiver up her spine. "You go in. I'll find you soon."

She cast a look behind her at Val. He was making little shadows dance on his lap then destroying them. Dance, destroy. Dance, destroy. "Be careful," she whispered. "I don't trust him."

"Don't worry. Val and I have an understanding."

She nodded and headed toward the ballroom. A strange, uneasy feeling sat in her stomach.

*"I hate him."*

But the words hadn't been said with hatred.

They'd been said with love.

# 23
# IN WHICH TIMOTHÉE DANCES ACROSS THE STARS

**A**S IT TURNED out, a lot of people wanted to dance with a god. And he was pretty sure it wasn't the god Timothée Greywick, who glowed on moonless nights and only survived the Dark Prophet by sheer luck. It was the god he was pretending to be.

Timothée swirled around the dance floor with everyone from first to fourth-years and even one of the cooks who said she needed to get her scare in for the night.

And not a single person called him by his name.

*Noctis.*

*God of Shadows.*

*King of Vampires.*

Everyone certainly knew a lot about his notorious dead brother.

And now, so did Timothée. Every day after class, he'd gone back to the Dark Star tower, devouring the tales of Noctis: his conquests and struggles, his desire to create, and his ever-present friction with his mother. *Their* mother. Noctis may not have been good, but Timothée had grasped an essence of him between the lines of legends. A god with the magic to destroy, who tried to use it to create, whose creations had been hated and hunted.

Being hated... *That* Timothée could understand.

A waltz slowed to a stop, and Timothée stepped away from his latest dance partner, a handsome second-year Morning Star. He had deep black hair pushed back from his forehead with a pair of fawn ears.

"Hopefully I'll see you later," he whispered in Timothée's ear. "This dance was fun, but I know how to make a heart beat in ways a waltz never could."

Timothée's stomach flipped over itself. That wasn't the first offer he'd gotten tonight. He watched the Morning Star boy walk off. A crowd still hovered at the edge of the glass dance floor, waiting. For him.

"I need a drink," Timothée mumbled and tried to weave his way through the crowd.

He didn't need to.

The crowd parted before him.

He couldn't blend in like he was used to. The boots added an inch of height to his already tall frame, and the wide shoulders and cape simply demanded space.

One thing this bold and beautiful costume didn't change was his voice or the way he held himself. He could almost hear Carmilla telling him to walk straighter.

*Is this what you wanted?* he thought absently, directing his thoughts to the castle. *For me to parade around and look ridiculous all night?*

The castle didn't answer back, but there was the slightest shift in the lights, a blink. A satisfied emotion rolled through Timothée. *I guess that would be a yes.*

Timothée searched the crowd until he saw his sisters over by the table of sweets.

Marion loaded up a towering plate of hard candies and pie and caramel apples before she led him to a quiet corner. Vivian placed a glass of water in his hands, and he drained it gratefully.

"How long was I out there?"

"Almost an hour," Marion said. "That armor is quite the fixation."

There was something about her tone he couldn't quite read. "You two must be getting so many compliments on your outfits. Your ears look great."

"Well, you can't very well be an elven queen without pointed ears." Marion ran a finger along the sharp ridge. "Don't worry, all this will go away at sunrise."

"Darius got his ears pointed too." Vivian smiled.

Timothée searched the crowd until he saw the Prince. It took a while to place him because his hair had been enchanted with magic. It was now a rich earthy brown, tucked behind pointed ears. He wore a woodland tunic with a finely crafted woven belt. "Ahh, Zacarius the elf and Daisia, the Sapphire Ranger."

Vivian smiled. "You need me to hunt something for you, little brother?" She touched the fake wooden bow on her back. Her costume consisted of a brown vest over a glittering blue tunic and black pants. They were stained with mud as if she'd been in the forest.

"A human and an elf." Timothée grinned. "Very star-crossed lovers of you two."

Vivian's smile wavered for a moment. *That hit a little too close.* He picked up a piece of pie.

"I saw Viv on the dance floor," he said. "But where were you, Mare?"

Marion stabbed the cherry tart on her plate. "I was, uh, getting air."

"With Khalid?" he teased. She'd tucked Khalid's pirate hat onto the seat beside her.

"Never mind that." She picked at a leaf on her dress. "You just... You just have a good time tonight, okay? Don't let anyone ruin it for you. You deserve to have a good night, Tim."

He stared at her, her crafted green eyes strange and unsettling. "Uh, yeah, okay."

"Speaking of dancing," Vivian said, "your crowd is getting impatient."

Timothée shoved a huge bite of pie in his mouth. The flavor was delicious, full of nutmeg and cinnamon. "Ugh, I guess."

A part of him wanted to fade into the background of the party like he normally would. Or take a huge plate of sweets back up to his room and place Yvaine on his lap and curl up with a good book. But Carmilla had a plan. *They* had a plan. After this, maybe people wouldn't treat him like he was normal... but they would treat him differently.

*Embrace what you are.*

Timothée cast one last look around the ballroom. *Where are you?* He hadn't seen Val for the last hour. He was no longer at the drink table, and he hadn't danced with anyone all night. And he definitely wasn't in the crowd waiting for Timothée to return.

"Lover boy went outside to get some fresh air." Khalid swaggered up, resting an arm on Marion's shoulder. He gestured to the huge double doors leading to the garden. "He was in such a state he rebutted even an offer of a dance from me! That boy knows how to break a heart."

"Val left?" Timothée put the plate of pie down. He wasn't hungry anymore. Of course, Val would think himself above the ball. "Is he okay?"

"He's fine! I checked on him. You know Val. Parties aren't exactly his thing, especially when they're not centered around him. Besides, you've got a whole bustle of people waiting to dance with you," Khalid said. "I can't even get one thorny druid to take a poor scoundrel's hand for a simple waltz."

"You know I don't dance." She rolled her eyes. "I'm going to the washroom."

Timothée bid goodbye to his sisters and made his way back over to the dance floor like a prisoner condemned, where he was immediately surrounded by Starlings waiting to dance.

So, he danced.

He twirled back and forth amidst the low sounds of the orchestra. He wanted to enjoy this moment, when everyone's eyes were on him, to truly feel like a god among mortals. But his heart refused to beat.

Maybe it was the fact that he knew all the attention had to do with his armor, or maybe it was something else.

As the night wore on, he decided he didn't want to be Timothée Greywick anymore anyway. He didn't want to think about what was bothering him. And he truly lost himself in the sounds and the steps and the revered looks. The long grazes of fingers down his arms, palms pressed against his hard chest, sensual whispers of the most intimate desires.

The darkness he'd brought on this haunted night was transforming the ballroom, transforming him. And no matter how many times he moved from end to end of the dance floor, there was always more people wanting him: to press against, to whisper at, to touch, to dance.

Between the songs, Starlings fed him tastes of cakes and pies, and begged him to lick the sugar off their fingers. They handed him drinks of bubbling sour apple liqueur and wine so sweet it tasted like nectar. They ran their hands along his hair and the ridges of his face and told him he was too beautiful to be real, and he wanted to tell them his face had always looked like this, that he hadn't changed at all.

He'd always been here.

But for some reason, he was starting to doubt that.

Stars shifted overhead, showering them with new constellations through the glass ceiling. And he was taken up in a feisty foxtrot with an Evening Star girl, whose gown of roses blew pink petals into the air as he twirled her.

The ballroom doors burst open, blowing in cold air and fog and all the shadows of an eerie autumn night. And standing in the center was the dark silhouette of Valentine Sun.

If the ballroom had been still when Timothée came in, it was now completely frozen. The only sound was Val's footsteps and the *drip, drip, drip,* of blood.

Val's lilac hair was windswept, and there was a rip in his shirt. A red slash across his palm scattered blood onto the floor.

The crowd parted before him. Students stepped back, forming a path that led straight to the middle of the ballroom. Straight to the dance floor.

And unfortunately, straight to Timothée.

He didn't think he'd ever been so afraid in his entire life.

Val stopped in front of him and the Evening Star girl. His gaze roved over them as if he were critiquing a less than impressive piece of art. A casual stance, as if he hadn't just brought the entire student body of the Celestial Academy to a standstill with his entrance.

"Move," Val rasped.

The Evening Star girl scrunched up her nose. "Do you know how long I waited for this dance?"

"Move."

From the corner of his vision, Timothée saw the Evening Star girl looking at him, but he couldn't be sure, not with Val standing there.

The girl made a sound of indignation before huffing off, and then it was just him and Val and nothing else in the entire world.

"That's better." Val gave Timothée a look as mischievous as it was deadly.

"Val," Timothée stammered. "Your hand—"

Val placed his bloody palm on Timothée's neck. The other hand tangled in his long dark hair, and then with a wild glint, Val stood on his toes and kissed him.

# 24
# IN WHICH MARION HEARS A REGRETFUL LULLABY

ARION STEPPED OUT of the luxurious washroom located in the corridor outside the ballroom. It was quiet and dark here, with the faintest din of laughter and music coming from the ballroom's double doors. It was good to have a moment of quiet; surrounded by people, she had trouble sorting her own thoughts.

As she started walking back, another sound drifted down the hall. A woman's voice, low and melodic. A song that transcended the music from the party. And it was coming from the opposite direction.

Marion cocked her head. It sounded strangely familiar, yet she was sure she'd never heard it before. Only felt it.

Slowly, she stepped toward the sound, her glittering green gown drifting across the foggy floor.

The song became clearer, the ethereal voice flitting like flickers of a candle. The song was in an unfamiliar language, no words she recognized from Liturgical or any of the three traditional tongues. Corridor after corridor, Marion traced the music, her speed increasing.

Surely, she'd heard this song before. She could almost complete the lyrics, even though she didn't speak the language—

She turned into an alcove full of portraits. Archpriestess Kassandra stood before a painting, singing. She wore a white dress with wide sleeves; it may have been called plain, save the obvious fineness of the fabric. Her white-blond hair was done up into three cones upon her head, resembling the spikes of a crown. She held that hideous staff tight with both hands.

Tears streaked her face.

*Oh bother.* Marion stepped back quietly, wanting to escape unspotted.

Archpriestess Kassandra turned, stopped singing. "Marion."

"I'm sorry to disturb you. I was just heading back to the party." Marion spun on her heel, expecting the Archpriestess to stop her from leaving. But she didn't.

*The blood remembers.*

Marion turned back to her. "Archpriestess, I don't mean to pry, but that song... What language was it?"

Kassandra quickly wiped her face with her sleeve, appearing almost embarrassed. "Oh, the song? It's a silly thing from the first language."

"The first language?"

"Yes." Archpriestess Kassandra sniffed. "The language spoken by the stars."

A language spoken by the stars, something older than the three traditional tongues. "I've never heard of it." Marion stepped closer. And yet, it had felt so familiar. "What does it mean?"

Kassandra turned to the portrait before her. "It's a lullaby. Something a mother would sing to her child."

Marion followed her gaze. A painting of Noctis, the same one Timothée had shown her their first night at the Academy. Now, having seen Tim done up in shadows and darkness, it could have been an exact portrait of him.

The alcove suddenly felt cold, and Marion wrapped herself in her arms. The painting depicted the God of Shadows victorious among a battlefield of bloody bodies. Of course the sight effected Archpriestess Kassandra. She was a disciple of Rhaemyria, who had waged war after war against Noctis.

Seeing him personified tonight was truly the epitome of evil for someone as pious as Kassandra.

Almost tenderly, the Archpriestess ran a slender finger across his oil face. "Noctis has a tragic story, you know. More tragic than you'd think from what they write in their history books or teach in lectures."

"He hurt so many people," Marion said.

"Not always." Kassandra's ice-blue eyes shone. "For an age, he was beloved by the people. He was a curator of the arts, of sports and games, and held a fierce sense of justice. How they adored him, idolized him. How they loved him."

And Marion knew it for truth, for she had seen it in her vision at Bøgelund. She and Vivian and Timothée standing before a crowd, but it hadn't been them at all, but Rhaemyria, Xydrious, and Noctis. She had felt the people's reverence.

"And he was beloved by the other gods," Kassandra continued. Her fingers clutched harder at the oil painting. "He was a blessing. A god conceived by mortal terms. He was a savior born from flesh and blood."

Marion took a step back, the coldness of the alcove creeping through her thin shoes and up her legs. "I suppose love wasn't enough to cure the darkness inside him."

Kassandra closed her eyes. "Maybe it could have been. He was beloved by his parents too. Maybe they should have told him that more." Then she threw her head back with a tinkling laugh, tears cascading off her face. "Or so I have heard in my revelations from the goddess. Isn't it an odd thing, Marion?" She turned to her fully. "That even the creator of our world can hold regret?"

Marion's vision sat heavy in her skin. "Perhaps the gods are more mortal than they'd like to admit."

A small smile quirked on the Archpriestess's ethereal face. "Indeed." Her hand dropped from the oil painting, and she cupped Marion's cheek. "I understand it's been hard for you to find your place here at the Academy, Marion. If you need anything at all, please do not hesitate to come to me." Her lip trembled and her next words came in a rushed exhale: "You are beloved too."

They were just words. And yet, something quaked in Marion's heart.

Was it true, Professor Barracus's theory? Had her father loved Kassandra many years ago?

"From the ashes. The Morning Star words. They suit you." Kassandra released a deep sigh and turned again to the portrait. "You should get back to your party. Have fun with your classmates. Be merry."

A strange sadness settled in Marion's chest. "May the skeletons dance and then sleep," she whispered.

Kassandra sighed. "If only that were possible."

# 25
# IN WHICH VIVIAN FEELS THE HAUNT OF THE HUNTER'S BLOOD MOON

VIVIAN COLLAPSED TO her knees. Each drop of Valentine Sun's blood hitting the glass floor was as loud as a thunderclap. No one noticed her fall to the floor, not with the Dark Star boy's mouth overtop of her brother's.

Her mind rung. Where was Darius? Her gaze swept across the ballroom. He'd gone to get drinks, but now he was staring stunned and stupid at the scene playing before them. Marion had left for the washroom a while ago and hadn't come back.

All she could do was look at the long trail of blood splashed across the glass floor. The scent of it filled every part of her mind.

*Your self is at war,* the castle's voice boomed. *And the god is losing.*

She splayed her fingers across the edge of the dance floor, looking through the glass to the swirling clouds below.

*Gods submit to no one,* the castle whispered, *no matter the strength of the blood.*

Nausea roiled through her. Her fangs sat heavy in her mouth, but it wasn't hunger she felt from the scent of this blood. It was something deeper, more primal—

"Hey? Are you alright? Let me get you out of here." Strong arms lifted her up and led her through the crowd. And it wasn't until she was halfway across the ballroom that she realized it was Erik Borstigsson—Darius's Dark Star cousin—that had his arms around her.

The rushing of her head stopped as they entered the quiet hallway. Erik kept a firm hand on her arm, and she touched the cold stone wall to steady herself.

"I know lots of girls get sick at the sight of blood," Erik said. "Thought you might need to leave."

Vivian nodded and blinked her eyes, vision slowly clearing. With growing horror, she realized Erik was dressed as a vampire. Painted red blood splashed around his mouth, and he wore a long indigo cape, the emblem of a bat hastily sewn on his black jerkin.

How had he felt when her little brother showed up, looking like the embodiment of Noctis himself?

And as she thought it, the castle laughed alongside in her mind.

"What a disgrace." Erik shook his head. "I know all the professors are spineless, but they just stood there gaping. Not one of them tried to stop that little show Valentine put on."

Little show. It hadn't felt so mundane. There had been an intensity in Val's eyes unlike anything she'd seen before.

"Can't speak to me after I saved you?" Erik quirked his head, mousy brown hair catching in the crystal light.

But she couldn't speak to him. Couldn't open her mouth. Her fangs hadn't retracted, despite being far from the blood. As if some deep, primal part of her still registered danger.

"I'm not mad about that match."

*When I kicked your ass?* When it had felt like her body had not been her own. When she'd had the vision of blood and sand.

"I'm curious about what power you used. I know Darius didn't teach it to you." Erik's voice dropped dangerously low. "My cousin may know how to wield a blade, but I've never seen him move like that."

She shook her head back and forth, the only signal she could give. She wanted him to leave, to get back to her dorm room, and crawl under the covers of her bed until these cursed fangs finally went away. Until she couldn't smell the lingering scent of Valentine's blood.

Vivian ducked to move away from him, but Erik still gripped her arm. He tugged her back, hard enough she bumped her head against the stone wall.

He didn't notice.

"What is your godly secret? Think a nasty Dark Star isn't trustworthy?"

She shook her head, but he still didn't let go.

"You know who's not trustworthy? My cousin. That boy you've been dancing with all night. You don't know what he's really like," Erik sneered.

The Dark Star boy was slightly shorter than her, but right now she felt as small as a mouse.

"I can see it by the way you look at me. Like I'm some *monster*," Erik said. "You don't know what a monster is."

But she did. She knew better than anyone. And if he didn't let go of her soon, he would find that out.

"Come on now, little lost star." Erik tugged her hand. "I want to know what power you have. Would it be so bad to share that?"

She tried to move, but he pushed her harder against the wall, her weak body manipulated so easily. He placed his other hand on her neck. His gaze dropped, pupils dilating. "And what about the power in your heart?"

Her fangs felt too big in her mouth. Her heartbeat, wild with fear, froze her movements. What if she lost control?

What if she didn't?

"Tell me to stop if you don't enjoy it," Erik said lowly. "But I've been watching you. You can't be good all the time. You crave the darkness."

And she was silent. So silent. How many times had she held her tongue in Wolfhelm, when Mrs. Meryladon the candle shoppe owner had berated her, when Tilda Dovetail and her friends had whispered nasty gossip?

And now she was forced to be silent again.

But only her words were silenced.

Magic simmered beneath her skin. She needed to bring it closer.

As an Evening Star, she couldn't create water, only change it. But there was water all around her, inside her. Inside him. The temperature dropped.

Erik felt it. His eyes wavered, lip trembling. "W-what in the Three are you doing?"

If she couldn't make Erik stop touching her, she'd make it so he didn't want to. A thin layer of frost covered every inch of her exposed skin. Erik looked down at his hand, blue ice spreading from her fingers to his.

"What the fuck are you doing, you crazy witch?" He slammed her against the wall—her head rang. But inside, her star burned hot and wild. She'd freeze his feet so he couldn't move, couldn't run. Then she'd bite his arm, drink every last drop of his blood—

"You're as fucking mad as your crazy prince." Erik clutched his blue fingers. "Where the fuck is he, anyway?"

"I'm right here."

Vivian took the moment of Erik's distraction to dart away from him. Darius stood down the hall, Carmilla beside him. He was looking right at her.

"I found you."

*You found me.*

"What are you doing to her?" Darius stalked toward his cousin. He was dressed like a fictional warrior, and now he truly was one.

Erik looked down at his hand, fingers still frosted blue. "Your crazy girl froze my hand—"

But before Erik could finish, Darius drew back his fist and slammed Erik in the jaw. Hard. So hard, Erik collapsed to the ground. "You would be wise not to speak to her that way."

Carmilla danced around the two boys and arrived at Vivian's side. "Are you alright? Darius was worried when he couldn't find you. I was helping him look."

Vivian could only nod. Before them, Darius loomed over Erik on the ground, a wolf circling its prey. "Why did you choose that costume, cousin? It is a mockery of our kingdom."

Erik rose to all fours. Gods, that was blood in his mouth from where Darius had hit him. *No.*

"Dressed like those loathsome creatures, you laugh at our fallen." Rage radiated off Darius in waves. His eyes were so dark. She'd seen him this way once before: when the Dark Prophet attacked Wolfhelm.

"You disgrace the Störmberg name," Darius growled. "You mock the death of everyone that died that night."

Erik's shoulders shook with laughter. "Whatever emerged that night was as crazy as the Dark Prophet." Erik sat up, blood spraying from his mouth as he snarled, "I may be a Dark Star and never sit on the Andúrigardian throne, but do not think shadowcraft the only form of evil. You will bring ruin to Thraina, *my king.*"

Carmilla stepped forward, heels splashing in Erik's pooled blood. "Go slither back into whatever hole you crawled out of, Erik."

Slowly, he stood on wobbling legs, before staggering down the hall. Just before he rounded the corner, he narrowed his eyes and said, "This is far from over."

Carmilla placed a hand on Darius's arm. His breath was ragged, gaze black as the sky outside. "Go get some air. I'll help Vivian freshen up."

Darius swallowed, then looked across the space at Vivian. It was all she could do to nod. She needed to leave this hallway, get away from all the blood.

"Good." Then Carmilla grabbed her arm and led her to the bathroom.

Like all things at the Celestial Academy, the bathroom was spacious, filled with settees and elegant mirrors.

Vivian fell to the seat, put her head in her hands and breathed. Away from the blood, away from Erik, her fangs retracted.

"Erik is nothing but a worm with the arrogance of a hyena. But he can bite."

Vivian looked up to see Carmilla leaning close to the mirror, brushing red lipstick across her lips. She turned to look over her shoulder. "But you did well. I don't think he'll bother you anytime soon."

Her voice was raspy, throat dry: "I felt so afraid."

Carmilla sat beside her on the settee. She wore a blue dress like crackling lightning that hugged her body. "Fear," she said, "can be as powerful as bravery."

"Then I must be the most powerful person here." Vivian laughed. "I'm afraid of everything."

Carmilla didn't break her gaze. "You Greywicks... You have no idea what I'd do for the power you have."

Vivian studied the former imperial princess, but Carmilla shook her head, said: "Let's fix you up. There's a rabid prince out there, and you're the only person able to calm him."

Vivian said nothing, smoothed an invisible wrinkle on her trousers.

"You're dressed as a book character, aren't you?" Carmilla pinned up the pieces of Vivian's hair that had fallen. At Vivian's nod, Carmilla continued, "Val loves those books. Reading was one of the first things he started doing again."

"Started doing again?" Vivian questioned.

"When I first met Val, he was different. Sad. The type of sadness that eats at everything you are. For a while, I didn't think he'd ever break out of it. I mean, he's still unhinged, as you've seen tonight. But that sadness is gone. Or very well hidden. Close your lips."

Carmilla dipped a small brush in a tiny pot of red, then brought it to Vivian's lips. "I think this color will suit you." She leaned in close,

and Vivian smelled the scent of her, honeyed and peppery, with a tinge of apricots. Her heartbeat was so steady.

The black Dark Star choker tightly wrapped around her thin white neck, and Vivian realized Erik hadn't entirely been wrong. *You crave the darkness.*

Carmilla pulled away, a knowing smile on her lips. "There. All done."

Vivian gathered herself, then looked back at Carmilla. "You know Valentine better than anyone. What's he doing with my brother?"

Carmilla smirked. "You saw it for yourself, little bird. Valentine is kissing a shadow."

# 26
# IN WHICH TIMOTHÉE REPEATS HISTORY

WHEN TIMOTHÉE HAD caught his star, when it had leapt down his throat, he thought nothing would ever come close to that scorching heat, the sensation that had taken over his body and lit every nerve on fire.

Val's kiss left it all behind.

Val was *kissing* him.

Timothée could have choked on his surprise. Died from it. His heart raced out of his chest, blood humming in his ears. He tasted sour apples and pomegranate and starlight. Val tugged hard on his hair, and fingernails raked over his neck, and Timothée couldn't breathe, and he never wanted to.

He gasped for air and Val broke away, falling back down to the ground, a curved grin on his face. A bloody handprint streaked across the front of Noctis's gravastarium armor.

And Val didn't look satisfied. He looked ravenous.

*Why? Why? Why?* He stared at the flashing expressions over Val's face. Not one made sense.

Timothée opened his mouth, closed it.

Val laughed and said: "It seems I skipped your line." And he took Timothée's hand in his.

"You want to dance?"

"We're at a ball, aren't we?" Val looked down. Sky and sea swirled beneath the glass floor.

"What?" Timothée stammered. "Afraid of falling?"

"Incredibly."

Timothée put a hand on Val's waist. He'd always been much taller than Val, but in this armor, the difference was staggering.

He glanced over at the orchestra, caught the stunned faces of the crowd. But mercifully, the music rose in cadence.

"Everyone's looking at us," Timothée said as they moved into step.

"Everyone's been looking at you all night." There was a bitter rasp to Val's words.

*So, you did see me.* Timothée wanted to touch his lips, wanted to ask Val a million questions, but it felt like they were dancing along the edge of a knife.

As they moved across the ballroom, he realized Val knew the steps far better than he did.

The song came to a close so fast—and Timothée's heart shuddered with it. *Are you going to leave now?* But Val cast a withering look at the waiting crowd and did not remove his hand.

"Unless you'd prefer to dance with one of them." His smile was positively wicked.

Timothée managed to shake his head.

The music picked up. They fell into the rhythm of another dance, and Timothée finally found his head clear enough to properly look at Val. Ripped shirt, blood around his choker, twigs stuck to his hair and clothes, and black smudges ran down his cheeks and rimmed his red eyes. *Was he crying?*

"What happened?" Timothée gestured to Val's hand, the one still bleeding all over his armored glove.

"Paper cut."

So, he was going to be like that. Timothée wanted to press more but changed his tactic. "Are you just dancing with me because you're bored of sleeping with Melissa?"

Val blinked. "Who?"

"Melissa Cormick?"

Confusion crossed his features.

"You kissed her outside of the Secret Society of Starbound Exiles?"

"Oh." Val laughed. "Her. She got annoyed right after you went inside."

"What? Why?"

Val just shrugged.

Dancers now circled them on the floor and conversation bubbled in the air, but there was a melody to the words, whispers as loud as any song.

Two names repeated over and over and over.

"They're whispering names," Timothée said. "Noctis and... the Prophet of Stars. Why?"

Val tilted his head back and laughed and laughed and laughed.

"What?"

"Don't you remember that book you read?" Val narrowed his eyes. "Let me remind you."

Then he looped his arms around Timothée's shoulders, pushed himself up and placed his lips to Timothée's neck, right over the bloody handprint. Val's mouth opened, long wet drags across Timothée's throat.

The sensation was igniting, and he grasped Val's shirt in his armored hand. Val fell back, and Timothée realized his dance part-ner had been lifted entirely off the ground. The song picked up. He dipped Val back. They were nose to nose, and blood was splashed across Val's mouth.

"Now, do you remember?" Val said with a red-lipped grin.

The image from the book flashed back: the Prophet of Stars, drinking Noctis's blood. And he remembered the castle's words: *The present is only ever an echo of the past.*

The look of Valentine in Timothée's arms, desperate, wild, tattered, lips blood-splattered... The sight of it did something to him.

Timothée had *never* felt want like this before.

He pulled Val up, somehow falling back into the dance. How he managed to find the steps was beyond him.

"Why are they calling us that?" Timothée asked.

"It's obvious, isn't it? Your *costume*. And," a slow smile spread up Val's lips, "the legends say the prince was the most beautiful person in all of Thraina."

"I think maybe it's the purple hair." Timothée laughed. But inside, he thought: *I couldn't imagine anyone, even a prince, being more beautiful than you.* "So now you've finally got a costume: the prince stolen for vengeance."

They twirled, stars spinning above and below.

"Or a prince stolen for love." Val looked up at him.

And Timothée realized something terrible as he looked down at Val's beautiful face, his eyes full of stars, his wild hair blowing with their movement.

"The tale of the prince with too many dreams," Val continued, "who prayed to the stars. But the stars turned out to be a man."

Timothée didn't remember anything about love in the text Taf read. But he was sure there were lots of legends.

Val ran his hands over the moon and star emblem on his armored shoulder. "What if it wasn't vengeance? Not at first. What if Noctis couldn't bear the thought of the mortal prince dying? So, he changed him. He couldn't make him a god, of course, but he... He made him something different."

"But if that's true, why didn't he stop at giving him the star? Why did he change him into a monster?"

Val's red lips quivered, and Timothée couldn't explain how, but he felt he was losing Val.

"So?"

"So?" Val echoed.

"So, how does it end?"

Val tousled Timothée's hair. "Who do you think I am, Setviren? Go ask him."

The song ended.

They didn't break away.

Val said: "How do you think it ends?"

Timothée dropped his hand. And looked down at his armor, the cape of shadows now pooled at his feet. "Well, even if Noctis made it so the prince didn't die... Noctis himself died. So, it's tragic either way."

"It is," Val said softly.

Timothée looked to the crowd around the glass floor. Was this where their dance ended?

A few people began heading toward him. In a heartbeat, he made a decision, grabbing Val around the waist and pulling him back against him.

"Again?" Val painted another red line down the armor with the palm of his hand.

"Tonight, I'm the God of Shadows," Timothée said. "It would only make sense I dance with the Prophet of Stars."

Val fell easily into step. "Then you don't know their history."

"What do you mean?"

"Noctis would never dance with the Prophet of Stars."

"Why not?" Timothée asked.

"The Prophet was his lieutenant. It wouldn't make sense to dance with your lieutenant, would it?"

"Weren't they lovers?" Timothée flushed the moment he realized what he'd said.

Val didn't miss it though, a wicked smile curving up his face. "Yes." The word sounded like a prayer. "They were."

Timothée's throat went dry. Was that how he and Val looked? Like lovers?

*You kissed me,* Timothée thought. *Kiss me again. And again.*

Timothée closed his eyes as Val's fingers explored his face.

"You are so ridiculously beautiful," Val whispered, a snarl to his voice.

Timothée shot his eyes open and grabbed Val's hand, returning it to his shoulder. Somehow, they didn't miss a step of the waltz.

"That's not good enough."

"What's not?" Val's purple eyes sparked.

"If I'm going to play this part, I want to do all of it right."

Timothée dipped Val back—but he didn't pull him up. He crashed his lips against Val's open mouth.

Something feral flashed in Val's grin as they rose from the dip, and he gripped Timothée's face. Val was chaos and beauty, a calamity of emotions and wild hair and flashing eyes, and Timothée wanted to lose himself in every part of it.

"I have never seen a look like that on *your* face." And then he licked Timothée's lips, trailed his tongue along his jaw to nibble at his ear.

Timothée gasped, grabbed Val's hair. He caught a glimpse of the rest of the ball, trying desperately to limp along. But he could see their eyes on him.

"We're making a spectacle." Timothée hadn't realized how low and raspy his voice had gotten.

"Isn't that what Carmilla had planned for you?"

"I don't think she planned on you." And the sight of Val's red-lined lips was too much. He lifted him off his feet and kissed him again.

Val writhed against him, and they lost all semblance of the dance. Their mouths came apart, bodies stayed pressed together.

"Good thing this armor is so thick." Val ran his palm along Timothée's thigh, swept it briefly along his hips before resting on his stomach.

But that brief contact—the sweep of it—had him blinking away stars.

The other dancers halted around them. But Val's lips were against his, tongue so deep in his mouth he almost choked on it. Val was practically crawling up his body, and Timothée knew his own hands weren't much better, drawing Val closer and closer and closer. And he wished he wasn't wearing these stupid gloves. He wanted—needed—to feel Val's skin.

Were they doing this? Kissing in the middle of the ballroom—in front of the entire school? In front of his sisters? And professors?

Some common sense still pulsed through him. "Maybe we should—"

"Don't stop." Val's voice shook. And he crashed his lips against Timothée's. "Don't stop. Noctis, don't stop."

Timothée pulled away. Val had called him Noctis. Everyone had been calling him Noctis all night. But it bothered him when Val said it.

Was that the only reason Val wanted him now? Because the school wanted him when he wore this dark armor? Like it was some sort of challenge to see who could bed a god?

"Ahh," a silky voice said. "Does the God of Shadows realize he is in fact a mortal and needs to breathe?"

Carmilla stood beside them. "It's my turn now."

"I'm dancing with him," Val said, not looking at her.

"Is that what that was?" Carmilla's voice trilled.

"He belongs by my side—"

"You're not yourself. You're drunk." Carmilla spat out the words.

Sour apple liqueur, that's what Val's mouth tasted of. Timothée could have kicked himself. He had seen Val indulging at the drink station.

He'd wondered why, and he'd gotten his reason. Val was drunk and wanted to have what everyone else wanted. Maybe if Timothée hadn't been so blind with desire, he would have seen it earlier. This was another one of Val's games, like the sewer and the forest and the bridge.

"And Timothée's not himself right now either, is he?" Carmilla ran a cloth over Val's blood-stained mouth before pressing it against his bleeding palm. "It's All Hallow's Eve after all, and we're playing pretend. Unless you think I'm really Niya, the lightning huntress?"

"I'm not leaving."

"Take a walk, *Prophet of Stars*." Carmilla's gaze drew up and down Val with great disdain. "I'll meet you for a drink later. The Three know you need it."

Val was still shaking, glaring at her.

Did she want Val for herself? A drink. *Sure.* Timothée wasn't stupid. He knew what that meant.

"But first," Carmilla placed her hands on Timothée's shoulders, "I'm going to have a dance."

Val pulled away, snarling. His lips were swollen, and he didn't look back as he stalked off through the ballroom.

And Timothée was pretty sure he was going to return to a destroyed dorm room.

Carmilla addressed the staring crowd. "Show's over," she trilled. "Now dance."

They settled into an awkward waltz, and Timothée realized Carmilla was leading. How embarrassing. But he couldn't regain his thoughts. He felt off-kilter.

"Timothée," she said, "do you know how many students could get away with what you did in the middle of the ballroom?"

He flushed. "I probably shouldn't have done that."

"No," she said, "and yet, no one stopped you. Not even Darius could have gotten away with that. No Starling here could."

"Then why—"

Carmilla looked up at him. "Tonight, you're not a Starling. Tonight, you're a god. And if we play our cards right, one day you won't have to play pretend to have all of this."

THE REST OF the ball passed in a blur. As the hours waned closer to midnight, the more desperate the attention for him—for the God of Shadows—became. And Timothée soon realized what all that attention could mean: a night of pleasure with anyone he wanted.

The idea enraptured him.

And he was furious.

Because the one taste he couldn't get off his mouth had gone for a *drink* with Carmilla.

Somehow, he made it out of the ballroom alone, 'no' coming off his mouth in waves. All he wanted to do was go back to his room and be angry all by himself with his cat.

Archpriestess Kassandra stopped him as he was heading for the Cauldron. She told him to leave the armor in Professor Barracus's office, and to not seek it out again. Before he could leave, she had gripped his face and stared at him long and hard until a single tear ran down her cheek. Then she bid him well.

Presently, he walked up the long stairs to his dorm. He felt strange without the armor: lighter, but there was a lingering weight there, as if he hadn't been able to take all of it off.

Timothée pushed open the door to his room. Yvaine slept before a purple crackling fire, and Valentine was lying on his bed.

Val sat up suddenly, eyes wide with surprise. His hair was damp, face clean of smudges, and he'd changed, wearing now a loose pale top and pants.

Timothée didn't move from the doorway. "You didn't think I was going to come here tonight?"

"I didn't think you were going to come here tonight."

## 27

# IN WHICH VIVIAN GETS TANGLED IN THE TRUTH

**A**FTER CARMILLA LEFT the washroom, claiming she needed to check on Valentine, Vivian stayed alone for a few moments. Steadied herself. Checked her teeth in the mirror. All flat at least. And the lipstick Carmilla had put on her certainly was striking.

Vivian took a path to the garden. There, standing on a stone veranda looking over the Tealight Garden, was Darius. The pale autumn moon cast silvery threads in his starcraft-darkened hair.

"Darius," she said lightly.

He turned to her, and his face melted as he took her in. "Vivian."

She crossed to him, letting him cloak her in his arms. "Are you alright?"

"Am *I* alright? Are *you* alright? I can't begin to apologize for my cousin. And for my behavior… I lost my temper. I know you can handle yourself. I just want to protect you from everything."

She pulled away slightly and narrowed her eyes. "I was glad you came. I knew you would."

He led her to sit on the edge of the wide railing. Below, marble statues of the gods lined hedges and rose bushes. Autumn leaves crackled in the icy wind, and the music from the ball was a soft lilt across the breeze.

"Darius, you can tell me if you're not okay."

His gaze was cast on the stars above, peeking out from the drifting clouds. "What if Erik was right? What if my rule will bring ruin to Thraina?"

She shook her head. "I don't believe that. So what if you lost your temper? Erik is awful."

"I know I'm better than that."

"He knows what haunts you. It would be a wonder if it did not affect you."

"I can't feed the wolf." His hands curled into fists, knuckles white, then his voice dropped to barely a whisper: "All of Thraina depends on it."

"What do you mean?"

"I'm not yet king, not officially. So many people—lords, ladies, *vultures*—circle, waiting for me to fail."

"But you're the rightful heir. You're the last Störmberg."

"And they know it. My father's control over Kirrintsova was tentative at best. They were their own empire for hundreds of years. Now the people find living under the laws of Andúrigard a challenge. And without my father on the throne, there have been minor rebellions, nobles pushing for more land. And with the return of the Dark Prophet…" Darius trailed off. "At least Medihsa has complied with trade and regulations. But there's madness at court. Jeremysson Borstigsson does a fine job as steward. But Erik constantly pushes his boundaries and tries to inflect his own ideals on his father. I fear Jeremysson will ask for a prominent position of power for him when he graduates. And there will be ramifications if I deny it."

So many worries swirled behind his gaze. "They expect you to be both a student and a prince, with no room left for the boy."

"When I'm around you, it's the only time I feel…" He ran a hand through his hair. "You make me feel stronger than I ever have before."

She narrowed her eyes. "I do? How is that?"

"I have my theories. Did you know the history books say Störmbergs were Xydrious's favored line? That it was the Father God who bestowed the name of King on my ancient ancestors?"

She didn't. Father had rarely spoken of the royals, and never of the gods.

"It is said he bestowed many gifts on my kin, even those who did not catch a star." Darius tapped a finger beside his brow. "Our blue eyes are a trait of his. If you look at the portrait hall, our family line has the same color as far back as anyone can see. My father and my sister had the same."

"So, you're drawn to my magic." She tilted her head, hair falling over her shoulder. "Drawn to me for the Evening Star I caught?"

"It was a theory." Darius leaned closer. "But one I have dismissed. There is something I cannot name. Something stronger than the bond between gods and kings."

Her breath caught in her throat, because the truth of his words resonated in a place deep within her. The blue fluttering ribbon caught her gaze.

"I will always fight for my people, for them to have a bright future, free of suffering and tragedy. But…" He hesitated, as if not sure how much more to say. Then he gripped her hands and pulled her up to stand before him. "It is you who makes me want to live in that future. Your light and kindness. You make me believe I can achieve it all."

"You will, Darius," she said. "I know you will."

"I must endure until graduation. Then Carmilla will return to Kirrintsova, and Khalid to Medihsa, and we can provide a united front. The truly unified Thraina my father dreamed of so long ago when he adopted Carmilla and Khalid into the family."

Carmilla and Khalid would return to their homes, but as vassals of Andúrigard, not true rulers of their nations. Or would Darius change that?

"They know you can do this, as I do." She trailed her fingers over the blue ribbon he wore around his wrist.

"The darkness will leave me one day," he said, gaze still skyward.

"When?"

"When I kill the Dark Prophet."

There was a terrible purpose in his voice. Her thoughts turned inward, dark and creeping. *What would he do if he knew?* She looked down at their hands threaded together. His were so much larger than hers, calloused fingertips rough on her skin.

But her body didn't react with fear as she thought of his strength versus her own. Her stomach tightened, heat dipping low in her core.

"Darius," she said. "Dance with me."

His gaze softened. "I can still hear the music."

"Until it ends."

They stood, and he kissed her lips once before she lay her head against his chest. For a moment, she enjoyed the beat of his heart instead of craving it.

He twirled her around the veranda, in and out of the orange light. There was hatred in his heart, that much was surely true. But she had seen him and knew there was love too.

Love for his kingdom, for Khalid and Carmilla, and... love for her.

And somehow, she knew deep within her own heart, love would outweigh anything. Even the truth.

The song dwindled to a stop, and he pulled back to look at her. His blue eyes sparkled in the starlight.

"Darius," she whispered. "There's something I have to tell you."

He tilted his head, hair spilling across his brows. "Anything, my darling."

*Anything.* She believed it.

"Darius, the truth is..."

Blackness passed over her vision, and between one breath and the next, something distinct changed within her.

There was humming in her blood. She stumbled past Darius, as if tugged by an invisible rope. When she looked out into the inky landscape of the Isle of Argos, all she saw was darkness.

*You crave the darkness.*

"Vivian?"

"It's nothing."

She turned, rubbing her neck. Darius's eyes widened, looking past her. "There's something in the air."

# 28

# IN WHICH TIMOTHÉE POISONS VAL

TIMOTHÉE STEPPED INTO the room. He had no idea what happened now. Did they continue as roommates, barely speaking? Or as dance partners, with their lips all over each other's faces?

Timothée shook his head. Of course, it was the former. The dance floor had been a game to Val.

Val lay back down on the bed, indifference playing across his features. He tossed a shadow ball up and down in his hands, choker discarded on the bedside table. "How did you make it past all your adoring fans with your clothes still on?"

"I did lose some." Timothée crossed to his dresser. Without the armor, he felt vulnerable.

Val tossed the black ball up and down, up and down. "You could be worshipped in any number of Starlings' beds right now."

"You can drop the act. I'm not playing dress up anymore."

"What do you mean, Morbis?" Val's face was clean and bare and unreadable as always.

As upset as he'd been when he'd left with Carmilla, Val seemed fine now. Maybe she'd calmed him down. Or maybe he really hadn't cared that much about dancing with Timothée.

And the room was intact, so he couldn't be that upset.

Timothée sighed. "Just admit you wanted to beat everyone who thought they could spend a night with a pretend god."

Val laughed. "Pretend? Are you not a god?"

"Not like he was. Noctis grew up in the stars. I grew up in a shack. But when I was dressed up, it was enough for the school to want me. Or maybe I imagined that."

"You didn't imagine it." Val let his shadow ball dissipate, sat up. "When I stepped into that room, do you know what I saw? They were all dripping with it."

"With what?"

"Desire. Desire for you to—"

"To be theirs?" Timothée almost laughed, it was so ridiculous.

"No. For you to make them yours. You're a god of darkness. You don't let anyone have power over you."

*You do.*

"Well," Timothée said, "you don't have to pretend anymore; I know you just wanted to prove something—that you could win or whatever."

"And I did win, didn't I? You're here. With me."

"I thought you'd be with Carmilla."

"I was," Val said simply. "For a little while."

Timothée did not want to imagine the details. He clutched the edges of the dresser.

"I am curious though," Val said. "You had the entire school willing to drop to their knees in front of you, and yet you're here... with no one. Why?"

*Because kissing anyone after you would have been as pleasant as kissing a thorn bush, and any other touch would have felt like sandpaper.*

But all he said was, "I was tired."

"Liar."

Timothée ripped open his dresser with more force than necessary. "Drop it. I'm not in my costume anymore. And there's no one around for you to show off to."

Back to Val, he gripped the edges of his shirt and threw it off, dug in his dresser for pajamas.

And in an instant, he felt Val's presence as if someone had lit a fire behind him.

Then shivering down his back: Val's fingers, tracing over the ridges of his spine.

"Tell me the real reason you're here," Val murmured, then his wet lips replaced his hands.

Timothée tilted his neck back and stared at the ceiling, blinking back stars. "I told you."

Val inhaled a disappointed breath. His hands snaked around Timothée's waist. "Come on now," he chided, "it's not like we both don't already know."

Timothée's mind raged. Because he didn't know. Didn't know if he hated this beautiful, intoxicating boy or if what he had felt on the glass dance floor was *real*.

Val's hands dropped lower and slid along him, grazing his length. Timothée hissed in a breath, and Val laughed, clearly enjoying his torment.

"Tell me." Val drew his tongue along Timothée's back and to the edge of his ribs.

"Fuck you, Val."

Val ducked to get between him and the dresser, caging himself in Timothée's arms. "What an idea, Greywick."

Timothée remembered what Carmilla had said and the taste of sour apple on Val's lips. He pushed off the dresser and stepped away. "You're drunk."

"Not anymore." Val padded after Timothée. "You're very sweet worrying about taking advantage of me, but I can tell you I am sane of mind."

Somehow, Timothée doubted it. "Didn't you go drinking with Carmilla?"

"Jealousy's cute on you, Greywick. She sobered me up with a nasty bitter drink."

"So," Timothée said slowly, "you two aren't…?"

"No. But if you say please, I could ask her if she wants to join us."

Timothée went red from his feet to his head. "W-what, no!"

Val placed his mouth on Timothée's shoulder, dragging along his collarbone.

What was going on? Yesterday, Timothée could recall with perfect clarity every instance Val had touched him. And almost every time, Val had done it with a deep simmering regret. But tonight, it was like Val would burn without his touch.

"Okay, even if you're not drunk," Timothée shook him off, "Carmilla was right. You're not yourself."

"Carmilla doesn't know me, doesn't know us—"

"Us?" Timothée almost laughed. He reached into his dresser, drawing out his nightshirt. As soon as he did, it dissolved into a powder of shadows.

He whirled to Val. Black rippled around his curled fingers. "You look better without it."

"That was my favorite nightshirt."

"You have others." Val sat down on the edge of his bed. "So, are you going to fuck me or not?"

Timothée's heart flipped in his chest. He couldn't breathe.

Val smiled wider, no doubt relishing in Timothée's dumbfounded expression. He casually started unlacing his own shirt.

"No—stop." Timothée held out his hand. "No… I'm not—we're not. We can't."

But his mind raced with the idea of it. His body was already reacting to the premise, growing hard and desperate.

"Why not?" Val flicked his eyes up but didn't stop unlacing.

"One, because you were drunk earlier—"

Val rolled his eyes. "I'm not *now*."

"And two: no matter what Carmilla says, *I say* you're not your-self tonight."

"Maybe this *is* the true me."

"So, you're not normally mean and closed-off and distant? Your true self is horny and clingy?"

"Why not?" He shrugged out of his shirt then stood.

Timothée was transfixed by the pale canvas of his body, the line of purple hair that ran down between his sharp hip bones. Val was slim, but there were muscles in his arms and chest: long and lean from practiced movement.

Val stepped closer and Timothée realized he had nowhere left to go. He'd backed into his own bed.

Val stopped an inch away, stood on his toes, and kissed him.

It had only been a few hours, but Timothée hadn't realized how much he'd needed this, how much he'd been craving the taste of Val's lips. He moaned into the kiss, didn't care how desperate he sounded.

Val broke away with a satisfied smile, then leapt at him again, lips on Timothée's neck, sucking at the sensitive skin. The feeling was like descending all the way to the fire at the heart of the world: a scorching blur.

And maybe Val was right, maybe half the school did want some dark god for a night. But Timothée knew he only wanted one person. Wanted to kiss Val so deep he wouldn't ever think of kissing someone else in front of him again.

He gripped Val around the waist, then roughly tossed him to the bed.

Val fell in a heap, then pushed his hair from his eyes, and leaned back on his elbows. "You weren't very hard to convince, godling."

"I didn't say we were doing *that*."

"Then just kiss me."

Shadows pooled at Timothée's feet, but he wasn't afraid. Because they felt like Val. The shadows spiraled up and around his legs, urging him forward. Timothée let them direct his movement until he crawled on the bed, knees on either side of Val's hips.

The shadows fell away, and Val gave a satisfied smirk now he had Timothée where he wanted him. Timothée lowered his head, long hair he still wasn't used to falling in his face. "You're so beautiful, Val."

Val bucked his hips up against Timothée's and the friction was staggering. A low carnal sound emitted from the back of his throat as he ground his hips down. *Fuck*, he was hard, knew he was straining against his tight pants. Timothée ran his hand along Val's leg until he felt the shape of him through the soft fabric. He moved his hand up and down Val's length.

"Greywick, you're drooling."

Timothée closed his wide-open mouth. "I was imagining how it would feel to put my lips around you."

Val's fingers tangled tightly in Timothée's hair, and he bucked his hips up against his hand. "Yes, Morbis."

*Say* my *name*, Timothée thought.

Val followed his lead, reaching his hand down between them. He captured the shape of Timothée through his pants, running his hand up and down, up and down. Val bit his lip. "I suppose you had to be godlike in at least one way."

Timothée grinned and laid his forehead over Val's. He licked his way across his face, along his jaw. He'd never wanted to impress anyone the way he wanted to impress Val, never wanted to take the time to explore, to savor.

His hand traveled further up Val's hips to his chest, but he stopped. The skin wasn't smooth like he had been expecting. He blinked, clearing his vision. Val's chest—it was covered in scars, old scars, fresh scars, large, small, all criss-crossing his body. The scars stopped abruptly at his forearm; while his upper arms were ravaged, beneath his elbow was smooth and soft.

Timothée began to speak. "Don't," Val said darkly.

Timothée grabbed Val's palm, where it had been sliced open earlier in the night. Now there was just a soft pink line.

"Starcraft," Val said by way of answer.

Timothée swallowed, but he said nothing. Instead, he brought Val's palm to his mouth and kissed it.

Val ripped his hand away. "Are you ready to do this yet, Greywick?"

"Not just yet," Timothée said. He knew he was stalling, but something didn't feel right. "I know exactly how I'd do it, if we did."

Val arched his back, letting his hands fall long above his head. "Thought about this before, disaster boy?"

"A little." Timothée traced patterns along Val's skin with the tips of his fingers. "I'd be slow. Very slow, and it would annoy you. Maybe you'd beg me to go faster."

"You want to see me beg?" Val cracked an eye open. His lilac hair tousled in front of his face.

"Slow touches, slow kisses…" He lowered, barely brushing Val's lips with his own. Val tried to deepen the kiss and Timothée lifted to his elbows, smirking.

Val fluttered his eyes closed and rubbed his hardness against Timothée's stomach. "I suppose I could beg for very good reasons."

"When we start," Timothée's hand drifted lower on Val's stomach, "it'd be inch by inch by inch."

Timothée circled his belly button, thumb brushing the line of hair between his sharp hipbones.

"When I'm inside you," Timothée leaned his lips down to Val's ear, "I'm going to make it last as long as I can, until you feel all of me, take all of me." He dipped his hands lower, just under the band of Val's pants. "And then we'll move and move, and it won't be slow anymore, and you'll beg in a completely different way, and once you're screaming and trembling, once you're mine, and limp and spent, then… Then I'll come inside you, and kiss you until you collapse in my arms."

Val pulled Timothée's hair so tight it hurt. His back arched, and his faced scrunched up, and he gasped as he came.

Timothée felt wetness over his hands, saw how it dampened Val's pants, spilled over his stomach. Val's chest heaved up and down. He blinked his eyes open, lips trembling.

They were staring at each other.

"Wipe that stupid expression off your face," Val said but there was laughter to his words.

"I made you come with just my words. Tell me that's not impressive."

"I'd say you'd get an ego, but it may be the one thing you've succeeded in at the Academy, so I suppose you can have that."

He grinned. "Anyone else ever do that to you?"

Val pushed him on the shoulder. "No one else is stupid enough not to fuck me when I ask them to."

Timothée leaned down and lapped up the wetness on Val's stomach. He looked up at him through his lashes. "I don't think that was stupid. I think it made you want me more."

Val blinked, stunned still as if entranced. Then he grabbed Timothée's face and pulled him up for a ravenous kiss.

"Do you have any idea how much I hate it when you're right?" Val broke away, slid his hand down Timothée's chest, over his pants, grasping at him. "You're so hard. I want you in my mouth. I need you inside me. Just like you said—*please*."

"I don't know, Val. Maybe not tonight," Timothée said, surprised by his own words. He had never been able to say no to anyone before. But then again, he had *never* wanted someone the way he wanted Valentine.

"I can beg. I can beg." Val looped his arms around Timothée's neck. "Fuck me now, Greywick."

Timothée sat up, bringing Val into his lap. "I don't need you to beg." His reflection danced in the lilac sky of Val's eyes. Wild long hair, swollen lips, makeup smudged. He looked lovesick.

Fuck.

He *was* lovesick.

"I just need one thing." Delicately, he wiped Val's hair back from his sweaty brow. Val closed his eyes, sighing into the touch. Timothée placed a kiss tenderly on each eyelid, worked his way down the side of his nose, his jaw, until they found each other's mouths. And this kiss was different from the others.

It was slow, exploring. He weaved his hands through Val's hair and Val's fingers dug into his arms. Their foreheads touched, dark hair tangled with light. "Call me by my name and I'm yours."

Val's breath hitched. He pulled away, no, *pushed* Timothée away. "What the hell was that?"

"A kiss?" Timothée said, confused. Though it had felt like more.

"Well, I told you to fuck me, not whatever the hell that was." Val stood up, staggered into the bathroom.

Timothée followed, waited outside the curtain. His cheeks burned. "Is it such a hard request? You never call me by my name. You call me Greywick, godling, Star Child, Morbis—whatever the fuck that means!" He heard water running, tried to scream over it. "You even called me Noctis!"

The water shut off. Val didn't come out.

Hot tears streamed down Timothée's face, and he brushed them angrily away. His mind desperately tried to play over the last few moments, to make sense of Val's sudden shift of mood.

But it was clear they had wanted two very different things from each other. He threw on a shirt and made his way to his study desk. Texts and half-finished potions lay scattered on top. With newfound fervor, he began to mix.

The curtain clinked open, and Timothée glanced over his shoulder to see Val had changed, his face splashed with water.

He turned back to his potion, taking the boiling mixture off the burner and straining it into a cup. Then felt the heat of Valentine behind him.

"Ahh," Val said, "the smell of poppy milk, lavender, and fire-snow. A sleeping draft. Managed not to explode it this time?"

The swirling mixture of purple and red sent curls of steam into the air. "I just want this day to be over."

"No. You just don't want to deal with me anymore." Val snatched the potion, drained it, and shoved the cup into Timothée's hands. "Now you can go back down there and fuck one of your little worshippers and have them scream your name 'til the sun rises."

Timothée stared down at the empty cup, then up at Val. There were tears pooling in his lilac eyes. "You're the one who stopped it!"

"No, you're the—" Val took a step forward, wavered, blinked. "Tim—"

Then he collapsed.

Timothée darted forward, barely caught him before he hit the ground.

"Val!"

Val stared up at him, confused. "What did you mix?"

"Uhh," Timothée stammered. "A sleeping draft? Professor Rosewyn said it was supposed to make you a little tired. Four parts fire-snow to one part lavender?"

Val choked out a laugh. "Other way, disaster boy."

Now his heart raced in a completely different way as he stared at the near limp boy in his arms. "Are you going to be okay? I can find Professor Barracus!"

"You're cute when you're worried." Val quirked a smile. "I'll be fine. I'm just going to have a *really* deep sleep."

"Are you sure?"

"You think I'd be this calm if I thought I was going to die?" Val asked. "Now help me up."

Timothée lifted him to his bed, but when he went to pull away, Val grasped his hand.

"What?"

"Are you actually leaving?"

Timothée sighed. "I've got so many people waiting to worship me."

Val's sleepy face fixed in a frown.

"No, I'm not going anywhere." Timothée hesitated, rubbed his thumb along Val's palm.

Val pulled, and then Timothée was on the bed with him again. But now Val's face wasn't lit with desire. He looked loopy with sleep and sadness.

"You better not hold this over me," Val said.

"What part? That I successfully poisoned you or that I had you begging for me?"

Val placed a hand on Timothée's jaw. "I know you won't."

"I'll forget it all. For one thing."

Val looked at him, confused.

"Just kiss me?"

Because he was pretty sure he would never kiss Valentine Sun after tonight, and he needed one last taste of him. One last kiss.

Val's fingers tangled in his hair, and he said: "I miss you."

Then Val kissed him, slow and long.

Timothée let the kiss grow sloppy, let his tongue slip into Val's mouth, and his lips glide off course to slide along the edges of his jaw.

"Now I wish I wasn't so tired," Val murmured.

"Me too."

Even though he knew it was for the best. Still, he would savor every moment with Val.

"You know," Val's fingers tangled in the back of his hair, "a bit of salt under my tongue and I'll perk right up."

"No one should have to endure that floral horror again." Timothée smiled against Val's wicked grin. "Plus, then I would have to move."

"That would be a problem." Val fell against him, movements heavy and slow as the potion worked its way through him. But it still felt like Val was fighting it, kissing him deeper, harder.

"Promise me you'll stay," Val whispered.

"Where would I go?" Timothée laughed.

"Just promise."

"I promise."

*I could kiss you forever and never tire of it,* he thought.

A crack sounded, and the door flew open. For a single flash, Timothée saw two figures, both with bloody daggers in hand. Then a sweep of darkness devoured them, cleaving their heads off in a cold strike.

Timothée startled, looked down to see Val's outstretched hand.

The squelch of blood dripped through the cracks in the floor.

"You…" Bile rose in his throat. "You killed two men."

"They didn't look friendly." Val's shocked expression mirrored his own as he gazed at the severed bodies on the floor.

A large boom sounded from outside, and a bright red light flashed from behind the curtains.

Timothée jumped up. Val fell flat against the bed, body going limp. "Shit, get me some salt, Greywick."

Timothée pulled back the curtains. Outside, the night sky was on fire. Dozens of floating airships circled the Academy, and alongside them, great winged creatures flew through the night. Down below in the courtyard, hundreds of soldiers stormed the front gates.

"The school," Timothée gasped. "It's under attack!"

More clatters and shouts sounded from down the stairs.

Val blinked his eyes rapidly. "Salt—" he demanded, then: "Check that one's hand."

Timothée knelt by the body. The body without a head. Picked out a piece of tattered paper from the limp hand. On it was a copied image, a hatch work drawing. A drawing of Vivian and Marion and him.

He showed it to Val, who could now barely move. "They're here for me and my sisters."

With incredible effort, Val pushed himself up. "Salt. Now."

Timothée's body made the choice before his mind could catch up. He shoved the drawing in his pocket. "I have to find my sisters. But no one's here for you. I don't want you to do something reckless for my sake and hurt yourself."

The look on Val's face could have killed, and Timothée felt shadows pool at his feet.

"You're not using shadowcraft on me." He swiped his hand, and they dissipated as if caught in a strong breeze. He registered only brief shock on Val's face before he shoved the choker around his neck. "I'm not letting you do something foolish like getting caught using magic."

"I *hate* you! You're so stupid," Val said, but his voice was so weak it was barely a whisper. "Timothée, don't do this."

"I have to."

Val's eyes shut; his head lolled to the side.

Timothée took a deep gasp, heard clangs and shouts from down the stairs. He needed to protect Val, then find his sisters. He carried Val into the bathtub. His body was limp, but his breathing seemed steady.

Then he ran back into the room, scooped up Yvaine, and placed her inside the bathroom. "I'm sorry, Val," he said, looking down at the sleeping boy in the tub. "I can't keep my promise."

Timothée shoved the dresser in front of the bathroom curtain, making it look as if the room simply went no further.

Then he stepped over the dead bodies and walked barefoot down the stairs.

The Cauldron was a calamity of chaos, students running, throwing vials, screaming, and there were more soldiers and mercenaries grabbing students, inspecting their faces.

*They're looking for me,* Timothée realized.

A mercenary caught his gaze from across the room and recognition shone in his eyes. He lifted his sword. Blood, there was blood on his sword, and he charged toward Timothée.

Fear rooted him to the spot.

The window shattered. A torrent of wind blew Timothée back, and a resounding boom echoed across the Cauldron as a giant monster landed on the ground.

Translucent wings, a furred hunched body, and a long snout with one glowing yellow eye. A giant bat.

The monster looked around and roared, "Where is Timothée Greywick?"

# 29
# IN WHICH MARION SPIES A PHANTOM FROM HER PAST

MARION YAWNED AND lay her head on the table, using Khalid's floppy hat as a pillow. The white feather tickled her nose. She had not done so much eating and drinking and mingling in her entire life. Though the sky outside was still dark, she knew dawn approached. She felt its nearness like a distant melody, a warm touch just waiting to caress the Isle of Argos.

The party was still in full swing, and she imagined people would celebrate All Hallow's Eve until the ballroom was flooded with light. Though, there was a different energy now. The dances had become more sensual, bodies pressed together. Pairs disappeared off to their dorm rooms.

*I wonder who started that,* Marion thought.

She sighed. Tim was going to get his heart broken by that strange Dark Star boy unless she did something. But she was always having to do things. Always having to meddle. Even Archpriestess Kassandra had wanted something from her that she didn't know how to give.

But it had been such a wonderful party. Maybe for tonight, it would be fine if she did nothing at all—

"You're drooling on my hat."

Marion shot up, blinking. Khalid sat beside her, a huge grin on his face. "So, you sleep with your mouth open, eh? Good to know. One time when we were children, Darius and I—well, mostly I, but he was there—snuck into Carmilla's room and placed a big fat spider in her mouth—"

"I wasn't drooling!" Marion shouted, wiping at her chin. "I wasn't even asleep. My eyes were resting."

Khalid touched her chin, winked. "Don't worry. A little drool doesn't bother me."

"You're impossible."

"Come on. Let's get you to bed."

Marion blinked instantly awake, not sure if there was a connotation behind his words or not. She let him drag her up with two hands.

"I can't believe we've been here all night and you wouldn't let me have a single dance." Khalid wrapped an arm around her shoulders. "And I thought we were friends."

Friends. What a mysterious word it was for them. "I told you, I don't dance."

"Do you want to say goodbye to Vivian?"

She nodded. After looking around for a few minutes, she glimpsed her sister outside the glass doors leading to the garden. Darius held her tight in his arms and they swayed to the hauntingly beautiful music in their own private dance. How slight and pale Vivian looked against Darius's huge shape.

"No, I don't think she'll notice if I'm gone." Marion smiled.

"Anyone else to say goodbye to, then?"

Marion looked around the ballroom. Timothée had pulled off his little stunt and long retired to his room. Carmilla had left for a while, then returned to be surrounded by her Dark Star worshippers—not that Marion wanted to say goodbye to her. Val was gone too.

Marion looked up at Khalid. His face was soft and tired, bright green eyes half covered by long lashes. "I only want to talk to you."

His hand ran along her crafted ear. "Then let's go home."

Home. The Morning Star dormitory. Yes, that sounded nice. With Khalid's arm around her, she thought tonight had not been so deeply unpleasant. Things may have been odd. But maybe odd could be a good thing.

They walked past the immense windows, heading up the stairs and out of the ballroom. A glint caught Marion's eye outside: something metal shining in the moonlight.

No. Lots of metal things.

She pressed her face to the glass. "What's out there?"

The ballroom was constructed at the back corner of the Academy, so it sat on the edge of the Isle of Argos. The Meadow of Shattered Stars lay in sight beyond the window. And glinting lights filled the field, flashes of steel.

People heading up the field toward the ballroom.

"Swords," Marion breathed. "And shields. Are they Celestial Knights?"

Khalid came up beside her. "No. They're not in formation. What's that in the distance?"

Marion peered past her own reflection. Three massive ships sat in the meadow. They looked like the wooden pirate ships out of a textbook, but they weren't on the sea. And instead of sails, they had white balloons emblazoned with a blue handprint framed by feathered wings.

More Starlings gathered around them and stared out the window.

"Is this part of the party?" Marion whispered.

Khalid's mouth twitched and then he snatched Marion's hand. "I don't think so." He looked behind him. "Professors!"

Setviren was already charging over. "Whatever is the problem?"

"Did you invite them?" Khalid grabbed the loremaster's arm and pulled him forward.

Setviren narrowed his eyes, stared into the dark. His face went ashen.

And then he screamed.

"THE ACADEMY IS UNDER ATTACK!"

Chaos erupted. Students began screaming, running to the window, running away from it. Marion's heart surged in her chest. "Under attack? The Academy can't get attacked! It's the bloody Academy!"

Suddenly, a bang exploded in the room. Professor Barracus stood on top of the grand piano, holding a bubbling vial. Everyone quieted and turned to stare at him.

"House leaders," he said, deep voice reverberating throughout the entire ballroom, "lead your houses back to your dormitories. Bar the doors and do not leave for any reason. The professors and Celestial Knights will handle this matter."

"Erik isn't here!" one of the Dark Star students screeched. "He's disappeared!"

"I'll lead you." Carmilla stepped forward, her face a grim mask. "Follow me."

Professor Barracus nodded. "Out the main doors. Straight to your dormitories. Now!"

A semblance of order formed as the house leaders for the Morning Stars, Evening Stars, and Carmilla began to lead their cohorts out of the ballroom.

Marion scratched at Khalid's arm. "We have to find Vivian. She's outside!"

He nodded. "Darius is there too."

They sprinted across the floor, pushing past the panicked students. Khalid heaved open the doors to the garden—

The glass windows erupted. Dark shapes flung themselves into the ballroom. Rough-clad marauders wielding hatchets and knives rolled onto the floor and sprung upward. Some held nothing at all. But each had a painted marking on their chest: a blue handprint with wings.

Glass rained down as the roof smashed open. Icy wind pummeled against her and the sound of beating wings echoed. Giant creatures plummeted into the room. Marion's legs went weak, her mind awash.

It couldn't be...

She had seen them in murals and oil paintings, in textbooks, and stained-glass windows in the cathedral...

But they didn't exist anymore.

Mythical beasts couldn't exist anymore.

And yet, the fabled animals—gryphons with eagle heads and lion bodies, and winged horses with jewel-tone eyes, and snakes covered in feathers—smashed toward them.

It was as if the entire ballroom took a deep inhale.

And then erupted.

Screams filled the air, students pushing and shoving, the sparks of starcraft bursting bright as cracking embers.

"Get the students out of here now!" Professor Barracus yelled at the house leaders. He ran forward, pulling from his jacket a spherical glass ball. He threw it at the marauders, and it exploded, sending several flying back.

Professor Kunuk ran into the fray. Great gusts of wind soared from her hands, pushing the winged beasts back toward the shattered glass ceiling.

And suddenly Setviren was behind Marion, face as green as his hair. "Where are your siblings? I'll see you to safety."

Marion's heart thrummed in her chest. A moment ago, she had been asleep on a table. Now her body was in the tight mob of students, desperately trying to escape the ballroom.

"Out here!" Khalid forced open the door and pushed Setviren and Marion through.

"Who are these people? Is it the Dark Prophet?" Marion gasped.

"I don't think so," Setviren said. "He commands an army of vampires. These are humans."

"Some of them are Starlings," Khalid said. "Look!"

Though many wielded basic weapons, some marauders matched the professors' moves. Wind raged against wind. Fireballs whipped through the air. And more and more marauders poured through the broken windows.

They hurried across the veranda to Vivian and Darius who stood together, staring at the sky.

"Vivian!" Marion cried and snatched her sister in her arms. "Are you alright?"

"Yes." Vivian looked upward again. "There's something—"

"We have to make sure Timothée's okay," Marion breathed.

"He went back to his dormitory," Khalid said. "He's safer than any of us right now."

Marion nodded. At least Timothée wasn't here—

"There's something in the sky," Vivian insisted.

The two nobles, the sisters, and the loremaster stared up into the inky darkness.

Flying through the air was a giant bat.

The giant bat that had stolen her father, had tormented her dreams.

And clutched in its claws was her brother.

# 30

# IN WHICH TIMOTHÉE GOES
# FOR A NIGHT FLIGHT

WIND WHIPPED PAST as Timothée hurtled through the air. The giant bat had done one quick scan of the room and crawled forward on the front of its clawed wings before it scooped him up and swept out into the night. And now he helplessly dangled in its grasp.

The Isle of Argos swirled beneath him, glass buildings glittering in the white moonlight. Timothée blinked rapidly, trying to make sense of the world around him.

Far below, people ran and screamed. Ships with black sails and a blue handprint docked on the field overflowing with armed men and women.

Timothée swept his gaze up. They weren't alone in the sky.

More flying ships descended onto the Isle. But that wasn't what stole the breath from his lungs. Flying alongside them were creatures. Magnificent, beautiful creatures.

"Mythical beasts," Timothée mumbled, awe lacing through the fear.

These weren't like the shadowling from the Enchanted Woods. These were the pure, uncorrupted creatures of legend. He spotted a pegasus with white wings, a gryphon, a massive raven...

Timothée had accidentally awoken a long slumbering panther shadowling in the woods. What had awoken these creatures? They swept down, defending the mercenaries as Celestial Knights charged from the school.

Was this giant bat a mythical beast too? None of the legends mentioned a beast that could talk.

A horrific memory flashed in his mind. The night of the Wolfhelm attack. His father had been dangling in the clutches of a giant bat. Was this the creature that had murdered his father? Fear lanced through his body. Was he to face the same fate? He needed to find his sisters.

"What do you want with me?" Timothée cried.

"You are to stand before the Exalted One," the giant bat replied.

The Exalted One. Images of blue handprints and raving cultists flashed through his mind. That same blue handprint was smeared on the sails of the ships.

"P-please. I have a choker. I'm not hurting anyone, promise. Let me go."

The bat flapped its leathery wings, circling the school. *It's looking for someone.* Timothée's body whipped wildly from its claws, his stomach lurching.

He gazed up at the pointed snout. "What are the invaders doing? Are they killing people?"

The bat said nothing, his stare concentrated on the night ahead.

"Please," Timothée tried again. "I don't want anyone else to die because of me."

A deep rumble went through the bat's body. A sigh. "Then don't resist, kid."

Did this monster... call him kid? Timothée wiggled in the giant bat's claws, though he wasn't sure what good it would do. He wouldn't survive a fall from this height. He cast an anxious look back at the Dark Star tower.

"The Exalted One sent all this?" Timothée cried. "Because of me?"

Cold air rushed over his skin as the giant bat beat its heavy, leathery wings. "We have one order," the bat growled. "Get the triplets out of the Academy by any means necessary."

Any means necessary? That meant anyone who stood between these villains and the Greywicks was collateral.

What had he been thinking, leaving Val unconscious in the washroom? He should have woken him up. But then Val could have done something stupid, like use shadowcraft in front of a professor.

The stars swirled above, and the ground was so far below, and no matter what Timothée Greywick did, he only ever hurt people. And now there was nothing he could do to protect his sisters, to protect Val. This was all his fault again.

In the distance, a floating ship with black sails and a blue handprint came into focus. Dark clouds shifted in and out of view.

*That's where he's taking me.*

He touched the choker around his neck… But he hadn't let Rayna and Taf disenchant it. There was no way of getting it off. And even if he could, he didn't know what would happen.

Last time, his star—that power of Noctis—had been completely out of control. Shadowcraft was not an option.

Icy fear laced its way up his body.

Fear of the ship, of this monster. But there was something deeper.

The memory of that power—a star burning so hot in his chest, pumping not blood but *shadow* through his veins. Darkness, so much darkness. It overflowed from him, casting out, out, out to protect.

To kill.

The giant bat twisted its neck to look back at him. "What are you doing, kid?"

Fear-tangled webs spread through Timothée.

The trees of the Enchanted Forest swayed back and forth. Breaking foliage sounded through the night air, and a shadow burst from the trees.

And it was heading straight toward them.

The giant bat swerved. "It can't be."

The stars dimmed, and the clouds quaked around them as another giant sailed forward. This creature was different. The giant bat holding him felt real: animal, furred, and primal in its existence.

But streaking toward them was a shadow cleaved from the night sky itself. Long and elegant black body with glowing purple wings, amethyst eyes, and mist trailing in its wake. Another bat, this one made of shadow.

"Fuck," the bat holding Timothée swore. Then he dove, careening toward the Isle of Argos.

Timothée screamed. His whole body flung upward, slamming against the furred body. The giant bat swept up before he touched the ground, but the shadow bat was right behind them. Timothée could *feel* it.

"That's not one of your friends?" he cried.

A rumbling laugh sounded through the great animal, but it cut off as the shadow bat lunged for them. The giant bat swept out of the way, a leathery wing cutting across the top of a Selene Crescent building.

Timothée saw the new creature up close, reflective purple eyes staring right at him. But the giant bat spiraled until he managed to steady them and swept back into the air. He was flying toward the Academy now.

"Faster!" he yelled to the bat clutching him. "Go faster!"

He didn't trust this giant bat, but he'd rather take his chances with him than whatever was chasing them. There was darkness in the way the shadow bat moved. Darkness given flight.

"There's no running from this thing." The giant bat swooped closer to the Academy.

A loud shriek sounded over the call of the bat, over the cries of the soldiers, and the students, and the giant bat twitched its head and groaned, "What is that racket?"

Running along the inner grounds of the Celestial Academy were his sisters, Prince Darius, Khalid, and Loremaster Setviren. And Marion was screaming loudest of all.

271

*That,* Timothée thought, *is my sister.* And who the giant bat was looking for.

Didn't they see they needed to get away? Then he was tumbling, head over body, as the giant bat dropped him on the rampart that circled the castle. He careened to a stop at the edge. Sharp pain exploded along his body.

Blackness spotted his vision, and he looked up. The giant bat landed with a rumbling thud in front of him. Separating him from the shadow bat.

The stone wall and walkway swept around the entire school, and it was barely big enough for the two bats. Timothée glanced over the edge: one side with its long drop to dark clouds, the other down to the inner gardens of the Celestial Academy, where his sisters were shouting up at him.

"Timothée!" Vivian shouted. "Timothée, are you alright?"

"I'm okay," he managed, touching his arms, his head. A few scrapes and cuts from the fall, but nothing too bad.

In front of him, the giant bat spread his wings in a threatening move, blocking the advance of the shadow creature.

"Come on, buddy," the giant bat said. "You know me. Don't do this."

The shadow bat gave a clicking hiss in return. But it wasn't looking at the giant bat. It was looking at Timothée.

This wasn't one of the mythical beasts under the Exalted One's control. This was a shadowling. And he'd awoken it... like he'd awoken the panther in the Enchanted Forest. Had this shadow bat been slumbering deep in the Isle as well?

*My fear awoke it.* Like the panther.

But he'd been able to control the panther, or at least it hadn't attacked him.

Timothée stared across the darkness until his eyes met the shadow bat. Something flashed in his mind.

A vision. A memory.

Dark caverns, a sweeping cape, a gloved hand reaching down to the stony ground. Something feeble in a puddle. The hand scooped the small thing up. A baby bat with a torn wing.

"If I leave it alone," a deep voice spoke, "this sickly creature will perish and die. But with my help, it could become so much more. Like you."

There was someone beside him, but he couldn't make out the face, covered by long, lilac hair. "I have seen a vision of this creature. I know its fate."

"And what is that, my little star?"

The person's full lips curved into a mocking smile. "It will become—"

Timothée blinked as the memory faded. But now he knew what this creature was.

"Dyamodius," Timothée said. "Dyamodius, the Siphon of the Starless Sky."

That name. *That name.* It awakened something inside him, a voice ringing in his ears: *Be fearful, holy Starlings, for fear is the compass of light in the dark. And the batting wings of unseen shadow are the eternal void in which the siphon of the starless night feeds.*

The creature looked at him, shrieking in response, revealing rows of sharp teeth.

"Noctis," Timothée continued, and his voice felt deep and powerful, like in his vision. "This was Noctis's steed."

The giant furred bat glanced over his shoulder. "So, you do know. And here I was thinking you were nothing like him."

*Nothing like him.*

He'd been trying to hide that part of himself, to shy away from it. To say again and again and again he was nothing like his brother.

But it was the biggest lie he'd ever told himself.

A lie that had came crashing down tonight.

Wearing the armor, commanding the room.

*Kissing Val.*

And now, more than ever, to protect his sisters, to protect the Academy, he had to be like Noctis.

*Embrace what you are,* the castle roared in his mind.

Timothée kept his gaze firmly on Dyamodius. He took a deep breath, then said: "Begone from this place. And take the bat with you."

The giant bat turned to look at Timothée—betrayal flashing in his single yellow eye—before Dyamodius swept into him, barrelling them both toward the edge of the Isle of Argos.

And unfortunately, toward Timothée.

"JUMP!" Marion shouted.

Fall fifty feet into the courtyard or off the entire Isle? He leapt into the garden just as the tumble of leathery wings lurched past him.

He rushed through open air but didn't hit the ground.

"I got you!" Darius had his hands outstretched. Magic crackled as the air around Timothée swirled, the density shifting, until Timothée gently floated to the ground.

Marion and Vivian's arms were around him in an instant.

But Setviren's hand grasped their shoulders, his voice dark and low. "Hurry, Greywicks. Danger has come for you. We must flee the darkness."

# 31
# IN WHICH MARION MEETS
# THE PHANTOM TWO

"WHAT HAPPENED?" MARION clutched at her brother's thin shirt. "Where are your shoes?"

He needed shoes. He could step on a thorn in the garden or cut his feet on the shattered glass from the windows and roof. Yes, it was vitally important she find him shoes.

Because she couldn't think about the other things. Couldn't think about the great animal that had held her brother in its clutches the way it had held Father. Instinctively, she snatched Timothée in her arms and held him as tight as she could. He was alive. He had escaped.

The creature was real. Flesh and fur and blood. She could hear its voice from when it infected her Celestial Rite last moon: *'Marion? Come with me now.'*

Timothée was out of breath and pale. Gasping, he shoved a piece of paper in her hand. "They're here. For us."

Setviren snatched the paper from Marion, opened it. A rough drawing of the three Greywick triplets. His throat bobbed.

Cold fear shot through Marion's veins. An entire attack on the Celestial Academy for Fallen Stars, all to hunt the Greywicks? She wanted to throw up. She wanted to go kick her past self for ever stepping foot on the Isle of Argos.

"I won't let anything happen to you." Darius's voice was full of dark promise as he grabbed Vivian's face in his hands.

Khalid shrugged at Marion. "If it's between my skin or yours, who's to say what'll happen?"

"We need to get inside. I cannot protect you if those demon bats return." Setviren looked around. "The five of you, come with me." Then he darted for the ballroom entrance.

Inside, nearly all the students had evacuated, but the professors remained with a host of Celestial Knights, battling a mob of marauders and mythical beasts.

Setviren waved them along the edge of the chamber toward Archpriestess Kassandra's golden chair. Marion fought back tears of fright as she ran. They were so close to the professors battling with the invaders. Led by Professor Barracus, they had formed a line to hold back the brigands.

Barracus moved fast as a lightning flash, grabbing the alcohol off the drink station and mixing it with a powder from within his coat. Bomb after bomb he flung at the enemies, their bodies flying like ragdolls. *He doesn't even have starcraft,* Marion thought.

Setviren pushed aside the curtain behind the Archpriestess's chair, revealing nothing but stone. "Hurry, children."

"You want us to run into a wall?" Khalid asked.

Setviren pursed his lips and stuck his arm into the wall. It disappeared. "An *enchantment,* Mr. Ali Bagheeri. Now *go!*"

Marion cast one last look behind her, at the battle raging where there had been dancing. But then she stepped through the wall and the dark consumed her.

A dim, narrow hallway lit by blue-flamed torches lay before them. "This way, this way." Setviren pushed ahead. "I'll take you to the Archpriestess's office. You'll be safe there."

They ran until Marion's sides splintered and she swore her lungs would give out. She really shouldn't have had *two* pieces of pie. And pumpkin loaf. And a cranberry tart. And there was the plate of smashed potatoes with mushroom gravy—

"Here, here." Setviren stuck his head through what appeared to be a stone wall. "Hallways are empty. Out we go."

The five students and the loremaster leapt through the wall and emerged out into one of the Academy's hallways with the sapphire carpet and mahogany walls.

"Almost there," Setviren said. "Just a little further. Then you'll be safe."

They darted down the too quiet hallway. What a sight they must appear: Setviren in his fluttering white robes, Khalid dressed as a pirate, Timothée with his bare feet, and Darius looking not himself one bit with his hair crafted brown and his ears elongated to points. At least Vivian looked a fighter in her hunter's garb. And Marion must look the most ridiculous of all, with her scandalous leaf dress and her stupid copper hair and her stupid green eyes and her stupid big ears. *This is what you get for trying to have fun,* Marion thought bitterly. *Running for your life with your bosom bouncing all about!*

A bright light surged out one of the windows. Marion slowed, stared.

Archpriestess Kassandra crossed the Meadow of Shattered Stars toward the marauders' airships. A host of Celestial Knights surrounded her, their previous path littered with dead bodies of the raiders and mythical beasts. The Archpriestess's white dress shone in the moonlight like a star itself. She rose her arms in the air.

And fire.

So much fire.

Marion couldn't be sure where it was all coming from, but she knew it sprung from Archpriestess Kassandra. The air ships burst into red flames. Blazing bodies ran from the ships, smacking at their clothes. But there was nothing they could do.

The Archpriestess was the very sun itself.

Marion's breath caught, and she touched the window. To burn so hot no one could ever get close to you...

"What are you doing?" Khalid snapped. "Come on!" He snatched her wrist and yanked her toward the rest of the party.

The hallway led to a T-shaped junction. "We'll take the path to the left," Setviren called. "I think we're in the clear—"

Marauders. Five of them skulking far down the hallway to the right.

Marion's first thought was how normal they looked, nowhere near as disciplined in their movements as the Celestial Knights. And not as organized as the Dark Prophet's vampire followers. These bandits wore a mess of rough-spun and pieced-together armor.

*Pilgrims.* That's what everyone had been calling them.

"There they are," a gravelly voice said, spotting them. "Don't let them get away!"

With a growl, Darius reached into the pocket of his costume, pulled out a cube of stellarite. The bristle of Evening Star magic surged through the air as the cube morphed, lengthened, shifted into a glistening sword.

"Do you keep that thing with you at all times?" Timothée asked, impressed.

"Loremaster, they're after the Greywicks. See them to safety. Khalid and I will handle these ruffians." Darius's handsome face had shifted into something menacing. There was a glimmer in his eyes unlike anything Marion had ever seen. Fear shivered through her.

"But Your Highness!" Setviren gasped. "I cannot let you put yourself in danger!"

"You don't have a choice. This is a royal command." The Prince turned to Vivian, dragged his hands through her hair. "I swear this to you now: anyone who wishes you harm will die by my blade."

"Be careful," Vivian whispered.

"There is no chance of me being vanquished while a single enemy of yours remains." His voice was rough. "I am Darius Störmberg, ruler of Andúrigard and all of Thraina. I will protect you and the Celestial Academy with a wolf's fury!"

He pulled Vivian in for a kiss by the back of her neck, his other hand still clutched to his blade. She raised up on her tiptoes to deepen the kiss.

Khalid turned to Marion, shrugged. "How about it, Marion? I'm Khalid Ali Bagheeri, ruler of nothing. I'll avenge you—"

She patted his shoulder as she walked past to stand beside Setviren. "Maybe let Darius do the fighting."

"Then let us go, children," Setviren urged and began running down the left path. The triplets followed. Marion looked behind her to see the marauders surging toward Darius and Khalid.

Darius stared at Vivian. "I'll find you." He kissed a blue ribbon tied around his wrist. Then turned and ran his blade straight through a bandit.

Vivian screamed his name, but Marion tugged her forward. "Trust them."

But it didn't stop her from turning back one more time to watch Darius's blade flash, and Khalid's palms explode with flame.

Then they turned a corner, and the boys were gone.

"We're here!" Setviren cried. They stopped before two mahogany doors with no handles.

Marion was instantly transported back to the memory of their first night at the Academy: the moving room had taken them up to Archpriestess Kassandra's office. "Do we have to take this thing?"

"Would you rather take the stairs?" Setviren snapped. He opened the doors with a whish of his hand. They filed into the small room.

As soon as the doors shut, Setviren breathed a deep sigh. His hands trembled as he moved the room upward. Marion could barely register the sensation; her heart was beating too fast, her breath too ragged.

She looked at her siblings. Vivian's eyes were rimmed red, staring at nothing, and she rubbed her neck. Timothée dragged his hands through his hair, still too long and too dark to suit him.

"Once we're up, we'll be perfectly safe," Setviren said. "No one knows how to get here besides me and the headmistress. Everything will be fine."

The room shuddered to a stop.

"Ah," Setviren breathed. "Safety at last."

He opened the door to the Archpriestess's office.

And leaning on her desk, looking perfectly at home, were two vampires.

Marion wasn't sure how she knew they were vampires. At first look, they were two dark-clad figures. One was massive, broad body in worn black pants and a dirty black robe. His heavy boots were scuffed and covered in dried mud. His cloak was torn, and bloody gashes ran across his chest.

The other was shorter, slimmer, neater, but held his body in the same arrogant stance. They wore deep hoods that shaded their faces to obscurity. And both had the painted emblem of the winged hand-print on their chests.

Their matching smiles flashed with moonlit fangs.

Marion stepped behind Setviren.

"Well, well, the boss was right," the tall one said. His voice was deep and husky. "The Greywicks have come straight to us."

"You're so right, brother," the smaller one said. "And I didn't even have to get my hands dirty."

The big one laughed and picked up an amber paperweight from the Archpriestess's desk. Examined it in the moonlight. "Lucky for you, I love getting my hands dirty."

"Don't touch that!" Setviren snapped. "You are trespassers in Archpriestess Kassandra's office. By will of the Archpriestess and headmistress, I must ask you to depart!"

The big one dropped the paperweight to the ground. The heavy *thunk* reverberated in the office, and then it rolled toward the Greywicks. "Aw, did you hear that, Allistar? He's asking us so nicely."

"Allistar..." Setviren whimpered.

The two brothers stepped forward, and in perfect unison, pulled back the hoods of their cloaks.

Two glittering yellow eyes stared back, one from each brother. The slimmer one had straight, long hair concealing the right side of his face. He held his expression in a sly grin, his half-lidded eye like a waning moon.

Setviren murmured, "It's impossible."

The other, taller than any man Marion had ever seen before, had his left eye covered by an eyepatch. His black hair was pulled up into a messy bun at the base of his neck. He had thick brows and bronze skin that shimmered with candlelight. His golden right eye flicked to her. His expression softened.

Marion's heart filled with trepidation. There was the strangest feeling she'd been seen through that eye before. She tugged on Setviren's robes, whispered, "Get us out of here!"

But Vivian stepped forward. Her pupils were completely dilated, mouth a perfect O. Her hand rubbed and rubbed the side of her neck. She was staring at the lean vampire, the one called Allistar.

"Vivian, stop!" Timothée grabbed for her wrist, but she held it out of his grasp.

She walked, straight-backed and rigid, out of the moving room and into the office. Marion and Timothée rushed after her, grabbed each arm. Again, Marion had the feeling she had entered a giant orb, the entire office a sphere of glass. The moon and stars were so close, she felt trapped. And this time, she was trapped with two predators.

"Don't get close to them!" Marion cried. The vampires held themselves with perfect stillness, save the wicked glint off their fangs.

And then Vivian screamed. She collapsed, hands clasped around her neck.

"Vivian!" Marion fell to her knees, tried to grab her sister, but there was nothing she could do. There was no wound on her neck. Marion looked at the vampires. "What did you do to her?"

The smaller one stepped forward, movements lithe and silvery. "I did nothing." He sounded... confused.

"Make it stop!" Timothée screamed. "Make it stop!" He snatched the amber paperweight off the floor and chucked it as hard as he could at Allistar. It smashed against the vampire's skull.

Silence echoed.

Allistar brought a delicate hand to his head. "Ow. That hurt."

The bigger vampire laughed, an almost merry sound, doubling over. "This one has guts!" Then he stopped laughing, and in a single movement, stood right before the Greywicks. "But we've got work to do."

Marion stared up at him. He was huge, cresting seven feet. He could crack her neck with one twist.

"Are you playing with your food, Balthazar?" In a flash, Allistar was beside him. "Don't leave me out."

Marion's heart sunk. Standing beside one another, each with a golden eye—Balthazar the right, and Allistar the left—they looked like a single entity, a terrifying monster.

Then the ground beneath the vampires roiled, the floor panels shifting, carrying the brothers backwards. Setviren stepped behind the triplets, arms extended. "Stay back, foul creatures!" He looked down at Marion. "Hurry to the transport."

Marion grabbed Vivian beneath her shoulders and Timothée hauled her feet. They sprinted for the transport.

The doors slammed shut.

The brothers had regained their balance. Balthazar had his arm outstretched. "Leaving already?" He turned to Setviren. "I don't think even your magic can pry those doors open, loremaster."

Allistar picked up the amber paperweight that had hit his head. It changed color, shifting to an iron grey.

*Evening Stars,* Marion thought.

"You don't need to be involved in this, old man," Allistar said, bouncing the iron ball in his hand. "The boss doesn't want you dead. But accidents happen." With frightening force, he whirled the iron at Setviren.

Marion closed her eyes, expecting to see a bloody pulp for a head. But when there was no squelching sound, she opened to see Setviren's hand extended, a bundle of feathers floating in the air where the iron paperweight had been.

The loremaster's white robes fluttered like a gull's wings. He placed one hand behind him and walked before the brothers, an instructor evaluating his pupils. "What master do you answer to now?"

Allistar stepped over to the pearl statue of the phoenix, ran a finger along the outstretched feathers. "Ha! We have no master. Our boss is whoever has the most gold."

Setviren rose a green eyebrow. "That emblem on your chest says otherwise."

"What can we say?" Balthazar's rumbling voice kept that edge of laughter. "The Exalted One has a lot of gold."

*The Exalted One.* Marion shook her head. The cult leader riling up the pilgrims around Bøgelund. "Help me get her to the transport," Marion whispered to her brother.

Timothée picked up Vivian's legs again. "They locked the transport with starcraft!"

"Evening Star magic. Maybe Vivian can unlock it."

Timothée looked down at his shrieking sister, clawing at her neck like she would tear the skin off. "I don't think—"

"We have to try!" Marion's eyes filled with tears. They wouldn't die like this, trapped like animals. Setviren would protect them.

But if he couldn't… They needed to escape.

Setviren stopped pacing. He drew a foot before him, then held a firm stance, like a dancer. One hand behind his back, the other extended out. "I have told you before. You are trespassers at the Celestial Academy for Fallen Stars. Begone or I will remove you by force."

The brothers looked at each other, single yellow eyes glinting. They laughed.

"Alright," Balthazar said, pushing up his sleeves and revealing thickly muscled forearms. "I'm always ready for a brawl."

The room sparked with magic.

Setviren moved, his arms both delicate and purposeful. The floor shifted beneath Balthazar, liquifying. He yelped, sinking as if he'd stepped into quicksand. Allistar leapt, doing a front flip over the Archpriestess's desk. His hand grazed across a map. It turned to netting, which he threw at the loremaster. It wrapped around Setviren's face.

Balthazar pried himself from the quicksand and growled. He held up his fists; his skin turned hard and golden, changing his own flesh to gauntlets.

"Watch out!" Marion screamed as the vampire charged toward Setviren like a bull unleashed.

Setviren whirled, each movement graceful and deliberate. Balthazar charged past him, smashing into a suit of decorative Celestial Knight armor. The pieces clattered to the floor with a crash. Setviren snatched the netting from his face; it crumbled into dust. "That map was an *original*," the loremaster barked.

"Vivian." Marion tried to hold her sister's spasming body down. "You need to open the doors to the transport. Do you hear me? We have to escape!"

But Vivian's eyes rolled to white. And as she screamed, Marion saw the flash of fangs in her sister's mouth. She sprung away from her. Her heart raced in her chest, and she could only wonder how loud it sounded to her sister.

Setviren traced his foot across the floor again. Now he held both hands extended. "In the name of the Archpriestess of the Celestial Church, I will bring you to justice!"

And the great pearl statue of the phoenix flapped its wings.

Giving a screech, the statue leapt from its perch of flames and soared toward Allistar. It smashed into him; he sailed across the room, crashing against the glass walls. A crack splintered where he hit.

The statue folded its massive wings and divebombed Allistar. He cried out, blood splashing across the glass.

Vivian screamed and tore at her throat, leaving deep red lines. Marion snatched her hands, but Vivian was too strong. No, no, Vivian wasn't strong. She hadn't been capable of lifting a box in the last three years. Except for that fight with Erik.

*There's something wrong inside you.*

"Brother!" Balthazar roared. He held his golden gauntlets aloft and charged at the statue. With a massive blow, he sent the pearl statue smashing out the window.

Allistar stood with the help of his brother, brought a hand into his long hair, pulled it back bloody. "I think I've had enough playing."

"This was fun," Balthazar said, "but it's time to get our job done."

Setviren stood, his stance as strong as ever, but sweat dripped from his brow. "I will protect the Greywicks with my life."

"Don't need you dead." Allistar rose his arms. His fingers were long and elegant as a pianist's. "We just need you out of the way."

Balthazar gave a chuckle and stood in a broad stance, hands extended out like his brother. "Nighty-night, Professor."

A strange blue glow surrounded Setviren, then radiated through his skin, out his eyes, from his fingertips and feet.

"No!" Setviren cried. "No! No! Greywicks, run—" His whole body burst: a flash of light and feathers. And where the loremaster had been now fluttered a green bird.

Marion gasped. Evening Stars had the magic of change. But to change a human into an animal… It was unheard of. Impossible.

How powerful were these brothers?

Nauseating spurts of adrenaline ran through Marion's body. "What did you do to him?"

Allistar snatched the squawking green bird and walked to the smashed window. "Have a pleasant flight, Loremaster." And with a surprisingly gentle toss, he flung the bird out of the tower.

It fluttered outside the window, darting its head left and right, and flapped into the night sky.

"Setviren! Wait!" Marion screamed.

"Don't get your vines in a knot." Balthazar gave a downturned smile. "Dear *Professor* Setviren will be his old self with the sunrise."

Allistar's fangs flashed. "Finally, we're alone."

Marion stared down at Vivian, now curled in a ball, sobbing. Timothée held his body over hers.

*I have to protect them*, Marion thought. *It is me who must do this thing. I am alone.*

She stood, legs trembling, mouth dry. "What do you want?"

The brothers circled, predators batting around their prey. Then in a movement so quick, Balthazar was in front of her. She swallowed, completely engulfed by his size. Beside him, she was positively doll-like.

"We want you." His gauntlets vanished and he placed a finger under her chin. Her heart thundered. "Well, the Exalted One wants you."

"And your sister." Allistar appeared beside him, one yellow eye flashing down at Vivian. "And the boy—"

"Touch them and die!" Marion screamed.

Timothée whimpered at their feet. "Just let my sisters live. Please. Let them live."

Balthazar ran a tender thumb along Marion's cheek, wiping away the single tear. "I promise your safety."

*Liar.* Only she could keep her family safe. And she had magic within her. The same magic Archpriestess Kassandra had. Archpriestess Kassandra who had brought the force of the sun upon those ships. She could do that too, burn this whole tower to the ground if she had to.

Like she had done in the Celestial Rite with her home.

"I will see you laid raw before me," she growled. "Charred and broken, a husk of who you think you are. You will beg for mercy and receive none. You will rue the day you threatened Marion Greywick."

Heat burned in her palms. Yes, yes, she'd create a fire that rivaled the sun, and leave ash in her wake. With a roar, she whipped her arms up to Balthazar—

He caught her wrists. No flame flickered on her fingers. "Very intimidating, sunshine." He covered her hands in his huge ones, the way one would put out a candle.

Tears streamed down her face. No, no. That was all she had. Their only chance—

"Grab the boy," Balthazar said. "I'll carry the girls."

Allistar pulled Timothée up by his choker. He shook his head. "It's uncanny, Balt. I don't like his face."

"Get a good hold on him," Balthazar said. "He's squirmy."

Allistar lifted Timothée in the air, feet dangling above the ground. "I feel like any moment he's going to snap his fingers and obliterate me. Do you remember when he—"

"Brother, you must not fear," Balthazar said. "See how the kid cages his magic? He cannot harm you."

"Not now..." Allistar said. "But you saw what he did on the ramparts, who he called. Brother, I cannot complete our task."

Balthazar whirled. "Allistar?"

"I will not stand idly by a second time."

"The Exalted One wants him alive!" Balthazar growled.

But Allistar's breath was ragged, voice deep as he snarled, "The Exalted One is no match for Noctis's magic."

*He's going to kill him,* Marion realized. *The vampire is going to kill my brother.*

Vivian was sobbing, and Marion screamed until her throat was raw, and Timothée cried, "Please! *Please!* Don't kill me!"

Allistar's fangs bared at Timothée's neck. "Noctis cannot reign again."

From the shadows behind them, a dark voice purred, "Oh, I have other ideas."

As if emerging from a portal of darkness, out stepped night embodied. A cape of writhing shadows, armor of pure gravastarium, a sharp angled obsidian mask.

The Dark Prophet.

"Hello, Greywicks," he said. "It seems you're in need of saving."

# 32

# IN WHICH TIMOTHÉE FALLS OUT OF THE FRYING PAN AND INTO THE FIRE

THE DARK PROPHET strode into the room, a trail of shadows in his wake. Though the mask hid his face, Timothée couldn't help but feel a sense of unhinged amusement emanating from him.

Allistar dropped Timothée and a wave of pain rushed through his body. *He was going to kill me.* The brothers turned to face the Dark Prophet. *What's he doing here?*

"Well, well, well." Balthazar gave a joyless chuckle. "We finally meet. You've been the talk of Thraina these last three years, *Dark Prophet.*" His recrafted golden gauntlets glinted in the lightening sky.

"You know me." The Dark Prophet's voice was a gravely rasp beneath the mask. "I do love a spectacle."

Allistar's body reverberated, heavy black coat shaking. He grabbed a knife from a scabbard at his waist and pointed it at the Dark Prophet. "Silence! Keep your forked tongue behind your teeth, liar."

The Dark Prophet circled the brothers. Shadows danced between his gloved fingers. "Heh. You call me a liar. Look at you. The Phantom Two turned hired dogs. You used to be part of the Prophet of Star's princeguard. What jokes you have become."

Balthazar grunted and slammed his foot down. The floor rippled with each massive step. "Imposter! Don't you dare invoke the Prince's name!" His golden gauntlets flashed as he surged forward, enormous arms swinging for the Dark Prophet's face.

"Whoever wins," Marion gasped, "we lose."

But Timothée wasn't so sure.

Balthazar's fist swung through the Dark Prophet as if he were nothing but smoke. The Dark Prophet stepped aside, chuckling. "The Beast of Briarmere. As slow as ever. Maybe it's time to use that head for once and look at the facts."

Balthazar stumbled, caught himself on the glass wall. Snarled.

"The facts?" Allistar stalked forward. His voice was raw, destroyed. "You are not the Prophet of Stars. You don't deserve to wear armor in his likeness. I'll take it off your corpse!"

Allistar leapt, his dagger growing into a thin rapier. The Dark Prophet dodged, his shoulder becoming smoke, then reforming. Allistar lunged again and again, each time barely missing the Dark Prophet.

With a cry, Balthazar charged and then both brothers flanked the Prophet, one thrusting with blade, the other pummeling with fists. But neither could land a single blow.

"Hurry," Marion whispered. "We have to escape while they're distracting each other!"

"How?" Timothée rubbed at his choker. Tight. Too tight. "Without Setviren, we can't use the transport. And he's probably perched in some tree!"

Vivian whimpered and writhed. Her neck ran red from her own fingernails clawing at the skin. But she had done that herself. There was nothing physically wrong with her. *It's something with the brothers,* Timothée thought.

"There's a staircase," Marion said. "Setviren mentioned it. They use it during the day when their magic is gone. We have to find it!"

The three vampires fought across the entirety of the room. Gold and silver glistened in the light of the waning moon as gauntlets and rapier flew at the Dark Prophet.

And yet still, they could not hit him.

*He's not fighting back.*

Timothée sucked in a breath. Watching them battle like this, he realized how much smaller the Dark Prophet was than the other two. Even with the armor, he was shorter, slighter. And yet he moved with such confidence, such unnerving speed and precision.

The Dark Prophet brought up tendrils of shadow that snatched the wrists and ankles of the brothers, slowing their movements. "You two never were the brightest, were you? Who's your new master? Were you so eager to abandon me?"

Allistar pulled back, rapier shaking in his hand. Though half his face was sheathed by his dark hair, his one yellow eye shone. "You mock him! The Prophet of Stars was a legend, and you are—"

"Pathetic," Balthazar said. "Three years ago, all of Wolfhelm saw you get thrown from the castle by that boy prince. The Prophet of Stars would never have been defeated by the likes of him!"

"He didn't defeat me!" the Dark Prophet roared. It was the first time his muffled voice was filled with emotion. "Darius Störmberg isn't worth my time."

Cold, ancient fear crawled over Timothée. These brothers... They were talking about the Prophet of Stars. But he had disappeared centuries ago when Noctis died. If they used to work with him...

They were as deeply rooted in the threads of Thraina's history as the gods themselves.

"Hurry," Marion said. "We have to find the staircase."

He nodded and together they grabbed Vivian, dragging her behind one of Archpriestess Kassandra's crescent moon bookcases.

Timothée squeezed Marion's hand. "See if there's a trapdoor by the transport. I'll check for one by her desk."

Marion squeezed back. "Whatever you do, don't get in their way."

Timothée scrambled off, keeping low and away from the three fighting vampires. The sky was lightening to a burnished red, sun threatening at the horizon, spreading light and deep shadows over the floor. One by one, stars winked out.

Presently, the brothers paced before the Dark Prophet.

"Take off the armor!" Allistar screamed. Bloody spittle sprayed out of his mouth.

"Oh, Alli," the Dark Prophet crooned. One of his shadows laced up Allistar's body. "Aren't you going to buy me dinner first?" Then the shadow threw Allistar across the room, smashing him against the desk.

Balthazar screamed and charged. He tackled the Dark Prophet. Shadows and glinting gold rolled over and over each other.

Timothée perched behind the desk, now shattered from the impact of Allistar's body. The vampire that wanted to kill him was so close. Timothée tried to still himself, to not even breathe.

Allistar pushed up to all fours, shook his head. And Timothée knew the exact moment the vampire realized he was there. He caught the sudden stillness of his head, then the sharp crick of his neck as he turned.

And Timothée had never seen someone look at him with such hatred. There was an ancient fury in that yellow gaze.

"Noctis will *never* reign again," the vampire snarled.

Three things happened in a single moment.

First, Allistar leapt over the desk, rapier drawn and thrust toward Timothée's chest.

Secondly, Marion screamed Timothée's name at the top of her lungs.

And third, the Dark Prophet, grappled to the ground by Balthazar, turned at the sound of Marion's scream. And every essence of darkness in the office came to life.

Shadows leapt up like hideous gargoyles, fangs made of gloom. The Dark Prophet roared, a hideous, rasping sound, and threw Balthazar off him. The entire tower shook. And the sun seemed to retreat behind the line of the horizon, if just for a moment.

Shadow whips snatched Allistar's wrists, pulled him up against the glass wall. His rapier fell to the ground. More shadows grabbed Balthazar the same.

"Timothée!" Marion rushed forward, not caring about the brothers hanging like puppets or the Dark Prophet. Timothée lay on his back, rubbing his chest. A thin red line sliced across his collarbone.

"It barely scratched me," Timothée said. He looked at the Dark Prophet.

The surging shadows, the shaking room, the complete darkness. With dawning awe, Timothée realized just what the Dark Prophet was capable of. He truly had not even been trying with the brothers before. And the power he'd shown against Ser Dedont and Darius in the square… That was nothing. He had been toying with them. If he wanted the Greywicks dead, he would see it done.

If he wanted *anyone* dead, he would see it done.

The Dark Prophet stared up at the brothers. "Do you doubt me still?"

Allistar and Balthazar looked at one another. They did not writhe against their bonds, nor try to escape. Allistar's voice was broken, weak: "You… You died."

The shadow bonds released, and the brothers fell to the ground. The Dark Prophet reached a hand down to each of them. "I was just sleeping. For a very long time. But I'm back now."

There was a single moment of pause. And then the brothers took the Dark Prophet's hands.

And fell to their knees before him.

"My Prince," Balthazar cried. His whole body shook. "I don't understand. All this time, we thought you were dead."

Allistar clutched the Prophet's gloved hands. "I dared ask you to remove your armor. Take my life as retribution, my Prince, I beg thee—"

"*My Prince.*" The Dark Prophet laughed grimly. "I never could break the two of you from calling me that."

Something terrible prickled at the edge of Timothée's senses. That magic, those shadows... There was something familiar about it.

Marion motioned for them to crawl back toward Vivian, hidden behind the bookcase. "What is going on?"

"The Dark Prophet really is the Prophet of Stars from the legends." Timothée's eyes were wide, unblinking. "His shadows... They feel so—"

"Shush, be quiet. We need to make a move before those three remember they're supposed to be fighting us."

The vampire brothers and the Dark Prophet seemed much more involved in their reunion. The Dark Prophet pulled each to their feet, clapped them on the shoulders.

"He really is short for a murderer," Marion grumbled, looking at the trio. Balthazar and even Allistar towered over the shadow prince.

"Now tell me, friends, what are you doing here? Are you truly now mercenaries?" The Dark Prophet's voice sounded so strange in normal conversation, not threatening world domination or the return of Noctis.

Balthazar looked down at the blue winged handprint on his chest. "Huh? Oh, our mission. It's the Exalted One, my Prince. Surely, you know who he is. Been working in the underdark for years. He's got gold, my Prince. So much gold. Had us organize this operation. 'Course he knew everything about the school and the headmistress's office."

"It wasn't just the verdallions," Allistar said. "We'd never have joined him if so. We owed him a debt, and he promised us vengeance on the ones that took you from us. Or so we thought."

"And is your loyalty to this Exalted One?" the Dark Prophet purred.

The brothers looked at each other, then in unison, placed their hands upon the blue mark on their chests. Using their matching starcraft, it shimmered away, and in its place appeared a crescent moon at the forefront of a four-pointed star. The same sigil was inlaid on the Dark Prophet's armor. The same sigil Timothée had worn for All Hallow's Eve.

"Our loyalty is to you," Allistar said, voice thick with dark promise. "Until the stars fall from the sky."

"Good." The Dark Prophet turned and waved his hands. A swirling door to darkness appeared out of thin air. "Then follow me."

Timothée's breath hitched. *They're leaving?*

"What of our mission, my Prince? The school's swarming with mercs," Allistar said.

"Your mercenaries can be left to face the Archpriestess's judgment. Let this Exalted One know who he's truly up against."

Balthazar turned to Timothée and his sisters. "What of them? The Exalted One wanted them. Badly. Do we leave them in this place? With *her?*"

Allistar's gaze fell heavy on Timothée. "And what of him? He summoned—"

"Dyamodius. I know," the Dark Prophet said. "Who do you think called her off? You're welcome, by the way."

"That was you?" Balthazar asked. "How?"

"She remembered me. I named her, after all." The Dark Prophet turned to Allistar. "If you touch that boy again, there will be no corner of Thraina that will hide you from my retribution."

Allistar stared at Timothée for one cold, hard moment before turning to the Dark Prophet and inclining his head. "Yes, my Prince."

Icy fear beat in Timothée's chest. It didn't make any sense. The Dark Prophet was protecting him and his sisters. And why was Allistar so adamant on killing him? Just because he looked like Noctis?

"Timothée Greywick." The Dark Prophet turned and stared at Timothée. Timothée stared back.

With purposeful steps, the Dark Prophet approached him and his sisters, who still sat huddled on the floor. Ancient power radiated off the Dark Prophet. They'd been playing at this act of gods and Starlings for a moon. This vampire had seen the rise and fall of kingdoms.

He stared down at them. "There are a great many wonders in this world, Greywicks. And you are one of them. You will be hunted everywhere you go. Wanted for your power and your blood. Your friends may turn out to be foes. And your foes may turn out to be friends." The rising sun splashed his cape with red. Timothée could still feel the flicker of his shadowcraft in the air. How much longer before it disappeared beneath the dawn?

The Dark Prophet turned back to his door to darkness. "If you're tired of being a pawn to the Celestial Church, follow me."

Marion gripped Timothée's arm. "Does he think we're stupid? That'd be like a deer following a wolf into the den!"

Flanked by the Phantom Two, the Dark Prophet stepped before his swirling black door. He was leaving—

"Wait!" Timothée called out.

Marion dropped her hand. "What are you doing?"

Timothée kept his gaze focused on the Dark Prophet. "Tell me, is my brother coming back? Will Noctis return?"

A dark moment passed. Then the Prophet said, "No."

A rush of relief shuddered through him. "Your vision was wrong then."

The Dark Prophet stood still as obsidian. "I have had hundreds of visions in my long lifetime, and all but my first has come to pass. This prophecy will eventually come true."

"But—"

The monster walked to Timothée. All remaining darkness in the room became a halo around him. "For I have seen a vision: your school bathed in shadows. But it wasn't Noctis beside me." The Dark Prophet brushed a gloved hand along Timothée's cheek. "It was you."

# 33

# IN WHICH VIVIAN MAKES A CHOICE OF BLOOD AND BOND

VIVIAN'S THROAT WAS so dry. Her head was pounding. She wanted to scream, cry, throw herself at the Dark Prophet and strangle him. He had tried to kill her in Wolfhelm. She would not let him have Timothée. But she could do nothing but stare at her brother, his grey eyes like a stormy sky. The emotion on his face… Was it fear? Or desire?

From the moment she'd walked into this room, pain had consumed her. Nightmarish memories barraged her, images flashing over and over in her mind: the night of the Wolfhelm massacre. A bite in her neck and blood spilling down her throat.

Had she… drank blood that night? Yes, someone had given her blood and it had flowed through her veins like an icy river.

She couldn't stay there, locked in that memory. Her siblings needed her. And that river still coursed within.

She was everything that night had made her.

Vivian forced herself up on shaky arms. "Get away from him," she snarled. "Now!" And then she hissed, lips pulling back to reveal her fangs.

Marion screamed.

The Dark Prophet laughed and walked back to his door to darkness, flanked by his two vampires.

"Girl." Allistar's yellow eye focused on Vivian. "You don't have to live like this. I know what it's like. The pain. The hunger. Come with us. I'll help you."

"Never!" Marion exclaimed at the same time as Vivian heard herself say: "You can help me?"

"No, Vivian," Marion said. "Don't believe him. You're not a monster. You're just sick. I can look after you."

Vivian took a step toward the vampire, and her movements were slow, as if her feet were shuffling over sand. The roar of a crowd rang in her mind.

"Leave!" Marion screeched at the vampires. "They'll never follow you!"

Vivian fought for control over her own thoughts. She blinked. Was that concern in his yellow eye? "Can you really help?"

"Yes," Allistar said. "Trust me."

"That's interesting." The Dark Prophet looked at Vivian, then Allistar. "It seems we have much catching up to do, my friend."

Timothée took her hand.

Marion looked at them in desperation. "What are you doing? Stop it!"

"What if they can help Vivian? That's why we came here, isn't it?" There was something strange on Timothée's face. Like terrible destiny had taken hold. "What if this is our path?"

Vivian took a step forward. "What if this is the way?"

Warmth bloomed bright inside her chest. It had been so long since she'd felt it, she could not place it at first. But there it was, simmering between her star and her heart. Hope.

She stared into the dark, churning door. The embodiment of the space between the stars. Pure darkness. A new awareness entered her. Within that space, possibilities among possibilities were being written within the universe. And if only she gazed deep enough, she'd see them all.

"Through that door," Marion said, "is only wickedness."

"The time is now, Greywicks," the Dark Prophet called. "The choice is yours."

Vivian squeezed her brother's hand. Marion was right.

But she was a little wicked. And so was her brother.

Together, they took a step toward the door.

*Marion will follow,* she knew in her heart. *We stay together.*

No matter the path.

There was the smashing of glass and the roar of a propellor.

A panel of the glass wall was shattered upon the ground. And outside in the cold rising dawn, was a sky skiff, piloted by Khalid and Darius.

Darius grabbed his hand back from where the glass had been, now broken by his starcraft. His eyes flashed like a lightning strike.

*Darius.* She halted, her star and heart both blazing at the sight of him.

But he wasn't looking at her.

He was looking at the Dark Prophet.

Khalid had a bloody gash across his nose and a black eye. "Greywicks, we found you! Hurry, get on!"

"Khalid!" Marion sobbed and scrambled up. "You've come to rescue us. Hurry, Tim, Viv!"

But Timothée was still staring at the Dark Prophet. As if he had looked within the nothingness and seen the paths no one else could.

"Come with me," Allistar pleaded.

Vivian looked from the sky skiff to the door to darkness.

"Get away from her," a gravelly voice said. Darius left the sky skiff and stalked forward, his sword of stellarite shimmering.

Khalid's eyes were wide behind him, hand outstretched. "Dare, no."

But Allistar didn't spare the Prince a glance, his gaze fixed on her. Vivian looked between them and wavered on her feet.

"Darius—"

Darius stepped between her and the door to darkness. Then he turned his sword not to Allistar, but the Dark Prophet. "I should have known you were behind this."

The Dark Prophet let the sword's point touch the middle of his chest. He quirked his head. "What can I say? Disaster calls to me."

Shadows swirled up and down Darius's stellarite sword. He gasped and dropped the dissolving metal. Black flecks fell like ash to the ground.

*The Dark Prophet destroyed his sword,* Vivian thought. If he could do that so easily, then why had he bothered fighting Darius in the square?

Marion grabbed Vivian's arm. "We have to get out of here!"

"I can't leave."

"Because of the Prince or the vampire?" Marion hissed. "It can't help you. It's nothing but a trap."

The Dark Prophet laughed as he looked at the remains of Darius's sword, then turned to his door to darkness. "Goodbye, little prince."

Darius's chest heaved, a black mark upon his palm from where the shadows had scorched him. Then he moved, quick as a falling star, and slammed into Allistar. He threw the vampire to the ground, grabbed the rapier, and thrusted between the slats of the Dark Prophet's armor. Red blood spilled out from the wound.

Whatever the Prophet was, he was still mortal enough to bleed.

"Thrice you have tried to best me," Darius snarled, blood dripping from the rapier. "Tried to take my castle, my kingdom, my school. But you will never win. You are nothing but a murderer. A monster."

A thin line of blood dripped down the Dark Prophet's gravastarium armor. The vampire brothers looked ready to retaliate, but the Dark Prophet waved them down. He bobbed his head up at Darius.

Like in the square, their movements seemed to freeze the world around them.

"You want to talk about being a murderer?" An unsettling cadence sounded in the Dark Prophet's voice. "Fine. I am one. I have killed for wars, for vengeance, for love, for those who do not have the power to defend themselves. But I have never killed like you, little prince."

Khalid shouted: "Darius, we have to go! The sun is rising. Hurry!"

"I wonder," the Dark Prophet mused, and he walked closer to Vivian. "Does she know the path you painted to reach me three years ago? How the hero prince of Thraina truly defeated me?"

Vivian expected to see Darius swing the rapier, brandish words of contention, but he was shaking. Face blanched.

"Oh, that's very interesting." The Dark Prophet started circling Darius.

"Darius!" she managed. But Marion grabbed her arm, dragged her closer to the window.

"Dare, let's go!" Khalid screamed.

"I've had quite enough of your rambling for one night, Medihsan." The Dark Prophet extended his hand, and shadows crawled up the side of the room, covering them all above and below, until it was as if they were suspended in the sky. Colors formed: swirling stars and galaxies.

Vivian screamed and clung to her sister. She could still see the shapes of Timothée and Allistar and his brother, and the Dark Prophet prowling around the Prince. But Khalid, beyond the window, was gone.

Where in the space between the stars had he trapped them?

"Let me take you back to the siege of Wolfhelm." The Dark Prophet's voice encapsulated all of her. "How many of my soldiers did you slaughter to get to me, little prince? How many did you leave broken and dying on the ground, their blood seeping through the stone cracks in your castle?"

Images flashed in the surrounding stars: castle halls so clear it was as if she were there. And there was a boy, wild, covered in blood, sword shaking in his hand. If Vivian didn't see his blue eyes, she would not have recognized the Prince of Andúrigard.

Brutalized bodies littered the path behind him as he stalked down the hallway.

*So much death.* Vivian trembled, a soft whimper escaping her lips.

"We are more alike than you think," the Dark Prophet snarled.

"I'm nothing like you," Darius roared. "They were nothing but monsters without a soul."

It was then Vivian saw the sharp teeth. The dead... They were all vampires.

*No...*

Vivian was falling through space. Marion clutched onto her tunic.

"Well, if it's only monsters you killed that night," the Dark Prophet said, his gaze cutting quickly to Vivian before flashing back to the Prince, "you missed one."

The images around them changed, lightning flashes across the sky, until Vivian saw the turrets of the castle. Darius Störmberg kneeled; blood and rain ran down his face. The Dark Prophet stood above him, unarmed, shadows coiling from his fingers like smoke.

"Your death would have been inevitable," the Dark Prophet continued, "had the stars not chosen that very moment to intervene. They sent me a vision. Unfortunately for me, they're a tad incapacitating."

Vivian watched the image before her, how the Dark Prophet's body stiffened. Then he slid, falling off the slanted roof of the castle and into the darkness below.

Darius had been lucky to survive.

"That is the true golden Prince of Andúrigard, of Thraina." The Dark Prophet sighed. "Not the hero who vanquished me, but a fraud, a little boy drowning in the blood of all those he's killed and all those he could not save."

The galaxy of stars snapped away as quickly as it had come. They were back in the Archpriestess's office, and Khalid was outside the window on his sky skiff yelling for them.

"Darius—" Vivian croaked, and tears spilled down her cheeks. So much death. If he knew what she was, would he have slaughtered her too?

The Dark Prophet stood over the Prince. Darius had fallen to his knees, lips trembling, eyes unblinking.

"There are only a few minutes left of starlight. It would take but a moment to kill you though." There was twisted humor in the Dark

Prophet's words. "But it would be rather dull if there's no one around to watch your fall."

"Dare, you need to stand," Khalid yelled. Wind ripped at his hair, sending his feathered hat sailing into the office. "Listen to my voice. I'm here."

Darius blinked and dropped Allistar's rapier. He rushed over to Vivian. His eyes cleared as he took in her face. He held out his hand.

She cast a look behind her. The door to darkness was still swirling, and Allistar was staring at her.

But she knew she could not, would not go.

Vivian took Darius's hand.

# 34
# IN WHICH MARION KEEPS A VOW

COLD FEAR RAN up and down Marion's spine. How similar she felt to that night in the square, helpless and defenseless.

How could this be happening? Her family... pulled away by these wicked creatures. No, no, they couldn't believe them. These were *killers*. Vivian wasn't a monster, she was just sick, and Marion looked after her. No one else looked after her. It was Marion's job, her job to keep them all safe—

"Marion." Khalid stared at her from the sky skiff, hovering outside the window. His emerald eyes held hers and he smiled. In all this darkness, here was something to hold on to. One piece of goodness, of light, amidst the nothingness.

She set her jaw and sprinted to the window.

Cold wind rushed at them. The sky skiff—a haphazardly put-together contraption with a propellor at the front of a covered engine, a stiff-looking wheel held tight by Khalid, two patched wings on either side, and a small standing space nearly filled by Khalid himself—seemed barely capable of staying in the sky.

Their feet tinkled on the broken glass. Darius jumped into the sky skiff then turned, holding out his arms. "Vivian."

"Go!" Marion pushed her forward, and Darius lifted her into the contraption.

"Your turn, Marion," Khalid called. "Mind the gap!"

Marion stepped to the edge of the tower. The roar of wind and the propellor sent her hair spiraling. She looked down. *Oh. Bother.* She'd known the Archpriestess's office was atop one of the tallest towers, but to stand at the edge—

They were so high, she could see everything: the whole of the Academy, the Meadow of Shattered Stars with the mercenaries' aircrafts ablaze, Selene Crescent now crawling with fleeing marauders, even the very edge of the Isle itself. The sky seemed close enough to touch, the sun blazing over the field, the last stars winking out.

"Come on!" Khalid called. "The halls are swarming with those mercs! They'll find their way up soon enough."

But she couldn't go. Not yet.

Timothée was still in the middle of the office, staring into the darkness.

"Come with me, Timothée," the Dark Prophet said. "I saw it. We will stand together at the end. You belong by my side."

"No." Marion ran to Timothée. "He belongs with his family." Then she laced her fingers through her brother's and found his gaze.

There was darkness there too.

*I'll fight it for you, brother. I'll fill the world with light if I have to.*

And pulling on her brother's hand, she ran for the window.

Darius yanked Timothée into the sky skiff. Marion stared at the gap between the tower and the contraption, the long fall. *One day I will plant my feet on the ground and never leave.*

The engine made a whirring noise. "It's time to go," Khalid called.

Marion gritted her teeth and leapt. Air and nothingness—then Vivian, Darius, and Timothée's arms were around her, pulling her tight onto the skiff.

Marion shot a look back. The Dark Prophet stared at them, fists clenched. Then he turned and disappeared into his door to darkness. Allistar shook his head and then followed. Last to go was Balthazar.

"Stay safe. Remember what you're capable of," he said, the deep baritone of his voice rumbling through her, "Marion."

Her name... Her name. Why did he have to say her name like that? And as he turned into the door to darkness, he bent down and picked up Khalid's hat that had blown in. He plucked the white feather from the brim. Magic pricked in the air and the feather morphed, turning into a strange blue flower with pointed petals.

He disappeared, tossing the flower into the breeze. It blew toward her, and she snatched it. The same flower had bloomed around her in the daylight the morning after her Celestial Rite.

"What I'm capable of..." And Marion remembered the vow she had made to that phantom: *I will see you laid raw before me. Charred and broken.*

This was a promise she would keep.

A trapdoor in the middle of the office swung open. A swarm of marauders poured out.

"And that's our cue." Khalid pressed some buttons beside the wheel and the sky skiff's wings buzzed to life like an insect, careening them off into the rising dawn.

The contraption made a horrible sound, smoke rising from the engine. "What kind of skiff is this?" Marion cried.

"A homemade one," Khalid called over the wind. His hands flew from levers to buttons back to the wheel. "I built it myself!"

"I can tell!"

The five of them were huddled so tight together on the tiny contraption, there was no room to turn around.

"I'm going to take us across the Meadow of Shattered Stars and over the Enchanted Wood. Doesn't look like there are any baddies over there."

"Are you sure we're going to make it?" Timothée looked down at the sky skiff. "I don't think it can take all the weight."

"She'll make it!" Khalid bellowed. The rushing wind blew his hair back.

Marion held her breath. Her stomach roiled. She wanted so desperately to close her eyes, but she couldn't take them off the dancing ground below. They made it over the Academy, and were now flying toward Selene Crescent—

The engine sputtered and coughed. The wings whirred. Then stopped. The sky skiff lurched downward.

"Khalid," Marion said, "is it supposed to be doing this?"

He yanked hard on a lever. Nothing. Pressed a button. "Shit."

The sky skiff plummeted. Wind rushed at them like a hurricane; they screamed as they fell and fell and fell. Her cheeks pulled with the force. Selene Crescent grew nearer: the cobblestone path and shoppes and the swarm of fleeing marauders.

And worst of all, they were heading straight toward that enormous marble statue Darius had commissioned of the three of them for their birthday.

Somehow, amid pure panic, Marion thought, *This is how I die. Splattered against my own bloody face.*

"Do something, Darius!" Khalid yelled.

But the Prince of Andúrigard didn't move. Didn't even blink.

As the skiff was about to crash straight into the marble, Vivian cried, "Hang on!" She thrust out her hands. And with the magic of the last stars, the statue shifted, marble changing into…

Snow.

The skiff collided with soft powder. Marion was engulfed by cold and wet then she was tumbling, ice shivering over her arms and down her back, and she was rolling through it and then she stopped.

She shook her head, pushed herself up. She lay on snow-covered cobblestone. The sky skiff was in pieces around her. Quickly, she looked for her friends. Khalid was sitting on his bottom, still holding onto the detached wheel. Timothée was near her, groaning, but awake. And Vivian pushed out of a pile of snow with Darius in her arms.

"It's disappearing," Marion whispered. The enchantments that had been put on her for All Hallow's Eve had vanished; her ears were round again, her hair back to its gold. Darius and Timothée too had lost their crafted features.

It was fully dawn, and there would be no more starcraft until the night.

They were entirely defenseless.

And as her vision focused, she stared around Selene Crescent. They had crashed right amongst the marauders, all baring the blue mark of the Exalted One. They did not need to wield starcraft, for they had swords and daggers and hatchets.

"It's them," one said, calling to the others. "The triplets Master sent us for. Grab them!"

Darius and Khalid stepped together in front of the Greywicks. There was something feral in Darius's blue fire eyes. He stalked forward with naught even a sword. "Stand down. I am... I am—"

"He's the bloody Prince of Andúrigard!" Khalid yelled.

A mercenary threw a hatchet. It embedded in Darius's shoulder. "Darius!" Vivian cried.

Khalid grabbed Darius in his arms as he fell. "Dare!"

His eyes rolled back, blood spurting from his shoulder.

"Face it," the mercenary said. "We ain't getting off this Isle. Look at that one. He's the God of Shadows reborn! The Exalted One promises us a heavenly end in the stars. But ain't no end for anyone if that boy lives. He'll smother all the stars one by one." He held a rusty dagger toward Timothée. "Let us take him with us in death and ensure Thraina's salvation!"

Timothée backed up. "No, I wouldn't—"

"You die." More mercenaries sauntered up behind him. His red-rimmed eyes darted from Darius on the ground, head in Khalid's lap, to Vivian and Marion standing shoulder to shoulder. "And anyone who tries to stop me will meet the pointy end of my knife."

Marion felt Vivian's heavy breath. "I can't let him do that," she whispered. "I won't let him."

And Marion knew what Vivian was going to do. The only weapon they had. The ones in her mouth.

No, no, no. *Protect them.* She wouldn't let this filth touch her brother, wouldn't let Vivian sacrifice her humanity for them. Couldn't. They were the Greywicks, *dammit.* It was them against the world. Always had been.

She thought of their little cabin, the smell of lavender, her father's voice singing as he strummed on his dulcimer. Sitting with Vivian and Timothée by the warmth of the fire. How that fire had bathed them in its light and warmth, given them comfort and courage.

It wasn't *fair.* All she wanted to do was sit by that fire with her family. She had asked for *nothing* and been given *shit.* A dead father. A sick sister. A cursed brother. Some stupid fate as some stupid god. Where was her damned fire?

No one gave her anything. So she would take everything.

Still clutched tight in her fist was the crumpled blue flower. *What I am capable of…*

There was heat. And a glow under her skin. A fever burning from the bottom up. It was all around her, covering her body: burning, bursting flames. Every piece of her ignited.

The ash in her turned to fire.

*From the ashes.* The Morning Stars' words.

She looked to the rising sun: a brilliant red orb filling the sky. Starlings didn't get power from the sun.

*But I am the phoenix,* she thought. *I take my power.*

Body writhed in flames, she brought her hand out before her, watched the fire dance across her skin. But it didn't burn. *I am made of flames. I do not burn; I ignite.*

She had done it before at the Celestial Rite.

The mercenary stopped, sneered. Then charged with dagger drawn.

Marion raised her arm, fire flowing beneath like flame-tipped wings. With a flick of her wrist, an inferno of thermal pressure shot out. A blaze engulfed the mercenary, scorching skin from his bone. Where once had been a man collapsed a charred corpse.

"Marion!" Her brother's voice. Distant.

She turned to the next marauder. The woman charged, ax raised above her head. Marion rose both hands: a whoosh of heat blazed forth. Only cinders emerged from the flame.

There were so many mercenaries. Some came toward her. Others ran away. But with each fling of her hand, flames and energy burst forth. *No one will frighten me again,* she thought as flame after flame surged before her. *Not the Dark Prophet. Not the Exalted One. Not the gods themselves.*

"Marion, enough!" Khalid yelled.

Marion shook herself, the fever dripping out of her body. Waxy heat hung in the air. Charred corpses littered Selene Crescent, screams seared forever on their faces. It smelled of burnt hair and... lavender.

Her siblings and friends stepped beside her. They looked afraid.

*Laid raw before me. Charred and broken.*

A vow she had made to one who had threatened her.

Here was proof she could keep that vow.

Here was proof she could lay the whole world before her if she wished.

# Mourning Sky Moon

Bitter winds and barren fields mark the landscapes of Thraina.
It is a time of rest for farmers, and a time of activity for merchants
and Starlings who work to keep citizens fed and warm.

Many choose this moon to connect deeper with the gods by
leaving offerings at the shrines or praying at the many temples.
Remembrance of the fallen rests heavy in the heart of Thraina as
nature begins its long hibernation.

# 35

# IN WHICH VIVIAN REWRITES
# THE WILL OF THE STARS

WITH THE DAWN came a new moon, the end of the Hunter's Blood and the arrival of the Mourning Sky.

Vivian Greywick walked the halls of the Celestial Academy for Fallen Stars as quiet and soft as one of the fabled ghosts they tried to ward off on All Hallow's Eve. She barely felt the cold stone beneath her bare feet or the chill in the corridors cutting through her thin medical robe.

She should be in the sanatorium right now awaiting a healer to check her vitals. But there were so many students and professors injured in the attack who needed help.

What she needed, no one could give her.

*Perhaps he could have.* Allistar. Vivian rubbed her neck. What would have happened if she had gone with him?

Outside, the yellow horizon was cut with black smoke, still rising from the charred bodies of those her sister had killed.

Marion had used her magic during the day when the stars were sleeping. An unheard of feat. She had saved their lives by murdering dozens of people.

Timothée, too, had blood on his hands.

*Shall I be next?*

Her brother was still waiting for his physical check in the sanatorium. Marion had been swept away by Professor Kunuk and Loremaster Setviren who blessedly had returned to human shape with the dawn.

She thought of her siblings, of Timothée sweeping across the ballroom, cloaked in fear and reverence. Of Marion, glittering in the dawn light, every piece of her ablaze in righteous fire.

Monsters, all of them.

And as fun as it had been to pretend to be a normal girl, Vivian knew she could do it no longer.

She arrived before a specific door in the Evening Star dormitory. Knocked. No answer. A quick twist of the handle revealed it was unlocked. She opened the door and walked in.

Darius stood in his room, staring out the window. Vivian wondered what he saw in the red of the setting sun.

He turned to her. "Vivian." He was shirtless, save for the white bandage wrapped around his chest, and the blue ribbon tied on his wrist. He wore loose trousers and his hair had fallen across his eyes. There was a frantic expression on his face, but it softened when he saw her.

She stepped into the room but kept her distance. *Am I afraid of him?* This was the reason she came. To see, to feel. *If you knew what I was, would my blood splatter your flesh like the vampires in your past?*

"I'm glad you're here." He turned back to the horizon, resting an arm against the window frame. "Be witness to my vow. I will not rest until I have that monster's head."

She knew he was talking about the Dark Prophet. *That monster saved Timothée's life. Perhaps all of ours.*

Darius pushed away from the window and crossed to her. "There is concern in your eyes."

She had to look away from him, stare at the stone floor. *Why did I come here?*

Darius gently reached to put his hand under her chin, but she jerked away.

"Are you frightened of me?"

*Incredibly.*

"Darius." She realized she was crying. "You were covered in blood."

"I... Your fear is the Dark Prophet's doing. I promise you. That isn't who I am."

She tried to steady her breath. She had to know what it all meant from Darius himself, and not just the memories of darkness. "So those images of you were false then?"

"Vivian." Darius shook his head, and panic crawled up his features. "The Dark Prophet—he forced us to see his memories. He was trying to turn you against me!"

"Turn me against you?" Vivian repeated. "I just want to know the truth of it."

"The truth of it? The truth of it..." His blue eyes were wild. "The truth of it... was that night he took everything from me. They stormed the castle, and pillaged and burned, and severed the heads of my parents and piked them on the gates. They killed my little sister then he came for me. He came for me, and I do not know who he found. But that is who the Dark Prophet showed you."

The setting sun turned Darius's hair a burnished gold, the ruler before her raw and open.

"I did not wish to deceive you." His voice was hoarse. "Now you know I am nothing but the fraud of a hero. I never defeated a great enemy those three years ago. And there is something inside me I have no control over. A beast that will not be tamed."

His words were a question: *Will you still love me now you see me? Truly see every wicked part of me?* It was a question she desperately wished she could ask him of herself.

*Tell him now. Tell him when he is raw and so are you.*

*Tell him.*

"Darius," she said, and her feet were moving on their own accord, crossing the room to him. She lay her head on his chest and held him around the waist.

His movements were slow and cautious, but he wrapped his arms around her. The tickle of the blue ribbon grazed her back.

*I love him through his darkness.*

"For a moment, I thought you might leave."

"This world is cruel," she whispered. "Sometimes it demands cruelness of us."

*I need to tell him now.*

"Darius, I'm—"

"One day I will know peace," he murmured. "And the souls of my family and the citizens we lost that night will know peace. Peace when I finally enact my vengeance."

He pulled away and his hands were on either side of her head. He did not wear a calm expression. Something feral glinted in his gaze.

"And I swear to you now, Vivian, I will not let anyone harm you. I will keep you safe."

"The church has deemed me a child of the gods. My very existence is danger. That is why they were here."

"It matters not." Darius's hands trembled on her cheeks. "The gods could spirit themselves from the sky and they too would lay dead at my feet for daring to get close to you."

"Darius…" She stepped away from him, and he whipped around, pacing the room.

"You understand what this world requires of me now. What the crown requires." His voice was too fast, movements jerky and strange. "Do not be afraid. Do not think me above the value of life. It was only monsters I killed. They chose their fate when they discarded their souls to become creations of the night."

*Only vampires.*

"I doubt all of them chose their fate."

"Then I freed them of their monstrous existence."

*Tell him,* a part of her mind still raged. She needed to know the truth. "What if instead of death, your sister or mother had the fate of being bitten? Would you think their souls gone?"

It was not telling him, but it was as close as her fragile heart allowed her to get.

But the Prince's face did not flash with consideration before he snarled, "I would have freed them too. It would be the only kindness left. And I would expect the same done to me."

Vivian flinched, stumbled back.

"Vampires killed the man you called father. You of all people must understand this!" Darius threw his head back, pinched the bridge of his nose. "I know it is a harsh light to see me in—to see the blood painted plainly on my face. But I have never taken actual life carelessly. I had to get to the Dark Prophet. Don't you see?"

"I—"

And she saw him, a valiant prince who was kind and overflowing with love. But he was also hurt and broken and covered in blood.

And for a girl who craved blood more than anything, it was dangerous to be so close.

"I will not let anyone I love come to harm again." He walked to her and grabbed her hands. "I swear it to you, Vivian."

*Love?*

And she thought, *I will always love him. Every dark part of him.*
*But he cannot love me, for it would be the death of him.*
*And therefore, the death of me.*

"I don't want that of you, Darius."

"What?"

"It's clear to me now. This is where our fates diverge." She made herself stare into his face, even as it fractured.

She took a step back.

He looked down at the space between them as if the world had cleaved in two.

"Vivian... What have I done?"

318

"It's not what you've done," she said. "It is what the future holds. I see now your path, and I cannot walk it with you. I do not yet know what the gods want from me, but—"

He stumbled closer to her. "No. The stars brought us together."

"They did." But she did not believe all the stars were good. And if she continued with him, that end was blood, and blood, and blood.

If she told him what she was, and even if beyond any wildest dream, he accepted her...

Then what?

There could never be a vampire queen on the throne. And if they kept it a secret and he was discovered... then it could be the downfall of Thraina.

One child of the gods had already destroyed the world.

She would not follow in her brother's footsteps.

"I can't let you go," Darius said, and his voice was so low. "This can't end. I lo—"

"Darius, so much has happened to me. I can't..." She wiped her eyes. "A moon ago, I was a girl in a candle shoppe. Would you be fighting so fiercely if that was all I was now?"

She knew she was being unfair, that her station had no bearing to him. But small truths leaked out where the large ones could not.

"Yes, yes, of course." Darius fell to his knees before her. "Vivian, Vivian... Don't go. *Please.*"

He took her hands. Her fingers slid over the blue ribbon, and she wished it was strong enough to keep them together.

"I would fight for you in every world." His blue eyes were so wide. "I would run away with you if you wished it. Leave the crown and the gods behind. Tell me what you want, I will give it to you."

"You care about Andúrigard too much." She shook her head, and her tears flung to the ground. "Do not speak things you do not mean."

"Then tell me what I can do. I need you like the flowers need the sun, like the tides need the moon. Anything you ask, I would give you."

"Your vengeance against the Dark Prophet," she said. "Would you give that up?"

He startled, stood. "Why would you ask such a thing?"

*Because it's driving you to madness. Because I cannot ask of you what I truly wish.*

Anger lined the edges of his words. "You would see that monster alive after what he's done?"

"There are many monsters in the world," she said simply. "What is one more?"

Darius let out a frustrated groan. "I do not understand you! I cannot change the things I have done but I can—"

"I want you to let me go."

His expression blanched and there were depths within depths in his eyes.

"Goodbye, Darius."

"Vivian, I'll—"

But she did not hear what he said. The door shut behind her.

For a monster without a heart, hers sure hurt a lot.

# 36

# IN WHICH TIMOTHÉE AND HIS SISTERS EMBRACE WHAT THEY ARE

**I**T HADN'T BEEN hard to sneak out of the sanatorium. The Academy was in a state of chaos since the attack. Timothée was covered in bandages from the various cuts all over his body, but nothing was serious. Sadly, the same couldn't be said for every Starling.

There was no way Timothée could stay in the sanatorium a second longer, not when every wound felt like his fault. Now, he darted down the halls, desperate to get to the Cauldron.

Images of the attack flared in his mind. The offer the Dark Prophet had made, the terrible purpose in his words: *You belong by my side.*

He tried to shake the voice, but it embedded deeper than any physical injury he'd received.

However, the thought of returning to his room, to Yvaine and to Val, was enough to keep even the Dark Prophet's voice at bay.

Timothée pushed into the Cauldron. It was early evening and starlight flittered over the Dark Star students. Classes had been canceled and students were confined to their houses. Groups talked loudly on the mismatched sofas and chairs. But it all quieted as he entered.

This was the first time he'd stood in front of his classmates since the ball. The ball where he'd dressed as Noctis and ignored everything in the entire world except Val's mouth on his.

All eyes stared at him, standing in the doorway of the Cauldron barefoot, with dried blood on his collarbone and love bites on his neck.

But there was no lilac gaze in the crowd.

He didn't care what they thought of him now. He shuffled past them, heartbeat quickening as he ascended the stairs. Would Val be mad? Probably. But Timothée could think of a few ways to appease him.

He hadn't been able to stop thinking about Val. It'd felt like he'd been beside him in his thoughts at every moment, even when the giant bat carried him above the Isle of Argos. Even when the vampire had tried to kill him.

Timothée made it to his door. Took a deep breath and slicked back his hair.

"Val," he said as he entered, "I'm back."

But the room...

It was destroyed.

Sickening fear coursed through him. The bookcase was turned over, contents scattered. Violent streaks of dark magic cascaded across the walls. Broken vials, torn bedsheets, and singed flooring lay in their wake.

A mournful meow sounded, and Yvaine jumped down from the windowsill. Timothée scooped her up and clutched her to his chest.

Then he looked to the bathroom. The curtain lay limp, half-ripped off its hanger.

Bile rose in his throat. Cautiously, he stepped into the bathroom. It was empty. Smashed containers of salts and creams littered the floor.

Two thoughts warred in Timothee's mind. *Where are you?* But even more prevalent: *Why didn't you find me?*

Something bled deep in his heart and his thoughts whirled.

But something made him still. His reflection in the mirror. Except it wasn't his reflection.

Not exactly.

Looking back at him was a man with long black hair, a wide jaw, familiar gravastarium armor.

Noctis, God of Shadows.

Timothée blinked. So did the reflection.

Then the room shook, and purple lines rose along the walls.

*Greywick triplets,* the castle's voice echoed in his mind. And somehow, Timothée knew his sisters were hearing this too. *You have done as I asked.*

*One of you has welcomed their monster.*

*One of you has fed their monster.*

*And one of you has emulated their monster.*

Timothée's reflection smiled, though his own face remained stunned, and the castle purred, *Lost Stars, it is time for us to meet.*

Thank you so much for reading Wicked Academia: Stormwind of Shadows! We hope you enjoyed the second adventure of the Greywick triplets.

We would be so grateful if you would take a moment to leave a review. Reviews help indie authors like us so much!

Leave a review on Amazon:

Leave a review on Goodreads:

Here's to catching stars and kissing in the shadows.
The adventure continues in…

# Wicked Academia 3: FROZEN BLOOD

Coming Soon

# About Us

Jasmine Jenkins and Sophie Suliman are sisters who write new adult fantasy. They live in British Columbia, Canada. They love telling stories full of magic, adventure, and romance. When not writing, you can find them exploring the beautiful forests of their home, playing Dungeons & Dragons, or connecting with their amazing readers on social media.

# DISCOVER YOUR MAGIC

What star would you catch at the Celestial Rite?

Are you curious, clever, and serene like a Morning Star?

Imaginative, determined, and resourceful like an Evening Star?

Emotional, passionate, and feared like a Dark Star?

Scan the QR code or visit

https://www.wickedacademia.com/discover-your-magic and take
the quiz to find out!

# ACKNOWLEDGMENT

What a joy it has been to return to the Celestial Academy for Fallen Stars and to bring you another adventure of our dear Greywicks.

As always, the building of Wicked Academia has been a labor of love from so many, and we are eternally grateful for all the support and encouragement from our family, friends, and online community.

Firstly, we want to thank our mother and father for all the love and support behind-the-scenes that makes this possible. As children, we were free to run wild with our imaginations, and Wicked Academia is a result of that.

To Graeme: for the love—both gentle and tough—; for your undying belief in our success; and for keeping the machine running.

To Auntie Jo, for always keeping us fueled during our writing sprints!

To Melanie G., Kendra S., and Lisa N. How did we get so lucky to have friends like you? You continue to believe in us. We are forever grateful.

To Rosie, Emily, and Rehana. Your keen eyes, kindness, and astute observations have helped make Stormwind shine!

To Yasmin, Chris, Callie, and Jack. We are so, so thankful to have your amazing talent on our team. Collaborating with you has been a great joy.

To the Wicked Academia community. Whether you're on Discord, Instagram, TikTok, or elsewhere... Thank you. Your fanart, comments, and humor are the best reward after a long day. You are a safe place to call home. The Celestial Academy will always be there for you.

And finally, to our Patrons. Without you, we would not be here. You have helped us create the world of Wicked Academia. Thank you.

Here's to wishing on falling stars, kissing in the shadows, and all your dreams coming true.

Love and Starlight,
Jasmine and Sophie

# Bonus Chapter
# In Which Khalid Keeps the Spirits at Bay

FOR SOMEONE DRESSED as a pirate, Khalid Ali Bagheeri certainly felt serious.

It was the night of the All Hallow's Eve Ball. Every year, there was a huge party, celebrating old superstitions about how merrymaking satiated the ghosts that would otherwise haunt freely the rest of the year.

Khalid was not afraid of ghouls or ghosts or the wild fervor that gripped all the students on the night of a party. Fear made you slow and desperate.

No, it was not fear he felt. But caution.

Opportunity arose during nights of fervor. And he would not be the only one looking for it.

Khalid wore the costume garb of a pirate: tight breeches, a loose shirt with a deep V, a red bandana, and a tricorn hat with a huge white feather that he was positively chuffed about.

And of course, he wore his gloves.

Khalid hurried down the hallway, using the appearance of running late, having spent a little too long perfecting the smudged liner around his eyes. Everything had to be calculated, including his look.

But Khalid had to let go of some control for tonight. Even his little whisperers couldn't tell him the future.

All good plans allowed for a dash of chaos.

Rayna stood at the end of the hallway, chatting with a group of Morning Stars. They were all dressed in their finest costumes: ancient royals and legendary saints and cosmic owls. Rayna was dressed as the mythical galaxy cat, with a tight bodysuit enchanted to shimmer like the night sky. A headband with two pointed ears crested her blue hair.

She barely flicked a glance at him before she dropped her hand to her side. Still laughing and carrying on a conversation, her hand moved in subtle, quick motions: two fingers down, tightly clenched fist, pinky out, three fingers touch on chin, then two, then drop.

*Carmilla Vladimirovna, you minx,* Khalid thought. *You went through with it. Alright, have your show tonight. Let us see if this plays out in both our favors.*

Khalid kept watch on Rayna's hand. With such small, delicate movements, no one could know complete sentences were being conveyed in their secret code. *Professor Barracus's office, eh? Thank you, Rayna dear.*

Khalid turned a corner and headed toward the Dark Stars' quarters.

From Rayna's signals, he had determined all three Greywicks were in the office. He hadn't been able to get a good read on Quincy Barracus yet but added it as a priority for the coming moon. If the professor let students use his office for this kind of activity...

*Schemes within schemes within schemes.*

Purple light filtered from under the office door. Khalid licked his lips, curled a strand of hair around his finger and dangled it between his eyes, then opened the door only a crack and looked inside.

Not for the first time, a small pressing voice in the back of his mind screamed for attention. A voice that flared in particularly precarious situations. He liked to think of it as an aspect of self-preservation, one that reminded him that he was just a man playing with lords and empresses, with prophets and princes.

But now, looking at Timothée Greywick dressed in night-dark armor, hair long and black, the voice screamed at Khalid a new reminder.

He was playing with gods.

Khalid couldn't see the Greywick sisters through the small crack in the door, but he knew they were in there. His attention was wholly focused on Timothée, pacing back and forth.

Whispers had traveled to Khalid the last few days; Carmilla had found some ancient relic. Of course, she would dress the Greywick boy up and parade him around like her personal graven image.

Khalid had been prepared for this. Knew this was her play.

But he hadn't realized exactly what that meant.

Timothée was dressed in gravastarium armor, black as pitch. A purple jewel embedded on each shoulder flashed with the violet torch light. His cape pooled like liquid shadows on the floor. But it wasn't just the armor. His hair was straighter, longer, darker. Black liner accented his eyes and hollowed out his cheekbones.

Timothée had always eerily resembled the portraits of Noctis. But dressed in his clothing, with his hair and face made up…

Khalid's caution began to feel like fear.

He wiped his sweaty palms on his pants, breathed deeply to calm his racing heart, and forced himself to stare at the boy god. He wouldn't let himself shrink away like the night Timothée swallowed his star: his shadows like whips, the violent deaths. And now all that stood between that magic and everyone at the Celestial Academy was a flimsy piece of fabric around the boy's neck.

But it didn't matter. Timothée Greywick didn't want to use magic. Rayna had recounted everything that happened when Timothée was introduced to the Dark Stars' precious Secret Society of Starbound Exiles. The boy thought shadowcraft wicked and buried his magic deep inside.

But Khalid was reminded of one of the first lessons he ever learned. It did not matter what someone *could* do, but rather *why* they wanted to do it. The why was always so much more powerful than the could.

It was why Carmilla was so dangerous. And why Darius wasn't.

It was why Khalid could stay in this game with all of them.

Let Carmilla try this risky move, getting Timothée to dance on shadow strings for her. Khalid wasn't sure what she was getting at yet, but he knew one thing. He had learned something vitally important that Carmilla had not.

The key to rule was not to scare the people into bowing. It was to get them to hoist you on their shoulders.

Khalid knew what happened to a people forced into oppression.

It made them want to fight back.

And so on his little game went until he wouldn't have to fight anymore.

He pushed the door open slightly wider. There they were: the Greywick sisters. His gaze involuntarily drifted, as it tended to do these days, to Marion. It had yet to be determined if her magic and will were so wicked. She sat tucked on a sofa, a scowl upon her cherub mouth, ripping a leaf from her costume into little pieces.

Did gods tick the same way as humans?

Marion Greywick certainty made him think so.

And didn't.

One moment, he knew all her desires and wants. She was the inner workings of a clock, one he knew so well he could take it apart and put it back together just how he wanted.

There were other moments. Stark reminders she was not just a girl, but something much more.

*She hasn't let herself realize it yet.*

Never mind Vivian and her affliction. The gods only knew what would happen if Darius found out…

So, Khalid's inner voice screamed inside his head, and his fear boiled as he looked at the Greywicks. As he looked at the children of the gods.

The thing was, Khalid had only gotten as far as he had by following one rule: ignore that voice at every possible instance. So what if he was a man playing with lords and empresses, with prophets and princes, and now with gods? With enough tricks and schemes, he'd be the only one to ever know the truth.

He opened the door and strode into the room.

"Wow, Timothée, talk about a statement piece. Love the cape. Always thought I should get myself a cape, but I don't know if I could pull it off—"

Khalid turned to fully face the sisters. Whoever had designed their costumes had not held back: they were dressed as legendary heroes from one of Thraina's most beloved fairytales. Vivian wore sparkling sapphire blue hunter's garb, hair pulled up high upon her head, a heavy application of rouge applied to her cheeks.

Marion uncurled from the sofa and stood. Khalid ran his eyes over her body. She'd allowed an Evening Star to alter her normally golden tresses a burnished copper and her gold-grey eyes an emerald green. Her ears had been extended and pointed to resemble the fairytale elves. Her dress was made entirely of leaves and vines that hugged her body and trembled as she moved.

She was a vision.

It made his next move vitally important.

Khalid's mind turned over like a water wheel rushing with ideas. Thoughts whooshed by, vanished, came back. His next words had to be carefully considered. He could lavish her with praise, tell her he was near blinded by her beauty, proclaim his heart had leapt from his breast. But no, such extravagance would only irk her, make her close up with embarrassment.

Perhaps an alternative approach would reap maximum reward. He could barely blink at her appearance, pretend as if today were any other day, and she was no more or less stunning than any other student. But she was prideful and insecure, for all of her pretending, and that sweet combination offered such an opportunity if only he could pluck the right strings.

No, he knew how to play this.

The scenarios flashed across his mind in a fraction of a second. So when Marion raised a brow, put a hand on her hips, and said, "Well?" his rush of breath was perfectly timed. The nervous blink, the push of hair off his eyes.

"U-Uh," he stammered. "Hey, M-Marion." Finally, he raised his eyes to meet hers. "You look beautiful."

And Marion stepped toward him, a slight sway to her hips and the barest hint of a smile on her face. She fixed the cuff of his sleeve he had intentionally left undone. "You're not so bad yourself, Mr. Ali Bagheeri."

Khalid never played a game he couldn't win.

WHAT A NIGHT! With Carmilla and Timothée's little scheme, the party had turned into a most interesting debacle. Now, Khalid stood outside in the Tealight Garden with Marion and the biggest wild card of all: Valentine Sun.

He was in a state.

For the flash of a heartbeat, Khalid felt pity for Valentine. Something—someone—had wounded him in the deepest part, a part no one should be allowed to see. And that wound had festered until the door to that dark part of his soul was forever pried open.

But Khalid's heart beat on, and the pity was gone. Val had chosen to sit in his wounds, to fester in the darkness.

Carmilla was fascinated with him. And Carmilla did not care for people. She cared only for their usefulness. Khalid knew this because he and Carmilla were one and the same. Forged in the same fire.

But why Valentine?

He needed more data. Data he could not collect with Marion hovering over him like a mother hen.

Thankfully, the cold of both the night and Valentine's personality had gotten to her, and she was heading back inside.

"Be careful," she whispered. "I don't trust him."

"Don't worry. Val and I have an understanding."

She nodded, and he watched the sway of her hips as she walked out of the maze and back into the ballroom.

The moment she was out of sight, Khalid rounded on Val. He snatched his shirt and shoved him into the hedge.

"Oh, Khalid," Val purred. "I love when you're rough with me."

"Enough, you little shit," Khalid snarled. He looked pointedly at the shadows swimming around Val's body. "Pull yourself together. I don't care what your problem with the Greywick boy is, but if you don't clean this up, we're both going to be royally fucked."

"Royally fucked." Val repeated the words as if they tasted delicious. "Worried your little prince is going to see you out here with me?"

"This is serious." Khalid released Val's shirt. "Why are you losing your mind, anyway? Don't tell me Carmilla didn't let you in on her ploy."

"No. She didn't."

Khalid's mind whirled. *What is your play, Empress? And how can I turn this to my advantage?* Val had been Carmilla's wild dog for the last year. But maybe she didn't know just how feral he could be.

Standing beneath the statues of the gods, Khalid felt wicked euphoria swirl in his chest. He felt like the gods were witnessing his grand moves and were helpless to stop him. "You know what she's doing, don't you?"

Val flicked shadows through his fingers. "What is she doing, Khalid." His voice was bored, not a question.

"You think this is about the Greywick boy dressing up to steal your thunder? Think, Valentine. He couldn't pour water out of a boot if the instructions were on the heel. This is all Carmilla."

Val's violet eyes flashed. "Carmilla would never betray me."

Khalid paced around him. "No. But she would replace you. Who better to have in her pocket than the literal embodiment of Noctis?"

"He's not Noctis!" Shadows sprang around the garden, shooting up with great ghoulish faces.

Khalid's body stayed entirely still, but his heart stuttered in his chest. Bright fear flashed and that cautious voice whispered that if he played these next moments wrong, he would die in this courtyard.

Val hunched over, trembling. The shadows surged around him like protective guardians.

Khalid stepped forward. Said: "No, he's not. But he's sure the closest thing we've got."

Val met his gaze.

"Let Carmilla play her little game. Let her torment you with that boy. But you're my dear friend, Valentine, so I'll give you my opinion." Khalid placed his lips against Val's ear. Prayed to the gods he didn't believe in. "Nobody should have him but you."

Khalid grabbed Val's hand, pressed the choker into his palm. "But what do I know? I'm just a Medihsan. And you're the only one who trusts me."

Val's hand closed around the choker. "I don't trust you."

Khalid smiled. "Yes, you do. You have to." He waved a gloved hand. "Just like I have to trust you."

Valentine squeezed the choker. Tighter, tighter, tighter. He held Khalid's gaze as he did so, a dark promise in his eyes. Blood oozed out between his fingers as the clasp bit into his skin.

"Goodnight, my friend," Khalid called as he walked back toward the ballroom. "I hope you get what you desire."

A clatter sounded as Khalid exited the maze. He looked back to see the headless statue of Niya, the lightning goddess. Shadows covered her severed neck.

Ah, did he ever love this game.

If you enjoy bonus scenes like this, please consider joining our Patreon!

We have a collection of Safe-For-Work and Not-Safe-For-Work bonus chapters, as well as chapter drops for upcoming novels! Your support on Patreon allows us to create more content in the world of Wicked Academia and helps us work toward our goal of being full-time authors.

Scan the QR code below or visit https://www.patreon.com/ wickedacademia to learn more.

CPSIA information can be obtained
at www.ICGtesting.com
Printed in the USA
LVHW030408170822
726158LV00005B/5